DEADLY

DECEPTIONS

By Elizabeth Munro

The Chronicles of Anna

Book 2

Blue Swell Books
Nanaimo, B.C.
Canada

Second Print Edition: March 2016
ISBN: 978-1-988257-08-2

Visit www.elizabethmunro.ca

By Elizabeth Munro

Anna

Chapter 1

"I figured the fresh air would tire her out."

Paul softly rubbed Camille's back. Her eyes slipped up as her lids came down and with a sigh, she fell asleep. We'd taken her to the pond south of the compound for lunch and afterwards she lay on her stomach, laughing at the noises Paul made under her chin. He risked wearing her lunch in his hair but with her head down, he was safe. We had her on a blanket between us under an umbrella for shade.

He stroked my nose with his finger, green eyes sparkling beneath a fresh hair cut. His wraparound sunglasses were pushed up on top of his head.

"Your freckles are showing up already," he teased.

"Maybe I'll get them everywhere this year... you'll have to look."

Sweet grass came up in earnest nearly as soon as the snow melted, making up for the cold blanket of winter. Paul talked about stocking the pond this year and teaching Camille to fish. We lay exactly where I'd fallen asleep with her; months before for me, years in the future for her. Exactly where I promised her the spring we were having together.

My sister Alina laughed behind me. She'd arrived a few days before to stay for a couple of weeks. Ray wanted to return to Toronto with her but she was already working her way in to an emergency position in Sacramento, a couple of hours away, because she wanted to be closer. They'd both been back and forth for the past three months,

1

unable to be apart and just as unable to decide where they wanted to be together. I knew the compound wasn't her style but she was always comfortable and got along well with Paul and his mother who was here just as much.

Ray leaned against a tree a few yards away, Alina sideways between his legs. He had an arm around her and a hand on her stomach. She hadn't laughed at us; Ray ran his fingertips up and down her back. She learned they expected a boy; which I knew already and as far as our father knew Ray had been a well kept secret like Paul had been with me.

Three months earlier she turned up first thing in the morning. It was the night after she and our father had come to meet Paul and Camille. She knocked on the door wearing the previous day's wrinkled clothes and apologizing for her jet lag before steering Camille and me into the kitchen. Camille was falling back to sleep and I'd hoped to get a couple more hours myself but with Alina still on Toronto time the possibility was fading. She put on coffee and started going through the fridge.

"Oh my God I'm so hungry in the morning now," she blurted out.

Blind with hunger. I'd have to keep my hands back.

"You want me to fix something? I know where everything is."

"I need to calm down," she said with a sigh so she took Camille and sat at the table while I got out toast and peanut butter, fruit and cottage cheese.

"I can't eat," she frowned after a few bites.

"Get it off your chest then you'll have room."

I waited for her to tell me what I already knew. Paul and I watched her go hand in hand with Ray into his cabin the night before and I didn't think they were going to talk sports.

"I slept with Ray," she said. There, Anna, her look begged. Give it to me. Tell me I should have known better.

"Okay," I said.

"Okay?"

"I slept with Paul last night and I can eat. Can you eat now?"

She shook her head and gave me Camille on her way to the coffee pot. I pointed to the cupboard the mugs were in so she helped herself to Paul's favourite and sat down. She stared at her black coffee for a few seconds before she realized she'd forgotten milk.

"Why are you worried about it?"

"I just met him," she shrugged.

She'd told me what happened with her baby's father Damian, every bit, in a long teary phone conversation. Maybe she didn't think she was ready to be with someone again. It was too soon. Or maybe she thought she was still too wrecked inside for it to be fair to Ray so I waited to hear her real objection.

"We started fooling around on his bed, undressing. He asked if I'm pregnant. I told him yes. He said he was falling for me, but if the baby's father was around he'd back off. I told him no. When he saw my shoulder he asked if the father had done it to me. I started to cry. He kissed me there, said I didn't have to talk about it but I did anyway because I wanted to tell him. He promised he wouldn't be any more than I was ready for, but I wanted him so I told him. Told him he was all I needed and then I slept with him."

"Okay," I said again.

"Aren't you going to say I'm irresponsible?"

"No," I said. "I slept with Paul two hours after I met him. At least you had three weeks of phone calls first."

"I can see why you don't think it's a big deal," she laughed.

"Are you worried you'll catch pregnant?" I whispered, making her laugh even harder. She tossed a bit of toast at me.

"I love you, Anna," she said as she pulled her plate closer.

"You too, Sweetie."

I found her some of my more practical clothes to wear and put the baby sling on her with Camille in it to disguise her stomach. She had her back to Paul as he came from the bedroom, our heads together as we adjusted Camille for our walk.

As we finished, he put his hand on her shoulder and pulled her hair out of the way. I lifted my head to look at her and she stared back, eyes wide. Paul put his nose on her neck then he kissed her, mistaking her for me.

"Good morning..." he whispered.

Alina's eyes went back to normal and she could see me trying not to laugh so she tilted her head, exposing more of her neck and letting him dig himself even deeper. He kissed her again. Fortunately, his eyes closed so he couldn't see my hand on my mouth.

"That smells so good. Is it Alina's? What's it called?"

"Ray's aftershave," she announced and we both burst out laughing.

Paul froze.

"I'm in so much trouble," he said as he doubled back to the bedroom, our laughter following him the whole way.

Now she laughed as Paul and I watched our daughter sleep on our blanket by the pond.

"Feeling better now?" Paul asked.

"Not really," I'd been crampy off and on all day and figured it was just Mother Nature getting things going again after the baby. I had Tylenol and a heating pad for a while then I tried being up and around for the exercise and at least it hadn't gotten any worse. No better either.

"I'm getting a drink, want anything?" I asked. The basket we brought our lunch in was too far away to reach.

"Yeah, can I get a beer? They're getting warm."

Chivalrous, I thought, spare the beer from getting warm. The refrigerator will save it without killing it. I pushed myself up sitting and definitely felt Mother Nature starting something.

"I think the cure for the cramps just turned up," I whispered to Paul. "I have to run to the house for a minute."

"Okay," he said, curling up closer to Camille.

I passed him a can and gave one to Ray then hurried back to the house. By the time I stepped off the path and onto the road north past the cabins, steady pain replaced the cramps.

By the time I reached the house I'd nearly doubled over in agony and screamed for help. I'd already bled through my clothes halfway down to my knees.

Paul's brother Joshua was the first one on the porch. Paul's men were just finishing lunch in the big kitchen.

"Jones!" Joshua yelled at the open door.

"Something's wrong, Joshua..." I whispered as he sat me on the stairs.

"I'll say."

Jones and another man ran out.

"Jones, get Ray and the Captain. They're at the pond... fast as you can. Matthews, call this lady a ride, medical evac."

Crap, I thought. But flying couldn't be any worse than the pain I felt. Someone else brought a blanket and they lay me down. I couldn't get out of the ball I was in.

"Are you pregnant again, Anna?" Joshua asked.

"I... what?" I managed.

"Stay with her," Joshua ordered. He ran in the house and had an I.V. started by the time Paul and Ray ran up. Alina must have Camille, I thought. I felt dizzy even lying down and tried to ask where Camille was but nobody answered. Joshua said something about helicopter and Ray said something about blood. I couldn't be sure. Maybe it was the

4

other way around. Paul's lips at my ear told me to relax, hold on. I remembered being carried and a lot of noise and wind.

Chapter 2

I flew.

Rows and rows of corn fields passed beneath; tall, green and covered in tufts of angel hair as far as I could see. The sky darkened behind me, both with clouds and with the coming of night. As I descended near the corn I heard voices; a murmur at first, then louder. I glimpsed men in the fields. They shouted, yelling and pleading.

The darkness behind reached above in spite of how fast I flew ahead. Loud, pulsing. I felt the vibration in my bones. I flew lower, trying to escape and I could see the men more clearly. Some raised their arms, calling to me for help, pleading, pursued by others armed with all sorts of crazy things. Metal pipes, crowbars. Guns and cleavers. Bare hands and teeth.

As I brushed over the tops of the stalks, water rose up through the ground, filled the space between and climbed the legs of the men. It quickly froze, holding them in place. The armed men remained on top of the thickening ice and attacked the others. A bone snapped and I shrieked in sympathy with the impossibly shrill sound of a man's scream. I didn't want to watch or be attacked so I went up higher, back up to the shaking sky and as I did the ice receded and the unarmed men were able to get away. They still begged me to help but at least the slaughter stopped.

I slowed down and could see them more clearly. Only their raised hands could be seen above the corn while the pounding above ravaged my chest. Hurting me, damaging me. I had to go lower, the pain was too much. But going lower brought the ice up. I struggled to adjust my altitude even though I couldn't find a place that didn't hurt me or the men. I tried to go low until they were close to getting caught then I went up again until the pain pushed me back down.

It went on too long. I tired and couldn't tolerate the noise from above. I weakened, dipping lower each time as the sky above sunk. Soon I couldn't fly high enough to spare the men below at all. I brought my hands up to cover my eyes as the thunder drove me down.

Chapter 3

I opened my eyes to the blur and spin of thunder overhead. The noise deafened and pressure smothered me. Ray stood at my side, grey like everything around him. My hand held one of his and he raised two bags in the other; one big and clear, the other deep red against the colourless everything around it.

"Hold still, Anna," I heard under the fading rumble. Ray hurried me away, the thundering above replaced by lights flying over. Something let go of my arm and he let go of my hand.

"Seventy over fifty," a woman's voice said. As the lights above fled past he popped the empty red bag off and attached another.

"That's funny, Ray," I laughed. "When I wake up I'll tell you you're in my dream. You're grey."

The lights above slowed and one took station above. I tried to pull away from pressure around my arm so Ray took my hand and held me still as the lights moved again.

"Still holding, seventy over fifty, doctor."

"Good," Ray said. I didn't understand why he looked so grey but sounded so relieved. He hung the bags on a pole above my head and put his nose on my forehead. "Alina has Camille. Paul's coming in the truck. He'll be here when you wake up. Everything's okay."

"Okay, Ray."

I must have fallen asleep with Camille at the pond. Paul with us in the sunshine and spring breeze cooled by its passage through the trees. Ray stayed with me under the lights, keeping the thunder away. After a bit he took me somewhere else and I lost track of things for a while.

I woke in a room full of hospital beds. Ray sat with me and a nurse saw to someone on the other side, her back to us. The curtains were pulled on both sides of my bed and he slumped back in his chair looking at his ankle up on his knee. His white medical coat pushed up at his shoulders with his shirt. He fussed with the Dr. Jackson tag and it dawned on me I really was in a hospital. I wasn't entirely comfortable. My stomach hurt and my throat was dry. When I tried to breathe my chest resisted like the weight of the room sat on it.

"Am I still dreaming?" I asked.

He looked up.

"No, Kiddo," he said. "You're in recovery."

"Why? What have I been doing?"

"I'm sorry, Anna. You had a miscarriage," he pushed my hair off my forehead. "You had to go to surgery to stop the bleeding."

I must have looked like I didn't know what he was talking about so Ray leaned over the bed, looking like he needed a hug. I put my arms around him and tried to reassure him.

"I didn't, Ray. It's okay. I would have felt him so I couldn't have been," but my eyes dampened and he held me tighter. "Does Paul know?"

"Yeah," Ray said as he straightened up, wiping his eyes. "We had a pretty good idea before the helicopter arrived."

I suddenly felt very alone. I wanted Paul and Camille, at home.

"I want to see him. He's all by himself."

"I know, he said the same thing about you. You were in a lot of trouble during the flight. He doesn't know yet or he'd have knocked the door down to get in here. Right now he's waiting down the hall. We'll have you in a room in half an hour. I got you a private one."

Ray stroked my forehead.

"He's hanging in there. Are you having much discomfort?"

I shrugged.

"Okay. I'll order you something. If I'm not back before you go to your room I'll see you there. I'm going to let him know you're awake. He'll let Alina know."

He knew it took a lot for me to admit I hurt. I didn't argue. Even though he'd read me correctly there was nothing he could do about most of the pain I felt. While he was gone, the nurse came and shot something into my I.V. then went back to what she was doing. A while later someone else came and wheeled me to my room. It was all the same colour, empty and sterile like I felt inside.

Soon I heard Paul and Ray in the hallway. They whispered outside the door for a minute then Paul came in. He didn't say anything; he didn't have to. The sadness on his face was the same as mine. I lifted the blanket so he kicked off his shoes and got in and held me.

We didn't talk much. I didn't want to know what trouble I'd been in and didn't ask. The nurses didn't say anything about Paul in the bed. Ray joined us after a while and sat in the chair. Alina started him texting then Paul and his mother. Alina talked to her more than I did. Paul's mother was delighted about Alina and Ray and thought of their son as her own grandson.

7

"Alina says Camille's gone to bed. She made a big dent in the milk you froze," he passed me his phone. "See?"

She sent a picture of sleeping Camille. Alina dressed her in the pinkest sleeper we had and I knew if she turned from her side there would be a giraffe on the front. Paul and I both looked.

"I haven't been away from her since the trip to Arlington," he said. The only time he'd been away from her was for the service for Denis when she was three weeks old.

"I'll send it to you, Paul." Ray said and a minute later Paul's pocket beeped. I liked the thought of Camille in his pocket.

"I didn't feel him inside me, Paul," I whispered. "I should have felt him. I should have known."

"It's nobody's fault, Anna," he answered as he wrapped himself around me, his jeans rough on my bare legs. "Please don't blame yourself."

"I just feel like if I'm quick enough, if I reach in the right direction and grab on I can get him back. I can undo it."

"Sshhh," Paul said. "I do, too."

He stayed with me until Ray took him to their hotel at midnight, long past the end of visiting hours. I smelled him on my pillow as I fell asleep.

Jack

Chapter 4

I didn't know the time when a familiar presence in the hall got my attention and set my heart racing. One of Damian's men. Alone. Moving to my room. Panic had me wide awake and I quickly read him. Definitely Damian's but his loyalty was weak, soft. My door opened and he stepped in, allowing a brief burst of dim light from the hall before he closed it behind him. He stopped at the end of the bed. I could tell he had short hair but not the colour and his white t-shirt seemed to glow brighter than anything else in the room.

"Anna Richards?" he asked.

I didn't say anything right away. Instead, I ran his line in my head to see what he would do. I saw him standing by the bed. He'd give me something then leave. I relaxed. I wanted to know what one of Damian's men would give me other than the pointy end of a knife.

"I'm Anna," I answered.

"My name is Jack Roberts," he said. He had a gentle east coast accent though not New York east. I imagined him from somewhere to the south. "I apologize for the timing of my visit. I've wanted to speak with you privately for a couple of months and this is likely the only chance I'll get."

"You're Damian's," I said, still reading him.

"Yes," he sounded surprised.

"His line. Close. Maybe his son." I compared Damian and Jack. He stood there. I didn't care about my manners; he snuck into my hospital room in the middle of the night. "I don't know your mother. Your loyalty to him is not what I've felt before. It's much softer; almost tenuous, doesn't stink.

"You're not here to kill me," I stated. I didn't have the strength to do anything about it other than scream for the unarmed nurse.

"No, Anna. I came to ask you to arrange a meeting with Captain Richards. Damian Howard has been missing for months. No word, no body. Our group is big. It's become difficult to control. Three of us have been left in charge and my men must find a way out or face elimination. The other two are as volatile as he is. They know we're wavering."

I thought a moment. If he wanted to separate himself from Damian's group it made sense to reach out to Paul. In a strange sort of way.

"How can the Captain help?" I asked.

"We want out. We're not looking to join you. We want a normal life; the way things used to be. We hope to have an understanding to watch each other's backs. The other two, Soros and Walker, are content to carry on hunting you. We think Damian is dead and they want to make as much trouble for you as they can. They won't move on you without his say so or without evidence they'll only see him again on the other side."

He didn't know exactly how dead Damian was. He wouldn't be regrouping with anyone anywhere.

Ever.

"I imagine you don't trust me. I'd like to offer something to open dialogue between our groups. Walker is in Toronto. Ray Jackson and his pregnant mate won't survive there for long. He's watching her apartment and has someone in the hospital she works at.

"Soros' team is in Calgary. He lost a man there a few months ago and has been trying to track him down. There are hints you might have men in hiding out that way. If you do, be careful. Soros is watching and will follow you to them. His inner circle is a small team of powerful readers, some of the best we have and he's tenacious. He'll never be convinced they're not out there.

"When they move on you, you won't stand a chance. Neither will we when our turn comes. Cooperation is a necessity."

We were both quiet for a moment.

"I understand what you're asking, Jack, and appreciate the heads up," I said. "I'll tell Paul what you told me. It's not my call. I do get where you're coming from."

His conversation drained me. I felt overwhelmed by what happened the day before and my interest in what he wanted faded.

"That's the best I can hope for," he said then he approached and gave me a piece of paper. "Leave a message at this number if you want to get in touch. Again, I'm so sorry to trouble you now."

Suddenly his head turned, looking back through the opposite wall. I turned my attention in the same direction and sensed Paul and Ray. It must have been closer to morning than I thought.

"Your men are coming. I have to go."

And with that he disappeared out the door. I lost track of him in the opposite direction. I waited only a minute before Paul came in.

"Hi, Paul," I said. I pulled the string for the light when he opened the door.

"Hi, Sugar," he came over and held me. "Ray's checking over your chart. Were you okay?"

"Yeah," I said. I didn't realize how much I'd missed him or how relieved I'd be he was with me and Jack wasn't.

"Whatever my chart says happened in the bathroom is way out of proportion." I'd buzzed the nurse to help me get to the toilet because I was still dizzy even sitting but she took so long and I really had to go so I went on my own. I made it to the toilet but must have passed out. She found me leaned over against the wall.

"Okay," Paul said, not sure if he believed me or not. He sighed and kissed the top of my head. Paul wore the same clothes as the night before since he left without taking the time to pack. He chewed gum and looked like he'd run wet fingers through his hair.

"Paul, I had a visitor."

"Mm?"

I hesitated, knowing Paul would be out the door and wouldn't listen until he failed to catch him. If Jack served with Damian then Paul would know who he was.

"Jack Roberts."

I felt Paul's arms stiffen. "Roberts? When?"

"He was sorry to bother me now, just came to talk."

"When, Anna," he demanded. He let go of me and went to look out the window in the door.

"He took off when he sensed you coming," I said but Paul ran out before I finished.

"Where is he off to in such a hurry?" Ray came in seconds later.

"I had company. I think Paul's pretty pissed about it."

Ray came over to take my blood pressure. I didn't really see the point. The nurses woke me up all night to check it. He also wore the same things as the day before including the white coat.

"Company," he said, somewhat absently. He set his doctor switch to 'on.' "Any trouble getting to the bathroom?"

"No, the getting there part went fine."

"So I heard." He squeezed my hand. "Otherwise how are you holding up?"

I sighed. "It was a long night. Can I go home today?"

"Yes, you're doing well. That plus a promise of a week of bed rest and two doctors next door is enough for me."

"Okay," I promised.

"Anna," he sighed. "If Joshua hadn't started dumping fluids in you and had all the extra blood bagged and ready to go you wouldn't have made it to the hospital. Your pressure crashed and I lost you for over two minutes. I was lucky to get you back. Joshua made the difference."

He reached for a tissue and wiped his eyes.

"Come here," I whispered and held my arms out. I saw how much he hurt and felt too numb inside for the miscarriage to bother me. "Thank you, Ray. I'm sorry you had to go through that."

He passed me a tissue after he let me go. "I'm used to treating friends. It's part of what I do. It doesn't sink in until later."

"Think about getting a hospital posting with Alina," I suggested. "Paul hasn't talked about resigning yet. We need military resources if there's any more trouble from Damian's men, but when we're sure it's over."

"Yeah, I have. I'd go to Toronto if she asked but she wants to be near you. I have privileges here in Redding and in Reno. Alina is a good doctor in spite of being so young. She won't have a problem getting on where ever she wants."

"If she's young what does that make me?"

"Kiddo," he smiled. "Where did Paul go again?"

"He went after Jack Roberts. He was in my room."

"What? Roberts?"

"You just missed him," I said as Paul stormed in.

"God damn security, Ray. Where the hell were they?" Paul came straight over to the bed and took a few deep breaths to calm down. "Are you okay?"

"Yes, Paul." I took his hand. "Jack's not a problem for us."

"Apparently not if we're on a first name basis," Paul sneered. "I'm sorry. Even if he just wanted to talk that's dirty him coming here."

"I don't know, Paul. He'd be in pieces if he went straight to you. Even alone."

Paul pulled up a chair next to Ray and sat down, putting his hand on my ankle through the thin blanket.

"You're right. I'm sorry I ran out."

"Ray says I can go home today. You doing okay?"

Ray pulled Paul out of his seat and moved him to the one closer to me, then sat in the one by my feet.

"It's hard when there's something wrong I can't fix," Paul said. "I guess that's why I ran out after Roberts. At least I can do something about him."

I rolled to my side. He took my hand and pulled his chair closer. "What did he want?"

"He asked me to arrange a meeting with you and he gave us some information in exchange for considering it."

"Do you want to tell me now? He's long gone. It can wait."

"Yeah," I said. He squeezed my hand.

"With Damian gone him and two others have been left in charge but they're struggling to keep control. Jack and his men want to leave. The other two know it and Jack's afraid. He's going to wind up with the same problems we have. His loyalty to Damian is so soft. It doesn't smell of Damian's insanity. I believe him.

"He's not looking to join us or ask you to join him but he says neither of our groups stands a chance without finding a way to team up. Even when they split it sounds like there will still be too many of Damian's men left."

"I remember Jack from before Damian lost it," Ray said. "He stuck with him a long time. Put him down more than once hoping he'd come back cured. Even then he talked about breaking away."

I could see Paul thinking. The lights came on in the hallway and I heard the cart with the breakfast trays.

"What information did he give us?" Paul asked.

"He said Walker is in Toronto. Watching Alina's apartment and has someone working at her hospital. Walker's going after Ray and Alina once they go back and they're separated from us.

"He said the other one. Sor..." I'd forgotten the other name.

"Soros?" Paul asked.

"Him. He's in Calgary. It was his man I took to the forest in December when we were in Edmonton. Soros is trying to find him. Jack said there are rumours we have a second group hiding in the area. Soros is convinced of it. Jack said he's one of their best readers and he's not going to give up until he finds them. He said if we go to them or try and contact them Soros will be able to find them."

"Did you tell him anything about us?" Paul asked.

"No, other than giving him a thorough and rude reading of his line right down to his mother which I thought was fair because he had the cans to come in here. I saw he would stand at the foot of the bed, hand me something, then leave. I didn't tell him that part. I said I'd tell you everything and it's not up to me to bargain with him."

"What did he hand you?"

I passed Paul the piece of paper. "He said to leave a message if you want to be contacted."

Paul put it in his pocket.

"We should tell Alina to turn around," Paul said.

"No," Ray protested. "We can't do anything different. It could push Soros' hand."

"She has my daughter, Ray," Paul said.

"You can't stop her, Paul," I said. "She sees too many drivers roll in from accidents while they're using their phone. It'll be off."

"Anna's right, Paul," Ray agreed. "She caught me in Toronto and threw my phone out the window onto the 401. Didn't talk to me for two days."

Paul leaned forward and buried his face in his hands.

"I don't need this right now," he said. His tight voice betrayed the strain he bore.

"See if the Colonel has anything on Walker and Soros." Ray suggested. "If it matches what Roberts said then think about calling him."

Someone came in with breakfast and put it on my bed.

"I have a few things to take care of," Ray said. "Alina said she'd pick up coffee when she got in if Camille isn't running on empty. Anna, you get a hand walking to the bathroom if you need to go. We're not picking you up off the floor again."

"I wasn't on the floor," I argued as he left.

Breakfast was, well, breakfast. Hospital breakfast. I gave Paul the coffee and ate the toast and eggs-like scramble. He remained quiet, watching me.

"Ray had a talk with me," he said when his coffee was half way down. "He thinks Camille's line is still tied to ours until it settles when she's older. We can conceive but it might be why we lost him. We can't give a son a line right now. Ray wants some time to try and figure it out."

I had to put my drink down because my hands shook.

"No, I didn't notice. I never tried to feel him." I took another tissue and wiped my eyes as I cried my first real tears since the previous day. "What if we can't have another? What if my line is too strong now? How the hell do I fix that, Paul?"

"Sshhh, our daughter's line is strong like ours and she'll have a son. If a strong line in a mother was a problem then she wouldn't have a baby, would she?"

"No," I agreed.

"There's no rush. I'm thankful for my healthy wife and daughter. I love being a husband and a father and I'm not risking one for more of the other. Ever. Even if Ray is right Camille won't be our last. We'll just have to wait longer."

That cheered me a bit. I didn't have the perspective yet that he had. Coming back. The patience to wait through childhood and the teen years to find each other again.

"Is Anna being childish?" I sniffled.

"Yes, but it doesn't mean Paul doesn't feel the same way."

Paul helped me to the bathroom and took my breakfast tray out while he waited for me to need help returning to bed. I had no plans to fight Ray on the bed rest if it took all I had to get six feet to the toilet. I was drifting off when I heard a familiar song coming from the hall.

"It's Alina," I said. "Our mother used to sing that Russian lullaby. Alina and I got the words all messed up because we never spoke Russian and our mixed up version stuck."

"I've heard you sing every goofy word to Camille," he laughed then he got up and poked his head out the door.

"Paul!" I heard her say as he stepped out. "Come hug me. My hands are full. Don't squish babies. I'm so sorry, Paul. Anything I can do you name it, okay?"

"Of course."

Paul brought her in and pulled a big bag off her shoulder.

"You shouldn't be lifting this up into the truck. It weighs as much as you do."

"Hi, Sweetie," she smiled at me as she put the tray of coffees on my table and started rooting around in the sling for Camille. "We ladies wouldn't drive that big ugly rolling man purse around. We took Mommy's pretty Lincoln. I told her if she made a peep in the hall and we got tossed out she'd be gumming biscotti at the caffeine station downstairs for breakfast. She's been so good. Here."

She passed Camille to Paul who buzzed his lips under her chin earning a laugh. Then he brought her to me.

"Hi, baby," I said as I tucked her in beside me to feed. Alina came over and hugged me.

"I'm sorry, Sweetie," she said. "You hanging in there?"

"Yeah."

"The marked decaf is mine," Alina told Paul. "Milk in yours. Bunch of muffins in the diaper bag."

I knew it wasn't decaf; she'd have told them to write it on the lid. I also knew it was her second from the big wad of minty gum in her mouth, disguising the evidence of the first.

"You sit," Paul ordered Alina and gave her the decaf. "I'll go get the nurse to tell Ray you're here."

"Thanks, Paul." She put the chairs together and sat in one with her feet up in the other. "I brought you clothes to wear home."

"You're a dear," I said. "Can I ask you something?"

"Sure." She popped open the plastic lid on her cup.

"Have you thought about marrying Ray?"

Her eyebrows went up as she looked to see if I was serious.

"I guess it wouldn't be unexpected for us to get married if we're naming him as the baby's father. What do you think?"

"About marrying Ray? He's like a brother to me. I look up to him. But I hadn't thought about marrying him. Do you think it would make things awkward with Paul?"

"What?" she tried not to inhale her coffee.

"I mean maybe they could swap weeks with me or something?"

Alina laughed. "Maybe it would be more convenient for everyone if I did it."

"Did what?" Ray asked as he and Paul came in. "Hi, Sweetie. Don't get up."

He knelt and held her tight. She held him with one arm so she wouldn't dump her coffee on his back.

I pointed at Ray on his knee in front of her and she snorted. Paul came over behind me and put his chin on my neck to watch Camille. He would have been as worried about her as Ray was about Alina since the visit from Jack Roberts. Camille slowed down so I decided to get the air out of her stomach and have her changed before I gave her any more.

"Paul, can you give her dry pants please and see if she has a burp?"

"Yeah," he said, scooping her up. "Come here, Miss Missy."

I moved my legs out of the way so he could change her on the bed. Alina whispered in Ray's ear and he smiled.

"Anna, you're a riot," he laughed.

I shrugged. "Give it some thought."

Ray laughed again and put his hand on Alina's stomach as he kissed her. Paul brought one of the chairs around to sit facing us and Alina demanded to see my chart so Ray went to get it.

"Thank you for bringing her, Alina. I feel less empty inside," I whispered.

"You're welcome. She was a treat. You know she's only slightly more stubborn than you are."

"Yes," Paul answered for me.

Camille was warm and sleepy and I wasn't far behind. Ray brought my chart in and I listened to Alina flip pages. She sniffed. Then she started crying.

Ray sighed.

"I told you to pass on reading it," he whispered.

"Ray," she sobbed. "Your handwriting is even worse than mine."

"Give it to me. Come on, let's stretch your legs."

She leaned over my bed and kissed my cheek before she let him haul her toward the door.

"Love you, Sweetie," I whispered once she was out. Then I opened my eyes and looked at Paul. His were red, looking down at his hands as his fingers examined each other.

"Paul," I said. "If Ray's right we could be in our forties and fifties before we can have another. Fifteen years is a long time to be careful, too many chances for mistakes. We need to think about doing something permanent, to be sure."

He didn't look up but he nodded. "I'll do it. It's minor for me."

"I have everything I need right here. If he's wrong it's a bonus. When he has an answer."

"Yes," he said, finally looking up at me. Then a smile. "I still have to pinch myself to be sure I have you two. This is tough, but it makes me more grateful for what I have."

Chapter 5

Paul drove us home in the truck ahead of Ray and Alina in the car. As we left the parking lot, I picked up Jack and another man on the road. I quickly scanned the second man. His loyalty was mostly to Jack. I read a tiny bit of weak loyalty to Damian before they left my range. It looked to me like their split from the other side had begun.

Paul was wary: constantly checking the mirrors, changing lanes, varying our speed. Ray did the same. Ray gained on us then lost ground in a strange dance. Paul did it much more aggressively than Ray because I knew why and Ray would be trying to avoid annoying Alina with what she would think was reckless driving.

"How do we warn Keith and keep Alina from leaving?"

"I'm taking suggestions." Paul replied. "I can't warn him without giving him away. I don't know what to do about Alina. I know Ray's trying to come up with something."

Camille's car seat occupied the space between us. I reached over her and walked my fingers on Paul's leg to get his attention and he took my hand.

"I'll come up with some version of what really happened that she'll buy. If she's mad at us Ray can take her side so she'll still feel safe with him. If we all piss her off she'll want to go home. Maybe Ray could get off his ass and marry her and then dawdle about setting up housekeeping in town."

"Sooner than you think, Sugar," Paul hinted. "Not a word especially with you in the running for him. I don't want you two fighting."

He squeezed my hand and laughed. Camille startled so I brushed my fingers on her cheek the way she liked and she went back to sleep.

We quietly drove for a while and I thought about Keith. I'd slumped down in my seat with my knees on the dashboard, still holding Paul's hand across Camille. The only warning they might get was Keith's reader Patrick picking up a bunch of Damian's men in the mall.

"Paul?"

"Mm hm?" Now we were on the two lane highway he couldn't change lanes but he still varied his speed and concentrated on everything around him.

"I always could jump, long before anything else changed. I can test it to see if I still can. If it works I can get you to Keith. I'll use my bike and take it down the highway a bit then try getting home. You can follow in the truck. We can rig up a two-way in my helmet."

Paul thought. We hadn't talked about Andre or any of the other terrible things I'd done in a couple of months. Not since Paul ran out of questions.

"I know Keith will never trust me again. I don't think any of them will. I just have to get you there. Patrick would pick us up and you could go see them. We'd be there and back in about as much time as you need with Keith."

He settled on regular highway speed and looked ahead.

"Give it some thought. I'm not running off to test it unless you want me to. But I feel like I owe him something after what I did. If it was just a bunch of men there it would be different but there's a child coming and we can't walk away."

Paul didn't say anything and after a while went back to working the accelerator. He stopped before the gate and Ray and Alina disappeared ahead as he turned off the engine. He reached and pulled me to him over Camille's seat.

"I need to know if something happens to me you'll think like a grownup and take care of Camille and the other children. You'll put them before me. We'll be together again and the children are worth the sacrifice of every grownup in the family. I need you to think like a leader. Consider everything and don't hesitate to act when you have to move forward with a difficult choice. I need you at my right hand. You're my reader. That's as important to my grownup side as being Anna's husband and Camille's father are in this life. Part of being a grownup is balancing the two: the memories and the present.

"There may be times we have to leave Camille behind to protect her. If I tell you to take her and run you must.

"When Ray says you can get up we'll take your bike out. I'm going to contact the Colonel and find out where Walker and Soros are. I'm not telling him why other than I want the go ahead to do a little clean up."

He tipped my head and tasted my neck with his lips.

"What have you left out?"

"I picked up Jack and another man as we left the hospital."

"Uh huh?" Paul whispered.

"The other man was loyal to Jack; just a hint of Damian. Then they were out of range."

"And you didn't say anything then because you thought I'd go after him again?"

"Something like that," I whispered. I put my hand on the back of his head and lifted my chin further as he brushed his nose on my throat. "I was hoping you'd pull over and force it out of me in front of your brother."

Paul stopped and pulled the front of my shirt back where it was before he started nosing it out of the way. Joshua stood in front of the truck.

"I think Jack's group is close to separating if they're so tightly tied to him. As long as there's a bit of the old loyalty I should be able to see what they're going to do. I just wanted to go home, Paul. I didn't want any more Jack today."

Paul climbed out and talked to Joshua for a couple of minutes then Joshua came around to my door. I opened it and hugged him.

"I'm so sorry, Anna. Are you doing okay?"

"I'm doing. Thank you for everything you did at the house. Ray said you made his job easy," I winked. "I owe you one."

"Glad you're okay. Paul and I are heading back to Redding in a few hours to get Mom from the airport. Nothing I can do to save you from that."

Chapter 6

After two days, Ray allowed me meals at the table. After four, he extended it to a couple of hours on the couch. I hadn't done any more than they said and they left me alone in the apartment for hours at a time while they took Camille out for fresh air. On the fifth day when they took her out I went downstairs as soon as I knew the house was empty.

My pack was still in the closet. Nobody touched it other than me to remove the knife and book for the Colonel a week after I killed Damian. His gun was still in it with mine. I removed the nine volt battery from the cheap alarm on the armoury door and took a knife from the drawer in the kitchen and broke in. I carefully cleaned and reloaded them both and helped myself to a stack of targets. I ran a couple down the long, dim and dirty tunnel under the house.

I started with mine and shot with my left like I used to. Did okay but I was all over the target. Nothing like the tight cluster in the centre I'd done before. My right was better than my left and I hadn't been able to hit anything right handed the last time. Same with Damian's. It wasn't much bigger than mine and was smaller than the guns Paul favoured. I felt his hands on my shoulders when I reloaded.

"I'm getting better," I said. "Left is sloppy still but right's improved. I guess Andre took his leftiness with him."

"I've been watching," Paul said.

"I don't want to find out how useless I am when it really matters."

"You're right," he sighed. "That makes sense. I don't recognize that one."

He pointed at the bigger gun.

"It was Damian's," I said. "He left it behind on the ground. Mine now. I forgot I had it."

Paul loudly sighed through his nose.

"Let's see them both in each hand again," he said. It sounded more like an order.

I did. Still improving.

"You do better with the heavier gun in your right because it's stronger. It's a toss up with your gun," Paul observed then he ran out two targets.

"I want you to alternate target to target as fast as you can and still hit them. I think you'll do better with your left handedness gone. You won't feel as steady but if you can shoot with both hands you should take advantage of it."

I thought I took it slow, concentrating. Didn't do any worse with either even considering the one handed hold I had on each.

"Were you rushing?" Paul asked. "I didn't expect you to go so fast."

"It felt like everything was slowing down."

Paul nodded as I put the guns down.

"I'll get you a holster that will hold both," he said.

"I need you, Paul. Are we just going to be friends while we wait for Ray to finish his puzzle?"

He didn't respond so we got the guns clean and I followed him into the armoury to put them away. He stopped me before we went out the door and closed it, turning the lock.

"I came prepared," he said as he patted the little packet in his pocket.

I spent the rest of the afternoon reading to Camille in our bed. Paul slept. He took a shift on watch every night. Alina was ticked at me for going down to the range. Ray was too but he understood why I did it. We were all a little on edge. Damian's men weren't done showing interest in us and it was just a matter of seeing how events leading up to their next visit would play out.

"The Colonel says Walker is in Toronto and Soros is in Alberta," Paul said. He hadn't opened his eyes but his quiet snoring stopped a few minutes before. "He called while you were downstairs in the range. He says he's very sorry to hear about our loss and Ray is right."

Ray was usually right.

"How did he know what Ray's doing?"

"He didn't," Paul explained. "He very diplomatically expressed his surprise you survived. He said that's quite unusual."

"I'm sorry, Paul."

"Don't be. We can't change it," he sighed. "Ross will take me for the vasectomy next week. Ray will go while Alina heals after their son is born. She won't know. She'll just think he can't."

Camille yawned. Paul reached around her tummy and pulled her close.

"The number was for a bar. I asked for Jack and the person who answered said I had the wrong number. He's probably monitoring the phone."

"Maybe he'll turn up when we're in Redding tomorrow."

"Don't know." Paul held Camille tighter. "If you pick up anything wrong, walk away. I'll be right behind you. I'm going armed. The Colonel is getting you licensed to carry. He gave us the go ahead to go after Walker and Soros. That just means we don't get in trouble if we take care of them here. In Canada, we're on our own."

"Do you think Keith will bring Marie here?"

"I would if I was him. We have over a dozen family plus the others, maybe Jack and his men but that's a long shot. Keith has such a small group and they can't stay hidden there for very long. There not prepared for an assault in any case. They've been fighters in the past but not in this life. They'd pick it up more quickly than normal with training but it doesn't just come to us. Muscle memory, reaction time. The mind remembers but the body still has to learn."

I recalled I knew how to breathe through labour and breastfeed through Catherine's memories. She'd seen babies come but I still had to figure out what really worked for me and Camille and we had our challenges with the feedings.

"Dinner, kids," Paul's mother interrupted us with a knock on the door.

"I've been putting away milk for Camille again. There should be enough for tomorrow for her. Are Ray and Alina okay with looking after her for a few hours?"

He nodded.

"Ray's not happy about us going alone but as long as Alina is pregnant his job is to be by her."

I understood what Paul meant when he said Camille was the only thing protecting me. She was more important than both of us because until her line set years down the road she wouldn't come back more than a few times if something happened to her. Then she would be gone. I would come back and now she was separate from me I wouldn't need that same protection. I didn't like it but that was part of my life since I'd taken Damian's strong line for my own.

Ray and Alina joined us for dinner so the five of us passed Camille around at the table as we ate.

"I can't believe you ran off to play cowboy downstairs," Alina said like she'd never done a questionable thing in her life. She sat across from me, next to Ray who was across from Paul. Paul's mother was at the head of the table where Paul usually sat. I thought she was through giving me an earful but she obviously wasn't. I tried to stay calm but it felt like pushy Alina and stubborn Anna were going to butt heads.

"Have you even been down there?" I asked, trying to sound nice but not doing a very good job. "You can lie down to shoot so I wasn't actually breaking any rules."

"There's a lot of things you can do lying down you probably shouldn't be doing yet," she primly replied. God, I hated it when she took that tone. I didn't see how letting a few rounds go could take any skin off of her nose and didn't know how she would have heard about Paul and I in the armoury. Maybe we weren't as out of sight as I thought.

Paul and Ray exchanged glances so I knew exactly how Alina found out. Paul's mother pretended not to notice.

I took a few bites while I decided if the silence in the room warranted backing down or replying. I chose replying and managed to sound completely sincere.

"You know, Alina, why don't you come down to see for yourself. It's not as bad as you think. Maybe in a couple of days?"

She thought; wondering how my nice offer could possibly sneak around and bite her from behind. I put my fork down and waited for her to look up then I smiled. She sighed and smiled back.

"Okay, in a couple of days."

I picked my fork up and loaded it with potatoes and peas.

"I don't know how much fun you'd have though," I said and mixed a little coldness into my sweet tone. "When you lie on your stomach you look like a see-saw."

Alina firmly put her fork down. I kept smiling as I reloaded mine. She hadn't seen that coming. She watched me take another bite. Paul and Ray hadn't heard us fight before and didn't know Alina and I secretly enjoyed ourselves.

"Hey, Anna," she said. "Remember when you took all those things from my room and had a garage sale with them in front of the house?"

"Oh yeah," I smiled. That was well done.

"And I had to pay you my own money to get it back before the neighbour kids bought it all?"

"Mm hm," I nodded. I'd completely forgotten until she brought it up.

This time I watched her take a couple of mouthfuls. I kept my smile up but inside I worried. I still found out about things she'd done to get back at me for getting back at her years after the fact. "Every day for a month I went into the cloakroom at morning recess, got out your lunch and spat in your sandwich."

I felt my eyes narrow as my smile fell. It transferred itself to Ray's face so I decided to dust off one that would have had Alina grounded for a year if she'd gotten caught.

"Remember that Easter when you went out as the sun came up and picked up every last bit of candy mother hid in the yard the night before? How you blamed it on Kenny?"

She glared at me. I waited but she didn't say anything.

"Remember how much trouble he got in?" I asked. "I still believed in the Easter Bunny, Alina. You ruined my childhood."

"I gave you half to keep quiet," she hissed. "I can't believe you're still holding that over my head."

"What if Dad finds out," I gasped, finger tips over my mouth in mock horror. "You'll be hauling out Kenny's garbage and cutting his lawn for a year like he had to do for us."

Her knuckles whitened around her fork. Paul snickered. Anything that got Kenny in trouble would please him.

"Dad never did find out how mother's sewing basket wound up in my room, did he?" She whispered.

"Alina..." I growled.

"You told Ray you never needed a doctor. Might have something to do with the sewing kit." She smugly stared back. I'd lost. She knew it and I knew it. The only thing left to decide was how she was going to rub it in.

"What?" Ray asked.

"She never told you?" Alina asked. "Paul never asked how you got the scar on your backside?"

"He's too much of a gentleman," I said as I put my hand up over my reddening cheek so his mother wouldn't see it. For some reason I wasn't comfortable with Paul and my butt being in the same sentence in front of her.

"Enough, Alina. You win," I said but she kept going.

"How you cut it open the second time you and Kenny swiped his brother's motorcycle? How you never got caught because it went down on the same side and he hadn't fixed it yet? How you begged me to sew it up so Dad wouldn't know?"

I felt my lips press together and my nose flared with anger.

"You stink, Alina," but Paul and Ray both tried not to laugh. The story was funny but not when she ground me into the dirt with it. I forced back the hilarious vision of Alina; forehead screwed up in concentration, tongue working the corner of her mouth and needle and thread in hand sewing up my bare ass as I shrieked into a pillow.

"You're lucky it didn't get infected. That kind of thread is like a vacuum sucking in germs."

I held my hand up flat in front of my face and tilted it back and forth like a see-saw while I made a creaking sound.

"Too little too late, little sister," she laughed. "Two more days in bed except for your doctor trip tomorrow or I start making phone calls."

"Fine," I said as I stood, pushing my chair back with my legs. I stomped off as their laughter started.

Chapter 7

My follow up with the doctor went as expected. He reassured us we could have more children and not to worry. We had one already

25

and a miscarriage wasn't likely to happen again. After a few other questions about my recovery, he said he didn't need to see me again. To me, it felt like a colossal waste of time but it was important to Paul I was physically past it. We were in and out in all of ten minutes.

Paul took me for lunch and we chose a booth for privacy. I hadn't cried about the miscarriage since I was in the hospital and decided lunch was a good time to do it again. The doctor told us to expect it. A postpartum ride like after Camille was born. I was over it by the time the waitress brought our food and felt better. We both missed Camille, being away from her for the second time in a week, but we also needed time away from all the help we had.

The doctor appointment had been so brief we decided to pick up motorcycle gear we needed. Paul looked warm. He had two guns under his jacket so he had to keep it on. I was down to a t-shirt and felt toasty in the sun. The dark black and red flames covering my arms soaked up the heat like a dark shirt. We kept the air conditioning on in the truck for him so he didn't cook and I didn't complain about my goose bumps.

Paul disappeared to the men's section for a jacket and boots. I found a nice fitting leather jacket with good padding and long enough sleeves. It was plain black with zippers in the right places so I wouldn't baste in my own sweat. Paul found me as I decided on the size.

"If I were a cop, I'd pull you over to get a better look at you," he said. "But you're not thinking about your accessories."

He had a few jackets in his arms so I followed him to the change room. After he pulled the curtain, he took off his jacket and tried on one he chose for himself. I saw what he meant. He had to be able to get two guns under it plus his Kevlar vest without looking like he had two guns and a Kevlar vest. It would have been too big without his accessories but with them it fit fine and was loose enough I couldn't tell he carried.

"Now your turn."

He put his jacket aside then he put his guns and vest on me fitting them as best he could. His guns were bigger than I would carry because I was smaller and couldn't hide as much under my arms.

"Try fitting this under the one you picked."

"The one I picked was cute," I pouted.

"Cute doesn't stop a bullet."

I gave him the point. He decided on one snug enough to keep the padding in the right places and loose enough to conceal the bulges under my arms. Or would be with armour and weapons the right size.

"Are you sure you want the other gun? I can get another like the one you already have. The Colonel will make sure there's no problem with the registration. You just have to decide."

"I like the two I have," I said.

I paid attention for Jack and finally sensed him when we were about to pay. Jack and the other man from the hospital were out front either in the parking lot or across the street. I made a note for myself to keep better track of my surroundings so I could be more useful than pointing and announcing 'over there somewhere.'

"Jack's out front," I whispered as our turn came.

Jack separated from the other man so I ran his line forward to see what he would do. The man with him would wait in the car and watch us talk to Jack. Paul would shake Jack's hand after we moved toward our truck and further away from the busy front door. Paul and I would both speak then I'd give Jack something. Jack would talk and I'd look at Paul who would nod and I'd talk some more. He'd lose interest after a bit.

When Jack returns to the car the other man will dial a number on his phone. I took the pen from Paul after he signed to charge our gear and wrote it down on the back of a business card I took from the holder on top of the register. Jack's loyalty hadn't changed. Neither had that of the man with him; mostly loyal to Jack with a lingering bit of loyalty to Damian. We took our things down the stairs from the clothing section and through the rows of motorcycles for sale.

"Are we going to have a problem?" Paul asked.

"No. The man from the other day is waiting across the street. Jack's coming our way."

"What's the number?"

I shrugged. "The driver will call it as Jack returns to the car. I'm going to ask him about it, if that's okay with you. He doesn't know I can fast forward their lines but he's less likely to try something funny down the road if he knows I can see it."

"Do it," Paul said. "We have a favour to return. Are they armed?"

"I wouldn't know unless I rewound their lines. I can if you want but I'm not sure how far back I can go."

Paul shook his head as we walked toward the front door.

"Don't bother. It's busy here. But if we have to meet him somewhere private it's the kind of thing that's a priority. That and if anyone with him is strongly loyal to Damian. Then we all have a problem including Jack if what he told you is true."

Jack fell in beside Paul as we walked out. I hadn't gotten a good look at him in the dark hospital room and I could see now he had a long scar running up past his eye into his closely cut blonde hair. I remembered similar marks on a couple of the men who came after me the day Denis died and I wondered how rough life with Damian was. He looked about Paul's age, mid-thirties, just more weathered from time outdoors.

"Thank you for calling, Captain," Jack said.

"Over here," Paul nodded. He indicated away from the door. There wasn't any shade in front of the store. We stopped about ten feet from the door, out of the foot traffic and somewhat out of sight.

"Jack Roberts," Jack said as he offered his hand.

"Paul Richards, Paul is fine."

"Jack, please," Jack said then he offered his hand to me.

"Anna," I said as I took it. His palm tingled in mine as I looked up at him then he pulled it away.

"I want to apologize again for the timing of my visit. If Anna's told you what I said I hope you can understand why I would do something so tactless. There was just no other way to reach you without prematurely putting myself and my men in danger."

I shifted my new gear to my other arm as Paul elbowed me then tipped his head toward Jack so I pulled the business card with the number I'd written on it out of my pocket and handed it to him, number side up.

He took it and visibly whitened as his mouth opened. He looked at me then at Paul.

"Where did you get this?" His voice wasn't much more than a whisper.

"Your driver will call it as you return to his car," I replied. "I want to make sure he's not going to call in reinforcements while we still have time to drive off with you in the back of our truck."

Jack emphatically shook his head.

"How did you get this? If you have it then Damian—"

"Jack," I said and he looked up from the card. "Put it in your pocket. I don't want it. I watched him dial it into his phone as you return to the car, which you won't do for a while yet. I was upstairs in the bike shop as I did it and I wrote the number down only a few minutes ago. I've never seen the number before and I don't remember it.

"I can run your line forward and backward like a video tape and see where you've been... where you're going... through your own eyes.

Consider it a security check. I did it when you came to my hospital room. That's how I knew you weren't there to kill me."

Jack sighed. He pulled himself together and challenged me with his tone.

"Where am I going after this?" he asked.

I looked at Paul. He nodded to go ahead.

"South. The sun is shining in the front window. You take the gun off your right ankle and shove it under your seat. The one down your pants will go in the glove box. Driver wants Mexican. He pays. Driver's license is upside down in his wallet."

There was something more about it so I skipped backward.

"Speeding ticket driving up here; he put it away upside down. I can make out Sacramento before he pulls it out and fixes it."

I paused to wipe my forehead. It felt damp and clammy in spite of the heat and I felt a wobble in my stomach. When I lowered my arm, I grabbed Paul's elbow so he looked at me.

"I think you've overdone it, Sugar," he said. "Back in the truck."

"Gimme," Jack said as he took the things I carried. His fingers brushed my arm and again I felt the tingling and shivered in the sun. Paul's arm went around me as Jack grabbed what he could carry from Paul. If I did a lip stand here and Alina found out she'd make me stay in bed for a month. We rolled down the windows and a breeze blew through. I sat sideways on the edge of the driver's seat on the shady side so I could listen to them talk. Paul put our gear in the back of the truck and brought me a bottle of cold water and an ice pack from the first aid bag. I put my hair up and he put the ice on the back of my neck.

"That was my fault," I said. "All this hair is like a fur coat in the heat."

Jack patiently waited.

"So what about the number, Jack?" I asked. "Are Paul and I going to have a problem getting home?"

I wasn't sure if Paul wanted me questioning him but I hadn't said anything I hadn't cleared with him first and knew he would open his mouth and take over if the conversation went somewhere he didn't like.

Jack chewed the inside of his lip as he thought then he addressed Paul.

"I gave you something minor in your wife's hospital room. I assume you verified it or you wouldn't have called. You've stepped up that trust by telling me what your reader can do. That's a powerful trick and tells me who I'd have to hurt to get an advantage. But I suspect there's even more to her if she's at your right hand."

Paul shifted his weight so more of him was between Jack and me. I reached for Paul and put my hand on his back so he would know where I was.

"Leaving this meeting without offering you something equally precious is only going to make anything we try to do together in the future much harder," Jack decided and I felt Paul relax. "Damian controls the growth of our family. He's taken many of the mates as his seconds. I don't know how many. Only he does.

"I found mine first this time. I was supposed to wait for him to decide if I could have her or not. Keep my distance. I didn't." He gestured at the scar on his face then he lowered his eyes. "Discipline. I'll see her next time."

I looked at my hand on Paul's back. He reached around and held it. Suddenly I felt very lucky.

"That's just the one you can see. My driver, Dana. That's his mate's number. Damian doesn't know about her. We have her in hiding. Under the protection of a couple of my men I found who Damian doesn't know about. Their son is due in a month or two, we're not really sure... he calls her a lot. The pregnancy has been rough and they don't have a doctor. Can't go to one... the risk of attention is too high.

"So unless you're afraid of a huge, uncomfortable pregnant woman there's no trouble at the other end of that phone number."

"Paul," I urged as I put my feet on the ground and my arm around his middle. He knew what I wanted. We had two doctors. Alina was an emergency doctor who looked after people usually after a paramedic or a doctor like Ray tidied them up and delivered babies who couldn't wait to get upstairs but Ray had training in obstetrics and had delivered Camille.

"Ray can't go, Anna. If we're being watched he'll lead them right to her," he thought. "If Damian doesn't know about them you could send them to us. He would think they're mine, or that group up north he believes exists. Ray Jackson delivered my daughter and you know his mate is a doctor too."

"Daughter?" Jack asked. That seemed to get his attention more than the offer of help but it wasn't surprising. The only children born in the family were male. "You mean living this life as a female?"

"No," Paul said. "She is female; strong line like ours."

I knew what they meant. Paul's father had lived his last life as a woman but he was male. I had done the same thing; a female line in Andre's body in my last life.

"She thinks it's something about organized crime or spies... witness protection," Jack explained, getting his thoughts back on track. "That's why she has to hide. She's not really sure but she's run for her life with them so she knows she has to stay hidden. She'd be good."

"That would work with Alina," Paul mused.

"I'm expected back soon. We've been holding off on splitting until we had somewhere safe for them to go. I have to get things straightened out with my group."

"I do, too," Paul replied. "For starters we can offer the help. Bringing our men together requires some preparation. Some might need help accepting an understanding as grownups. The biggest challenge will be the men who aren't family. You're still wanted."

Jack nodded in agreement then he looked at me. I'd been watching him over Paul's shoulder.

"I need to speak with you privately, Paul," he said.

I didn't move. I wasn't going to be dismissed by Jack Roberts.

"It's a matter of Courtesy," Jack said.

Paul turned to me. "Excuse us, Sugar. I'll be fine."

I hadn't taken my eyes off Jack and waited a moment before I let them narrow. He better be, I thought.

"I'm going inside for a few minutes."

I walked past the motorcycles. Compared to what was new my ZX-9 was almost ancient even though it was only a decade old. I had to wait for the ladies room and took my time walking to the front door. By the time I stepped out, Jack left the parking lot and waited for a break in traffic so he could cross. Paul picked me up and hauled me away from the door.

"Did I tell you today how beautiful you are?" he whispered in my ear.

"Yes," I laughed. "This morning."

"Are you sure?" he asked as I got my arms up around his neck. I was still laughing.

"You make me happy," I said.

"I'm glad." He put my feet down and steered me toward the truck. "Would you tell me anything I wanted?"

"Mm hm." As long as he kept brushing his lips on my ear I was helpless.

"Do you trust me completely?"

I nodded, pushing my head closer to him. My eyes were closed and I knew he wouldn't let me walk into anything.

"Would you do anything I asked of you?"

"No," I said. He had me on the seat of the truck, hidden by the open door. His hands started to reach up into my shirt but they froze and he leaned back, withdrawing them.

"No?"

I'd surprised him so I hooked a foot around his thigh and pulled him toward me.

"Not until you twist my arm some more."

His hands went back up into my T as I unzipped his jacket and pulled up his shirt to feel his warm stomach.

"Would you do anything I asked of you?" he tried again.

"Yes..."

"Because you trust me it's right even if you think it's wrong?"

I pushed myself back on the seat and opened my eyes.

"I'll damn well speak my peace. If I'm unhappy you'll know."

"I can always count on that," he muttered, straightening his jacket as he took a few steps back.

"Are you going to tell me now?"

He looked across the street and I followed his gaze. Jack stood by the car, watching. Dana had the phone to his ear, oblivious to Paul and I.

"I already said I'd do whatever it is. You're not sending me with them, are you?"

Paul looked at the ground and shook his head. Sunlight lit the greys around his temples. Whatever it was I was going to be mad and I could feel it building already. He looked like a man listening to the windows rattle from a coming hurricane.

"Jack believes his father handed you down to him."

I jumped from the truck and charged at Paul, stopping just short of knocking him over. I pushed my chin up in his face and stared into his eyes until he looked at me. I was so mad I couldn't think of anything to say so I turned to Jack and took a step toward him. Even across the street, he took a step back. Then I crossed my arms and glared up at the sky. The only person I had to be mad at was Jack's dead father Damian.

After a minute, my anger crumbled and I looked at the ground as I started to cry. Paul put his arms around me and walked me to the truck.

"I know it's not what you wanted. We need to talk about it rationally. Not now."

I curled up on the seat with my head on Paul's leg. This wasn't his fault. There was no point in wasting energy being angry at him. After only a few blocks I'd cried a big wet spot on the leg of his pants. He stroked my face with his fingers until I stopped then rested them on my cheek as I watched his keys swing back and forth with the movement of the truck; the aged leather fob slapped the steering column. I didn't think I could feel any deader than when I woke in the hospital but I did.

Chapter 8

By the time we returned home I felt exhausted both inside and out. Camille woke up fussy so I took her to bed to feed her. Alina needed to get off her swollen legs so she joined us. Paul had gone to talk to Ray.

Alina touched the bags under my red eyes.

"You don't look so good, Sweetie," she said. I would have worn sweats if my legs were as bloated as hers but she opted for a skirt and pantyhose.

"Everything hit me all at once today," I admitted, barely even able to whisper. "I'm not leaving the house ever again."

"It'll be okay. Just take your time."

"I know. I look at what you went through and I'm ashamed of how sorry for myself I feel."

"Forgive yourself," she said. "It wasn't your fault and what happened to me wasn't mine. We both have something wonderful now. Good men, children; a year ago we were both alone."

"We have each other again," I smiled. "It took expecting a child of my own for me to stop thinking only about myself. After we lost mother I stopped trusting anyone to ever love me again."

"I did, too," Alina said as she slid down in the bed to put her head on Paul's pillow. "I never told anyone about Damian. After he hurt me I still didn't tell anyone until you called to tell me about Camille and Paul. You have no idea how much it helped to hear happiness in your voice again. It let me know it was okay to be happy, too. Ray is so good. I feel like he's been mine forever. He's never judged me. I still have some really bad days and he always picks up the slack. I feel full inside again. He says I make him feel the same way."

"Have you thought about names?" I reached and rested my hand on her stomach.

She nodded, eyes closed and covered my hand in hers. He moved like he knew we were talking about him.

"And?" I asked.

"When did you pick Camille's?" she asked.

"After she was born. Are you going to tell me or surprise me?"

"Julian," she said. "Neither of us knows a Julian. And John; Ray's father was named John, too."

I successfully stifled a laugh. Julian John Jackson. That was a lot of J's.

"I like it," I said. "It's old fashioned like Camille."

I was happy for her. Paul said Ray waited a long time to be with her again. I didn't know how many lives he'd lived without her, waiting for the time when her presence in his life wouldn't bring her pain. With Damian gone, Ray had her to himself. I thought it would just be me and Paul but I had to accept it wouldn't.

Jack wasn't crazy. He had a first mate he loved, men he looked out for and children coming into his family. He was a lot like Paul, driven to do the right thing for so many when he could have just quit. In part it was those things about Paul I found attractive. I knew I could do worse than Jack. A lot worse. Jack was a leader, he stood out among the men he felt he served and that attracted me to Paul, too.

Alina's breathing softened. She napped in the late afternoons, mostly because she slept so poorly. I sat up to let Camille burp before I lay down on my other side to feed her some more.

I suspected Jack would have to get me in bed to accept him, like how Keith described a man asking for a second mate. He would have to ask her mate first and if she accepted him in her bed he would be responsible for her just as much as her first.

That meant I had a choice. I could refuse him. He would go away and it would still be just me and Paul. I didn't think it would be that hard. Now I knew what he would do, I could resist his grownup charm. I'd send him on his way. He'd never get close.

Paul came in and took Camille and I fell asleep with Alina.

Alina and I reheated dinner after we got up then Ray took her back to his cabin. Paul's mother would fly home early the next day so she went to her cabin after helping Paul bathe Camille. I'd been sent to bed. We read to her for a while until she fell asleep so Paul tucked her in her crib and left me with a book as he went downstairs to organize the night watch. He took the night off since he and Joshua would leave at dawn to take his mother to the airport.

He came to bed late and I shivered against his cool skin as he wrapped himself around me. I waited for him to start talking about Jack but he sighed and relaxed further into the mattress.

"I'm going to refuse him," I said.

"Really?" he said with a disinterested yawn.

I moved my legs finding more cool spots on his to warm up and wondered why if it was so important it scared him to tell me would he care so much less about it now.

"Really."

"I suppose your new line has made you very powerful. No mate has ever refused an inheritance. It's only ever happened when a man has asked for her. And then not very often."

"Just because I would never turn you down for sex doesn't mean I couldn't."

"You're usually the one keeping me up," he laughed through another yawn. "But then I've never used what you call my charm on you either."

I pushed myself deeper into his arms.

"You're always shamelessly charming," I whispered as I tickled his forearm with the tips of my fingers.

"That's different, Anna. We'd never use it if we ask a man for his mate as our second but when it's an inheritance the man has no choice. He'll use it if he has to and you can't resist."

I felt tears starting and wiped my eyes.

"I don't want Jack. I don't want anyone else. If I refuse him he has to go away."

"If you give me permission I'll show you. I won't touch you. I'll just make you sit still. You just have to try and put your hand on me. That's all."

I turned and put my arms around him. "I trust you, Paul. I'll show you I can."

We sat facing each other.

"Just try and get your hand to my chest. You're allowed to tell me to stop if you want me to but that's it."

"Okay, you have my permission," I said but I already had a plan. I kept my hands behind my back like when he'd examined my line at his father's. The pleasure had been so embarrassingly great I dislocated two fingers trying to distract myself.

"Ready?"

I nodded, grasping the fingers of my left hand in my right. He said I just had to sit still.

First, I noticed an ache in my bones and numbness crept up my neck and into my brain. Pressure built in my chest. The aching felt good until I tried to adjust my position and felt pain.

"Sit still, Anna," Paul said. His voice rumbled in my ears, deep and irresistible. I stayed still for a minute as the pleasure of obeying him grew then I tried moving again. Again pain. I could think whatever I wanted but the more I tried to move the more it hurt. I squeezed my fingers but it only added to the aching in my bones. He didn't say I could do it.

"You want me. Say you do," he said and suddenly I did. So very badly. I looked him over wanting every inch of him.

"I want you, Paul," I whispered. Then I tried moving again. Each time I tried the pressure in my chest built with the pain. Paul concentrated, his breathing sped up, as if he worked to keep me still. I tried to move my arm through the pain as I put my sense into my chest to figure out what he was doing. After a few gasps of air I moaned as I got my arm to move a bit and I sensed Paul in my chest. I tried to read him but there was so little of him where he should be. When I sensed myself I caught glimpses but it was all Paul in me. His line smothered mine.

I stopped struggling and as we relaxed I saw more of my line in me as part of his withdrew. He didn't read me in the way I used the extra sense under my nose to read others. This was something different and if my line was as strong as his there was no reason I couldn't do it. I pulled my sense back into my chest and tried to examine my line. It wasn't one line like a solid chain. It was more like a loose rope. Innumerable twisted strands bound together to be stronger than the individual ones. I concentrated and separated some out, spreading them so they looked the same size, the rest I moved out of the way.

Then I tried moving again.

"Sit still, Anna," Paul repeated but I didn't.

I kept trying as more of him came into me, binding the piece of my line he had. As I pushed my arm against the pain I concentrated on surrounding his line with mine. Not touching it. Just encompassing it. It was hard. The pain it took to keep him in my chest fought my concentration.

"Don't move," he said. I heard the effort in his voice. I could see how effective it would be against someone who would take the path of pleasure and submit. Paul was right. It would take away the will of anyone not expecting it.

As I ran out of reserves to fight him, I snapped the strands of my line around his. The pain disappeared as I put my hand on his chest. We both breathed hard as my line held his tight. The numbness lifted. I still felt the pressure of his line in my chest but I held it now and he had none left to try and take control again.

"Sit still, Paul," I said. "It feels good when you don't move, doesn't it? You want to feel good, don't you?"

"Yes," he answered. I could see the effort on his face as he tried to move his hand then I let his line go.

"How did you do that?"

"I figured out what your line was doing to mine and I did it to yours."

He looked puzzled.

"You shouldn't be able to resist."

I shrugged. There were a lot of things I shouldn't be able to do.

"Did I hurt you?" I asked. "I have no idea what too hard is."

But he shook his head. "It only hurt when I tried to move. Is that what it felt like to you?"

"Numbness in my neck and head. It felt so good when I did what you wanted but the more I fought the more it hurt. Your line was in my chest binding mine when I fought. When I relaxed you took most of it back into yours so I split off most of mine and started fighting you again. You brought your line back to mine holding it tight, so I wrapped mine around yours and did the same thing to you. It's a terrible thing, Paul. It shouldn't be allowed."

"I had no idea what it would have felt like," he said. "Listening to you felt so good. I can see why it works."

I lay back down, pulling Paul with me. He put his arms around me as I curled up in my favourite spot under his chin.

"What did Damian say when he told you he was giving you away?"

"He never did. He never said anything like that."

"Jack felt it when he touched your hand. You felt it. Try and remember."

I brushed my nose across the little hairs on his chest. Then I sighed in defeat as I found the memory.

"He said it made him feel good to see his ex looking like shit," I said. "I thought he just meant I was with you."

"No, he was telling you he had no tie to you anymore."

"If he liked hurting me so much then why would he give me away?"

"I don't know. Can you think about the reasons why this is right? Remember what Keith said about me backing him up? When Damian asked for you he was good or I would have refused him. I've protected you on my own for a very long time, even from the man who agreed to care for you himself when he asked for you. It's right for me to have someone helping me and you. If he finds you first I'll back him up. You deserve that. So does our daughter. He'll look after her as much as he would his own even if he was with his first.

"This is different for Jack than if he asked for you. He has no choice. You saw at the motorcycle shop after he touched you. He couldn't leave. He stood at the car and watched. It's distracting him now. In a few days he'll become indecisive. Little things like not being able to pick out a shirt or which route to take to some place he's been to a million times. As time goes on he'll forget more important things. All he'll want is to get to you. There are men and a child coming who depend on him and he won't be able to do his job."

Paul's arms held me tighter as I started to cry again. This sucked. He asked me to put aside everything I believed a marriage should be and everything I promised him to give our daughter something we promised her. To give my husband the peace of mind he deserved.

"You'll start feeling that same distraction now it's started. You'll take risks, maybe when you have Camille. You can't let that go on."

"I know what you're struggling with, Sugar," he whispered. "Your husband feels the same way. But we're the grownups and we understand it and will get through it... easier than you think. Our promise to Camille is bigger than both of us. I know there is nobody for you but me.

"Just because you can fight him doesn't mean it's the right thing to do. Trust me, when it's over it will be about as important to you as what you ate for breakfast last week."

"That doesn't help me feel any better, Paul." I sighed. "I get how it's right. I get it. But in my heart it still feels like infidelity. How are you going to feel about that?"

"I've always shared you, Anna. It's the same for most of us. Jack's first has another. He shares her, too. It's how things work. When you grow up you'll see it the way I do. Next time around, you'll understand."

Keith

Chapter 9

Two days later, Alina let Ray let me out of bed then Ray ordered Alina to bed; her blood pressure was up and she wouldn't fly home any time soon. It seemed pregnancy complications stepped in and solved the problem of how to keep her in California. He unfolded our sofa bed for her and they came up to watch Camille. Alina approved of us going for a date and readily agreed to play with Camille in our living room.

Having her upstairs meant we could leaved armed without her seeing us. Paul had already taken the truck down to the gate and would double me there on my motorcycle in case Alina peeked. She had a few words to say about me not burying the damn thing in a hole since we had a child. I reminded Alina about her blood pressure and maybe she should go have a nice decaf on the sofa bed. The remark nicely quieted her down.

I'd put the bug in Ray's ear about Alina and the decaf. Made him swear she'd never know I tattled. Unless he wanted her blood pressure to stay up to keep her with us but with it being a real health issue for her she'd likely smarten up about the coffee all on her own.

He agreed.

Paul and I left about four in the afternoon to allow for travel to Redding and dinner before the movie. At least it's what Alina thought. As soon as we reached the gate he got in the truck and followed me down the road. He'd spent the afternoon installing radios in our helmets plus two backup handsets on the same channel in our pockets. I was used to feeling sleek against the wind when I rode but with a Kevlar vest and a bulky jacket to conceal the guns under my arms I felt like a big sail. Even hugging the tank I felt the wind pushing back.

First we tested the range of the radios. I could get a mile or so ahead before we started to lose each other depending on the terrain. Then I slowed down and let him catch up. I didn't like the oncoming traffic. The gusts from the side as the pressure built sometimes pushed me over the centre line. I liked to be in the middle of the road since they would try to push me into the ditch but it put me closer to the oncoming cars.

"Turns aren't going to be as bad for the next dozen miles or so," Paul said.

"Copy," I replied. I started by focusing on my little Camille safe at home: warm, full and sleeping. The thin spot on the back of her head from rubbing it on her sheet and the dark brown curls coming in underneath. Our apartment, filled with family and great people. Pressure started in my spine, slowly at first then steadily climbed my back. I wanted to get back to her, be near her. I imagined the sound of her breathing as the bike picked up speed.

"Pressure's coming," I said.

"Copy," he replied.

I continued to focus as the bike wandered, first a little then as the pressure got up into my neck, the first push from the side hit, shoving me into the oncoming lane.

"You sure about this?" Paul asked. He'd never seen me do this on the bike, only with me in a vehicle and the radio couldn't disguise the tense apprehension in his voice.

"Affirmative. Too late to stop it. I'll be going," I replied as I got hit on the other side. At least I'd prepared and didn't go onto the shoulder. I pushed my focus as pressure built in my helmet and pushed me to the tank. "Almost there."

And I was.

"See you at home," I said as I closed my eyes and dropped my wrist on the throttle. The last thing I remembered before I found myself by the sheds was Paul's shout in my earpiece and the squeal of brakes.

Then silence. I turned off the engine and took off my helmet. The only way out involved backing my motorcycle while struggling for footing in the gravel. Once clear, I started it up and rode it back to the gate. If Alina heard I'd say I forgot something. If she even remembered.

Ross waited at the gate when I got there and we talked a bit. He'd started calling me Ma'am following my brush with insanity after Christmas and never warmed up to me. He didn't like how I'd run out on Paul for two months. For me it had only been a few hours but the men had to babysit Paul while he drank his way through my absence. Ross was polite and spoke when I spoke to him but he never sought me out or spoke to me first.

It took less than ten minutes for Paul to roar up in the truck. He jumped out and threw his arms around me.

"Oh my God, I thought I hit you. I saw your wrist drop and the front tire came up. Then you just froze on the road. I threw on the brakes and drove right over you. Saw you pass right through the truck. Scared the hell out of me."

"Sshhh," I whispered. "I turned up right where we always do."

Ross disappeared into the trees down the path they patrolled. It paralleled the road east for a while before sweeping wide around the pond then north on its way around the compound.

"Want to go see Keith?" I asked. "Maybe he'll feed us."

Paul sighed. "Yeah, I'll get my helmet."

I put mine on and waited. It wasn't likely Keith would feed me. I wasn't even going to try getting into the mall. His mate Marie would be there and it would set Keith off if I walked in the door.

I started the bike up and got on, then Paul.

"How do chicks get their feet up on these?" He asked about the passenger foot pegs.

"If you're good I'll let you drive home. I feel better doing it myself until I'm sure nothing is going to go sideways for us."

"I feel like I'm balanced on a bee's ass."

"Don't show fear, Paul."

"Undignified," he grunted.

I put it in gear and took us down the road. He started out holding the handles on either side of his butt then switched to having his arms around my waist.

"Bike feels you back there," I observed. "If we're doing this a lot I'm going to need something bigger. Maybe I'll get you that black ZX-14 for your birthday. You can let me ride it."

"Nope, that will be mine," he laughed through the speaker by my ear. "Get your own."

I kept my eyes on the mirrors as we made our way to the stretch of road I'd used to jump home. Paul didn't complain but he held on tighter when I pushed through the turns faster than he would. He wouldn't admit riding the bee's ass was more fun than he thought it would be.

I focused on Keith and his family but felt no pressure to jump build in my spine. Probably because Keith was likely to shoot me on sight. I'd threatened to kill his pregnant mate as a ploy to get Paul safe and away while I dealt with Damian Howard. So instead I focused on our hotel in West Edmonton Mall. The place where Paul woke me on my birthday with the beautiful gold necklace to promise he would look after me the next time around. The place where we dressed up and gone on our one and only date. I started to feel pressure in the base of my spine. Growing steadily. Paul looked so good. We were so relaxed, rested. As the pressure grew I kept up my concentration.

"Hold on," I said and his arms tightened around me.

This time when the pressure pushed from the side we didn't go as far off course as when I rode alone. The extra two hundred plus pounds plus his gear helped keep us in place. It was still unnerving. I hadn't ridden much with a passenger and had to remind myself how much slower the bike would react.

"Okay up there?" He asked.

"Dandy," I replied as I checked the mirrors again. Still nobody. I wished Paul had more on his legs than jeans in case we went down but I hadn't been able to convince him. At least his boots came up over his ankles so his feet would stay on if we got crumpled.

As I kept my focus we were pushed to the other side.

"That it?" Paul asked. I didn't answer, trying to avoid distraction. I would let the pressure build more than when I jumped alone because the bike would be sluggish to respond to the throttle with two people on it.

After another minute, Paul's weight mashed me down on the tank. He let me go with one hand and grabbed one of the handles next to his seat. We were running out of somewhat straight road so I picked up speed as we were hit again. My nose hurt from the build up and I hoped we were ready to go.

"Close your eyes."

"Copy," Paul replied.

I made sure I only thought of the hotel then closed mine as I flooded the carburetor with gas.

We jumped.

Chapter 10

The engine shut off as my eyes focused. Paul unstrapped his helmet while I stared into the sunlight outside the parkade. We stood on the mezzanine of the massive parking lot circling West Edmonton Mall about as far from the door as we could get.

"You couldn't park us closer?" He teased and his green eyes wrinkled up with the smile his helmet hid.

"Apparently not. We're by the hotel?"

"Yes."

I opened my visor and brushed the stray hairs off my forehead.

"Let's get closer. You drive," I said. That made it two trips and the third one home would likely put me at my limit before I had to start using Paul as a battery.

I yawned as we rode down the ramp to the bottom level. Paul parked us away from the entrance leading to Keith's restaurant where the bike was less likely to be hit by someone parking in a hurry. He took my hand as we walked to the mall and I picked up Keith and a couple of the others before we got half way.

"Keith, Warren and Reg are coming out. I don't think he'll risk his reader around the nut bar."

"That's not it," Paul said. "He and Patrick had a bit of a falling out when I was here protecting Marie. Patrick saw right through you. Keith didn't. I was stuck in the middle hoping Patrick was right and having to be prepared for Keith to be. He'd have told Patrick to stay put before he could sway the others to be nice to you."

I knew what Paul meant. If I'd shown up and my threat to kill Keith's mate was real it was Paul's job to do whatever it took to stop me. Even if it meant killing me.

Patrick remembered how I lured Soros' missing man away from Keith and Marie before he could lead Damian to them. How I made Patrick swear on the life of Keith's unborn son he would keep his mouth shut to Paul until I had the man away from here. How I'd also sworn on Keith's son's life. We stopped a few cars back from the road between the mall and the parking and watched as Keith and his two biggest boys came out.

"Hi, Keith," I put on a big smile and waved but Keith glowered.

Paul took my hand and stopped with his shoulder in front of mine.

"Just trying to be friendly," I said.

"I know. You'll have to wait at the bike."

I stretched my sense to the restaurant. Patrick waited there with Marie.

Keith and the others finally crossed and approached us. Paul dropped my hand and greeted them with handshakes.

"There's some troubles, Keith," Paul said. "I need to fill you in then we'll go."

"Looks like you brought the trouble with you," Keith stared at me until I looked away. I felt Paul tense up so I put my arm through his elbow and held him tight as I lowered my eyes.

"Take the high road, Paul," I whispered. "He can be angry at me. He hasn't had a chance yet to let it out."

"How is your son?"

"Daughter," I said. "We have a daughter."

Keith laughed. "What the hell is wrong with her? She can't give you a son?"

Paul tensed again and relaxed as I stepped around to face him. I wouldn't wipe the tears from my face in front of Keith.

"Can I shoot him, Paul?" I asked.

"No."

"Please? Just a clean one through the fat part of his ass?"

"No, Anna." I heard footsteps behind me; probably Warren and Reg moving in front of Keith.

"I'll stand back, make sure the powder doesn't burn him," I tried. Keith really rubbed me the wrong way and I didn't care if he thought any worse of me.

"Be nice, Anna," Paul said. "You're not making what I have to do here any easier."

I blinked to squeeze the last of the tears from my eyes as I turned to Keith. I was right. Warren and Reg stood in front of him. By the time I returned to the bike, Paul had gone in with Keith. Warren and Reg waited on the sidewalk by the door. I watched them for nearly an hour, taking turns smoking so it looked like they weren't loitering. Patrick could read me from the restaurant so keeping Warren and Reg guarding the door came off as some kind of insult. It didn't bother me. At least watching them gave me something to do.

Paul came out alone and said goodbye to Warren and Reg.

"Hi," he said, putting his arms around me. I held him tight. "Keith listened after he finished going off on me for bringing you here. Once he understood there was no other way for me to get to him without giving him away he settled down and let me talk."

"Does he know what he's going to do?"

"No," Paul said and let me go. "Anna, I need you to take me to Jack."

I sighed. I didn't want to see Jack.

"Keith and Jack were good friends a long time ago. Before things changed. Keith wants to see him before he decides what he's going to do. I need you to take me to Jack and then bring him here."

"I don't have the energy for it, Paul." Yeah, that was a good excuse that would get me out of seeing Jack. "I can get us home but that's all I can do today."

"Use him for the trip, use me," Paul pushed. "The sooner we're ready to help Keith keep Marie safe the better."

I crossed my arms and chewed my lip.

"But he won't be expecting us," I complained. "He'll be upset we found out where he is."

"Please." Paul brushed my cheek with his fingertips before lifting it to him and putting his cheek to mine. "There are things in motion we have to deal with. We won't have our quiet happy life again until it's over."

"I know, Paul. I just want to go home."

I let Paul drive. Hopefully we'd wind up somewhere completely random. Then I could avoid Jack. Paul took us north to the highway then west out of the city. Once on clear and straight prairie road Paul settled into a gap in traffic. I hugged him from behind and watched the road ahead over his shoulder.

"Okay?" he asked.

"Yeah," I glumly replied, wishing we really had gone to dinner and a movie.

I thought of how to get to Jack. I had to really want to see him, which I didn't, even though I already started to feel the distraction Paul warned me about. This morning I left the water running in the bathroom sink after brushing my teeth. Then when I went to fix my breakfast I found cold toast waiting for me from half an hour before. Nothing bad, but what if I left a burner on? Paul was right. He'd noticed the water but not my extra breakfast. He didn't comment but I knew what he thought. I had to let myself think about Jack and why I needed to see him and try and ignore how horrible it made me feel.

I guessed he was somewhere near Sacramento which helped. Dana's driver's license showed that city so they must be nearby. I wouldn't distract myself with when, just who. If we made it we'd have to convince him to come with me without telling him where we were going. I tried thinking about what Paul needed from him. The peace of mind and someone else as devoted to Camille as we were. I felt a bit of pressure in my tailbone but nothing with any promise of building.

"Anything?" Paul asked. "We're down to half a tank."

"Every time I think about wanting to see Jack I feel sick," I said.

He reached back and rested his hand on my leg.

"Do what you have to do," Paul said.

I tightened my hold on him as he put his hand on the grip. I remembered how my hand tingled when Jack shook it. My surprise at the time left me confused. As had his reaction. He wouldn't have known I'd seen his father then feeling the same thing in his hand I'd felt in mine confirmed I was Jack's. And he was mine. Just the formalities to get through.

The second time he touched me on my arm. At the time I thought by accident as he took the gear I carried but now I imagined he did it on purpose. Either to be sure or just to feel it again. The shiver it set off passed through me from head to toe. Almost unwelcome then but my mind kept going back to that moment causing my forgetfulness in the morning. Catching myself wondering what it would feel like on my lips or my neck but stopping myself before I imagined anywhere else.

Pressure built as I let myself want to touch Jack. Touch him just a bit.

"Hold on," I warned. We were hit hard minutes after entering a big break in traffic so we could ride the dotted white line between the two westbound lanes. We swerved all the way to the rumble strips on the right, put there to wake up sleepy prairie drivers wandering off on to the shoulder.

"Shit," Paul muttered.

Maybe just put my nose near Jack's neck. Or better his nose near mine. Just to see what it would be like. Maybe I'd feel the shiver again. Since I knew to expect it I wanted it.

We swerved just as hard the other way. Pressure climbed up past my shoulders and into my neck. I tilted my head to the left and felt a little pop in my neck as it stretched and the pressure surged up into my helmet.

"Soon," I said. "Speed up."

The first big gust hit us from behind, heavily pushing me into Paul. He kept the bike going straight and moved to the centre of our lane as we gained speed and he pushed us in to top gear.

"Ready?"

"Yes."

I closed my eyes and thought of Jack.

"Go."

Chapter 11

A strong hand around the back of my neck pushed me to my knees as my bike shut off. Paul struggled with someone and the four men who had us belonged to Jack.

"Do what they say," I whispered into my microphone. Paul stopped fighting. I quickly ran the line of the man who had me and saw them search us and take our guns. In a few minutes Jack would come out of the bush. By then Paul and I would be flat on the ground.

I asked if I could take my helmet off and the man who had me nodded. I wasn't going anywhere very fast. They would have me on my face before I could get to my feet. Once my helmet was off he told Paul to do the same. Trees lined the road and it sloped up and to the right a couple of hundred yards ahead.

"Richards," the man said.

"It's been a while," Paul replied.

"Shut up."

"Jack's coming," I said to Paul and had my head slapped.

Paul glared at the man behind me but didn't move. He'd be flat on the ground with a gun at his head if he tried anything. I ran the line of another man to be sure. They would hold us until Jack arrived. I couldn't read him yet.

"Three minutes," I said and was slapped again.

"How'd you like my boot in your face?" I asked then I said oof as I landed flat on mine.

Paul tried to get up but wound up on his stomach with me. He looked mad enough to break someone in two. Anyone. I winked at him and gave him a smile and his face softened somewhat. Lying down was a lot easier on my spine than being on my knees with my hands behind my head anyway even on the rough pavement.

It seemed like a lot more than three minutes before Jack burst out of the bush and onto the road, gun drawn. One of the men had radioed in after we were disarmed simply reporting two subdued intruders. He stopped in his tracks when he saw us and put his gun away before he approached. He squatted down on the ground between us.

"Why is she on the ground?"

"She offered to put her boot in my face," someone said behind me.

"That was after you smacked me in the head."

"You want her boot in your face or mine, Simmons?" Jack asked.

Paul's lips tightened as he worked to keep his face still. It was the kind of thing he'd say. The man behind didn't answer. I giggled, Simmons didn't say no talking.

"You need some time to think about it?" Jack asked.

"Yeah." A sigh.

"Are you two going to fill me in on the security problem that let you find me?" Jack asked.

"Yes," Paul answered as I asked "Can I get up now?"

"So what is it?" Jack asked.

"Let us up first," I said. Paul gently shook his head at me but didn't say anything.

"Please," I added.

"Get up," Jack said after a few seconds. Paul stood on his own but Jack took my elbow. I didn't feel anything through my jacket. All the dirt brushed off revealing a couple of scuffs in the knees of my leather pants. I took off my jacket and put it over the seat of my bike.

"Can I have my weapons back, please?" I asked.

"Give them their guns," Jack said. Paul and I checked them and put them back in our holsters. "How did you find out where I am?"

"We don't know where we are," I said.

"Not a good answer."

"Give me a minute. There's a better one," I said then I quickly read each of Jack's men ahead until they saw Jack and I return and Paul unharmed.

"Is there anyone else here?" I asked.

"My question first."

"Privately, please?"

Jack pointed down the road and we started walking but he stopped.

"You stay with my men, Paul. You two are up to something and I think that's fair."

Paul hesitated.

"It's what we came for," I said. Me taking Jack to Keith while Paul stayed behind. He stared at Jack for an uncomfortable moment before he went to wait with Jack's men.

"Be nice," Jack ordered.

I didn't know if he really meant it or if it was code for something else. We went about forty feet away.

"So?"

"You were right, Jack," I whispered. "There's a lot more to me than what we told you. I can find people, places. Just by wishing for them. Then I take a shortcut to get there. We're a long way from the place I remember being before we came here. Wherever here is."

"We left home an hour and a half ago," I said. Sort of true.

"You're more than three hours from there now," Jack said.

"I'll take your word for it. Is there anyone else here? I need to decide if it's safe to leave my husband here while I take you somewhere."

Jack stared at me, his expression not giving away a thing. "Just Dana."

"I have no concerns with Dana," I said.

"Good. You shouldn't."

I nodded and looked over to Paul. He stood off to the side, ignored by Jack's men. I guessed that's what it meant to be nice.

"What kind of things can you find?" Jack asked.

I needed him to trust me and he wouldn't if I lied. I had a feeling he could tell. "Both your uncles; Damian Howard's two brothers. In hiding. I've been to see them both. I found Paul when I lost him. Twice. I found you."

"Where do you want to take me?"

I took a half step closer, looking at his neck, suddenly finding myself not close enough.

"I can't tell you. I need you to trust me and do what I say. Paul will stay here under the protection of your men until I bring you back. I'm willing to trust you with my husband's safety in exchange for a couple of hours of your time. Your presence somewhere now is that important."

"What did Paul tell you about you and me?" Jack asked.

"Everything, but I need you for something else first."

Jack swallowed. He'd been watching my lips and now he lifted his head and looked at Paul.

"I'll get my motorcycle."

"You ride with me. You have to do what I say or we won't get where we need to go. I need to gas up. Any place near here?"

"Yeah, mine." Jack walked away, back to the others and I followed.

"Take it around the road," he pointed. "We're just up the hill and will meet you there. It's a big U turn, about a mile."

Then Jack and his four men disappeared into the trees.

"He'll go," I told Paul. "You'll be safe here. All four see Jack and me returning in a couple of hours and you're in good shape when we do. Dana's here and I'll give him a quick read when we get up the hill."

"I thought we'd have to do something like that," Paul said. "Your chin is scuffed."

He rubbed the dirt off with his thumb before he kissed me there. I glanced down at his part open mouth as he pulled away. "All better."

"Thank you."

Then he pulled a strip of four condoms out of his pocket and shoved one into mine.

"What are you doing?"

"You can't get pregnant again," Paul said.

"A rubber in my pocket will work for that?" I asked.

"I'm serious. I told Jack but we surprised him so he might not be prepared."

"Shit, Paul."

I would take Jack to see Keith. Nothing more. Paul could stick it.

Paul doubled me up and around the road to a house just up the hill. The house was on the right of the road and the whole dead end was surrounded by trees. Jack waited out front and one of the others had a red gas can nearby. Dana was there and Jack made proper introductions. His men were much more at ease than when we turned up. Jack had a black helmet and a jacket much like Paul's.

Jack's house was big; two stories with a full porch across the front. The grey exterior had faded, if grey could fade, and new glossy white trim highlighted the doors, windows and deck. The generous front yard was nearly free of the enormous trees surrounding it and the driveway. It appeared to be fenced merely for decoration since there was no gate at the end of the walk and an opening further down wide enough to park in and drive past to get to the backyard. An old brown sedan parked there with a newer car behind it.

Paul and I said our goodbyes then Dana slipped a can of beer into his hand. It was a good sign if they treated this like a reunion.

"Phone, Jack," I said, putting out my hand. "Please?"

He gave it to me. I opened the back and put the battery in my pocket before I returned it.

"We can't be tracked."

He sighed and put the dead phone in his pocket.

"Anything else?" Jack asked.

"Yeah," Paul said. "Close your eyes when she tells you to. She wants to see her daughter tonight, not spend it babysitting you worshipping at the porcelain altar."

"Amen," I said. "And take Paul's helmet... radio in it."

Jack traded helmets with Paul as I locked up the full tank. I started the engine as Jack got on.

"Nuh uh," I said. "You ride bitch."

"This keeps getting worse," Jack said as he got off but Paul seemed to enjoy his displeasure. I did, too. I got on and patted the rear seat.

"Hop on, Mister Battery."

Paul laughed as Jack got on.

"Can you hear me, Rachel?" Came into my headset. Paul tested the hand held.

"Copy."

"Passenger?"

"Copy," Jack replied. We wouldn't use our real names on the unsecured channel. I spun up the rear tire while I held the front break on and drifted it around to turn us.

"Don't show fear," I told Jack. Paul and Dana laughed as I let the brake go. The front tire came up as Jack's hands went around my middle and we disappeared down the road.

"Love you, John," I said.

"Love you, Rach."

I kept our speed down past the place where Paul and I turned up. After a couple of miles the trees opened up to farmland.

"I need twenty-five or thirty miles of road that's not too twisty."

"For what?"

"That's where the wings pop out the sides and we get airborne," I said.

"Can you tell me where we're going now?"

"No."

Jack gave me directions to a stretch of road that would do. I started thinking about the hotel again, imagining Paul on the bike with me and we were going to the hotel again. Just him and I. Pressure slowly built until Jack tucked a stray strand of hair up into my helmet, touching the back of my neck. The tingle from his fingers drove the pressure hard into my head and suddenly I imagined Jack and me going to the hotel.

"Hold tight," I warned. We were pushed hard first from one side then immediately from the other.

"Turbulence," I said as he was pushed into me from behind. I picked up speed well past the speed limit.

"Close your eyes. You'll be sick for hours if you don't. It's rough."

"Copy."

"I know you heard me, are they closed?"

"Yes," Jack said.

"Good, we're going."

I closed my eyes and opened up the throttle.

Chapter 12

The bike idled a couple of feet to my left so I turned it off.

"Jack?" I called. He stood motionless half a dozen feet away so I walked over to him and put my hand on his shoulder.

"Jack?" I tried again. His head turned and he looked down at me.

"We're here."

He looked around.

"That doesn't help me."

"West Edmonton Mall. Paul and I were just here. The group Soros thinks we're hiding isn't ours. We found them by accident last December. I think you'll remember the leader. He was eager to get reacquainted with you."

"How did we get here?" He asked.

"I moved our lines. Our bodies followed."

"I need a drink," Jack said.

"Double me." I gave him directions around to the restaurant. Riding would take less time than the three block walk in full gear in the early summer heat.

"I have them," Jack said when we dismounted. In a minute I did, too. "I recognize the one out front."

"Keith Waters. The other two are to keep me from killing him."

"Coming?" Jack laughed.

"No, I'll wait here. I promised Paul I wouldn't kill Keith until you talk to him." I put my helmet over one of the mirrors and took Paul's from Jack. Then I leaned on the bike.

"You're serious."

"Keith thinks I am. He'll listen if I'm not around. I threatened to kill his pregnant mate a few months ago. He'll have plenty to say about me."

I brushed my fingers on his cheek, over the scar running from his hair to his chin and felt the tingle in my hand. His eyes closed as he inhaled deeply through his nose.

"Jesus," he whispered.

I looked past him and saw Keith step out the mall doors.

"Go. Keith is waiting." I put my hand on his elbow and shoved him on his way.

I waited nearly two hours for Jack. After a brief trip around the outside to another entrance for something to eat, I use the bathroom. I figured Keith would give Jack dinner and he could always get something at home later if he hadn't.

Jack drove and I gave him directions around to the hotel and told him to park. I could always back out. The distraction wasn't too bad. Yet. But when would there be another chance? I felt brave about it and decided I might as well try.

"Coming?" I asked Jack as I hopped off the bike.

My bravery faded with every step to the door and fear stalked me. Jack followed. He didn't say anything.

I recognized the woman at the front desk, pretty sure her name was Carol and she recognized me. A cold ball of something I didn't like caught up, settling in my stomach.

"Mrs. Lund, so good to see you again. Are you staying long?"

"Hi, Carol, just the night. My brother and I are riding to Saskatoon to surprise our parents for their anniversary. He wants to ride through but my fanny can't take another five hours in the saddle. Got anything with two beds?"

"You bet, Rachel," she replied as she got busy with the computer. "I still have your card on file. Charge it up?"

"Naw, cash. John and I are trying to pay the damn thing off." I didn't want my card traced if Jack's brother Soros had his eye on Paul and me.

"Brother's name?" She asked.

"Willem Larson," Jack replied.

Carol hadn't batted an eye at the two tall blondes who claimed to be brother and sister. As long as winking at Jack didn't count.

"Any plans for tonight?" She asked.

I pointed in the direction of the huge mall's amusement park.

"I thought I'd show Willem the rides," I said.

"Good choice. Enjoy the 'coaster," she said, passing me a key. "You're on the third floor."

"Thanks, Carol," I said and we turned to the elevator.

Once around the corner, Jack took my hand as we waited for the door to open. The tingling I felt when he shook my hand at the motorcycle shop started again building in to a buzz I imagined I'd see if I looked. I glanced at him and he looked away after offering me a shy smile. As the door opened, I lost the nervousness I tried to hide in front of Carol. Jack turned to face me as soon as the door closed.

"I need to ask you something," he said.

"Sure, Jack."

"Why do you think I'm unworthy of you? Is it because of my father?"

I felt surprise on my face.

"I don't feel that at all," I said.

"Then what is it? I saw how upset you were when Paul told you but now you've brought me here."

The door opened and we stepped out, taking a left as the numbers on the doors grew larger.

"It's childish, I think," I said. "My parents were deeply in love every day until my mother died. That was more than ten years ago. His pain is fading but he still loves her just as much. They're like eagles. When one loses their mate the other lives out their life alone never seeking another. Growing up with their monogamy made it one of the most important values I have. When Paul told me I knew we would wind up some place like this... but I take my responsibility to my daughter just as seriously. Reconciling the two has been very difficult for me."

We stopped at the door with the number Carol wrote on the little envelope holding the card key. I didn't make a move to open it. Jack still held my hand, his fingers between mine, his thumb running slowly over the back of it.

"It's not childish. Monogamy is one of the most important values in the family. Most of our rules revolve around it. People like your parents mate off for the long term like we do, they don't remember of course but they'll find each other again."

"Thanks," I said. He pushed a small tear off my cheek and I tried to reach for more of his hand with the side of my face but he laughed softly and put his hand on my shoulder.

"I remember your father from the past. He's hurt me, Jack. Killed me. You're nothing like what I remember of him. I see the depth of compassion in you. You're probably the last man who still believes someday your father will come back cured.

"You could have hit the reset button after you lost your first," I whispered. "But you didn't. You continue to serve your men. You lead them that way. You protect them and their children in spite of the pain you carry."

Jack looked away. I put my hand on his cheek and turned him to me. He took a quick breath as we both felt the tingling increase where our skin touched.

"I saw it in your face when you spoke of her. Will making love with me ease that burden?"

He nodded.

"Did I answer your question?"

"Yes, Anna."

I opened the door. He had his arms around me and his lips on mine before we crossed the threshold.

Chapter 13

"Jack..."

At some point, Jack removed my braid. I held a little section of my hair and traced the long scar on his chest with the tips. It lined up with the one on his face, started at his collar bone, passed through his ruined nipple and swept down before it curved gracefully up just under his navel. Two similar parallel slashes ran diagonally across his back. We were still damp with sweat, tangled with each other and the hotel sheets. A trail of motorcycle gear and guns led from the door to the bed.

My skin still vibrated where it touched his and I felt it in my fingers through the inch of my hair touching his chest. A shiver caught Jack's breath and he reached around the small of my back to pull me closer. I didn't give a shit about getting back to Paul. And I didn't give a shit about that either. I guessed it was something he'd done to me or I'd done to myself to make this easier.

"Again, Jack."

"You're beautiful, Anna," he whispered as his hand moved up my side, his mouth to my throat. "Desirable. But no."

"Please?" I pouted.

He laughed and put his fingers on my bottom lip. "I bet that gets you your way all the time."

I added a pleading gaze as he replaced his fingers with his lips.

"You've accepted me. Again would be unforgivable." He didn't stop kissing. "You're not thinking clearly. I can't take you back to Paul until it wears off."

"Okay," I sighed. No was no. I went back to tracing the scar on his chest. "I think I got off easy."

"Why?"

"Can I trust you now?" I asked.

"Have you ever read Paul's loyalty? He leads your group. His men are loyal to him regardless of whether they've found their mates or not. He would be different."

I never thought of reading Paul. I just assumed his loyalty would be to his father.

"I know how loyalties work but I can't read them. Read me again."

I rested on my pillow as I did and he put his head on my shoulder, his arm gently resting across my stomach.

"Only loyalty to me," I said. "There's no Damian in you."

"None?"

"No."

He was quiet for a minute.

"I'll be loyal to you for the rest of this life. My first is gone. If she wasn't it would be hers."

"Will you still miss her?" I asked.

"Yes, I still love her. My loyalty was broken off when she died; my connection to her torn from me. I don't have that pain any more. I'm surprised my father is gone from me and I didn't know he got close enough to hurt you."

"It was this one," I said as I put his hand on the eye shaped scar above my belly button. "It never hurt. I was more upset about the bruises around my neck than the knife wound."

"That son of a bitch. He did the same thing to my first."

"The way I brought you here. It took me home at the last second. I couldn't fight him."

He traced around the outside edge of the scar with his fingers. The attraction I had only half an hour before was fading but nowhere close to gone. I felt comfortable, comforted by his presence.

"Are you feeling what I'm feeling now?"

I felt the stubble on his chin move as he nodded.

"I wouldn't have been able to sleep with you without it. You're someone else's and when it fades we'll go back to feeling the way we did before. Or somewhat the same way. There will be trust between us. We can find friendship. Love like siblings would have. But never intimate contact unless we were both unattached. This is what could be if we found each other first or if you lost Paul. I'll keep you here until it's gone from both of us. It would be bad manners to show up in front of Paul when we're still all clingy."

"I really don't care to go back," I said. "Yet, I guess."

He held me tighter and kissed my jaw.

"Can I ask about the other marks? Was that him, too?"

I pulled my shoulder out from under his head and turned to face him.

"The first man your father sent after me didn't touch me at all. He went down easy. The one on my back was from the man Soros is looking for in Calgary. The leg and arm are from the fight with the four who went to my house in February."

"You killed them all?"

"Damian sent three to Paul's. The first came alone, hit Paul in the back. I took Paul's knife and disappeared with it. It was a reflex, defensive. I appeared over him bringing it down into his neck."

"It was really like you said on the phone? I was with Father when he made that call."

"Yes," I pulled myself closer to Jack.

"He was so angry at you, never seen him so mad. I thought he would take it out on me but he said I was soft and deserved a bitch like you. That's when he gave you to me. He regretted it after but it was too late. Once it's said it can't be taken back. It must be finished. Then he decided he could hurt both Paul and I by killing you and it pleased him."

That wouldn't happen. I had Damian's long life line in me now. He was like anyone else. No strong line to connect him to the memories of his previous lives. He would come back on the other side but completely unaware who he had been.

"The last time I saw Damian Howard he called me his ex. I guess it was sufficient," I shrugged. "The other two he sent; I can only see their past and future if they carry some loyalty to him. Paul and his men took care of them. They didn't drown in the pond but that's where I knew they would be. I can't see your future now because your loyalty to Damian is gone but if you have someone in your group who's not on your side I'll tell you. I can tell you what's going to happen to your men until their loyalty fades completely, too."

"What about Soros' man?" He turned me around to look at my back.

"He took the bus up here so he couldn't be tracked. Boredom maybe? He didn't want Damian finding out, that's for sure. I picked him up in the mall, caught up with him. Let him take me down one of the service hallways. When he pulled his knife I took him into the bush miles from my home. He got hold of my hair before I could get out of reach. I kicked him in the junk to get him on his knees and opened up both sides of his neck with a steak knife I stole from the dinner table. Paul sewed me up in our room a floor below."

Jack thought.

"You're not making that up," he stated.

"No."

"And the four sent to your house?"

"Denis Martin got two. I got one. I think we split the fourth. I was going in to labour then so I was slow. Someone messed with me, Jack. Loaded me up with some extra gifts. A lot of what I was given disappeared when my daughter was born. Death by a knife in my hand was permanent for someone like you. Those men won't come back. I cut their lines from them.

"The last one to come for me was your father. His line is in my chest now. I took it. He won't be back to hurt anyone again. Ever. That's what I was made for. The permanent solution. The cure for his insanity."

My nakedness felt uncomfortable so I pushed myself up. If he'd lost interest in me he might be more than a little upset about what I did to his father. Insane or not, permanently losing a family member after so long together would be a surprise.

"I'm so sorry. Whatever Keith told you... I was insane. I did some terrible things. The knife skills were Andre's. The man I lived as before. I can't do it anymore. He left when it was done."

Jack sat and pulled me back down to the mattress. I put my arms around him and held him for a while.

He put his right hand over my chest.

"May I?" he asked, wanting to know if it was okay to feel my line.

I nodded then his hand moved as we watched his fingers. He sighed and let his hand drop on me.

"It's so strong. Was it quick?"

"He didn't want it quick. I'm sorry. I was the mouse."

Jack's arms tightened almost imperceptibly around me.

"Someone's coming," he said after a minute.

I cast my sense down the hall, toward the elevator and picked them up.

"Keith," Jack said, "and the other is familiar but he wasn't with Keith before."

"Patrick. They know we're here. They won't go away," I said as Jack found his boxers. Then he put them on and pulled the blanket up over me.

"Are you feeling ready to go?" He asked.

"Soon."

Jack waited for the knock and answered in his underwear.

"Hey," Jack said.

"Really, Jack? Taking another man's mate to a hotel room?"

"Come in friends."

Keith scoffed as he and Patrick came in and stopped when they could see me in the bed. Jack pushed past them and sat on the bed between them and me. I'd pulled the blanket up and I knelt behind him, my arms around his shoulders. Just because I didn't want to sleep with him any more didn't mean I wasn't still protective.

"Hi, Patrick," I said then switched to glaring at Keith over Jack's shoulder.

Patrick gave me a half wave but didn't say anything.

"My father passed her to me, he properly informed her. I followed Courtesy and spoke with her mate and she has accepted me," Jack said. "We'll leave when her head's back on straight."

Keith frowned at him. I lowered my eyes and put my lips on the back of Jack's neck, inhaling him again while I would still enjoy it.

"That one's head will never be on straight," Keith said.

I felt Jack straighten in response to my touch. His head wasn't on quite yet either.

"If you weren't in my line, Keith, I'd go ask your father for you, bring you up here. I think you'd like me more than you care to admit."

"Lunatic," Keith sputtered and took a step before Patrick grabbed him around the middle and pulled him back.

One of Jack's arms went around me and his other went up to block Keith. I ran my cheek down Jack's shoulder, ignoring what I set off. I'd done it entirely to piss off Keith and was satisfied with the result.

"Does Keith have to be here?" I whispered to Jack, loud enough for Keith and Patrick to hear.

"He has no business here," Jack said.

"No business here, Keith," I echoed. "Nice to see you again, Patrick."

"Bye, Anna," he replied as he pulled Keith out the door.

Jack locked it behind them and we waited until they were going down in the elevator.

"I can't see them as far away as you can."

"You've lost them already?"

"Yes."

Jack watched them for a minute longer.

"You know he's your line?" Jack asked.

I nodded.

"And you knew who my mother is?" He asked, recalling what I'd said in my hospital room.

"I just subtracted Damian from you. I didn't recognize who was left. I can show you if you want." I pulled him down on the bed to sit facing me then I took his face in my hands and brought him close.

"Close your eyes," I said and he did. "Focus on me; just under my nose."

"Got it," Jack said. Hopefully this wouldn't be too hard. "I'm just picking up you."

"Perfect. I'm going to put what I recall about someone into the spot you're reading and I want you to tell me who it is."

I put Jack there and waited for just a few seconds before he laughed.

"It's me."

"Yes, look closely, can you break it down in to its pieces?"

"Mmm," he said, "flavours, smells, it's stimulating all my senses. There's words. Other things."

"I'm going to add another."

"Father," he shifted position and his nose brushed mine.

"Break the other down. Remove everything that matches from both." We did for a few minutes. "See what's left of you? Is it a mate you know?"

His nose bumped me again as he nodded.

"She is your mother."

"Amazing," Jack whispered.

"Do you want to know who her brother is? We just have to make a mirror image."

His nose bumped mine again. So I discarded what was left of the fingerprint of Damian and created the reflection of the woman we'd found. It took a little longer.

"Keith," Jack laughed.

"That's a surprise," I turned my head and sneezed a few times into a handful of blanket.

"Bless you. But how can we be together if I'm related to him and he's your line?"

"Your line is from your father. Not from her, right?"

"Thanks for that," Jack said, kissing me on the mouth one last time; watching my face, returning my smile. "You ready to go?"

"I think so, I feel a little uncomfortable wearing a blanket."

"Okay," he picked up his clothes. "Holler when you're dressed. I have to take a leak."

I waited for the bathroom door to close and stuffed myself into my clothes as fast as I could. It wasn't that I didn't trust him to stay put. I missed Paul and wanted to pick him up and get home to my baby.

"Okay," I called. I found my hair tie and went to look in the mirror when he came out. My hair was a mess so I combed it with my fingers and put the braid back in. Jack had our guns laid out on the bed when I came out and double checked his as he put them back. He had two under his jacket and another on his ankle.

"When do you want to be back for?" I asked.

"What do you mean? We've been here for hours."

"I can get us back whenever you want: next Thursday, last week, two hours after we left. What's your pleasure?"

He briefly looked at me. "Couple of hours sounds good."

"'kay." I pulled my vest on over my t-shirt and checked my guns before putting them on. Then my leather pants and boots. Jack had his jacket on by then and held mine for me. I checked my pocket for my key and ID and we left the room a lot further apart than we'd been when we came in.

"I'm responsible for you until you get back to Paul," Jack said as the elevator took us down. "Physically and for your state of mind. What are you feeling now?"

I thought about it.

"I remember what we did but it's numbed some how. I care as little about it as I did at the time about Paul. I'm not guilty or upset but I'm anxious for him even though we'd talked about it."

The elevator door opened and we walked out to my bike. I started the engine and he turned me to face him then he put a hand on my cheek and stepped closer, putting his lips near mine.

"What do you feel now?" He asked.

"You're in my space," I said, warning him with my voice.

"Good, you're ready to go home."

"I need to ask a favour," I said.

"Anything."

"I need you touching my skin for the jump. I drained most of my energy with the trips I've made tonight and need to use yours to get us back."

"Sure," he said.

We took the same route out of the city that I'd taken earlier with Paul. When the traffic thinned, I focused on our jump back. I didn't know where Jack had been when we found him so I concentrated on Paul.

"Grab some skin." I spoke into my headset.

I expected him to put his hand on my exposed neck but instead it went up my jacket and shirt and onto my stomach.

"Got it."

"'kay, hold on... remember to close your eyes when I tell you."

Getting the jump ready went fast with Paul for a focus. I concentrated on two hours after we left which was about as much time as Jack had with Keith. I hated the idea I would need a bigger bike if I was going to be doing this with passengers. I hated the thought of doing this with the extra two hundred plus pounds on the back of my old bike even more.

It didn't take long before we were hit hard from behind. I decided to take enough from him to recover the energy I used to get around this evening plus enough to get home. Jack could sleep it off and I didn't feel bad about it at all.

"Close them, Willem."

"Copy."

I thought of Paul and snapped the throttle down.

Chapter 14

Damian's stink filled my nose as I became aware the jump was over. I held the seat of the bike and killed the engine.

"Jack, where are you?" I whispered as I pulled off my helmet.

"Behind you." Jack's boots disturbed the gravel as he drew closer. I didn't recognize the place under the nearly-dark sky. My timing was off. It should still be light out.

"Where are we?"

"Behind my house," he whispered.

"Who's with Paul?"

"Archer. Why?"

"He's all Damian. There's nothing loyal to you in him and he's two feet from my husband. You got neighbours?"

"Not out here."

I unzipped my jacket and unsnapped the leather tabs securing my guns. Jack opened his coat and did the same. Then I put my hand over my nose. I narrowed my eyes against the smell. A light came on inside the house, revealing a low row of shrubs and well worn patio furniture.

"It's bad," I said as I ran Archer's line forward.

"They're on the front porch. Dana's just inside," Jack said. "I'm going to grab him. Can you see what Archer's going to do like before?"

"Already doing it," I said. Jack put his hand on my shoulder then disappeared in the back door. Paul and Archer's conversation reached my ears. After less than a minute Jack returned with Dana.

"I'll get myself between Paul and Archer," Jack said. "He's finished."

"You won't be fast enough. They heard the bike and Paul told him we're here." I ran his line again to see how our delay changed things. "Archer's anxious."

"We're making our move against Soros and Walker," Jack said. "Dana, go around the other side. Anna, stick with me."

"Too slow," I protested but ran with him, held his hand in the dark and trusted he knew his way around the hidden obstacles. As I re-ran Archer's line, I found him seconds from pulling his gun. He'd hold it under Paul's chin and shoot before Jack took him out. Through Archer's eyes, I saw Paul's blood all over Jack's grey paint. Paul's attention would be around him looking for me, not on one of his new friends.

I let go of Jack and pulled out a gun with my right then I sprung, starting my turn in midair as I disappeared. I reappeared and hit Paul with the middle of my back. With both hands on my gun, I aimed at Archer as I flew past. If Paul saw me coming he could have braced and stayed up but I clothes-lined him right over the railing and onto a hedge below.

"Jesus," Paul and Archer said at the same time as Archer went for his gun. Then I lost sight of him the moment before he stepped to the railing, gun coming down at us in the darkness. Two guns discharged at once. I hit Archer in the shoulder from the front, barely missing my airborne foot and Archer's round whizzed over my head. Paul and I tumbled off the hedge and onto the lawn in the darkness below. Archer grunted when two more quick shots followed. Then Paul covered me on the ground as Archer fell on the wooden floor under his feet. Dana jumped over us as Paul pulled his gun and got his bearings.

"Anna?" Jack called.

"I have her," Paul said and Jack stuck his head over the railing. Paul straddled me with his hand on my chest to hold me down, his gun pointed at the dark sky.

"Take her around and in the back door. I have to talk to Mister Archer."

The shaky breathing above came from Archer.

"Who else shot him?" Jack ask as his head disappeared.

"I did," I yelled.

"God damn bitch," Archer wheezed then elaborated with more vulgar terms than I'd ever heard in a single sentence.

"I didn't think he knew me so well..."

"Come on, Sugar," Paul said as he got me up and we made our way around to the back of the house. He let us in the kitchen and we went through a double wide door to our left into a living room full of big dark furniture against bare white walls. Then he took my gun and after making sure the safety was on, he put it back in my coat.

"Are you okay?" I asked.

"Yeah," he said and put his arms around me as I lifted my chin and tucked my face into his throat. "You?

"I'm okay. When we turned up in the backyard I picked him up right away... loyal to the core to Damian. We ran around front but as I read him I realized there was no time. I jumped to the porch to get you clear and shot him from the hedge before we fell on the grass. I think Jack got him, too."

I felt sick. Some from shooting someone. More from nearly losing Paul.

"I need to sit down, Paul. It didn't bother me when Andre needed the killing but I feel ill."

My ears picked up two gun shots off in the distance and I jumped.

"It's okay, Anna. Archer wouldn't have told them anything. There's no point in leaving him to suffer."

Paul took off my jacket and tossed it on one end of the couch then I pulled off my boots and leather pants. I didn't need the extra layer over my jeans in the warm house. We sat at the other end. I folded myself up in to Paul and listened to him breathe for a long time. When the door opened, Jack, Dana and four others came in. I didn't look, I just read them. Their loyalty to Damian had completely gone. Either because I accepted their leader as my second or because they turned on one of Damian's men. Maybe both.

"You two okay?" Jack asked.

"We're okay," Paul said. He put his free hand on my head and his touch warmed my scalp.

"I'm sorry we squished your topiary, Jack," I said.

"It'll recover."

Glasses bump together and curtain rods rattled as they closed the house up. Paul let go of my head and said thanks then I smelled scotch. Paul's breathing changed as his nose went in the glass. Jack dropped into the armchair to Paul's right and Dana stood by him as the others spread through the house, locking doors and windows.

"Can you stay a bit? I've called the rest of my men in. They'll be here within the hour. We need to move tonight. We have a safe place to go. Nobody knows about it but me and Dana."

"I want to see Camille," I said.

"I need to ask you to read the rest as they get here. I can't afford any more surprises."

Paul tightened his arm around me.

"We can stay," he said.

"Unless you can read the men here and see what will happen," Jack suggested.

"I can't read these men like that any more," I admitted. Since no loyalty to Damian remained I couldn't see what they'd do. Jack would understand.

"What happened with Keith?" Paul asked.

"I think he'll come or at least try and get Marie here. But he's not sure if he'll come to you or to me. He'd probably come to you if Anna would stop trying so hard to antagonize him."

"Anna, you promised you'd be nice," Paul whispered.

"He called me a lunatic, Paul."

"That was after you offered to ask his father for him and bring him up to our room because you think he likes you," Jack said.

"Jack," I buried my face in Paul's shoulder and tried to be invisible as Paul rubbed my side with his hand.

"It's okay, Anna. I guessed," Paul softly said. "Jack's watch is an hour and a half fast." Of course he could see Jack's watch. It rested right in front of him on the arm of Jack's chair. He didn't sound angry. I knew the men shared everything but I felt they had pretty bad manners to talk about Jack and me in front of everyone, especially Paul. I decided to leave. They could talk about me behind my back all they wanted.

"Wait, he followed you?" Paul asked.

"Seems so," Jack said. "I explained and they left."

"Will you two stop it?" I hissed, desperately trying to become even smaller.

"She's shy about things like this," Paul apologized.

"Shy isn't a word I thought could describe her."

That did it. I pushed myself up and found my boots. Keeping my head down, I pulled them on and zipped them up then I pulled my jeans down over top. I got up and headed for the door Jack and the others had come in.

"Where are you going?" Paul asked.

"You jerks can compare notes without me, thanks. The stink all over the porch is so bad I can't see a thing out front. I'm going to find out if there's enough left of Archer to see what he was doing before he got here then I'll find a better smelling spot to assess your men, Jack. I can show you what I read from Archer. It would mean more to you than it does to me anyway."

"She can do that?" Jack asked as I walked out the door. The air still held the afternoon's warmth and my guns cooled my bare upper arms.

I didn't look to my left as I crossed the porch to the stairs. Archer's blood would be there. Not just where it ran from him onto the wood but also the mist from the exit wounds on the railings, wall and window and even the hedge below. I stopped about thirty feet from the house when the air improved. Paul and Jack followed.

"It smells worse than a freezer a month after it's been unplugged. It's not just in their lines. Damian's a poison. It's in their blood. It's covered the whole end of your front porch. You might want to get out the pressure washer. I don't think it's good for your new paint."

"He's over—" Jack said as he started to raise his arm but I interrupted.

"I can find him," I said and stomped off. The porch lights lit the ground enough to save me the trouble of stumbling around in the shadows. I stared into the darkness toward Archer's body and felt Paul's arm around my waist.

"You don't have to see him," Paul whispered in my ear.

"I don't want to. I can pick him up from here." I turned to face Paul and looked up into his eyes. Jack came and stood beside us as Paul got both arms around me.

"Ready, Jack?" I gestured under my nose. "Can you follow me?"

"Yeah," Jack said.

After a second I sent my sense toward Archer.

"His line is still here," I said, still looking at Paul but not seeing him.

"I don't see anything," Jack said.

"Just a sec," I started to rewind it. A pair of loud explosions behind me made my knees buckle and Paul's arms tightened to hold me up as my hand flew behind my right ear. Jack staggered but stayed on his feet, his hand grasping the same spot on his head.

"Anna?" Paul asked. My sudden movement startled him; he hadn't heard the gun shots.

"Sorry, never been shot before…"

"Holy shit, Anna," Jack stammered. Patrick said the same thing the first time I showed him something like this.

Then I was pushed, foot first through the forest as I watched it in reverse. Two men dragged Archer by his arms as Jack followed, checking his gun. Archer had only been on the ground a few seconds before he'd been shot.

I'm glad he didn't have to wait around for it, I thought.

I wouldn't do that, Jack's voice in my head.

Jack? I thought.

You can hear me? He asked.

Yeah, that never happened before.

Pushed up the stairs then right on the porch. Paul still had a good grip on me so I stretched my neck and kissed his chin. He sighed and leaned forward, burying his face in the side of my neck.

Cripes, you two.

Sshhh, Jack.

"Seen this," I said. "Going to skip backward. He's talking with you, Paul."

I saw myself fly past, a blur of black jacket and blonde hair appearing in front of Archer half a foot from Paul before colliding with him. Then Paul and I disappeared out of sight over the railing.

"You got to him the same way we got back here?" Jack asked.

Paul and I. Our shapes in the darkness then the flash of my gun.

"I don't think when Paul's in trouble."

"No you don't," Paul muttered into my neck.

"He's getting out of the car. Dana greets him. They go in. He's surprised to see you Paul... for some reason he thought you left with me."

I went back further.

"He's stopped in the car, looks around."

"He's about a mile from our gate," Jack said.

"Looking down... five one three seven... pushed into his phone to unlock it."

Keep going. I'll be right back. Jack took off in Archer's direction.

"He's reading emails. They're confused. Has pictures of us leaving the compound an hour and a half before pictures he thinks are of us leaving here but we're three hours away. He doesn't know it's Jack and me. Archer was supposed to check the camera here. Someone's going to be checking the one watching the road to our place to find out which one is having the problem to explain the missing hour and a half."

Jack returned, tapping the four numbers into Archer's phone. I saw the road in front of Archer as he drove then I was looking at Paul.

"That's it. I can't go back any further."

"That was amazing," Jack said. "I didn't know about the cameras. This is going to take a while to read through. He's got email going back weeks in here."

Jack? I thought but didn't get a response.

Paul's hand slipped down to my butt as I reached up around his neck.

"When are your men coming?" Paul asked.

"Maybe twenty minutes," Jack absently guessed as he headed to the house.

"Perfect," Paul whispered and pushed me into the darkness of the forest.

Chapter 15

Paul and I crossed the road and were half way up the walk to the house when the first of Jack's men showed up in an older truck.

"Come," Paul said but Jack was already out the front door when Paul got to the stairs. I hadn't followed. I went right out to the road as soon as Paul turned his back and stepped in front of the truck. The four of them jumped out, surprised by the tall armed blonde blocking their way, staring them down. None of them was completely loyal to Damian but I didn't move. Jack and Paul both ran down the walk and stopped in front of me.

"They're okay," I announced. First rule of being one of the guys was establishing dominance. By giving Jack permission to let them in I'd done just that.

"Take the truck around back," Jack said to one of them and he sent the others in.

"Can you do that from the porch?" Paul asked. "You don't need to be run over tonight."

"It smells up there," I answered but I backed up to the far corner of the yard near where the cars were parked. "Better?"

"Yes." Paul waited with me.

"When we watched what Archer was doing before he got here, Jack and I could talk to each other in our heads."

He raised his eyebrows. "And now?"

"No, not now or he's ignoring me."

"Not liking that much," Paul said.

"It was like we talk on the radio. He could only hear me if I wanted him to."

Paul still looked unhappy about it. His nose wrinkled as he tugged on his collar, loosening it a bit.

"I don't want him in your head. Just because you can't pick up his thoughts doesn't mean he can't pick up yours."

"I hadn't thought about that," I said, looking at the ground. "I don't want to be hearing voices again, Paul. How can I even be sure it was Jack? Andre talked to me in my head."

"You're not insane, Sugar," he softly said.

"Keith thinks I am."

"Keith is being an ass. And you're encouraging him."

We didn't have to wait much longer for the next car load. Just two this time. Mostly loyal to Jack as before. He already had as many as we did. Paul went to talk with Jack where the walk to the house met the road. I sat on the ground in my corner of the yard and yelled the all clear twenty minutes later when two vehicles carrying six more arrived. Jack sent them in and Paul waved me over.

"We're missing one," Jack said. "I can't reach him."

"Could he be the one sent to the camera by my place?" Paul asked.

"Maybe."

"Is he in Archer's phone?" I asked.

"Not the email," Jack took the phone out and unlocked it again. "I'll check the text log."

He read, pushing buttons for several minutes.

"Yeah, Bates. Son of a bitch," Jack glanced up at Paul. "He's gone to check the other camera."

"Try him from Archer's phone," Paul suggested.

"Found problem. Roberts called us in asap," Jack said as he typed.

"Good turning around eta 90 min," Bates typed back. "Were Richards and his woman there?"

"Long gone now."

"It's what we thought. Kill Roberts. Get out if you can."

"Can I tell him you're taking me to the group you're hiding in the west? I need him to keep quiet and come here."

"Yeah," Paul grudgingly said. We waited as Jack typed. Dana hauled a hose around front as another man brought out a bucket of soapy water and a brush. I felt a little queasy and turned my back so I couldn't see them clean up.

"I'll send Dana and most of the men on their way. We'll stay and take care of Bates."

Paul nodded.

"What?" I asked.

"I'm going with Jack so I know where to find his men," Paul said. "You're going home."

I glared at Paul then at Jack who turned and walked away, followed by his long shadow from the porch light.

"I'll be back tomorrow morning with Jack. He has some things to square up with the Colonel if he's coming to our place."

I wasn't happy but Paul knew best how this had to work.

"How does it help Camille if you two are in the same place?"

"Right now all three of us are in the same place," Paul replied, "and I can't feed her. You go home. You're Commander Richards now. We're going with the witness protection story. You're protecting Jack and the others. Anyone in the compound who's not family will fill in the blanks that it's about Major Howard. Jack is going to bring Dana's mate and the others to us soon.

"Most of these men are wanted. It's the only thing that will make sense. Get Ross and Joshua on that camera. I need it disabled before we come in."

Jack pushed my bike around front.

"Go home to baby. Tell her how much I love her."

"Okay," I said as I wiped my eyes on my arm.

"Jack said he's loyal to you now."

"Yes," I looked away.

"Just like I am. The men will listen to you. Like when you told Jones to radio me at the pond when you warned me Damian's man doubled back. Give attitude to the men who aren't family. Insist the Colonel assured you of our cooperation. We didn't do anything like protection and they don't know what you did. They'll buy it."

"Why are you talking like you're not planning on coming home?"

I watched his face as he answered.

"I am coming home." His face said he would do everything he could to make sure he did. "Ross will get the Colonel on the phone. We're negotiating with Roberts for assistance cleaning up after Damian in exchange for getting the names of him and his men off the wanted list. Colonel Iverson's approval would help but he'll know we're going to go ahead anyway."

I knew why. I'd figured out Sig Iverson was family. Paul knew now but nobody else did. Sig told us that we couldn't even talk about it with each other.

Jack brought out my jacket and pants from the house. I quickly checked the loyalties of all Jack's men; none were loyal to Damian at all.

"This gives us thirty, Paul, if everyone will be nice and we're still outnumbered?"

"You're starting to think like I need you to," he whispered in my ear.

"We need to go after them while we can still put together teams bigger than the little groups they have spread out all over."

"Yes," Paul and Jack said at the same time.

I leaned on my bike to get my boots off one at a time while my leather pants went on. Then my jacket. That meant Paul would be leaving to go after them. I pushed away my upset about it since I needed to be able to focus to get home. I took Jack's phone battery from my pocket and returned it to him. The condom Paul gave me was gone. He'd been right.

"I might have some of the return trip to sleep off if I didn't gauge how much I needed from him. I wasn't counting on the jump to the porch. Jack will probably be down for eighteen hours like you were. He paid for all the travel tonight. Don't trust him with heavy machinery past noon tomorrow but that's just a guess."

"Pardon?" Jack asked.

"Sorry, Paul can fill you in," then to Paul. "I'll have everything as you wanted by the time you get in."

I put my arms around Paul and held him tight for a minute, breathing in the warmth from his skin before I kissed him. Then I started my bike and got my helmet and gloves on.

"Rubber side down, Rachel," he said. His voice sounded far away already coming out of the little speaker in my ear.

"Come home to me, John. Bye, Willem."

Jack nodded. I pulled out and the house lights disappeared quickly as I rounded the corner that took me in the big circle to their gate. The two men there watched me pass.

"Remember where you're going?" Jack's voice asked.

"Affirmative," I replied and half a minute later I passed out of radio range.

It took fifteen minutes to get to the stretch of road I wanted and five minutes after I jumped home.

Chapter 16

I pulled my bike backward and out of the dark lane. The garage keys were in the common room on the main floor of the house so I left my bike in front of the heavy garage doors. I stashed my riding gear in the closet before I went into the common room. Ray had his feet up on the couch, eyes closed. Baby monitor sat on his shoulder by his ear.

"Ray?" I whispered.

"Hi, Kiddo," he answered as he opened his eyes and looked at either side of me. "Where's Paul?"

"I came back alone. He has a few things to do. Should be back with one of our new friends in the morning. How's Camille?"

He held the monitor to my ear. I could hear her breathing.

"Had to give her formula tonight. She was displeased. It's almost twenty-three hundred."

It felt a lot later for me. I had the extra two and a half hours in Edmonton under my belt. Ray let me go and I went over to the desk and tried to make sense of the watch schedule.

"Where is Ross? I'm too damn tired to see."

"Watch."

"Can you hold the monitor up for a little longer? I have a few things to clean up for Paul."

"Sure, Anna," he said and returned to the couch. I picked up one of the radios and tuned it to the channel for the men on watch.

"Control Delta," I called.

"Delta Control," Ross replied.

"What's your twenty, Delta?" I asked.

"Station Three, over." Station Three was the gate. Thank God. I didn't relish the idea of tramping through the bush in the dark to any of the other stations around the compound to find him.

"Stay put, Delta. I'm coming to you, over."

"Copy, Delta out."

I took the radio with me and grabbed a jacket from the closet.

"What's going on?" Ray asked.

I knelt down on the floor next to him.

"Walker and Soros have a camera somewhere on the road to the compound. I get to tell Ross to stay up all night to find it and shut it down."

"'kay Kiddo," but Ray was dozing off already.

It only took a few minutes to get to the gate when I hurried. And I did. I still had to clean my gun and get a shower before going to bed and if I wasn't quiet about it there would be a feeding for Camille.

"Evening, Ma'am," Ross said.

"Hi, Ross," I quickly filled him in on the camera and Paul's plan to bring in Jack Roberts in the morning.

"He's under my protection. We'll say it's what I did up north before coming here. The men can call me Commander now."

"Okay, Commander," Ross laughed. Not all that nicely.

"You know it's just for the base pay and benefits, Lieutenant Wells. I never set foot on a steam boat."

"As long as we both know the truth. What about the mate and her guard the Captain is expecting?"

"I think he's making those arrangements now. They're under my protection or so the story will go for the men who aren't family. I don't know if they're family of witnesses or witnesses themselves. I'll play as dumb as I can to avoid talking myself in to a background story I can't support."

"They'll buy that. Family will have no trouble keeping to it. We all want Walker and Soros in travel size pieces."

"I think you'll get some action sooner than you think. Who do you need for the camera? We need it found and off by dawn. Captain will be coming in one of Roberts' vehicles."

Ross thought. "I'll boot Joshua out of bed and a couple of others good with electronics. Nobody needed for watch. Two teams, hopefully everyone will get back to bed that much faster. If it has a radio or satellite transmitter it shouldn't take long to pick up. We'll check out a few miles to make sure there isn't another."

"Alright. You're relieved, Lieutenant. I have the gate until next watch sends me home."

Ross gave me the automatic and took off up to the house. Within fifteen minutes the two trucks stopped at the gate and I stepped out to meet them, approaching the truck Joshua drove. He was Paul's second in command.

"Commander," Joshua said when he rolled down the window.

"Lieutenant Wells filled you in?" I asked.

"Yes, Ma'am," Joshua replied. "Had no idea you were in to witness protection."

"You do now," I said. "I've been assured of your cooperation and appreciate it."

Joshua nodded.

"Let's get that camera down before the Captain brings in my charge. I have at least one coming tomorrow. You'll know him and I'll break the nose of anyone who makes my job any harder than it has to be. Clear?"

"Clear."

"I need the watches doubled starting tomorrow. Put me in the rotation when the Captain's back. Don't put us on back-to-back shifts at night. We'll have a hard time getting a sitter."

"Ma'am?"

"You can delegate that task to Wells for first thing tomorrow if you want, he's day officer I believe."

Joshua nodded. He heard me right.

"Report to me when you get back. Just let yourself in."

"Yes, Ma'am."

"On your way, Lieutenant," I said and reached in to pat his shoulder.

"Commander," Joshua said as the window went up and he pulled away. Ross nodded to me as he passed.

Half an hour later I was back in the house.

"Ray, I have a gun to clean and reload before I can turn in."

"Gun?" Ray sat straight up and the baby monitor tumbled to the sofa cushion beside him. "You shot someone?"

"Yes."

"Did he make it?"

"No," I replied.

Ray stood. "Sorry, Kiddo. I know that isn't easy."

"I winged him," I shrugged. "I found a bad man in Jack's house. He finished him off."

"I guess I'll wait for Paul to fill me in. Go take care of your weapon. It won't save your life if you don't look after it."

"I know," I gave Ray a quick kiss on the cheek then I turned off the alarm and got the key for the armory. It was easier to break in than it was to get the key to work but it didn't give me too much trouble.

"Alina is going to hate this," I told Ray when I came back upstairs. "I'll give her the cover story so she can be mad at me. She needs you more than anyone here so if you have to pretend to be mad at me too I understand."

"Don't worry about Alina," Ray said.

"Thanks, Ray. Give her a hug for me."

I took the monitor and went upstairs as quietly as I could then I closed Camille's door and ran a bath. As it filled I got a glass of wine and pyjamas. I washed my hair and combed out all the knots then I washed off Jack and the fine spray of blood from Archer I imagined I carried in every pore. I soaked until the wine was gone then I dried as much water as I could from my hair before putting on the pyjamas.

After turning off the bathroom light, I opened Camille's door and listened to her quiet snore. So much like her father's. Her eyes were turning green like his already. I gently picked her up and took her to the table for a change. She woke but didn't fuss. Her little nose sniffed at my shoulder as I carried her to my room. She rooted around looking for food. I tucked her in with me to eat. I told her Daddy would be home soon. That he loved her with all his heart and I did too. She let go for a moment and giggled then went back to gulping. I stroked her warm head until she fell asleep then I joined her.

The blue lights on Paul's digital clock said half past four when I heard a key in the front door. Camille still slept but I picked her up anyway.

"Anna?" Joshua quietly called. He knew I got ticked when rank was used in my apartment; or business talk for that matter.

"Hi, Joshua," I whispered.

Camille snoozed on my shoulder as I took her into her room for another change. Joshua followed.

"There were two within five miles of the gate," he whispered. "Both are out of commission. We thought about rigging them up to transmit to us but we couldn't be sure they wouldn't still transmit to whoever set them up. Ross and I will take another look at them tomorrow and decide if we can use them."

"Thanks, Joshua."

I picked Camille up and swayed with her as she went back to sleep.

"How did you find out about them?" He asked.

"It wasn't my intelligence that found them. The orders to remove them were from your brother."

"Okay," Joshua said as I gave him a one armed hug. He yawned.

"Sorry you got woken up. Paul should be back in the morning."

"'night, little sister." Joshua said and patted the top of my head. He wouldn't be getting away with that anymore anywhere but up here.

Marie

Chapter 17

Joshua arrived for breakfast at ten in the morning. I played with Camille on the floor when he knocked at the door. I had a radio on the watch frequency and stayed near it for news of Paul coming in. Joshua felt I owed him so he got down on the blanket to entertain his niece and I started eggs and sausages for him.

"Station Three Romeo."

"It's for you," Joshua called.

I ran in and answered. "Romeo Station Three."

"Report to my station, over."

"I gotta get this. Don't set my kitchen on fire," I told Joshua. "On my way, Station Three. Romeo out."

"I've got Camille," Joshua said.

I pulled on my guns and ran out the door, radio in hand. I tied up my runners from the downstairs closet and ran down the road, surprising Ray and Alina as I passed. If Jack turned up without Paul he would be on the ground at gunpoint.

I was right. Jack waited on the ground next to the faded brown sedan which had been parked by his house while North stood over him with the automatic. North wasn't family but had been around long enough to know Jack.

"Why is my guest on the ground, Corporal?" I asked. Fortunately I remembered his rank. I'd have to learn them all if I was going to insist they use mine.

"Side arm on his seat, Mrs. Richards. I ordered him out. And he's wanted."

"Going forward its Commander Richards or Ma'am, Corporal North."

He blinked at me from behind his sunglasses and I stared at him for a full minute before I gave up waiting and repeated myself.

"It's Commander or Ma'am. Do I need to order you to see Lieutenant Jackson for a hearing check?"

"No, Ma'am."

I helped Jack up then he dusted off his jeans and black t-shirt. I didn't feel anything now with my hand on his bare elbow. North's boots shuffled in the gravel under our feet.

"Sorry about that. We were expecting Paul and a passenger, not a stray."

"No worries, Commander."

"In the car, Jack," I said.

"No, Ma'am," North firmly said.

"Pardon?" I asked with all the authority I could pull together. North visibly cringed but the automatic still came up. I moved in front of Jack.

"I don't think you realize who that is," North said so I stepped right up to him. Not right in front of the gun, that would be stupid, but close enough I could look down on him. He was one of the few men in the compound who stood shorter than me.

"I know exactly who he is," I forced out through my teeth. "Perhaps you would care to explain to the Colonel why you are the only man here who has failed to provide me with his complete cooperation. Roberts is in my care and custody at the moment."

North swallowed and the automatic pointed back at the ground. His cheeks seemed to redden.

"Get in the car, Jack," I tried again.

"No, sidearm is still on the seat, Ma'am," North said. I heard Jack's feet stop in the gravel.

"Are you going to make the case it would be more comfortable for him to drive all night sharing the front of his pants with it?"

"No, Ma'am."

I heard Jack clear his throat as he tried to hide a laugh.

"In the car," I said as I turned my back on North and walked to the driver's seat. "Move over."

Jack slid to the passenger seat and I closed my door.

"You might want to put it away until I get you out of sight."
Jack lifted his butt off the seat and shoved the gun under his belt.
"Where is Paul?"

"We decided on separate cars. I drove straight through. He's
stopping in Redding to call Colonel Iverson from a pay phone. He said
if he didn't get through he'd come straight here and call again."

I put the car in gear and drove us past North and up to the
house. I felt my connection to Paul so wherever he was he was alive. I
trusted Jack told the truth but I still wasn't confident trusting my trust
in him.

The front porch was deserted so I parked at an angle in front
of the house. I caught a glimpse of Ray in the living room window as
we pulled up but he wasn't in the part of the window I could see when
we stopped. Joshua and Ross would have their own radios monitoring
most of the channels we used so there shouldn't be anyone on the main
floor.

I realized Joshua didn't know what Damian had done to Alina.
He should be sensitive enough to my so called assignment to keep his
mouth shut about Damian. Jack's presence would make it obvious who
he would be testifying about. I decided not to chance it and switched
my radio to the everything else channel.

"Romeo Kilo."

"Kilo Romeo." Joshua replied after a minute.

"10-35 my station." It's confidential, I told him.

"Copy, Kilo out."

"What's so private about me? I thought they knew I was
coming." Jack asked.

"Damian Howard hurt my sister to try and draw me out. She
doesn't know we know about him. Paul's brother Joshua doesn't know
he can't mention him around her. Ray's mate... she's my biological sister.
The three of them are upstairs with Camille."

"What are the odds of that," Jack said.

"I'm surprised you didn't know."

"Ray's mate is your sister? Father kept a lot of what he did from
us."

"Can you stay in the car a minute?" I asked as I got out. Joshua
came out the front door and stopped when he recognized Jack. His
right hand reached across to scratch his arm near his gun. Alina was
used to the men being armed. All of them but Ray so he hid his in the
cabin. She thought they were all a bunch of yahoos.

"That's your charge?" Joshua asked. His expression looked far more composed than his voice let on. He'd let his hair grow longer than Paul kept his and his blonde curls shook with the anger he tried to keep inside. "Do you have any idea what him and the rest of those traitors did?"

"A little. I can't discuss why he's here."

"The Captain knows about this?"

"Yes," I whispered. "Joshua, Damian Howard hurt Alina to try and hurt me and draw out Paul. She doesn't know we know him. Nobody speaks about him here... ever."

"And why does Roberts have to come here?"

"He's going to be with Paul and me for the next while."

"Commander, you have a baby upstairs. That's reckless."

I looked at Jack and smiled. He smiled back. "Jack's not going to be a problem."

Joshua's eyes narrowed, his nostrils flared as the entire lower half of his face tightened beneath them. "How do you know him so well? He an old flame or something?"

"Joshua!" I exclaimed but I felt my cheeks darken as I recalled the night before.

"Oh my God, he is," Joshua exclaimed. "Is that why he was sent to you here? Does Paul know about you two? Does he have anything to do with why you ran out on Paul last winter?"

"Cooperation, Lieutenant," I said but he had me flustered. His right hand came up and rested on the butt of his gun.

"Off the record, Commander Richards, this is complete BS," Joshua spat out and stomped down the stairs to the car. He slammed his hand on the roof above Jack's head but Jack politely waved and Joshua stormed down the road. I was sure he'd be good once he had a chance to calm down. And after Paul spoke with him. So far, I'd done a really good job of ruffling feathers.

I watched Joshua's back recede toward his cabin as I went to the car. All in all it hadn't gone that badly. At least he hadn't run after Jack to try and kill him like Paul had.

"You have luggage?" I asked as I opened Jack's door for him.

"Couple of bags," he took the keys from the ignition and went around behind the car to open the trunk. As he did, he grabbed the back of the car for a moment and closed his eyes. I knew what it meant. Jack didn't say anything but I knew he'd be sleeping soon to recharge all the energy I'd taken from him to get us around the night before. Looked like he'd spend the night on my sofa. I couldn't leave him passed out anywhere else considering the welcome he received.

Jack? I tried. Nothing registered on his face he heard. I sighed and took one of his bags for him. He didn't look like he had the energy for both. I led him upstairs and into the house. The main floor sounded as deserted as I hoped it would be so I took him up to the apartment. At least Ray would know to keep quiet about Damian.

I took a deep breath and pushed open my door. Alina curled up with Camille in one of the big chairs and Ray sat near her. In the few minutes I'd been gone she'd dressed Camille in something impractical and frilly.

"Hi, Sweetie," I told her as I came in.

Ray stood to get himself more in front of her and her eyes dropped from my face to the guns I carried.

"Anna," she stiffly said. She didn't approve. Then Jack came in behind me. I put down the bag and he put the other with it.

"Ray, Alina... I want you to meet Jack Roberts."

"Ray Jackson, my sister, Alina Creed."

Ray wasn't surprised and was friendly and Alina got a hand out from under Camille to shake Jack's. Jack gave Camille a little smile. She was the child he would protect now.

I took my guns off and put them on the coffee table and Jack pulled his out of his pants and put it with mine. Alina glared at both of us.

"What are you up to, Anna?" she whispered.

I leaned over and took Camille from her then held her a moment before passing her to Ray. Alina would be furious with me. Betrayed. I didn't want my baby in the middle. Alina wouldn't want it either. I knelt down on the floor in front of her, my stomach against her knees.

"Sweetie," I said. "I wasn't planning on going back to work so soon. Or ever, actually."

"What do you need the guns for if you're going back to work?" The pitch of her voice rose. She didn't like being surprised or finding herself disadvantaged because she'd been left out. She needed to know everything and sensed something big was going on that hadn't included her.

"You don't know what I do," I said. "I couldn't tell you before but I have to now."

"You take pictures of half naked women for semi-pornographic automotive magazines," she firmly said.

I shook my head. "That's what Paul did when he wasn't out of the country. I mostly did catalogues and newspaper articles about the bike rallies. I needed a legitimate job for my taxes. If anyone ever looked too closely I had to be making a living. The money from my real job is deposited into a bank account in another name by the Canadian Government."

She stared at me. I just needed her to believe me and to stay calm. She looked at the guns on the table again.

"What the hell have you been doing, Anna?" she demanded.

"For the past five years I've spent a lot of time away from home. Helping soldiers and federal employees doing sensitive work. Or helping their families. Sometimes they need a safe place to go for a while until whatever brought them to my team blows over or permanent arrangements are made for them."

Her hand came up over her mouth and her eyes started to tear. She knew where this was going.

"They're brave. They do some very important things we never hear about. Their families are so scared; women, little children. Those are the ones who come to me. I take good care of them. Help them deal with what's going on."

She shook her head, silently crying. Tears ran over her hand. I realized I cried from seeing dear sweet Alina hurt because of me. But I had to push even more. Her eyes still held the strength to fight me and I had to take it from her.

"I've had to hurt people, Alina," I whispered. "Keep them away. I've never lost someone in my care. The marks on me aren't from any motorcycle accident last fall. You work in emergency. You know what made those marks."

"No..." she sobbed.

"I have some coming here, a few days maybe a week. If having them here would bring danger to any of us I'd tell my CO to screw off. My baby is here, Alina. The ones coming, I don't know how many or exactly when. I only know one is very sick and they'll only come out of hiding if they can get discrete medical care. They're too scared to go to a public hospital. I have to tell you because I need your help. You and Ray."

"You couldn't get a real job?" she blurted out, her face now past red.

"Damn it, Alina, open your eyes." I hissed. "What do you think this place is? Some kind of weekend Army club? Do you think these men drink beer on some Florida beach when they're not here?"

"Please walk away, Anna, please? You died ten days ago. Your heart stopped for two minutes and I lost you and I can't lose you again."

Everything happened at once. Camille screamed in Ray's arms, Jack grabbed the door frame as the black sleep made its move to take him to oblivion. Alina stood, belly out back arched, knocking me over and charging over top of me.

"For a genius you're pretty fucking stupid," she yelled as she went out the door.

I scrambled to my feet and steered Jack to the middle of the couch as fast as I could. He could tip over either way and I could still get his feet up on it.

"I've got Alina," Ray said but he was obviously upset, too. He put Camille in my arms and ran out after her.

"Have you ever tried not being a man—" Alina's voice cut off as the front door slammed.

Jack's eyes rolled up in his head as he went over. I stood, breathing hard as Camille bellowed before I sat in the armchair to settle her. Air poofed out as it took our weight.

"Whiskey Romeo." Paul's voice squawked from the out of reach radio.

Shit.

Camille's breath hitched in her lungs as she stared angrily straight ahead filling her tummy but I got up anyway trying not to move her. She turned as red as Alina as she got herself going again. I sat back down with the radio beside me and gave Camille another minute so she wouldn't deafen Paul.

"Whiskey Romeo," Paul tried.

Camille let go and started crying again so I turned down the radio and stood with her on my shoulder, rocking side to side.

"Romeo Whiskey," I replied. I should have just held the talk button down by Camille to tell him everything he needed to know. As it was I held it down a lot longer than I had to. My patience ran thin and I wanted to calm her down before I did anything else.

"Disregard, Romeo. Whiskey out."

Paul came in an hour later. By then Camille settled down to the hitch, hitch, mmm that meant she would still be going at full volume if she had the energy to do it. Her eyes were closed on my shoulder now after my hundredth slow trip from the front door to our bedroom door and back.

"Hi, ladies," he whispered then he kissed us both. He wore yesterday's clothes and his voice was deep and rough from being up all night. He pointed at Jack, still tipped over with his feet on the floor. "When did he pass out?"

"Just before you radioed; at the same time Alina knocked me flat on my ass and Camille melted down. I woke her up to come to bed with me and again when Joshua reported back about the cameras so she's all out of sorts," I whispered. "Ray's upset. That was right after I pissed off your brother and bullied Corporal North in to letting Jack in. I have a hundred percent stirred up rate so far today... except for you."

"Shit disturbing is my job," Paul whispered, laughing. "I talked to Ray, Joshua and North on my way here."

Great. I didn't want to hear their sides. Except for Ray. I hoped Alina was calming down.

"Was Bates cleared up?" I asked.

"Yeah," Paul said. "I got him."

Paul put his bent elbows up above his shoulders and stretched. I noticed the legs of his pants were dirty and I imagined him and Jack digging a hole in the woods.

"Sorry, Paul," I knew he didn't like that side of himself.

He waited a few seconds before his arms dropped.

"The men have no idea what hit them," he changed the subject. "Word's out that crossing you is crossing me. You won't have any more trouble. For most of them it confirms what they thought about you all along. I gave you a promotion to put you on par with me."

"You're sweet but I think I outranked you already. Did you get briefed on the cameras?"

"Yes, you took the gate?"

"I had to man up in front of Ross. If I make him stay up late I should take some of the load. Ray was downstairs with the monitor and knew I'd be a bit."

"Good call. It's what I would have done. You impressed Ross and that's hard to do," he yawned. "He doubled the guard up like you ordered. I saw you pencilled in."

"Yes, what I lack in knowing what I'm doing I more than make up for with being able to see them farther out than any of you. Hope I didn't go too far during my brief reign over the compound."

"No," Paul smiled. "If you're sure you want in that's fine. I'll pair you with someone for a while but I'll take you out when your guests start arriving."

"Fair enough. Go jump in the shower. I'll heat you something up."

He nodded and I followed him down the hall to tuck Camille in before I went back to the kitchen to deal with Joshua's dishes as Paul's lunch heated up. I looked forward to joining Paul for a nap if Camille would sleep for a while. The breeze moved the tree branches outside the window over the sink as I washed up, listening to the microwave hum. Hopefully Alina would calm down soon. I needed her on my side for whatever might come. If trouble came to the compound I might have to take her and Camille and run. The dishwater drained as Paul put his arms around my shoulders.

"Ray said Alina is sorry for what she said but she's a long way from admitting it to you," he said.

"I'll suck up to her first, make her think she was right. That will make it easier for her. Not today though. Tomorrow."

The microwave beeped but Paul kept me pressed against the counter. I sighed and relaxed my head back on to him. He wore boxers and a t-shirt, ready for sleep.

"Did you use it?" he whispered in my ear.

"What?" I asked.

"The condom I gave you."

I pulled my head away so he couldn't see my face.

"Did you?" he asked again.

"Yes," I mumbled, looking down at the suds left in the sink.

"Did he hurt you?" Paul asked. I crossed my arms and kept looking down. I didn't want to see our reflections in the glass.

"Please tell me."

I shook my head.

"Okay," he said.

"I'm so sorry, Paul." I'd completely forgotten about it until now when he wanted to talk. "I don't know how you feel about it."

"It's over now, that's how I feel about it."

"I understand if you're upset. I feel ashamed of myself."

Paul turned me in his arms and put his hand on my face until I looked up.

"I'll only be upset if you're ashamed. You did the right thing."

While he ate, I gathered up our dirty clothes from the night before. I went through all his pockets and put everything in them on top of his dresser then put all the clothes in the washing machine for later. We wouldn't sleep well with it running. Then I locked the front door and pulled off Jack's shoes and put his legs up on the couch. After the window was open I put a light blanket over him then I put his gun on a side table and mine in the bedroom. By then, Paul was done eating so we curled up in bed.

"Remember your appointment tomorrow," I said. The one Ross was taking him to.

"Looking forward to it," he sleepily replied.

"Sure you are."

But within a few minutes he was still. I woke to the sound of someone trying the doorknob later and then by Camille at dinner time. Paul stirred so we made our way to the kitchen and he cooked.

"Do we have somewhere else we can put Jack?" I asked. Paul heated a big tub of his mother's beef stew which was usually the first thing we ran out of after she visited. Most of it went back in the fridge. The table was so quiet without Alina and Ray with us.

"No, not right now. Until we get something official from the Colonel he needs to stay out of sight. I have a couple of men I'm worried won't be professional. They're going to get shipped out if they don't get along. They had a hard time after the mission where Damian turned on us and they'll do better somewhere else for a while."

"There's no loyalty to Damian in any of Jack's men any more. Since they turned on Archer."

Paul nodded. He was still a little groggy but was more himself. Camille was in a better mood too. He got up for seconds while I poked mine around my bowl.

"When do you leave?" I asked.

Paul looked down at his bowl. He knew what I meant. I would be here with Alina and any of the other women who turned up and he would leave. Gone. Maybe with Jack, maybe a couple of teams. I knew he wouldn't take his time with the plans. He'd have as much information from Jack as he could gather and all the possibilities would be running through his mind.

"Sooner the better."

I pushed my bowl further out of Camille's reach. She sat on my leg facing him, my arm around her. It was almost out of my reach already but I didn't want her getting it. Her arms could grow a foot in the next minute.

"You'll have Ray at least. Ross. You'll have to work with him. He knows the compound and the men. You'll pick it up fast but your focus needs to be Camille and our guests."

We were silent for a while.

"I'll need to keep a truck. Packed and ready to go. I'll keep Jack's men who are coming in with Dana's mate. They'll know how to run and hide better than I do and she'll trust them. You'll need Jack for whatever you're doing."

"Whatever you need is yours," he said.

"It doesn't matter anyway, three pregnant women will make this place so unbearable every man here will volunteer to go with you."

Paul thoughtfully nodded; my humour lost on him. "I hadn't considered that."

"I'll need a van, not a truck. I can't get everyone and car seats in six seat belts. Big engine. Trailer. When are they coming?"

"Dana's gone to meet them, he'll bring them here. Could be a week. Maybe more. Maybe less."

Paul pushed his empty bowl away and wrapped his hands around his half full glass of beer.

"I'm sorry. I know this isn't what you thought we'd be doing."

I shrugged.

"Are you scared, Sugar?"

"Of some things, I guess," I said as I tightened my hold on Camille. "It feels like the end. I'm trying to shake off the feeling of resignation that's seeping into me before it starts guiding my actions."

"I'm with you on that... don't cut it loose completely. Part of leading is knowing when you need it to get through acting on a painful decision."

I sighed. "Is there any point? Won't we all be doing it again?"

"We're protecting our children. We can hope with Damian not coming back that side of the family will be more reasonable."

"Here," he said reaching out his hands. "Finish your dinner. I counted the carrots before you started and I know you've been pushing them around."

I passed him Camille over the table and pulled my bowl closer. He was right. It was cold and other than a piece or two of meat I picked out, still intact.

"Take care of the ones in the US first. Thin the ranks as much as you can where you have the Colonel's support. Draw their leadership to us." I thought out loud.

"Are you sure you don't want to go and I'll stay here?"

I smiled and shook my head.

"You after Sig's job?"

"Aiming higher than that," I replied.

"Don't step on him on your way up," he laughed. "I'm going to show Miss Missy how to get the watch out."

Nobody came up after Paul took Camille downstairs. I had a second load of wash churning in the machine and the dishes done when Jack sat up. Eyes open but not seeing. He walked a few feet from the sofa and started to unzip his pants. Damn it, this was a guy's job. Or his mother's. Not mine. I pushed him to the bathroom, fighting to keep his pants up the whole way. Once we were in there he figured out where we were and then found his way back to the sofa. Hopefully he'd remember next time he had to go.

I got the vacuum around and mopped while Camille was off the floor for a while. She didn't like the noise and I couldn't get everyone to stop wearing shoes in the apartment. It wouldn't be long before she started going off the blanket I put down for her.

"She could hear it from downstairs," Paul said behind me as I shoved the vacuum back in the closet.

I looked down at his boots.

"She's going to be crawling through everything you step in soon. Can we start leaving them downstairs?"

"Sure..." he conceded but I knew his complaint was the time it took to lace them up and he still had a few months to put off losing the argument.

We took her to our room to eat before she got her bath and bedtime. I usually fed her in one of the big chairs in the living room but with Jack sleeping out there it felt like there was a big awkward corner in the house.

"Next time he has to pee you help him," I said. "That wasn't part of whatever bargain."

Paul let out a forced laugh.

"It was either that or let him go on the carpet. He doesn't know were he is. I had to fight him to keep his pants up but once I got him past the bathroom door he was okay from there."

"Okay," he laughed a little easier. "Camille's learned almost all the call signs already."

I stroked her head, picturing him at the desk reading the list to her.

"I forgot about being Romeo until today."

"Everyone here has one. Jack's Hotel."

I stiffened and glared at Paul.

"Is that supposed to be some sort of joke?" I demanded. It was barely twenty-four hours since the hotel room.

"No," he said then he understood. "Ah, shit. I'm sorry. It's the only one left. Nobody ever wanted it because they think it sounds lame. I need a two letter system now. It's on my list of things to do over the next couple of days while I recuperate."

"It's okay. Irony sucks."

Paul kissed me and took Camille.

"You're flushed. Still getting your energy back?"

I nodded.

"I'll bathe her. Then we'll get some sleep."

She smelled clean while I fed her in the rocking chair in her room. We only used it at bedtime and she seemed to know it was the end of the day. Dark, quiet rocking. Sometimes I'd sing the Russian lullaby we heard Alina sing at the hospital. I didn't feel like it tonight but I did anyway. After she'd been up on my shoulder for a few minutes I tucked her in bed and Paul came in to say good night.

When we got in bed he turned his back to me but he didn't fall asleep. I listened to him struggle with his breathing for a minute before I realized he silently cried. I made my way around to his side of the bed and pushed myself into the narrow space between him and the edge, shoving my arm under his neck. He put his arms around me and I held him to my breast. I pressed my nose into his hair and ran the tips of my fingers through it as his soundless tears dampened the front of my shirt.

Even the Captain had to fall apart sometimes. I hadn't seen it before but it had been a rough couple of weeks for him. Any one of the things he'd been through or would be going through would be too much. He'd lost a son to a miscarriage and his wife had died for a couple of minutes. He had to send her into the arms of another man and he'd killed someone. He was going to say goodbye to Camille and me, maybe more than once and who knew for how long. Our bedroom was the only safe place for him to let himself be washed in all the feelings he kept away when he was outside our door.

Eventually his breathing evened out and he pulled up my soft pink tank top then rolled me over him to the middle of the bed.

"Thank you," he whispered as the top came off.

Chapter 18

Paul rose early since his appointment in town was first thing. I slept in a chair in the living room to keep an eye on Jack since he'd wandered into Camille's room instead of the bathroom during the night and Paul jumped out of bed to shove him in the right direction. I heard them talking behind me in the kitchen and when I opened my eyes, I faced the empty couch.

"She's not what I expected," Jack said.

Camille laughed as Paul stalled her for breakfast.

"You were expecting what you expect?"

"Something like that."

"She's loyal and trusting to a fault but obedient? No," Paul said. "If she can't back up her decisions with loyalty and trust you need to stay out of her way."

I hadn't thought of it like that before and I had to agree.

"She's deeply generous though," Paul said. "She thinks she's selfish but I've never seen it."

"That's the impression I get."

Camille giggled.

"Let your Mom have five more minutes," Paul said. "You heard her give Alina the story?"

"Most if it. Then I woke up on your sofa. I think it hurt her as much as it did for Alina to hear it. They seem very close."

"Yeah, they were mistaken for twins growing up. Most of what they say to each other doesn't come out of their mouths. Even when I hear every word I know I miss most of what goes on between those two."

I heard someone get up then the thunk of shoving the coffee pot back into the machine.

"Speaking of that, I thought I heard her in my head when she showed me what Archer had been doing."

"Really," Paul said. I was relieved I wasn't nuts though Paul sounded as unhappy about it as when I told him.

"Mm hm. Either she's ignoring me now or it's not working any more."

Paul waited a few seconds. "She said the same thing about it."

"Hm," Jack said. "I don't like the idea of her in my head any more than you like the idea of me in hers. If we're splitting up we need to know as little as possible about each other. Walker and Soros, they'll have no problem forcing it out of her. Or us for that matter."

Paul coldly laughed. "Anna calls that our charm though there's nothing charming about it and they won't get anywhere using it with her."

"Oh?"

"I used it on her, to show her she couldn't resist it. Her plan was to refuse you. She didn't understand the decision had been made and she didn't have a choice. She agreed to try and put her hand on me and I used it to tell her to stay still. It only took her a few minutes to figure out how it worked, break it, and use it on me."

"No way," Jack said. "What was it like?"

"Doing what she said felt incredible. I tried to fight her but the pain was unimaginable. She said it's a terrible thing. I agree, it's so easy to do but until you've had to fight it you don't know what having your will taken from you really is."

"So it's no different from a mate than it is from a man," Jack said. "The cut on my face runs to here. It hurt less than fighting the order to do it. Father doesn't lay a hand on his men. He makes them do it to themselves."

I thought Damian cut him, made him stand still for it. Now I felt sick. He chose between the pain of fighting and the pain of cutting himself with the intense pleasure of doing what he was told thrown in.

After another round of baby laughter I decided she shouldn't wait any longer and got up with the blanket. I wanted to see Paul before he left and didn't think I should do any more eavesdropping even if it was about me.

"Good morning," I yawned then kissed Paul. "Hi, Jack."

Camille heard my voice and fussed so I covered up with the blanket and tucked her in with me for breakfast.

"Sorry, Sugar. Did we wake you?"

"No," I yawned again as I rubbed the side of my head. "My ears were burning. It woke me up."

"Told you," Paul said as he and Jack exchanged glances. I wasn't going to let on how much or little I'd heard.

"How'd you sleep, Jack?"

"Never slept like that before."

I waited until he had his coffee at his lips. "I had to help you pee."

Coffee sputtered up his face and he coughed. Paul laughed. "You pushed him into the bathroom once. I got him in there the second time."

"That was helping," I said.

Paul put toast in front of me and I tried not to rain crumbs on Camille. Jack put down half a cup of coffee in a single pull on his mug.

There was a quiet knock at the door as Camille let go so I put her on my shoulder.

"Anna?" Alina let herself in so I took Camille with me to the door.

"Hi, Sweetie," I said as I went around the corner. Her puffy eyes indicated she had a difficult night. "Awe, you look rough."

"You do, too," she firmly said.

She was right. I hadn't rested much. And she did a much better job of keeping a straight face than me. Overnight was a record for us to stay mad.

"Ray says I should come hear your apology before my blood pressure gets any higher."

I heard Paul snicker around the corner. Alina glared at him through the wall. Her hair was up and in her little suit jacket she was all business.

"Alina," I took a deep breath. "I'm sorry I kept my job from you. I'm sorry I dumped it on you all at once. I'm sorry I made you cry."

I honestly regretted her pain and felt tears as I said it.

"I'm sorry I made you knock me flat on my butt and swear at me and call me a man." Her stern glare weakened as Paul laughed again from the kitchen. She reached and took Camille. "I hope you can forgive me."

Camille burped and Alina smiled before she clamped it back down.

"I would say no but they only send them to me if there are women or children. There are only a couple of women who do this and it makes a huge difference if a woman can look after them. I know one needs a doctor... what if it's a sick child? How can I say no? How could we ever refuse to help?

"Remember that single mom who broke her leg? No family? New to the city? Remember how you rearranged the whole Emergency so you could work straight nights for six weeks and babysit her three kids so she could get to physical therapy to get better and get back to work? You took two weeks off with exhaustion after. You know how I feel."

She nodded and wiped her eyes.

"I know when you saw me running down the road packing two guns you thought I'd lost my mind. Then you hoped it was some kink of Paul's and I had some see-through lacy gingham number... spurs."

Alina snickered. Paul and Jack remained quiet enough to keep listening.

"And it's such a funny coincidence. Paul has these matching short shorts and leather vest and sheets that look like table cloths."

She burst out laughing and covered her mouth. She reddened but not with anger as she pressed her knees together.

"And you'll never guess what's in the picnic basket." I whispered in her ear, naming several items one would only find in an adult shop.

"Oh my God, Anna, you are so bad!" She stammered as she shoved Camille in my arms and ran for the bathroom before her bladder could give out.

"You want breakfast, Alina?" I called to her.

"Yes," she yelled from behind the door.

Paul and Jack were still laughing when I sat back down to finish filling up Camille.

"I think she accepted my apology so I'll fix her breakfast when baby's done. Just watch, she'll have Ray blushing at the table."

"Picnic basket?" Paul whispered in my ear before he took it between his teeth and gently tugged.

"Paul," I whispered. I glanced at Jack and he rolled his eyes. "You want one for the road?"

Paul laughed as a truck pull up out front.

"I'll take a rain check, sheriff. My ride is here." He stuck his face under the blanket to kiss Camille goodbye.

"Bye, Paul," Alina called to him as he went out the door.

"You should warn a pregnant lady before you do that, Anna. I barely made it," she said. "Oh. Hi, Jack."

"I'm really sorry, Alina," I said.

She smiled at me this time. At seven in the morning and even with her rough night she already looked better than I would after hours of trying.

"I'm sorry, too," she said.

Jack finished the third cup of coffee I witnessed so I put on more since Ray would be coming and started cooking.

We had some good fruit in so I sliced up strawberries and bananas for their pancakes as they browned in the pan. I knew Jack would be up for a second breakfast only because I knew how hungry I felt after sleeping off a bunch of jumps and I cooked enough for everyone to get started by the time Ray arrived. I ate standing up as I kept the pan busy. Jack, Ray and Alina took turns with Camille. Ray kept an eye on him his first couple of turns. Understandably suspicious but he relaxed quickly.

After Ray and Alina left, I set Camille up on the floor to play with her. They would be back soon then Alina and I would get a nap while Ray caught up with Jack. He went for a shower and started up a load of his clothes. Then he came and watched us for a while. He hadn't bothered to shave and rubbed his hand on his chin like he wasn't sure why it felt so rough.

"Sorry you're stuck in here," I said. "Are your men safe where they are?"

"Yeah, Dana's got a backup place if they need it. They're relieved we've split. Morale had been desperately low. I don't think you can appreciate how long we've been waiting to make a break and get on with things."

I couldn't. It could have been lifetimes. Maybe hundreds of years.

"Ray says he remembers you from a long time ago."

"Yeah, Ray, Paul, Keith and I always got on well. We always thought of ourselves as the oldest with our Fathers being the first three. Damn, we were full of ourselves," Jack laughed then his mood changed. "Things are sure different with the old men out of the picture."

Camille had a cloth book in her mouth. Something in the bright pages rustled when she squished it so I squeezed and wiggled it in her hands. She shoved it further in and pulled her feet up. I sat up and put her on my knees and tried to interest her in something else but the book was her favourite and she wouldn't be tempted.

"What do you know about near death experiences?" Jack asked. His change of subject surprised me. I must not have been paying attention if we had switched to that topic.

"They happen?" I said. "Alina would be the one to talk to working in Emergency. She's told me some stories."

"I'm interested in yours," he said as he leaned toward me with his elbows on his knees. "It's been a hobby of mine for a while. We all have them, when we pass. Remember them. I get them from the men whenever I can. I have books of them. The difference with a near death experience is we don't die then. Later of course."

I didn't remember floating around the helicopter looking down at myself or anything else. I blinked and shook my head.

"No or you don't think you did?"

"I remember some crazy dream. Nothing like you'd be interested in."

"That's exactly what I'm interested in," Jack said. "If you could find meaning or spirituality in our constant cycle of living that's where it will be. I find patterns looking at the same man's experiences. Things relevant to the rest of their life if it was only a near death experience. I've never had the experiences of a woman in the family to look at."

Camille needed a change so I excused myself with her before I got her book off the floor and we joined him on the couch.

"I remember Catherine's death in 1777. Your father killed her and whoever Paul was then. My memories of her made me realize Paul was her lover. Your uncle told me a lot more when I went to see him, to find out what the hell he'd done to me. I remember Andre's death in the South Pacific. Andre was crazy even then, killed the enemy by the hundreds. Your father sent him first up the hill they were taking as payback for a little insubordination."

I rubbed my throat as I remembered.

"Andre finally found someone better with a knife than he was and he gratefully died, leaving the pain he carried behind. Or he thought he had at least. It's more the circumstances I remember, nothing else."

"And a week and a half ago?" Jack prompted. "Father's group knows a woman won't survive a second pregnancy with the same man. She can with another. His line is sufficient to give the child one. He was persistent in his... research. He didn't keep them around after the child was born anyway. They were just talking incubators to him."

I remembered what Damian said to Alina when she told him she was pregnant. That summed it up well. I told him my dream. About the corn, about having to choose between saving the men and saving myself, how I tried to find a way to save us both, then just one. That I realized I couldn't save anyone as I fell into the slaughter on the ground. Jack quietly listened, staring off into the kitchen.

"I woke up being taken from the helicopter. Ray was there, keeping the thunder away but it was just the blades thumping away above me. I thought because I was flying I dreamed I was in the air. The noise of the helicopter above and people below. I'd never flown before and was scared."

Camille grew dozy in my arms so I offered her a top up before her nap. I didn't bother with the blanket. I didn't put one over my head to eat and nobody else in the house did either. No reason why she should. Jack got up for another cup of coffee and brought me a glass of water.

"She's had more to drink today than you have," he absently said as he passed it to me.

"Thanks, Jack."

"You know you're the most powerful person here," he said after a few minutes. "Both leaders are loyal to you. You're responsible for us all in a way. And there are two groups of men. Yours and my Father's. They'll figure out how valuable you are to us. You tie our loyalties together, our bond as a group."

"I don't like where your thoughts headed." I put my glass down and took Camille to her bed. When I came out he was still thinking.

"What I've seen when I die has always been the answer to some big question I will have. Like a key to solve some problem I didn't understand yet. The key is there somewhere, Anna. When you find it, it will help us all."

Chapter 19

Paul was back up and around after his day trip with Ross and Camille still fussed in the morning and stayed up half the night. She slept in time for me to join Paul and Jack for breakfast before I would crawl back in bed myself. Paul had paired me with Joshua for my first night watch and he was civil showing me the ropes. His feelings were hurt with Jack Roberts seeming more welcome in my home than him.

Paul appeared just as sullen when the alarm went off as the previous morning, the day after his procedure. Just because family healed quickly didn't mean it hurt any less. I knew he felt uncomfortable and couldn't stand leaving the camp in Joshua and Ross' hands when he was right upstairs. More than once I'd been shushed so he could try and make out what they said downstairs then he would try and silently guide them through sheer force of will. Paul and Jack quietly talked as I put Camille down and fell silent when I joined them. Old habits, I guessed. Family man talk kept among the men. Paul and Ray still shut up around me and Jack wasn't used to a woman who knew all about them.

I quietly helped myself and took the seat next to Paul. He was dressed today unlike the day before he'd spent in his robe. His arm slipped around me and he squeezed just under my ribs.

"Morning," I laughed as I got an elbow down to protect my sensitive skin. "Feeling better?"

"I think I'm mostly over the shellfish," he replied. Jack snorted. When Ross brought Paul home he had Ray see him regarding alleged food poisoning acquired during our faked dinner and movie. The ruse moved Alina out of the apartment for a couple of days and gave Paul some privacy to get over his true discomfort. If having Jack within the same walls could be considered private.

"I'm glad," I said. His mood seemed somewhat improved with breakfast in him. His crankiness the day before challenged even Ray's cheerful bedside manner. Jack got up and took the coffee pot before refilling his cup and Paul's. Then he got himself a glass, sat, and filled it with apple juice. Something very Jack invaded my nose and I sneezed into my elbow.

Juice?

I sharply inhaled and stared wide-eyed at Jack. He winked.

"How the hell, Jack?"

Yes or no?

Yes, I thought at Jack and he topped up my glass.

"Ha!" I exclaimed and elbowed Paul as I pointed at Jack. Paul looked at me then at Jack and shook his head. "He figured it out. How'd you do that?"

It was stupid obvious. I was reading you here the other night, he answered, pointing under his nose. *Then I piggybacked on you after that.*

"Stupid obvious is right," I laughed out loud.

"Pardon?" Paul asked but I ignored him. Figuring this out was way more interesting.

Let me try, I sent and felt Jack remove his sense from under my nose. I waited a moment and pushed mine under his and was rewarded as he turned aside and sneezed into his shoulder.

Can you hear me? I asked.

Jack nodded.

Try reading something else, he suggested so I tried to read Paul. I could but I lost my contact with Jack as he was sipping his coffee so I reconnected and he slopped trying to avoid sneezing into his mug.

"Damn it," he muttered while I laughed. Paul elbowed me and I waved him off.

"You try," I told Jack; napkin ready. He dropped the connection as soon as he tried to put his sense somewhere else and reconnected.

I guess we can't read when we do this, Jack sent. *I can read while you're connected to me but not when I'm connected to you.*

I shrugged and smiled.

I wonder how far it works? I asked.

Guess as far as we can read, Jack answered as Paul abruptly stood, got his knee on the table and went over it.

Dishes flew as I fell backward off my chair when I avoided his foot. Paul roared as they crashed to the floor and I pulled myself up in time to see Paul haul Jack half up by his shirt and clobber him in the side of the face. Jack's head snapped to the side, blood already dripping from the corner of his mouth.

"Paul!" I shrieked as I tripped on his overturned chair and stumbled into the counter. I looked up to see Paul straightening his shirt as Jack awkwardly stood and gave Paul some space.

"Not that whispering *shit* when I'm around," he seethed at Jack. Jack tested his jaw, eyes lowered.

"Paul," I tried again as I moved in front of him, between him and Jack.

"It's okay, Anna," Jack said, barely louder than the drip, drip of someone's toppled drink running onto the floor. Paul worried about his men having a go at Jack and he did just that.

"It's not okay Jack—" I started but Paul's icy stare stopped me. I'd never seen the full alpha patriarch in him and realized I stood in the middle of something deeply family, something a woman in the family shouldn't know about. I dropped my eyes like Jack had in involuntary submission.

"That's better," Paul said as he stomped off down the hall to the bedroom. "I'm entitled."

I watched his back in silence as my arms crossed. Jack sighed behind me and I glanced at my destroyed kitchen.

"Jack, I—" I started but he interrupted.

"Stay out of it, Anna," he said. I turned and blinked at him in the morning sunlight shining off the top of the glass coffee table.

Hurried boots rushed up the stairs. Ross, I read, and probably Joshua in the second pair then an urgent knock at the door. Jack wiped his mouth on the back of his hand when he answered.

"Roberts," Joshua said suppressing a laugh. "Wearing out your welcome?"

Ross elbowed him and Jack walked away to the kitchen.

"The Colonel says to get you a cabin," Joshua called to him. "Three West. Bigger than you deserve but the *Commander* has a couple of her men coming and they'll bunk with you. Right next door to me, buddy. I'll have my eye on you."

"Joshua," I hissed but he pointed two fingers at his eyes then at me before he walked out, leaving me alone with Ross.

"Surprised it took Paul that long," Ross muttered. "Anyway, ball is rolling. The Colonel will be calling this afternoon for the Captain."

After he left, I walked past the opening to the kitchen. I heard Jack picking up dishes but didn't look in. Paul sat on the far side of the bed in the dark with his back to me in the curtained room. My hands tightly gripped the knob as I leaned back on the door.

"Sig will call you this afternoon," I said after a moment.

"Thanks, I heard," Paul said.

"I thought you went after Jack like you were worried your men would and I didn't understand," I said, trying to be a grownup about what I guessed just happened when all I wanted to do was tell Paul he acted like a child. He got up and walked around the edge of the bed and put his hands on my waist.

"Balance sucks sometimes, Sugar," he said. "The grownup in me believes every word I told you about Jack's inheritance. I've never seen one but knowing the ins and outs is part of my grownup life. It's something the men talk about to make sure everyone knows the rules. I had to help make sure it was done quickly before anyone got hurt. Delaying because of Paul's feelings or yours would get someone hurt or killed if Jack got out of control and shot his way in here to finish it. Or if you had gone after him."

"I get it," I curtly answered as I pulled on the door to leave. Paul put a hand on the door next to me and held it still.

"Wait, that's not all. Courtesy says the man in this life is entitled to stand up for his wife's honour; to do what any man would do to someone who'd been with his wife. Jack knows. I'm embarrassed I claimed that right in front of you. I know you're protective of us both now and I put you in a difficult spot. I'm sorry."

I reached one hand for his chin, stroking his jaw with my fingers.

"Jack told me to stay out of it."

"Yes," Paul said, threading his hands through my hair and pulling me close. "I'm asking you to do the same thing."

I nodded. Knowing why Paul hit him only reminded me every family rule was ninety percent testosterone.

"Alright," I said.

"Good girl," Paul kissed my cheek. "How did that work? You and Jack?"

"When I read I take my sense from here," I gestured under my nose, "and push it out of me to what I want to read. If I don't do it then I don't read. If Jack puts his sense under my nose I sneeze and we can talk or if I do the same to him. If I make the connection I can't read anything else."

"Look, Sugar," Paul said as he pressed into me. "I'm not impractical. I see how useful it can be—"

"It was impolite and I'm sorry."

Paul sighed as I got my arms around him.

"Jesus, I need another day, Sugar," he growled in my ear. "If Sig ships me out today I'm going to be one grumpy bastard until I see you again."

"That'll make two of us," I laughed.

"I'm getting Camille up. I'll bring her in here to eat while I help Jack clean up then I'm taking him to his cabin. Between your watch and her mixed up hours I want you getting some rest. You're only a couple of weeks out of the hospital. I'll put her down for an hour later and then to bed at eight."

Light and the sound of running water in the kitchen filled our room as he opened the door.

"It's really happening," I whispered at his back. "You're going aren't you?"

I was too quiet.

He didn't hear.

Chapter 20

My cramped cot in Camille's room felt too firm. Moving it in with her was my first action following Paul's departure. He said goodbye in the apartment and I sobbed on Joshua as the helicopter faded to the east. Virtue and Dana shared my bed. His formerly lanky Southern auburn haired charmer put on about a hundred pounds by Jack's reckoning but in spite of her poor health she quickly endeared herself to everyone, in particular Camille whose eyes went wide every time she heard her musical voice. She might have been all of seventeen but her deep attachment to Dana was as strong and timeless as mine to Paul or my sister's to Ray.

Virtue's health didn't do much for Alina's blood pressure and every drop in Virtue's blood sugar corresponded to an improvement for Alina. She felt it was her own personal challenge to undo the damage the men she called 'Jack's Bastards' had done. Between insulin, exercise and food that didn't come in a grease covered bag Virtue got better every day.

Jack shared his cabin with Jeff Halford and Bob Mason, his men who managed Virtue. Alina didn't like them right from the start and felt they'd be ideal caregivers if they sported spears in their chests. I had yet to break it to her they'd hit the road with us and was as disappointed as she would be. I knew the men would be useful and were loyal to Jack but they stunk of chauvinism to the point I'd have to be someone I really hated to work with them. Alina knew we waited for one more person, Marie, before we'd leave. Because of her trust and loyalty to Ray she didn't question why we'd drive away in the van Sig outfitted for us.

I rolled over for what must have been the twentieth time when a cell phone on Paul's desk in the living room rang, shoving my heart up into my throat. It only rang three times before I reached it. Paul's phone. A seven-eight-oh area code.

Keith.

"Yes?" I answered.

"I need Paul," he said, real fear in his voice.

"He's shipped out, Keith."

There was a pause.

"Do your magic, Anna. Come get my girl."

I reached my sense to Jack in his cabin and locked on.

"Of course," I answered.

Unh, Jack said.

Get a truck fast, Jack. Keith needs us to get Marie now.

Already out the door, he answered.

"On our way, Keith," I said but he started rambling.

"Warren called from the restaurant. Someone shot Reg and pinned down in the office and shooting."

My stomach knotted at the mention of Warren's name. He'd been mine and Paul's. I hadn't spoken to him during our time in Edmonton with Keith's part of the family and never asked Paul if he'd told Warren we were his mother and father. The only thing that would terrify me more would be news Camille was in trouble.

"Dana," I whispered as I stuck my head in the bedroom door. "I need a sitter."

Blankets shuffled. "I'm all ears for her."

"Get a damn bagged packed, Marie," Keith yelled. "She won't fucking listen. She won't leave. They're half an hour away once they find out where we are."

"Keith," I said as I pulled on pants, vest and guns. "Get her in the car and go, we'll find you."

"Now God damn it, Marie. I want you the fuck out of my house," he bellowed. Marie cried in the background followed by a crash.

I ran downstairs with Paul's phone to my ear, nearly taking out Jack at the bottom. Keith and Marie continued fighting.

"Stuff her in the damn car and drive, Keith. I'll find you," I yelled but the phone clattered to the floor and their voices grew distant. Ray barged in and disappeared down the hall with Jack. The bright lights on the main floor half blinded me in spite of having nothing to reflect on but the dark wood panelling I'd managed to ban from our apartment.

Ross is getting a truck, Jack sent.

Hurry. Keith's trying to throw her out and they're both screaming and he says there was shooting at the restaurant.

Damn, Soros found them.

I ran out as Ross pulled up in one of the trucks and jumped in followed by Jack climbing in the back seat. Both were armed. Ross wore the compound's usual casual dress uniform of army boots, jeans and a button up shirt under his bullet proof vest. He'd just come in from watch but Jack had shoved his bare feet in his shoes and wore a shiny pair of long black basketball shorts. His decomposing t-shirt would have said *I Like to Fuck* if half the letters hadn't rotted off.

"Anna drives," Jack said. Ross didn't argue and swapped with me. I floored it, sure the entire compound woke from the sound of my gravel tossing demonstration. We took off south from the house, cabins flashing by on either side.

"When I say so, close your eyes," I shouted. "Hold on."

I focused more effectively when sick with fear. We were only five minutes past the gate when I hollered and without waiting for them to say they were ready, we jumped.

Silence found us on a dark street lined on either side by nineteen seventies cracker box shaped houses, unfenced front yards and immaculate lawns.

"Holy fuck," Ross whispered when he figured out it was over. I'd never heard him swear.

"This way," Jack said and led us two houses down the street before he took a left up a paved walk. Ross and I hustled to catch up. We heard Marie and Keith yelling before we got to the door and Patrick quickly let us in. The three of us armed would get us some attention on the way out if it hadn't already.

Marie was an angry mane of sleep tousled red hair pleading with Keith against the backdrop of their toothpaste green living room. He wore his black and whites from the restaurant. She held her arms out to him and sobbed before she wrapped them around herself. Keith helplessly looked at us over her shoulder.

"Marie?" I said.

She spun to face me as I tried to get my arm around her.

"I'm not leaving him, Anna," she sputtered and her hands gripped the sides of the oversized dress shirt she wore. Her stiff legs pinned her in place. The big shirt couldn't hide her pregnant belly.

"Come on, little one. He'll catch up," I tried.

"I know he's in trouble," she sobbed. "He said he's been running coke through the restaurant to cover some fucking gambling debt and—"

"Marie," Keith warned.

"Now he's in for a quarter million and they won't wait—"

"I'm not going to your damned parents," he yelled.

I turned to Jack. Ross stood quietly next to him as Patrick took a step closer to Marie. The three of them were as calm as Keith and Marie were hysterical. I was right in the middle feeling as upset as Marie and trying to be as all together as Jack.

"Keith," I pleaded. "Let's all get in the truck. They could be here in minutes."

"No," he looked at Jack and tilted his head at me.

"Marie," he bellowed and as she turned to him Jack spun me to face him. He gripped my elbows in iron and held my eyes with his.

"I don't want you," Keith said then her teeth snapped together, leaving us in silence. Patrick stepped past me and caught her.

"Please, save her," Keith whispered as Patrick and Ross took Marie and Jack dragged me to the door. Marie's head lolled to the side as she blinked, trying to clear it.

"I'm gonna cut his fucking nuts off," she growled and as I forced myself around in Jack's arms I saw it took the both of them to keep her from doing just that. I'd only ever heard of a man breaking it off with his mate. I never imagined the fury the disgusting blow would unleash.

Her hands slashed at Keith like claws and spit flew from her as the cursing worsened. Jack grabbed me around the waist and picked my feet up off the ground, carrying me through the door. "It's normal," he whispered.

"Fuck you, Jack," I struggled. "That's not normal. Fuck Keith. We could have got them both out."

"Don't disrespect them by judging his decision, Anna," Jack grunted as we took an awkward step down the last stair. Marie's screams filled the street. "Be a good child and respect Courtesy."

"Fuck you, Jack."

"What the hell is going on?" A man yelled from across the street.

I gave in and ran with Jack to the truck. Two men hauling off a pregnant neighbour would bring the police for sure. Jack opened up the back door for them then ran around and got behind the wheel and fired it up. I turned to see Ross and Patrick twenty feet away. Marie flailed like an angry cat. Night blackened blood ran from Ross' nose from a swing he hadn't dodged. Patrick stayed between her and the house, half-carrying her along as she fought to get back in and get her hands on Keith. Ross furiously blinked to clear his watering eyes and see in the streetlight as he pushed them along.

Patrick pulled her in as more shouts came from the house across the street. The front door of the house we parked in front of opened.

"You're not taking her anywhere, assholes," the neighbour shouted. The flash and bang of a gunshot followed. I shrieked as the front passenger door opened and Jack pulled me in by the waistband of my jeans. Ross piled in after Marie as Jack put it in gear, squealing the tires.

"Which way, Patrick?" Jack yelled over Marie. The front seat shook as she pounded it with her feet. Blue and red lights dimmed by the tinted rear window appeared behind us a few streets back.

"Left in two blocks then right at the lights."

I didn't even buckle up and knelt on the seat next to Jack, saying Marie's name over and over in a vain attempt to calm her down. Houses flew by as Jack pushed the truck hard.

"She's going to hurt herself," Ross said. Blood stained his collar and he'd wiped what had run from his nose on the sleeve. Marie's bare foot slipped over the back of the seat and nailed me in the shoulder. I hit the dash and landed wedged on my back in front of the seat.

"Here," Jack said. He lifted his butt and pulled something from the pocket on the side of his shorts. The sirens behind us hadn't become any louder or if they had, Marie's cries bloomed to match.

Ross grabbed it from him. "Hold her arm."

"Go over the freeway then left to get on it," Patrick yelled at Jack.

"Got it."

Marie's screams turned into sobs. I squirmed myself upright in time to see Ross pull the cap a off a syringe with his teeth and jab her in the arm. He dropped it on the floor.

"You're sedating her?" I demanded, horrified.

"Jesus, Anna," Jack yelled. "What do you think? And before you get started whining about your feelings maybe think about getting us somewhere in southern California so we can put some miles on this damn truck to make it look like we actually drove somewhere."

I glared at him until his hard left at the light rolled me back on to the floor.

"We have three police cars a block behind," he said. "If Soros isn't right on their heels or dealing with Keith's distraction I'll kiss both of Joshua's bare ass cheeks in front of the whole compound. She could carry on for hours and we can't let her. The stress will cost her the baby. You're going to take us to San Diego or fucking Sacramento for all I care and you're going to use her like you used me."

"No, Jack," I moaned. Marie's thrashing weakened though the front seat still shook when she kicked. She'd been through enough without me using her like a soda.

"Damn it, Anna. Hurry," Ross said. He sounded as impatient with me as Jack. I pulled myself up again and saw half a dozen sets of red and blue behind us. "The rest you can give her is better than what Ray will have to do to keep her calm."

"Anna," Jack said and got his arm around my waist as I hooked my elbows over the back of the seat. Marie buried her face in Patrick and wept. Whatever they gave her hit quick. Jack's eyes were on the rear view mirror as he wove between the few slower moving cars on the highway. "Hurry. Time was the last thing Keith felt he could give her. Don't waste it."

I turned and looked at Jack then back at Marie, finally able to put some reason behind what happened to the now single and possibly widowed young woman in Patrick's arms. Breaking it off would spare her the pain of losing her connection to Keith when he died. She resisted at first when I took her hand and relaxed it as I stroked the back with my thumb.

"Please, Anna," Patrick whispered as he pressed her head to his shoulder. "She won't remember this. The trauma is too much."

"Don't touch me, Jack," I whispered. "Or I'll drain you."

Chapter 21

Marie slipped from my arms at the side of a road. I hadn't aimed for anywhere other than southern California as Jack said and hoped we were there. Once I had a better grip, I heard Ross calling my name. They ended up in a field and Marie and I huddled ankle-deep in dank water hidden by a low cement wall. It took the three of them to get her out. Once she made it over the wall, Patrick carried her to the truck, silently refusing help. The GPS on Ross's phone said we were forty-five minutes south of Sacramento which put us nearly four hours from home. He got himself an ice pack from the first aid bag in the back of the truck and held it on his nose.

The truck clock said two am. We left the compound just after midnight and had been gone less than half an hour but I'd added some time to our absence to help put some weight to our story that we'd gone somewhere. I hoped not to wake Alina when I called Ray. It wasn't likely. He'd be downstairs in the house waiting for whatever mess I brought back and could hear Camille squawk from the other side of the compound.

"Paul?" Ray said when he answered.

"No, it's me," I said. "Is my baby okay?"

"Yeah, Kiddo. Not a peep."

I straightened and turned sideways in my seat so I faced Jack. My speech was ready. The one that said if I was at Paul's right hand then why the hell were they just using what I could do to get from point A to point B without connecting the dots for me. Ray knew Keith's backup plan if he'd taken Jack to the back room for a needle full of peace for Marie. Ross knew and so had Patrick. Jack knew exactly what Keith was going to do and dealt with me. Hell, it looked like he'd even invited Ross along in advance.

I had the line of a man and if they weren't going to treat me like a grownup they could at least treat me like any other family member with a strong line. Raise me in the ways of the family like they would a son even though I'd known about them for less than a year. If they couldn't give me respect then what was my daughter going to expect? She was already mated to Alina's son so she wouldn't even have independence. She was headed straight for the life of a mate first. Full family member second. Maybe.

"Ray?" I said as I decided it was a conversation to have with Paul.

"Yeah?"

"It's quiet here too. I think we'll be back for breakfast. Go back to bed and hug my sister. We're hitting the road in a couple of days."

"Okay, Kiddo."

Ray disconnected and I tucked Paul's phone in my pocket. Marie shouted something about Keith's dick and his ass and went back to sniffling. Patrick was right about the trauma. Losing her connection to Keith was more traumatic than I could ever imagine.

I know you think what Keith did was harsh, Jack sent after he connected to me. *I've been through the death of my first. More than once. The physical pain outlives any emotional damage or grief. It's there every day, shredding you inside.*

Imagine her going through that now instead of this temporary rage: unable to work or raise her son, going from doctor to doctor to try and understand what's wrong with her. The pregnancy is too far along to avoid this. In the first month or two this doesn't happen.

Her acting out can last for hours, maybe a day and the physical stress of her loss could take another day after that to pass. That's why I told you to use her. He hit her. It's sick. Jack feels your revulsion. The grownup in Jack knows the alternative.

I sighed and turned my head away to look out the window.

I get it, Jack said. *Being angry at me is okay. This isn't the first time a woman's given me the silent treatment.*

I'm not angry at you, I replied. *I don't think I'm even angry. My eyes were ripped wide open tonight.*

"Yeah," Jack said out loud as he sunk down behind the wheel and pulled his sense from me. "Anyone else need coffee?"

"No," Patrick said. Ross mumbled a few words under his ice pack.

Sacramento lit the sky ahead for a while and Jack pulled us into an all-night drive through, shutting off the big truck engine so he could hear well enough to order. He got himself two extra-larges and a big double-double for Ross.

"How's the schnoz?" He asked Ross as he passed it back.

"Not broken," Ross said as he dropped the ice pack on the floor with the used needle. I could see the shadows forming under his eyes. "She bruised herself up pretty bad."

In the parking lot lights I could make out the marks Marie left on herself. She still squirmed in Patrick's arms. At least she stopped striking everything in reach though her vocabulary wasn't anything I'd expect from the lips of a sober person. It was obvious by the

107

tenderness he showed her she was his responsibility now. She held him tight. She knew it and wasn't letting him go. In a few days she'd be living in a hotel with the rest of us. Being separated from Keith would be shock enough and I felt grateful she had Patrick.

The Edmonton Journal
May 30, 2011

Five people are dead including an Edmonton City Police Officer after gunfire and flames erupted around Edmonton last night in two separate incidents.

Police responded to reports of shots fired at 1am at a restaurant in West Edmonton Mall's Bourbon Street and arrived on scene to find it fully engulfed in flames, say the ECPF in a statement. Shortly afterwards at 1:30am ECPF responded to an apparent abduction in north-west Edmonton.

Neighbours called 911 after hearing a woman screaming and reported seeing three or four armed males fleeing outside of the house and leaving in a black truck. The ECPF arrived on scene with the abduction occurring and pursued the truck but called off the pursuit. The vehicle and occupants remain at large and were last seen heading down Yellowhead Highway.

Police began investigating inside the house when witnesses report that 15 minutes later two separate vehicles arrived and at least half a dozen armed men stormed the house when gunfire erupted.

ECPF have confirmed that one officer was killed in the gunfire and an unidentified male is also confirmed dead. The house and neighbourhood remains closed off this morning as ECPF continue to investigate. ECPF have confirmed that the unidentified deceased male was not known to police. Dead is Officer Jason Barrett, 32, of Red Deer, Alberta, a veteran of eight years on the force. He was married with three children.

Three badly burned bodies were found in the remains of the restaurant and a large section of West Edmonton Mall remains closed. Edmonton Fire Department and the ECPF are on scene and investigating and so far have only said the fire appears to be deliberately set but won't be able to release any more details until they investigate further.

Wendy

Chapter 22

"I'm not saying it again. On your knees or I shoot."

I didn't recognized the voice and he wasn't family. One of the extras the Colonel sent during the month and a half I'd been away, I guessed, but this one didn't sound like he could be bullied. He revealed no fear or patience in his voice and I had the impression he could care less if he walked away leaving a big hole in me.

I got down, one knee at a time, and raised my hands. My bruised ribs wouldn't allow the left up as high as my right.

"Higher."

"Injured," I said in my helmet as I pushed them a little more.

"Sure you are. Don't move."

I waited a few seconds but he didn't say any more.

"Weatherman Control." Weatherman wasn't one I remembered from Paul's new list. My arms drooped as my ribs hurt more.

"Control Weatherman."

"Intruder Station Seven. Send two."

"Affirmative Weatherman."

"I'm Commander Anna Richards. Can you tell the Captain I'm here?"

"I'm the Captain," he said like I'd spent any tolerance he'd had for me. I sent my sense back to the house and found Paul there. Hopefully this yo-yo would figure me out and take me to him.

"Control, please invite the Major to my station."

"Control copies."

The Weatherman's boots shifted in the gravel.

"You're in my sights. Take the helmet off. Slowly."

As I complied I heard the two men he'd radioed for run up. I put it down beside me and lifted my hands again.

"Half assed job of complying. Claims to be Anna Richards," the Weatherman said.

"That's not her," one of the voices said. Great. My short brown hair wasn't helping.

"Search her," the Weatherman said. "We'll cover you."

I stayed still and glanced up at the man who felt my coat before unzipping it and relieving me of my guns. Didn't know him, another import.

"Captain?" It was Paul's voice. I hadn't followed him and didn't know he'd come too.

"Intruder, Major. She claims to be your wife. She's been disarmed. Jones says it's not her."

Major? I'd missed a lot. I heard footsteps behind me.

"Hi, Paul," I said. He took my hands and lowered them to my sides as he got down on the ground.

"Brunette?" Paul asked as he put his arms around me and I leaned on his shoulder. "Where did it all go?"

"Garbage can in a Bismarck hotel... my God I missed you."

"On your way, Captain. I'll see my wife to the house."

"Sorry, Major. Commander," he said as he and the other two left.

"Easy," I winced as he squeezed me tighter. "I've been testing my vest."

"Jesus, Anna," he muttered, helping me up.

"I'm glad you're safe, too."

"Been back about a week. It's been a long six weeks with you away." He gave me my guns and pulled the bike out then he wrapped an arm over my shoulders and walked me to the house.

"When did you get the promotion?"

"About a month ago."

"Well, congratulations," I said. "I'm sorry I wasn't here for it."

Paul stuck his nose in my ear. "You have no idea how much I've missed you. Is Camille okay?"

"Fantastic, she has three teeth now. She bites."

Paul laughed. "You didn't come all this way just to tell me that did you?"

"No, but I need to be your wife for a while first."

His hand slipped up inside my jacket as he kissed me. I wasn't going to get any argument so we went to our room for a couple of hours to get reacquainted.

Paul introduced me to the new Captain. Captain Taggart. He told me before we went downstairs he called himself the Weatherman because he decides where the shit falls. I thought that was stupid. He might as well carry an 'I'm the man in charge' sign around in front of the enemy and Paul agreed. He hadn't caught Taggart doing it in a while and would speak to him about it again. He said Taggart was a good soldier but still pretty green when it came to command.

Taggart apologized for holding a gun on me so I thanked him for doing his job and told him I hoped all the men would hold me up if they weren't certain it was me. He seemed pleased with the compliment and Paul whispered "nice" in my ear as Taggart walked away.

"It seems I'm more and more like you as time goes on," I said.

"Not unusual, I'm more like you, too. It's our connection to each other."

I laughed. Paul kept his arm on me since we got out of bed. He was upset about the bruising from the gunshot. I'd told him we relocated after Ray and I cleaned up two men who found us. Paul glared at the ceiling as he listened. I knew he didn't want me out hunting people. I said it was likely all the blonde hair gave me away so Alina had cut and dyed it for me. I'd done hers. She was a redhead now and Ray seemed partial to it. I was the only woman without red hair in the group. I knew it was more likely they'd come upon us by chance but it made Alina feel good doing something simple to protect me. She hadn't spoken to me through the whole cut and colour or since.

"How much time do you have?" Paul asked. We whispered, much too close to each other, in the corner of the common room and didn't give a damn about the looks from the men. It hadn't changed much. The furniture clustered closer to the front of the house and the extra space now held a weapons lockup by the radio and desk. Papers and charts plastered the walls. My mind lingered in our room where Paul found his way around lean muscle I didn't have six weeks earlier. He said he'd thank Ray for not letting me wait in some coffee shop while he finished our run on his own.

"The sooner I get back the better. I need Dana and A-negative."

Paul raised his eyebrows.

"It's been a bad couple of weeks," I lowered my voice. "Alina heard Halford and Mason talking about Damian. I told her he's a deserter and you were after him forever. He hurt me and went after her to get to you but we didn't know until January. She thinks we're on the run from him. She won't talk to me at all or Ray unless she has to.

"Ray delivered Virtue. Alina wanted her to go in for a C-section, to Hell with hiding, but Ray wouldn't. He didn't have his line yet. She delivered okay but her blood pressure had been too high for a while and she had a seizure while she was pushing. She lost a fair amount of blood. Ray transfused her with some of mine, more than he should have but she needed it more. I'm the only one the same type and she perked up a bit. She'll be okay with rest but more wouldn't hurt, we've been in the same place too long and I need her able to travel. Baby's doing well. I've been wet nursing him. She won't give up trying to breast feed but it's not coming in. He's taking a bottle while I'm away. She wants Dana before she names him."

"Wet nurse?" Paul asked. "I don't know if we have a commendation for it but if there is I'll put in for it with the Colonel for you. How's Marie?"

I laughed.

"She's doing okay. Patrick's really good with her. He knows he's not good for much else other than our radar system right now. I'd like to send him here. I don't sense Jack so you could probably use him."

Paul shook his head. "The children are more important."

"I know," I sighed and rested my head on his shoulder. "I'm glad you're safe."

"We've had a few incursions but the Colonel has us sufficiently manned. Taggart's expertise is security and he's thorough. We've shut them all down and haven't lost anyone here. Our away trips have had wins and losses but overall we've taken out more of them.

"Dana is with Lieutenant Roberts. The Colonel reinstated him as part of his deal. Jack got some seriously dirty lips pulling that off after everything that happened. I'll get what you need to take back. I can't help you find Dana though. Security is tight for obvious reasons. I don't know where he is." Paul looked around to make sure nobody watched. "If I put together a care package for Jack can you take it to him?"

"Sure, Paul."

Within half an hour we said goodbye. I carried a few units of blood for Virtue along with the other things on Ray's list in the small pack on my back and I didn't see what Paul put in the heavy saddle bags. I felt the extra weight as I shifted the bike side to side and adjusted the rear suspension for what felt like a passenger.

"If you wipe out, take cover," Paul said.

"Oh."

Ammo run.

"Jack's overdue," Paul whispered. "Be extra careful. We don't know if he's in trouble or just delayed."

"I will, Paul. I love you."

"I love you too, Sugar, let's not leave it so long before we do this again."

He followed me on my bike until the straighter stretch we'd used before, staying back as I got pushed around. I waved and Paul honked then I disappeared.

Chapter 23

I only missed a few hours with Camille. She was ready for bed so I filled her up as Ray unpacked the bag and set Virtue up with the blood I brought.

"Where did you get it, Anna?" Virtue asked.

I tried to look guilty.

"I stole a nurse's uniform and broke into where they keep it in the hospital. I only took a bit. Thanks for telling me what to look for, Ray."

"No problem, Anna," he said without looking up from the chart he and Alina kept on Virtue. Alina glared at me. She'd sleep with Camille after I left but she was still beyond angry. It had been over a week and she wasn't softening. It was worse I'd been shot and taken her man with me to do it. She thought we escaped with them on our heels. I couldn't imagine how mad she'd be if she knew I'd been lookout for Ray so he could dump them in a ditch while she piled in the van. She was safe because of what Ray and I did that night. I'd make her watch me spit in her shoes to keep her that way if I had to.

"I hear clicking," Virtue quietly said. She sounded relieved. "That means he's swallowing something, right?"

Alina sat behind her and rubbed her shoulder. The pregnant ones became close while the division between Alina and I grew and not just the past week. It started as soon as we drove out of the compound.

I was one of the guys. Closing the curtains and turning down the TV and coming and going at odd hours, bringing back cold take-out. Lurking around outside.

"I think you're right," Ray said. He put her chart away and turned off the lamp by the bed. "You had a rough time so it took a while."

"I got a message to Dana," I lied. "Might be a couple of days for me to bring him in if he meets up with me but it could be a lot sooner. Do you want me to top baby up before I go?"

"Please, Anna. Just in case it comes in slow. Ray has formula but mom's milk is better. Just feel my boobs. I think they're filling up."

"I believe you," I laughed. She was so young.

Her little boy clung to her for a long time and wasn't interested in me at all. I checked in with Halford, Mason and Patrick and let them know where I was going. Then I repacked the bag I brought Ray's medical supplies in with things for a couple of days before I softly kissed Camille's warm cheek. With her starting solids and half on formula she'd do okay if I wasn't back tonight. Ray caught up to me as I started up the bike.

"Did you see Paul?" he asked as he hugged me.

"Yeah, he's a Major now."

Ray laughed. "He turned it down two years ago. I'm surprised he took it this time. You look more relaxed."

"Ray..." I looked away as he chuckled.

"Anyway, Dana's with Jack," I continued. "They're overdue so I don't know what I'm going to find. Baby needs a name and a father so I'll be back as soon as I can."

"You're a good kid, Anna. Alina worried terribly about you while you were gone. She just doesn't have any other way to show it."

"I know. If she didn't love me she wouldn't be so angry," I agreed. The sun was almost down and I didn't relish the prospect of appearing in a strange place in the dark. Gone were the days when I wanted to arrive at night so I wouldn't be seen. "I'll find you if you're not here."

He nodded.

"Thank you, Ray. It means a lot having my big brother here."

I held him again. Alina peeked out the curtains after I let him go and I waved but she snapped them shut.

"Take care. Jack's Bastards know what they're doing. You need to move on as soon as Virtue can. I think I might be sleeping off my trip to Jack. If Dana takes a while to show up it'll be a day or two before I return. If he's there we'll be back right away.

"If Virtue can travel I want you out of here before dawn. If I've been compromised you can't be in the last place I saw you."

"I know, Kiddo. Be careful. I love your daughter like my own."

"She loves you, too. Hug Alina for me if she'll let you close enough, just don't say it's from me unless you really want to piss her off."

Ray laughed. "I'll cheer Alina up when she feels she's been angry long enough to make her point."

"Okay, bye," I said as I took off.

Chapter 24

The sun still lit the narrow road I found myself on. Not much, maybe half an hour away from setting. The old and weathered pavement showed no sign of a painted line. Even though it was July, white topped the mountain in the distance.

I rode up hill into the trees about fifty feet and turned the motorcycle off then I lay it down out of sight, making sure nothing hot touched the dry brush underneath. Even if I couldn't pick Jack up, I hoped he was close enough to read me since his range was so much better. Nothing leaked from the gas tank or any other part of the bike so I sat. The day's heat still radiated from the pavement but the ground was cool under the skinny broad leaf trees surrounding me.

I relaxed and closed my eyes, searching. First, scanning everything close then focusing as I sent my sense out as far as I could in one direction at a time. The farther I sent it out the smaller an area it covered. The recovery I needed from the travel was already in its first stage. Fatigue and sleepiness. Tomorrow the black sleep to recharge would hit for twelve to eighteen hours. Then I would feel hungry and out of sorts.

With the sun almost down, I felt a familiar tickle under my nose and sneezed as Jack focused in on me.

Social call? Jack asked.

Something like that. How are you doing?

There was a pause.

We've been better. Hope you brought some cheer.

Care package from Paul and news for Dana. I'd like to borrow him for a while, I said.

I'll come to you. Which side of the road are you on?

I looked through the dimly lit trees in the direction of the road.
Did the sun set on your side of the road or the other side? Jack asked.
Mine. I'm about fifty feet into the trees, hopefully out of sight.
Good girl, Jack said. *I'll be there in about half an hour for you.*
Thanks, Jack.

I closed my eyes and waited. After twenty minutes, I picked him up a hundred or so yards away. Him and another man I recalled from when I checked all Jack's men after we took out Archer. I focused my sense under Jack's nose. He was right at the edge of my range and I struggled to hold it but as he came closer it became easier.

Gesundheit, I said.

Ha ha. We need to figure out how to not give out each other's positions.

I pushed the bike up enough to feel the clips for the hard saddle bag underneath and disconnected it, then the other. They both held something sloshy and seemed to weigh as much as I did.

I think Paul sent you lead. You can each carry one.

Nice, Commander... that a rank thing? Jack asked.

No, Lieutenant. It's a 'gave blood twice this week' thing. I'm not sure I can even pick them up.

After what felt like another ten minutes I saw their flashlights through the trees. No need to call them over. Jack knew exactly were I was. When he reached me I stood up and held him and he hugged me back. It was like hugging Ray or Joshua, close and connected.

"Hey, Jack," I said.

"This is Finn," Jack said. "Richards."

I shook Finn's hand.

"What do you have for us?"

"Don't know," I said. "Someone else packed them. Said if I dumped the bike to take cover."

"Excellent," Jack said and gave me his flashlight. "If your bike is stolen you're walking out with the rest of us."

I was glad I had good boots on.

"Son of a bitch," Jack said as he hoisted up one of the bags. Finn grunted as he picked up the other. The ground was more level than I expected. A few wind fallen trees to step over but otherwise we made decent progress up a gradual hill then back down. We stopped once so they could take a break with the heavy bags. Jack let out a funny whistle as we approached their camp. They had a small fire going under an overhanging rock. Just three others. No Dana.

I started to take my coat off to sit on but Jack stopped me and gave me a dirty shirt instead.

"You want to stay covered. Mosquitoes are bitches out here. Close your eyes tight."

Glad I was quick because next thing I knew he hit me with the bug spray. I rubbed my hands on my face then wiped it on the backs.

"Thanks," I managed when the air cleared.

Jack introduced me as Richards again. He didn't bother with the names of the others. Didn't matter. Hopefully I'd be out of here soon and 'hey you' worked for me. If I didn't know who they were then I couldn't say where they were.

"Let's see what you brought us."

Jack popped open the first saddle bag and shone his light in. He tossed a package of cigarettes at one of the guys who ripped in and pulled out a piece of burning firewood to light one. There was water and food: mostly chocolate and jerky, dried fruit. Underneath there were boxes of ammunition.

"Mmm, explosives," Jack said as his light picked out the plastic wrapped loaves, then he opened the other saddle bag.

"Aahhh," he sighed as he pulled out a big bottle of scotch. "No cake?"

I laughed. Jack uncapped the booze and took a swig before passing it around. When it came to me I passed it on to Jack but he pushed it back.

"Drink, Richards. You're not going to sit there watching us."

I guessed I wasn't. It tasted as bad as it smelled and I managed to get down a couple of swallows without coughing like a rookie. The bottle went around again before Jack capped it and put it aside.

"No Dana?" I asked, warm from mouth to stomach and my arms and legs numbed.

"No," Jack said. "He's thirty-six hours overdue. Him and the two with him. We think they're being held down the road but we're skinny on manpower and ammo. Or were. They'll move them soon. I don't think Walker is going to come here. Walker and Soros are back in the US now. Walker is going to want a chat with them.

"You said news for him?" Jack asked.

"Yeah. His mate delivered four days ago. It was pretty rough. Baby is fine but I'm the only one her blood type so I donated twice to get her through. She won't name him until Dana is there."

Jack smiled though in the firelight he looked unnaturally wicked. "He'll be happy. We're going to spring him first thing. I hear you're decent with a rifle."

I was glad I practiced before I'd left with Alina and the others. Both in the range and outside. Still one of the best in the camp.

"I'll give you a thousand dollars if you find something I can't hit."

"Good. You'll be with Finn, providing cover."

"This little girl ever hurt anyone before?" One of the nameless three asked.

"She took out Soros' missing man with a knife hand to hand when she was six months pregnant and gave Archer his appetizer. You don't want to fuck with her."

I sent an adorable smile across the fire and he laughed but inside I knew it wouldn't be as easy for me now as it had been when Andre took the revulsion and remorse of killing from me. It wouldn't be a permanent goodbye for those men but still …

"Don't get her drunk then. She can't hit anything if she's half blind."

I laughed as Jack took the bottle out and passed it around then split up the ammunition based on who needed what. He kept the explosives for himself. The food and water were divided up six ways then he put the saddle bags out of sight.

We watched the fire for a while as the flames settled to embers. I pulled off my jacket then squeezed my shoulders together but it hurt and I couldn't get the holster off. Jack noticed and gave me a hand. He also noticed the damage to my vest.

"What happened here?"

"I have a matching hole in my jacket and a bruise the size of a salad plate. We've had some trouble."

Jack helped me with the vest and lifted up the back of my shirt to look.

"Ouch," he said.

"It doesn't feel so bad now. We had to show a couple of guests out. That's why the hair is gone. I stick out less if I look more like a man."

"You'll never be mistaken for a man," Jack laughed.

I rubbed the bumps growing on my arms and Jack helped me get my jacket back on.

"It'll be cold by morning. You bunk with me."

I nodded. Didn't know where my bike was and if they left I'd be lost.

"Lights out, we'll be on our way before dawn," Jack said and passed the bottle around as the last of it disappeared. Finn dawdled by the fire and the other three disappeared into the woods. Watch for Finn, I guessed. Jack led me a ways into the trees to a small and well hidden shelter with a sleeping bag in it.

"We should both fit," he said as I took off my boots. He stripped down to his shorts and put his guns with mine by the opening to the bag. "Take off your pants and jacket. We'll share heat better."

The cold sunk into my skin and I felt the temperature drop even as I undressed. Jack got in first and I slipped in front of him, putting my head on his upper arm for a pillow as he turned off his flashlight. He smelled of smoke and the forest. Scotch. His other arm went around my middle; not tight tucked in between me and the ground underneath. His fingers rested in front of me instead. He had me with him for my protection. I understood. That's why I would be up the hill out of the way with Finn who could probably handle our assignment all by himself.

Jack shivered so I pulled the sleeping bag up a little higher over his shoulder.

"Thanks," he murmured. "They're in a small out building. Four men watching them from outside. Usually two in front and two in back. You and Finn will get the two in front when we're in place and we'll get the other two. You won't be able to see the camp but you'll have a good view of the path leading down from it. Once they're out, I'll blow the building and we'll clean up the rest as they're figuring out what the hell happened."

"Is there a truck or something we can use?" I asked. "I don't care about the bike, but if we can all get in the truck I can jump us back to the compound."

"Yeah, an older one. I doubt Dana and the other two will be able to walk out. The men who have them aren't very nice."

I adjusted Jack's arm under my head. "Don't waste time looking for the keys, Jack. I'll have it started before everyone gets in."

"Unless I beat you to it."

"Okay. You know what it felt like?"

"What?" He sounded sleepy.

"My dream, in the helicopter. When I went up into the thunder. The aching in my bones, numbness climbing into my neck and head. Such pressure..." I rubbed my chest. "Sounds rattling in my ears like when you talk into a table fan or something. You've felt it."

He didn't say anything. It was just like when Paul's line was in me, smothering my line to make me sit still. Jack experienced it from his father when he made him cut himself as punishment for being with his own mate. He took his arm from around my middle and put his hand on my shoulder.

"How did you fight it?" he whispered.

"Our lines, they're not solid," I answered. "Not like fishing line. They're like a rope, strands upon strands, tightly bound for strength. Mine is made of three now. My own, the one I told you I took, and strands from the man I killed back in the compound. Accidentally tangled with mine as it drifted away.

"When Paul showed me how the charm works I knew he was doing something in my chest from the pressure I felt. I pushed my sense there. All I saw was Paul. I couldn't see me at all. There was so little of his line in his own chest. His line was in me, crushing mine when I resisted. When I did what he said he left me, I could see me again. I split off most of the strands and pushed them behind me then I fought him again, bringing him back in. The pain made it so hard to concentrate, to keep the strands safe but I had to keep him in me, as much as I could get then I snapped mine in, strangling his. The pain went away and I used it on him. I held his line in me, just for a minute to show him I'd resisted then I let him go.

"If they use it on me I have to comply while I keep most of my line free, when they're not in there holding it. Leave just enough to be a normal mates line. They won't be expecting any more than that. I might only get one shot. Paul wasn't expecting it. They could still crush what I have if they're holding a reserve, too."

Chapter 25

Jack hadn't said any more and it was still dark when the watch on his wrist vibrated, waking us. Even in his sleeping bag my feet felt cool. I crawled out first and quickly pulled my clothes on. Jack passed me half a roll of toilet paper and a spade.

"Over there," he pointed as he gave me the flashlight. "Watch your step, one of the idiots doesn't know how to dig."

When I returned, Jack took the roll so I checked my weapons and brushed my teeth while I waited. I had a bottle of water in my bag and drank half and gave the rest to Jack as we walked to the rock where the fire had been the night before. The others were already assembled around the remains. Finn handed me a rifle and took the other. It was similar to one I used back home. The extra clips went in my pocket and I adjusted the strap to where I wanted it before putting it over my shoulder with my pack.

I sneezed into my elbow as Jack made a connection with me.

"Bless you," Finn said.

"Mm, thanks."

Connect with me when we're closer. Keep it going as long as you can and I'll keep an eye on what's going on around us, Jack said. *If you drop it, wait for me to reconnect with you. I'll do it as soon as I can.*

Okay, Jack, I replied. I wasn't as nervous as I thought I'd be considering I hadn't done anything like this before.

Once the explosives go, you and Finn shoot everything that moves, other than us. The sun will be up by then. He knows. We've had our plan for a while, just been waiting for more ammo or fewer enemy.

Got it. If we're not out of here by noon we're here until tomorrow. I still have trips to recover from.

If we're not out of here in an hour, Jack said. *We're not leaving.*

He disconnected and we walked a while in silence. I had no appetite but ate anyway knowing the dried food would sit like a rock in my stomach for the next week. It was still dark when we crossed the road then headed left through the trees. The ground sloped down before us as the sun came up.

Jack looked at me and rubbed his nose so I focused in on him and he sneezed.

Be careful. You're safest up there with Finn. I'll get you home, he said.

I'll do my job, Jack.

"Remember where you're going, Finn?" Jack asked. He looked up at the brightening sky. Overcast and light didn't come urgently.

"Yeah, Jack."

"Watch for us to move in fifteen. You'll be in position first."

Finn and I nodded and Jack disappeared into the trees with the other three.

"Come on," Finn said and led me uphill a ways before he got down on the ground. We crawled the last dozen yards to where the grey tree trunks opened up to a view of a small rotting building not much bigger than a shed. My ribs complained the whole way but I kept my mouth shut. These guys weren't here to listen to whining. Beneath us, a set of tire ruts led up the hill on the other side of a decrepit shack then disappeared to the left thirty feet further on. There were two men in view as we expected; Jack and the others still out of sight.

"That leads up to the road we crossed," Finn whispered.

We set up a few feet apart where low grass clung to our little ledge concealing us. I opened my jacket for easy access to my side arms if I needed them and readied my spare clips. Finn unsnapped the knife at his side. I tested the feel of my rifle then tightened the strap a little more. It had to be steady. The distance was less than I shot outside at home but this time it mattered.

"Marry me," Finn whispered as he reached for the end of my barrel and screwed on another six or eight inches, changing the weight. I moved my left elbow away just a bit and nodded thanks.

"Set?" Finn whispered.

"Affirmative."

In position, I sent.

Copy.

"Four minutes," he said as he checked his watch. "Yours is on the left."

"See that white mark on the back of his jacket? I'm going to bulls-eye it."

"Sure you are. Five bucks says I have to take yours down too."

"You're on, Finn," I said.

Finn's target lit a cigarette and passed it to mine. They talked, glancing around as they shared the smoke. Keeping my finger out of the guard, I sighted the man and imagined pulling the trigger. Reminded myself what he would do to me or my daughter if he came close enough. Told myself the gentle reset I'd send did him a favour. With his leader gone, he might come back on the other side a little less smelly.

"Two minutes," Finn said.

Two minutes, Jack sent.

I closed my eyes and thought about my daughter and my husband, imagined them waiting for me around the turn a few hundred yards outside the gate. We would jump there. It was one thing for me to appear on an off-road bike by the warehouses where I could argue I rode in but if I aimed for home there would be nine of us staring off into space and a vehicle idling by the house. Big security hole to explain to the Weatherman since nobody would see us drive in.

"Thirty," Finn whispered.

I opened my eyes and pressed my weapon to my shoulder, my cheek to the cold wooden butt of my rifle. Slowed my breathing as I aimed at the centre of my target.

Ten.

Finn picked up the count at five as there was movement in the bush near the far side of the shed, at two my finger went on the trigger as I inhaled and held it so my moving lungs wouldn't throw my aim off.

At zero both men silently dropped and I exhaled.

"Nice," Finn said as we quietly popped the hot casings from our rifles, setting up the next rounds. It seemed to take forever for Jack and another man to run to our side of the shed and drag the two we hit into the trees as the other two of Jack's men appeared and opened up the shed.

"There," I whispered. Two men appeared coming down the road.

Two incoming, I sent.

Take 'em.

"When they round the bend and they're out of sight from the camp," Finn said. "You take left again."

I relaxed into my rifle and put my finger on the trigger and waited.

"Two, one," Finn called it.

Those two dropped. Jack and his men had gone into the shed and carried Dana out. The other two were on their feet as he sent a couple of men up the hill to pull the dead men out of sight. Dana looked bad. His face was bruised and the movement caused him pain. I couldn't see where Jack put him. Jack made sure the healthy ones were armed then he disappeared into the shed alone.

Things are going to move fast now, he sent.

Gotcha.

Jack ran from the building and into the trees.

A few seconds later, the building went up. Tiny pieces flew everywhere and I pressed my face down into the cold damp grass as the sound and heat pushed over Finn and me. After counting to three, I cautiously raised my head. The building was gone, only smoke and broken pieces remained. Men appeared on the road in slow pairs, hugging the trees on either side.

"Wait," Finn said.

I took a breath and waited.

"Go."

After the first two went down, the men on the road sought cover in the trees and Finn and I shot a few more before we lost sight of them. Then I heard a pop behind me and pink mist clouded my vision as warm wetness hit the side of my head. I tasted copper as Finn's rifle dropped. I put my hand to my face to try and figure out what covered it as I was hit hard over the ear.

I tried to call to Jack but my connection to him was gone. As I started to roll over, someone hit me in the face. Once I was on my back, he took my guns as I blinked up and tried to focus. All I could make out was dark hair sticking out from under a ball cap. Finn was dead and I knew I would be too as I felt cold metal press up into my throat.

"Looks like I get the first taste of you, Missus Richards," he growled as his weight pushed on top of me and he grabbed a hard handful of my breast.

I tried to get my hands up but he let go of me and gave me a left as the gun dug in. Then he grabbed both my arms with one hand and put his gun down as he rolled off me enough to start taking his pants down. As I fought, I earned a fist in the stomach and my lungs flattened. I struggled to breathe and heard gunfire and shouting below. Then the cold air and grass on my skin as my jeans came down to my knees. He pressed himself on me as he bit my neck.

When I could get air in again I tried to scream. Nothing but a short bark came out as he laughed at me and got up, throwing me face down on top of Finn.

"Bitch-wich," he breathed in my ear from behind.

He kept control of my arms as he kicked my pants down further, putting his knees between mine as he grabbed my ass and sunk his fingers into my flesh. My legs ached from the kicks as he got to work.

I felt sharp pain as he found his mark and my unwilling body tried to keep him out with every muscle it had. I tried to scream again as I threw my head at him but he was out of reach and I sneezed as Jack made contact.

Where's my fucking support???

The force of his voice in my head hurt, freezing me for a moment as I was pushed over and over again into Finn's still body.

What the fuck are you two doing up there???

!!!!!!!!!!!!!!! I replied. No words, just pain and rage, kicking Jack from my head.

The man on me took my sudden paralysis as submission and let go of my arms, taking a fist full of my hair as he pulled me up and twisted my face almost all the way around to his. He stunk of Damian and I shook my head, trying not to breathe him in as he put his mouth on mine. I got my hands under me and tried to push us over but his weight was too much. He bit at my lip as I dropped a hand to Finn's side, found his knife and pulled it out.

The man's body stiffened as he sputtered in my ear and I shouted and swung the knife around, sinking it deep. Could have been into me, I didn't know, I couldn't feel anything anymore.

"Aahhh..." he shouted. His hands went to his side as his body still trembled and he tried to pull away but I got my other hand around onto the knife and pulled up, tearing him as I went. When it slipped out of him, he fell off me as he tried to reach past the hole in his side for his own knife on his belt by his feet. I picked up his handgun as he freed his knife and hit him hard in the face with it, stunning him, before I tucked it under his chin.

Then I knelt with my bare cheeks on my muddy boots and my borrowed rifle at my shoulder, squeezing off rounds at any of Damian's men I sensed. Even the ones invisible in the brush. My hands shook and I wasted a round or two in the dirt for every one connecting with its mark. Each shot pushing the rifle into my bruised face. Pumping a round or two into the dead ones when I had nothing else to hit. Stay down, stay down, I pleaded. I paused, pulling out the spent clip and snapping in one of my blood covered spares, then the other.

Do your job, Anna. Do your job do your job Anna ran through my head. I kept the rifle up as I scanned below for more of Damian's men, finding nothing, but still looking.

Footsteps behind me. I dropped the rifle and grabbed one of my pistols. Both waited on the ground in front of my bare knees. Two some ones behind me. I couldn't find the trigger as I panicked though my finger kept reaching for it. When he took it I realized I held the muzzle.

I felt gentle fingers on my face.

"Oh, Baby. I'm sorry."

I looked where the voice came from and saw Jack crouching next to me. His other hand reached, hesitated then withdrew. He glanced down at my bare legs and the half naked dead man next to me.

"Shit," he swore. "How close did he get?"

I looked at the man on the ground as Jack decided and put his arm around me. Slowly, cautiously like he didn't want to hurt me. The handle of Finn's knife stuck up out of the dead man's chest, the front of his jacket torn up with furious bloody holes and his cap gone. I must have done that, Finn was dead before the man laid a hand on me. Doing my job, doing my job, doing my job.

Jack eased off my coat and my holsters, putting my guns in their places before handing the whole thing to the other man and putting my coat back on me. The other man took the rifles and the backpacks and made off down the hill as Jack stood me up and helped me get my clothes back on.

"How close?"

"Doing my job, Jack," I smiled up at him. "Doing my job. Can we go home now?"

"How close, Baby?" he whispered.

"Home," I insisted, already picturing Paul and Camille down the road and around the corner from the gate. If we got out of here fast enough then it didn't happen. Jack held me up, his nose and lips on my hair. One of my knees went and I slumped against him.

"Please," I whispered. "While I can still get us there."

Jack led me down the hill, past the rubble remains of the shed and along the road to the camp. His arm locked around my waist and he kept me from collapsing when I had to stop to throw up. I must have killed ten of the bastards and hadn't planned on seeing the damage up close. The truck idled and had four in the back seat, one in the front. Dana sat wedged in the back with a man on either side to keep him upright. That meant we'd lost another besides Finn.

Instead of taking me to the truck, Jack led me into a building next to it. A dead man lay prone on the floor and several pieces of electronic equipment cluttered the nearby desk. Headphones and a microphone for the radios, everything soiled with a fine red spray.

"I need you to show me what he was doing," Jack said.

I looked at him for a few seconds and nodded. The man's line lingered so I connected as I watched Jack's face and he watched mine. I shook as the bullets hit the man and Jack held me up.

"Sorry, Baby," he quietly said.

He'd been at the microphone, talking, numbers on the radio in front of him. A set of six, the dial. Jack took a small notebook and a pen out of his pocket and wrote behind my back, his arms still holding me up. We went back further. The man changed the frequency and the six digit code to something else. Then he left, or ran in.

"Okay," Jack said. "He made two call outs after the building blew. We have the frequencies and encryption codes. Let's go."

Jack pushed me into the middle seat and helped me with the belt then he climbed in, put the truck in first and let out the clutch. I quickly glanced at Dana behind me but couldn't take the stares of Jack's men as they took in my bruised up face.

"Move your legs," Jack said as the truck went into third and I shoved them both over into the legs of the man next to me as we got on the road.

"He was calling for help so you need to get us out of here."

Jack told the others to close their eyes when he said so I pictured Paul and Camille at the destination I'd already picked. Waiting for me to come home. I imagined Damian's men were all dead and we had peace and quiet. We'd take Camille to the pond and when she went to bed we'd go to ours, staying up late playing until we wore each other out. The pressure slammed in to me, I was so desperate to be home, but Jack's swearing interrupted me.

"Get down."

He shoved me over as the others did their best to sink in their seats. It didn't do much good. Seven people six feet tall or more in the older crew cab would look like seven people no matter what. The smell approaching in the oncoming lane was the worst I'd ever picked up. I put both hands over my nose, pinching it tight until they passed us.

"My God, Jack. What was that?"

"Walker," he said.

Tires squealed behind us and the smell followed.

"Please hurry, Anna," Jack said and pushed the truck hard.

I covered my ears and refocused as the truck swerved. The smell closed in, catching up. I ignored it as best I could as the windows rolled down and shots rang out from behind. Jack pushed me down further in the seat as I heard the rounds from Walker's truck strike ours. I went back to my little domestic fantasy as the pressure climbed. After breakfast we'd play with Camille then she'd go down for her nap. We'd go catch up on our sleep but would wind up all over each other again.

There was a loud grunt from the rear seat. The front seat jumped as one of the men fell into it and then shifted a second time as another took his place. Dana moaned as the four men in the back seat rearranged themselves. I pressed my hands on my ears and the truck swerved sideways from something other than Jack's driving.

I remembered the way Paul smelled, coming in from watch, my goosebumps as he warmed up with me setting my skin alight.

Another hit from the side.

"Faster, Jack," I urged. "Almost time."

I forgot the gunshots, the smell of fresh blood. The pain. In my mind, I only thought of Paul as the pressure pushed us from behind and one of the men slammed into the back of the seat and the truck recovered. I needed more. My energy was so low I took hold of the arm of the man to my right and let his seep into me. Just enough. I wasn't going to be denied the black sleep taking my pain away. Pressure burned my nose as a fresh batch of bullets peppered the tailgate of the truck.

"Now, Jack!" I yelled seeing nothing but my husband and my baby, smiling, waiting to welcome me home.

"Close them!" Jack shouted. The old truck roared as the rear window exploded.

Chapter 26

At least I stood. The back of my head stung and when I put my hand to it sharp little pieces of glass dug into my palm. I heard a couple of men throwing up as I opened my eyes to find myself behind the truck, looking through where the rear window should have been. Jack opened doors and directed his men in then opened the tailgate and put the ones who were throwing up in the back.

"You'll listen next time," he said then he put his arm around me and put me in up front with him. Dana was in the back seat again with two others. We were where I wanted to be but no Paul. No Camille.

"I know where we are," Jack said.

I pulled my knees up to my chest and looked out my window as I listened to one of the men throw up over the side. My fingers found a crack in the vinyl seat and dug in. Jack got the truck going and drove us the half minute to the gate, where two men I didn't know flagged us down to stop.

"Lieutenant Roberts," one of the men said.

"Corporal," Jack replied. "Radio us in. I have Commander Richards and five others. We need medical to meet us."

"Yes, Sir," he said as Jack drove on.

When we reached the house I stayed in the truck. There was nothing for the men in the box other than time and Gravol. Dana and the man who'd been shot as we fled were urgent. The other two could puke in the dirt for the rest of the day as far as I was concerned. I glanced up as Paul ran from the house and stopped when he saw the shot up truck. I looked away and put a hand over my mouth as I realized I was scared to face him.

I don't know what I felt. Pain for sure. Shame and humiliation. Embarrassment. I wanted to go back and stab that man over and over until he was jam. My eyes wouldn't come up far enough to meet Paul's as he helped me out. I shouldn't have been there with Finn. I should have sensed the man behind us. I'd let everyone down. The rape was just a prelude to the bullet I had coming, when they'd all had a taste of me. I would have preferred a quick exit to what I felt now.

"Sugar," he said as his arms went around me. I buried my face in him. He put his hand on the back of my head but he found the broken glass so he tried the side and found the lump from the first blow I took.

"What happened?" he asked. He tipped my face up to him but I looked away as I kept silent. I wasn't going to cry in front of everyone. Paul led me into the house, pausing to let Jack pass with Dana.

"Brief me," Paul told him and Jack nodded.

Then he took me upstairs and sat me on the couch. My hands shook. There was still blood on them from knifing the man and Finn's blood was on my bruised face and in my hair from the bullet that shut him down.

Paul put a blanket around my shoulders and knelt on the floor to face me.

"You know how it works," I whispered, my voice shaking. "It's not like sonar... sitting back picking up the echoes. It's like a flashlight in the dark. If it's not on and pointed in the right direction we don't know he's there."

I couldn't get my lungs full enough for more than a few words at a time.

"I was with Finn, up the hill out of the way. Linked in to Jack. We had to get Dana. They had him. Had to tell him if more were coming. After they got Dana out someone behind us got Finn... went after me.

"Lost my link to Jack, couldn't tell him. By the time I fought him off they were in trouble... I got as many as I could so Jack and his men could finish them off. When we left Walker was coming in...

"Jack couldn't see him behind us. There were so many everywhere. It's not his fault."

"What's not Jack's fault?" Paul asked.

"That I got hurt."

Paul put his hands on my face.

"Where else did he hurt you?"

"Nowhere," I said.

"You're not going to tell him, are you," Jack said. Paul had left the door open for him and he stood just inside.

"Nothing to tell, Jack."

"Anna, you need to see the doctor," Jack said.

"What the hell happened, Jack?" Paul demanded as I glared at Jack.

"When I lost my covering fire from Anna and Finn it was a shit show, still out manned two to one. There were a lot more of them there than we expected. By the time there was firing from their position again and it cooled off enough to pick them up on the hill Finn was dead. It was just her, picking his men off. When I got up there, Walker's man Stanton was naked from the waist down, top of his head opened up from a shot under his chin. Her jeans are round her ankles. She drops the rifle, terrified, trying to shoot me with a pistol but she's holding the muzzle and can't figure out why it doesn't work.

"She just says she's doing her job and wants to go home. I asked her how close he got but she wouldn't say."

Paul had put his arms around me as Jack spoke but now I felt anger build in him and he was going to let it loose on Jack. It wasn't Jack's fault.

"He didn't hurt me, Jack," I said as I tightened my hold on Paul.

"I think he did, Anna," Jack said. "You sunk Finn's knife in his chest more than a dozen times after you shot him."

I put my hand on Paul's shoulder to hold him down. If anyone was going after Jack it was me.

"If he made you that angry, he got everything he wanted."

"You God damn liar!" I charged at Jack with my hands ready. My left elbow came up ready to drop and give me the momentum I needed to drive my right into his head. He stood his ground as Paul grabbed me around the middle.

"I don't want to hear it," I hollered as I struggled to get at him. "I don't want to hear it."

I tried to pull Paul's arms off me and when they wouldn't budge I swung at him, yelling the whole time. He easily dodged and wouldn't let me go. It didn't take long for my rage to turn to tears.

"No," I cried. "It didn't happen."

Paul turned me in his arms and held on as I got my one hour warning the black sleep was coming. It couldn't come soon enough.

"It didn't happen."

"You can be mad at me as long as you want. You can't keep that hurt inside," Jack said as he left.

Paul took me to the bathroom and sat me on the toilet in my blanket as he filled the bath, then he went to the kitchen to get me a glass of wine. I turned and put my feet up on the edge of the tub and sobbed as he combed broken glass from my hair. He turned off the bathroom light before he helped me undress and get in the water. Even in the dim light coming in the open door I could see the fresh dark purple bruises on my legs. I was sure Paul could, too. My wrists were just as sore but the tattoos hid them.

He passed me my glass to sip as he gently washed my hair and soaped me up. Then he rinsed me off. He got me clean pyjama pants and a tank top as I finished my wine. Paul pulled the plug and helped me dry off and dress before taking me to bed.

"Do you want me to get in with you?" He asked.

I nodded.

"Yes," I said as I tucked my head under his chin, as close to him as I could get. Everything would be okay now I was back in his arms.

"Was Jack right?"

"Yes," I sniffed, cried out for now.

"I'm sorry," Paul said.

I didn't have much time left.

"It's nobody's fault, Paul. I love you."

"I love you, Sugar," Paul said as I dozed off.

Chapter 27

The blackout curtains kept dawn away as I curled snugly into Paul. His arms tightened and I moved a enough to touch my nose to his skin. My neck complained as I brushed it over his collar bone.

"Mmm," I said. After being away for a month and a half I still had to convince myself I was home, even with my brief visit a night or two ago. The memory of the rape stung, raw and intact. It was better that way. I preferred to have all my damaged pieces in one place over clinging to some imaginary healthy life raft. The shock of the cold water as it eventually sunk under me would be far worse than treading water now. Jack would hear an apology even though he wouldn't feel it necessary.

"Yes, you're really here," Paul whispered as I gingerly reached my arm around him. I felt like every muscle I tried to move had a Charlie horse.

"Ow," I said as I relaxed.

"You were beat up pretty bad," Paul sighed.

"No, I fought hard."

We lay still for a long time until his alarm went off.

"Crap, sorry," he said as he rolled over and turned it off. I glimpsed five am. "They can get by without the Major this morning."

I wasn't sure if Paul wanted to hear what happened but I needed to let it out.

"Jack put me up out of the way with Finn. They gave me a rifle even though they probably thought I'd hit one of them instead of being any help. Dana and the other two were in a shack down the hill, two guards for me and Finn to take care of, two for Jack and the other three on the ground. Dirt road to their main building curved up to the left out of sight.

"Finn and I took out ours as Jack and his men came out of the bush for the two we couldn't see. Jack opened up the shack and they got Dana and the other two out. Hid Dana somewhere and armed the other two who seemed okay. Then a patrol came down the road so Finn and I waited until they were out of sight from up the hill and took them. Jack blew up the shack to call the rest down. Finn and I let them get close before we started on them. We got five or six more I think before the rest ran into the trees and more were coming.

"Then there was a pop behind us to our right on the other side of Finn. I lost track of things for a second when I got hit in the head."

I put my hand up on the bump. Paul's hand followed mine then his fingers started stroking the back of my head.

"I rolled over to figure out what was going on and got hit in the face. Before I knew it he'd taken my weapons and his gun dug into my neck. I fought but I got it in the face again and he held my wrists in one hand and put the gun down to start getting my pants off. He said he was going to be the first to get a taste of me."

My heart sped and my need for air increased with it.

"I kept struggling and he hit me in the stomach. By the time I could breathe he tossed me face down on top of Finn's body.

"I don't know how long it was before Jack made contact, yelling for help, so loud, it froze me. Jack yelled in my head again and I blasted him back and kicked him out. The Damian smell was so bad. My hand found Finn's knife and as he... when he started to..."

I couldn't say it and took a deep breath. Paul's hand stopped moving on my head as he listened.

"I swung at him and hit something. Thought it was me for a moment but he tried to get away so I got my other hand on the handle and pulled, tearing him. I picked up his gun and put it under his chin.

"Then I was on my knees with the rifle. I could nail them in the trees without seeing them... just sensing them. When they were all gone I kept watching the road... searching. Someone ran up behind me so I dropped the rifle and picked up my gun. It didn't work then he took it. I heard a voice and when I looked it was Jack.

"There was a radio room by the truck we took. I read the man in there and got some numbers Jack wrote down. It helped me focus, I was so close to losing it and if I did we wouldn't get home. On the road, Walker passed us going the other way. He turned around, chasing us.

"I could be in some stinky gas soaked bonfire now. If I were a man I would be. I'll take what I got any day over being dead. I could have been face down on my rifle like Finn, Jack and his men dead down the hill. I made it home to you. I'll see Camille again.

"I'll take Dana to them but I know I can't be with her for a while. If Walker didn't know what I can do before he does now and they're going to want me even more."

"I don't know what to say, Sugar," Paul said. "I'm so sorry. The doctor came up to see you. Jack came back up. I sent them both away."

We heard people downstairs, muffled through the floor. Cooking sounds, voices.

"Can you help me up?" I asked. "I think I can eat."

Paul got me upright on the edge of the bed then he dressed and helped me to the bathroom. He started breakfast and was making coffee when I came into the kitchen. He came over and touched the bruises from Stanton's fingers where they showed above the low neckline of my top. I didn't look away and let him pull me close as my arms went up around his neck.

"It's okay," I whispered. "They'll go away."

He nodded.

"I wish I'd been there for you."

"I know you do, Paul."

We pushed our chairs close together to eat then moved to the sofa. He brought a blanket for me to curl up under and poured himself another cup of coffee. The sounds downstairs settled. Chatter from the radio. A door closed. I dozed for a while on Paul's shoulder until there was a quiet knock at the door. As I blinked, I realized I'd pulled myself into a tight little ball under my blanket. Paul kissed me as I unfolded and he went to let in Jack, Captain Taggart and an older man I guessed was the doctor. Taggart scowled at Jack. He didn't seem to mind. It looked like he felt the same way about Taggart.

"Commander Richards, I'm Doctor Flood," he introduced himself.

"Hi," I replied.

"How are you feeling?"

"Good," I said as I stood. Paul's arm went around my waist.

He nodded. "I have a few tests I'm required to complete. Can I join you in your room for a few minutes?"

"Rape kit?" I asked with angry cheerfulness. Jack looked away and Paul's arm tightened. Taggart hadn't really looked at me since they came in. The doctor's visit obviously wasn't why he was here. "I bathed."

Flood looked at Paul. "The Major declined to let me examine you yesterday. He said you were sleeping."

"I was."

"There could still be evidence," he said as he held his hand out towards my room.

"For what?"

"Charges, court."

"The man who assaulted me is very dead, doctor. I don't feel right wasting everyone's time." That got Taggart's attention. I knew mission details were only known by the men involved and the Colonel coordinated our intelligence.

Flood sighed. "Can we talk privately?"

I gave in and he followed me down the hall.

"Are you certain he's dead?" He asked once he'd closed the door behind us.

"Yes. I shot him in the head and according to Lieutenant Roberts I stabbed him over a dozen times. I just remember putting the gun on him."

"Okay, did you lose consciousness?"

"I don't think so. Just the memory lapse," I said then I let him examine my head and shine his light in my eyes. He checked my belly where he'd hit me and I pulled up the legs of my pyjama pants so he could see the bruises. The ones on my arms were visible through the tattoos in places and he looked at those as well. I wouldn't take anything off for him. Then he pulled the armchair over to sit near me.

"Are you on the pill or anything?" he asked.

"No."

"Okay," he said as he started pulling things out of his bag. "Emergency contraceptive. Take half now, half in twelve hours and a couple of pregnancy tests to save you asking me later. Wait a few weeks on those. Talk it over with your husband, but most women in your position would prefer not to be pregnant."

I nodded.

"If its positive whisper in my ear and I'll arrange for a quiet termination, if that's what you want. I'm taking you off duty for the next few weeks until that's resolved. Paperwork is already in for the Colonel. Paul says he's your liaison."

I nodded and crossed my arms.

"I'm sorry, Anna. I would have preferred to meet you under other circumstances. I've known Paul a long time. I was curious to meet the woman who would be the match for him. You don't disappoint."

"Thanks, Doc," I smiled.

"Russell," he told me as he left. I took a moment to straighten my clothes and decided on something with longer sleeves.

I sensed Jack's presence under my nose a minute after I heard the front door close.

Hi, Jack.

Hey, girl. You doing a little better? He asked.

Sorry I tried to shoot you and called you a liar. You're not and I feel terrible about it.

You don't have to say sorry. I know you don't think that of me.

Thanks.

Taggart's alone in your living room waiting for you. Paul wanted me to link and give you the heads up. He hasn't talked to any of us yet about what happened because he knows we'll just stonewall him claiming mission security. He hates that.

I can handle Taggart, I said.

He's in charge of camp security... can be a real dickhead about it. Paul wants me in on whatever you tell him in case he tries to backup your story with us. Paul told him you report only to the Colonel, I'll relay the play by play to him. Taggart's still trying to figure out how you got in here two nights ago.

Alright, Jack, I sent.

I went out to the living room to find Captain Taggart right where I left him.

"Captain?" I sounded surprised to see him. "I thought I heard you all leave."

"No," he said. "I like to get a feel for anyone new to the camp. Meet and greet sort of thing."

I stiffened and pursed my lips. I'd been thinking whatever I said and heard to Jack.

New? Does he not know he's in my house?

After a few seconds, Paul laughed downstairs.

"Have a seat," I invited as I pulled my blanket up over myself on the couch. Taggart sat in one of the big chairs.

"I'm so sorry to hear what happened to you," he started. "I hear Lieutenant Roberts' team had some losses as well."

"Possibly," I shrugged. "I haven't been keeping up on the details of any of the teams. I have enough to keep track of with my own duties."

"Indeed. Were you interrogated, Commander?" he asked.

"Is your function here to offer counselling to soldiers who have been through such a thing?"

"No, but anything endangering the security of the people here, including you and your husband, I need to know."

I adjusted myself on the couch and waited for the aching to settle down. I could understand his concern anyone held in their custody for any amount of time might have been encouraged to release information about the compound and our security practices.

"Then no, I wasn't interrogated. Any other questions regarding my recent command of Lieutenant Roberts' team or their absence from the compound must be directed to Colonel Iverson."

Awesome, Jack sent. *Paul says you're being nice.*

I hoped so. This guy was supposed to be looking after us and the last thing the family needed was for Taggart to become a nuisance.

"How did you get in here the other night?"

"This is my home, Captain. I know it very, very well. I'm sorry I can't be of any more help to you."

He leaned back in his chair, looking like he was still unsure what he thought of me.

"Major Flood said Lieutenant Roberts' man was shot within fifteen minutes of your arrival yesterday. My concern is there could be a cell of Damian Howard's men very close to us. That's a security issue I need to know about. I'd appreciate your honesty about the incident."

I gave a little laugh.

"Not all Jack's men have a military commission or training. I don't know everyone's history but from my own background I know not everyone had the same idea of firearms safety we had drummed into us. I see a lot of 'nothing bad ever happened before' working closely with organized civilians.

"I was understandably shit-faced after the assault. Jack had a big bottle of whiskey he'd been holding on to for coming home and I think I helped myself to at least half. My naughty little mistress. Never wonders where I've been or is angry when I've been away. Never found another man's boots outside her door. We don't see each other regularly any more but we still flirt."

I paused to play with my fingers, looking ashamed and avoiding eye contact.

"I heard someone say something about 'chamber' and we hit a bump discharging the gun, but yeah that was right before we hit the gate."

I can work with that, Jack sent.

"Paul saw how drunk I was and brought me right in, he doesn't know what happened. I might have been in shape to command after the assault if I wasn't drinking. The lapse in judgement that allowed the accident to happen was entirely mine. I hope it stays under the radar."

"And the two throwing up... had they been drinking, too?" Taggart asked.

"No, I wasn't going to share. I wouldn't be surprised if you see more get sick in the next little bit. I wouldn't have used that slime pit they were drinking from to piss in."

Taggart stood, laughing.

"Thank you for your time, Commander. You've been a lot more forthcoming than I expected."

I shrugged and stood to see him out.

"Captain Taggart, in my home please call me Anna. We don't use rank in here and I won't stand for shop talk. I've made an exception today because I know there is gossip about me in all corners of the compound and I'm not in the mood for the silence that will greet me when I leave my door."

"Okay, Anna. It's William."

"William," I shook his hand again. "It's been tough being the new guy when I'm not even a guy. Different background..."

"I know how you feel," William said. "These are good guys but it's like moving to a small town."

"Yeah, I appreciate your understanding."

He smiled and left.

Paul says good job, Sugar... Jack sent and disconnected.

I took half the pills the doctor left me and got in the bath. I still hurt all over and the hot water felt good. I knew Paul would agree about taking them. The bruising on my face was limited to my jaw on one side and a bit of swelling on the other. The bump above my right ear was the worst. The hardest part of the whole thing would be staying away from Camille. That and watching Paul leave when he had to go again. I wondered if I would be assigned to him or to Jack. Or just left behind.

I heard Paul's key in the door.

"Anna?"

"Bathtub," I answered then I heard him put some things down in the kitchen. I'd noticed when he made breakfast there wasn't much in the fridge or cupboards. He took his meals downstairs while I was away.

"Get you anything?" he asked as he stuck his head in the door then he sighed. "They're all over your back too."

"Really? I don't remember that. I guess that's why my back hurts."

"Doc says he's pulled you from duty for the next few weeks."

"Yeah, gave me some emergency contraceptive pills. I took half already, the rest at ten tonight. Can you remind me or wake me up if I pass out?"

"Sure," Paul said as he sat on the floor beside me. "Jack says you don't have to worry about catching, um, anything else."

He looked at the floor. "They're like us that way. Keep ourselves clean. It would be unforgivable to share something like that with a mate. Even the men who haven't earned one yet are meticulous. It would be disgraceful beyond belief."

"Okay," I said. That was something I hadn't considered. Getting something I could give to Paul.

"Do you really still feel like an outsider here?" he asked before I could ask him to elaborate.

I rested my elbows on the edge of the tub. "No, but Taggart does. He's got a tough hill to climb and he needs to feel he has something in common with someone. I gave him a big fat story and if he believes I'm confiding in him he's more likely to trust me.

"Being away has been so hard. I think half my stress disappeared as soon as I was back here with you. The rest will go when Camille is home with us."

"Mine, too," Paul said. "I could feel you while you were gone. Knew you were alive. But it wasn't the same."

We quietly sat for a while. I put my head on the edge of the tub and Paul put his hand on it.

"I'll get lunch," he said then he stayed on the floor. "The Colonel is sending your replacement."

"Sig?" I asked. I wanted to make sure we were talking about the same Colonel. So much had changed while I was away.

"Yes."

"Replacement?" I asked as I lifted my head. If Sig was sending a replacement to be with the children in my place this could be another of his men like Rice. Rice had been family like Sig and had been placed to watch Denis, to see if he would prove himself worthy of a mate through his actions toward another man's mate.

Neither of us spoke and I knew he had the same thought. I wasn't so sure I wanted another man looking after my daughter even if Ray was there with her.

"Commander Wendy Vega," Paul said. "Sig says you go way back."

I pulled my knees up and wrapped my arms around them, pulling myself into the tight little emotional ball that seemed to suit me now. I shook my head. Paul nodded. He knew it was fiction.

"When are they coming?"

"Tonight. Can you come down and greet them with me?"

I frowned and dropped my eyes as I nodded. What I agreed to felt like parading out the door and past the cabins to the helicopter pad. Right up front with Paul and the rest of the officers in tow.

"Dana wants to see you," Paul added. "Jack gave him your news. He's in the infirmary downstairs. Doc says he can travel in a couple of days."

"Okay, Paul," I agreed, hoping the front door would jam shut so I didn't have to leave.

"I'll get lunch, Sugar," Paul said again and this time he got up, putting a couple of towels in easy reach.

By the time I dressed, Paul served lunch. He sat beside me again instead of his usual spot at the head of the table.

"I guess I'm taking Commander Wendy Vega and Dana to join Ray," I said.

Paul nodded. "Sig says she's very good. No concerns with her doing what's needed to protect them."

"Yeah," I sighed. "I was hoping just two wheels. After that I come back here?"

"Mm," Paul replied. I sensed he was about to change the subject. He only made that sound when he had to choose between not answering and lying to me.

"Any concerns with Halford and Mason? Jack says they're old fashioned."

"They're much happier not having to be involved with Virtue," I explained. "Her health was bad... they kept her locked in a hotel room passing fast food through the door for six months. We got her moving around and she actually lost weight the last month and a half. Blood pressure and sugars better.

"When the baby was born Halford asked me why she's still around. He said if I can feed the boy and she can't she's a waste of resources."

"What?" Paul cleared his throat and swallowed.

"I told him we'd turn around and put him in the ditch with the two Ray and I took out if I heard any more shit like that from him. Those two are loyal to Jack but they have no business around the women or children."

Paul glared at his food.

"I'll fill Jack in," he said after a minute. "I don't want them around my daughter or my wife. I'll send Jack with you to straighten them out or ship them off."

"My vote is to get them out of there," I said. "Ray and I learned enough from them. We should be able to stay safely under cover."

"Who do you mean by we?" Paul eyed me.

"Ray, I meant," I said quickly. "I know I have to stay away."

I got up and went to the couch and pulled my blanket up. I hadn't eaten much. Paul cleared the table and I listened to him shuffle around the kitchen for a few minutes.

"My cooking that bad?" he asked as he joined me.

"No," I smiled. "I feel like crap, inside and out. I don't know the woman in the mirror any more. I'm so far from happy I don't think I'll ever get back."

Paul sat carefully beside me and let me curl up next to him.

"I think we're close," Paul said. "Hold on with me, Sugar. We'll get there."

I nodded and wiped my eyes.

"I'd go through it every day for her."

"You shouldn't have had to go through it once. Jack knows I want his head for letting you down. I'd take it if it would make him feel any worse."

I knew that. Paul was wondering what the hell I'd been thinking. What got into Jack's head that made him think I'd be safe anywhere near that place? Wondering why Jack hadn't thanked me for the bullets, told me Dana wasn't there and sent me on my way. Why he let me ride away two nights before.

"I'm one of the men," I said. "I know what I'm in for."

"Women shouldn't be involved in this," he firmly said.

I didn't reply. Debating gender and family right now was a shouting match waiting to happen. Paul wanted to put the blame for the rape somewhere. He knew as well as I did placing blame was futile and unfair. It would be just as ridiculous to blame Jack or me as it would be to blame Dana's newborn son for coming when he did. If he hadn't then I wouldn't have come to the compound to get the supplies Jack needed to pull Dana out. Dana's son would be without a father and I'd be going back with bad news. What happened to me felt like a fair trade.

"I can help, Paul."

"No!"

I jumped as he shouted. He hadn't raised his voice to me since our big fight at my house the night I attacked him and took off. I slapped my hands over my ears and burst into tears. The volume was too much for my shattered nerves.

"No," he said as he wrapped himself around me. "I'm sorry, Sugar. I'm sorry."

I nodded and sniffled in my blanket as I realized my knees were under my chin again and willed my feet back toward the floor.

"There won't be another chance for anything like that to happen to you again. You're out. No argument, please?" Paul turned my head to face him. "Please?"

I hadn't noticed the pain in his eyes until now.

"No argument, Paul," I whispered.

"You're with Jack or with me until this is over. Nobody is going to fight harder to protect you than we will. We both let you down once, we won't again."

I let my nose touch his and closed my eyes as he pushed himself closer.

"I don't feel let down."

"You wouldn't," Paul laughed, his lips brushing mine as he spoke.

"Mm," I mumbled as I reached for him and stole a quick kiss.

We kissed for a few minutes until there was a knock. He leaned back and sighed as I read the man on the other side of the door.

"Ross is here to see you," I said.

He started to push the blanket off me.

"He's not here to see me."

I raised my eyebrows as Paul stood and took my hands to pull me to my feet. He held me for a moment as Ross knocked again.

"Get the door."

A loud sigh pushed its way out my throat as I stomped over and opened up.

"Hi, Ross," I said with a reasonable amount of forced politeness. Paul should have known I didn't want company and should have told Ross to bother me some other time. Ross wrinkled his nose at me and crossed his arms. He wore a short sleeved shirt and two tattooed naked women smiled at me from his forearms.

"I don't like you, Anna," he started.

I opened my mouth although I couldn't begin to reply to a greeting like that. His arms looked friendly but his words certainly weren't. When I looked at Paul to try and figure out if Ross was serious or if Paul was in on some joke he looked away like he was trying not to be there. After everything I'd been through the past couple of days a dressing down from Ross was the last thing I was in the mood for. Ross's words and Paul's apparent letting them happen had me in tears inside already and close on the outside. I looked back at Ross as Paul put his hand on my shoulder.

I put my hand on the door wondering if he was far enough in I could break his nose with a quick push. Paul seemed to know what I thought and put his other hand on the door with mine.

"I don't like you because you ran out on Paul last November," Ross went on. "I don't like you because you attacked him in January."

He paused and I felt tears on my cheeks as I nodded. I knew this had been on his mind for a while and it hurt he had to straighten things out now.

"I don't like you because you refused me."

I hadn't known about that. At some point in the past Ross had asked for me and I'd sent him away in failure. I looked at Paul again. He looked at the floor like he wanted to disappear into the fibres. Just like I did.

"I don't like what Stanton did to you," Ross said, his voice softening. "As much as I dislike you, you didn't deserve that."

I looked up to meet his eyes and realized he was sincere and wasn't here to hurt me.

"There is one thing you've done that I simply won't put up with," he said. I tensed as I waited for it. "I just can't forgive what you've done to your hair."

I blinked with surprise as Paul squeezed my shoulder.

"I thought you could use a little cheering up, if I may come in."

"Yes, Ross. Of course," I said and opened the door wider. He leaned over and picked up a big leather case, the kind that opened at the top, and took my elbow. Paul disappeared out the door as Ross came in.

"Kitchen?" I asked.

"Yes."

Ross pulled a chair out from the table and guided me to it. He opened up the case and looked at me for a second.

"The cut is worse than I thought," he muttered. "I'll try and spare as much of it as I can."

"Thanks."

He sprayed my hair down and started combing and I felt the teeth ride over the bump above my ear. I pulled my head away as my knees came up.

"Sorry," he said.

"Pistol," I told him as I wiped my eyes.

Ross nodded. "I'll be careful... any others?"

I shook my head and put my feet down as Paul came back in with a bottle of wine. Ross started putting my hair up in chunks so he could even out the ends and I heard the cork pop. It was a little early for drinks but I didn't comment.

"Did you do this yourself?" Ross asked.

"Alina."

He paused as Paul gave us each a glass. "Alina? They let her operate on people and she can't hold the scissors straight?"

"Yes," I answered.

"Doesn't surprise me. They let Ray prescribe meds and he can't cook."

I laughed and put my glass to my lips. It felt good. My first laugh since I came home. Paul sighed in the living room and I heard the couch settle under him.

Ross pulled out a black cape and put it around me and the chair. He evened out the ends bit by bit as I sipped with my eyes closed. I realized I didn't really know him at all. He never did like me. I assume he avoided me like most of the men in the compound and hadn't thought anything of it until I returned after I ran out on Paul. Then his simple avoidance turned in to overt dislike. I didn't mind. Can't please everyone.

He was quiet as he worked, letting a little bit out of the clips at a time. He fussed with the ends; comparing the sides to make sure they were even then he pulled out a chair. When I opened my eyes he sat, facing me. He topped up our glasses.

"So what about the colour?"

"It'll grow out," I replied.

"Are you sure you want to wait that long? I can fix it."

I watched him for a moment then he raised his eyebrows and nodded.

"Or I can dye your eyebrows to match," he added.

I put my hands up and ran them over my head. "How do you do that? All you put in was water and it feels cleaner than when I washed it."

Ross smiled. "It'll feel even better when it's blonde."

"Okay, Ross."

He pulled a bowl out of his case and mixed up the colour.

"I didn't think there would be much demand for colour in a place like this."

"You'd be surprised," he replied. "Some of these guys are pretty vain when it comes to grey hair. I hope you don't mind being the same shade as Joshua as it grows back."

Paul burst out laughing from the other room and I laughed again, too.

"Not a word, Major eavesdropper," Ross warned as Paul kept laughing.

It was another peaceful half hour until Ross took me to the sink to rinse then he sat me down to fuss a bit more with the ends before he got out the blow dryer. When he was finished he gave me a mirror.

"What do you think?" he asked as I held it up.

I ran my fingers over my hair as I looked at it. Even considering the pile on the floor it looked longer than when he started.

"There's someone I've missed," I said as I looked at him. "It's really great, Ross. Thank you."

"You're welcome."

"Don't dislike me so long before you fix my hair again, okay?"

Ross laughed. "Okay, Anna. Paul? You're up."

Paul groaned as he rolled off the couch.

"Awe, there's my girl," he said when he came in. He gently put his hand on the side of my head. "I bet that feels more like it."

"Ross is amazing." It already felt like the rape happened to someone else. I knew it hadn't but at least I didn't look as much like the shaken woman I tried to avoid looking at in the mirror. Ross lifted the cape off me and held it out of the way as I stiffly stood up and Paul took my place in the chair.

"You want your greys done?" Ross asked.

"Joshua will never make Captain if he insists on looking like a kid," Paul said. "I've seen Sig's check list. He has 'hides greys' right at the top of the 'vanity' section."

Ross laughed. "He gets me to fill out that part of the evaluation."

"I knew it," Paul said.

The clippers snapped on as Ross got to work on the back of Paul's head. I pulled my knees up in the chair next to him so the edge of the seat didn't dig in.

"Come down and see Dana after this?"

"Yeah," I answered. I felt less conspicuous now that I looked more like my old self. "When is Wendy coming?"

"Mm, eighteen thirty."

Right after dinner. I shrivelled inside as I realized I might be stuck downstairs for the rest of the day. Ross made quick work of Paul's hair and packed up.

"I still don't like you," he smiled before he hugged me.

"I know. Thanks again, Ross."

He gave my cheek a quick kiss and Paul closed the door behind him.

"Are you going to get dressed?" Paul asked.

"Um, yeah," I said. When I looked down I realized I put my pyjamas back on after my bath.

"I'll be right back."

I changed into clean jeans and a t-shirt. I knew it would be warm downstairs even with the windows open. In the mirror I ran my fingers through my hair again, impressed by how much better I felt. Even though letting Ross clear the air with me had been brief and difficult it was well worth the results. I reminded myself of someone happier, stronger. Less bruised and vulnerable. I gingerly knelt and opened the cupboard under the sink and pulled out the makeup I bought when Paul and I had been in Edmonton. Somehow it remained intact in the bottom of my pack through everything then and in the months after. I took out the little bottle of cover-up and smoothed some over my face and was pleased with the job it did hiding the bruises.

Paul came into the bathroom as I finished up. He had my guns with him and eyed the makeup as I put it away.

"This stuff really works," I commented.

He lifted my chin to look.

"As long as it makes you feel better. Don't hide behind it for my sake."

"It's for my sake," I said as I wrapped my arms around him.

"I know he hurt you. Whatever you need is yours, you know that don't you?"

"Yes, Paul," I whispered. "I love you."

"Sorry it took so long to get your weapons back," he said after a few seconds. "Taggart had them. They were unprocessed."

I looked back, puzzled.

"He's thorough. You can have them back as long as you promise you won't try and shoot Jack again."

"I promise."

Paul helped me with them. "Ready?"

"Yes," I answered. As I'll ever be, I thought.

His arm went around me and we stepped down the stairs together. Jack went over something on a clipboard with one of the men I recognized from when we sprung Dana and started to make his way over. Joshua stepped in front of him before he got half way and with a smug glance at Jack he walked up to me, blocking Jack's path.

"Hey, Little Sister," Joshua said. Paul let me go so he could hug me.

I sneezed as Jack connected unexpectedly and Joshua was too close for me to get my elbow up so I turned away but I still got his shirt.

"Shit, sorry," I muttered.

"You doing okay?" Joshua asked.

"I think so," I said. "I'm glad to be home."

Joshua nodded and glanced back at Jack, still waiting his turn to talk to me.

Joshua still out to get you? I sent.

Yeah.

Nobody's fault but the dead man's, Jack. I'm glad you were there for me.

Thanks, Jack sent. *I'm glad I was, too. I'm so sorry.*

Nobody's fault.

Thanks... Jack disconnected and walked away. Joshua seemed pleased. It looked like Joshua still believed Jack and I had been a thing at some point in the past and still did whatever he could to keep Jack away. Getting hurt on what he saw as Jack's watch hadn't improved Joshua's opinion of him.

"Need anything the next couple of days just say so," Joshua said.

"I haven't told her," Paul whispered.

Joshua made an O with his mouth. "Sorry. See you at dinner."

"Told me what?" I turned to Paul.

"He knows you're going for a couple of days."

"You haven't told me he knows I'm going for a couple of days?" I asked. It didn't make much sense.

"The Colonel is taking some of us in the morning for a while. You'll be gone before I get back."

I closed my eyes and put my hand over my mouth. Paul knew the look. His arms went around me as he pulled me close.

"Sugar, I'm sorry. You'll have Jack and Joshua."

"I want you, Paul. I don't want to be a referee."

"You'll be in good hands. I've spoken to them both and they'll behave. They'll look after whatever you need until I get back."

"Commander?" I didn't recognize the voice right away. "Have you come down to see Mister Reid?"

I turned and saw the doctor. He talked about Dana.

"Go ahead, Sugar," Paul rubbed my arm. I used my eyes to plead with Paul to stay and he sighed and put his lips on my forehead. I knew he had no choice and where ever he was going I was safer here with Jack and his brother.

"Yes, Doc," I said.

"It'll be good for him to see you," he said as he guided me away from Paul. He pushed the pantry door open and led me in. I stopped in my tracks. Four hospital beds replaced the fridges and shelves of food. Dana occupied one and the rest sat empty.

"I had to fly out the other man you brought in. Reid's been all alone."

Dana pushed himself up when he saw me, a smile on his face. He looked so much better than the morning before.

"Just a sec," Flood said and gently held my elbow. "Did you make a decision on the things I brought you?"

I nodded. "I'll take the rest at ten. Otherwise I'm stiff and sore. Adjusting to being home."

"Okay," he said. "I'll get you a chair."

I walked over to Dana as Flood dragged over the big armchair from the common room. Dana held his arms out and I leaned over and hugged him.

"You look a ton better than you did yesterday," I said as I eased myself into the comfy seat. I pulled it closer so I could get my elbows on the bed.

"So do you," Dana said. "Jack says I'm a dad."

"Yes," I smiled. Dana's grin was contagious. "He has her red hair. Six days ago. I fed him for her. She lost a lot of blood so Ray drained me for her. She was doing well and feeding him on her own by the time I left. Ray and Alina took good care of her. She's so happy."

Dana sighed. "I can't stand to think how it would have turned out if we hadn't been able to bring her to you."

"Don't give it any thought, Dana," I said. "It didn't matter what was going on. She kept everyone in a good mood. All she talked about was you and the baby. I bet she's on pins and needles waiting for us."

Dana reached for me again and I stood to hold him. He quietly cried as I heard the door open behind me. His grip loosened and he kept me close so whoever came in couldn't see him.

"Anna," he whispered. "You fed my son, gave your blood to his mother. You gave up your innocence to save his father. I don't know how I can ever show you my thanks."

I put my hand on his cheek and wiped his tears away.

"Seeing you together will be thanks enough. I can't explain how complete my life feels having Paul and Camille. How deep my feelings for them go. Every second of what I went through was worth it because you and Virtue have that joy in your lives. Don't feel sorry for me. I feel pain... broken inside. Nothing can change that. You have no idea how I'm comforted knowing the good it did."

"You're right about her, Jack," Dana said.

I stood and turned to see Jack beside us. I held Dana's hand as Jack put his arm around me.

"None of us would have gotten out without her," Jack said.

"Enough flattery," I protested. "The last thing anyone around here needs is Anna with a swell head."

Jack laughed and got his other arm around me. "Okay, Baby."

"Too tight, Jack," I whispered. His arm found a sore spot.

"Sorry," he said.

"In two days I'll take you to them, Dana. I need you packed and ready tomorrow night, we go before dawn. I have to stay away for a while. I did some serious damage yesterday plus the Doc pulled me from duty for a few weeks."

"Paul briefed me," Jack said. "I'm coming along with you."

Dana nodded. "I can sleep now. I've been in knots worrying about you, Anna. I think you won the lottery with this one, Jack."

"Yeah," Jack whispered. Dana's eyes were already closing so I smoothed his blanket over his shoulder and pulled the string to turn off the light above his head. Jack took me out of the infirmary and down the hall, his hand still around my waist. The food smelled good. There was a seat between Paul and Joshua so he steered me to it. Joshua glanced at Jack's arm on me so Jack glared at him and shoved it a little further around before he pulled my chair out and sat me down. He served me before he took his down to the end of the table to sit with his men.

"I think he's doing better now," I told Paul.

"He's been a wreck," he said.

I agreed. Watching Dana relax as relief enveloped him proved it.

Taggart sat on the other side of Paul, glancing around the table. He chewed his food the way I did. Ever so gently so the noises in my mouth didn't cover up the conversation around me.

"Twenty minutes, Major," Taggart said between bites. Almost absently. Almost. He seemed completely aware of everything around him and kept one ear pointed directly at me. He acted friendly enough during our morning conversation but something about him made me cautious. I took a quick look around the room and realized I felt the same vague mistrust for all the new faces.

After a few bites I poked my food around, troubled about nothing in particular. The radio squawked in the other room and Joshua got up to answer it.

"ETA five minutes," he told Paul as he came back in.

"Let's get this show on the road," Paul said as he helped me up. "Captain Taggart, Lieutenants Roberts, Wells and Wight."

I didn't know who Wight was and guessed he was the man on the other side of Taggart who stood up at the same time as the rest of them.

"Join us, Commander?" Paul asked.

"Bells on," I replied. Since I technically outranked him it was appropriate for Paul to invite me. He looked at my untouched food and then at me. I shrugged. He knew I wouldn't let myself starve to death.

Joshua led us out the door. Paul and I behind him then Taggart. Ross, Jack and Wight taking up the rear. It took a few minutes to walk to the heavy raised wooden platform which served as the landing pad. Five wooden stairs led up from the dirt below to the top and we stopped maybe twenty feet away. We already heard the helicopter in the distance. I held on to Paul's elbow and watched the sky. It grew louder and louder and I put my hand on my chest as I thought about my dream. I looked over at Jack. He glanced at my hand and looked away. He knew what I was thinking.

Chapter 28

The Colonel's helicopter appeared above the trees. It slowed and lazily turned overhead before descending into the clearing and touching down on the pad, one skid just before the other. Through the reflection on the windshield I could make out the pilot as he reached up and started flipping switches. The engine exhaled as it spun down and the blades slowed. I turned toward Paul and blinked away the dust in my eyes until the wash stopped battering us.

The side door popped open and slid aside and I watched the Colonel step down to the platform. He turned and held out his hand and instead of another hand reaching for his, a long brown leg in a plain black pump and topped by a dark blue skirt reached out. It hesitated for a moment then she jumped, straightening up a bit in the air just before both pumps hit the platform. I immediately knew her even though I'd never seen her before. She was all arms and legs, long graceful neck. She wore what I remembered to be a Canadian Forces woman's dress uniform, her short tight black curls covered with the Robin Hood style hat held down by her hand. A pristine brown leather case attached to her belt concealed her side arm. Her dark brown eyes turned to me and her wide mouth split in to a glorious smile.

"Wenns!" I waved as I started toward her but Paul hooked his arm around the middle.

"We have to wait here until the rotors stop," he whispered in my ear.

I quietly growled at him as she waved back.

"Anns!" she called in reply then turned to grab her bag of gear and glared at the ground as she wiggled the heel of one of her shoes out of a gap in the platform. I burst out laughing. She shook her head as she waved. Free of the wood's hold, she took her bag in one hand and followed the Colonel to the steps as the blades became visible as individuals rather than a big noisy circle. She rushed past Sig as Paul let me go and I ran into her arms. Sig looked at us with amusement as I held her tight and blinked away tears.

"Wenns," I said again.

"Hey, Anns," she replied and tipped back and forth in her pumps, swinging me with her. "What have you gotten yourself in to this time?"

She stepped back and put her hands on my face. I held on to her arms. I couldn't let her go. The love and comfort I felt from her was indescribable. She wrapped herself around me again. The helicopter became silent and I heard the awkward shuffling of boots on dirt behind me. I didn't care. The arms of Commander Wendy Vega made everything okay. When she finally let me go I held on to her elbow.

"Look at you in your monkey suit," I said, laughing as I wiped my eyes.

"Where's yours again?" she asked. "Oh that's right, you never got one."

"I'm never getting stuffed into one of those. Remember how I got out of getting measured for mine?"

"Yeah," she laughed. "You hid."

"Under the barracks," we both said at the same time, laughing hard.

"Anyway, Harry said *one* of us had to make a good first impression."

"Who's Harry?" Paul asked behind me.

"Our C.O.," we said at the same time and burst out laughing as she seemed to notice the men behind me for the first time. It dawned on me there must be a reason why I knew exactly what to say to her.

"Colonel," I said as I reached past her, remembering my manners. It was up to me to start the introductions. Wendy let me go long enough to take Sig's hand.

"Commander Richards," he said as he kissed my cheek. "I'm pleased to bring Commander Vega."

"Thanks, Sig," I quietly said.

"Come, Wenns," I said as she stuffed her hand into mine and stood shoulder to shoulder with me. That lasted until we got to Paul. By then her arm was around me.

"Wendy, I want you to meet my husband Paul. Major Richards."

"Husband?" she said. "I'm not surprised you got the eye of the man on top. Come here, husband." She let me go and wrapped her long arms around Paul.

"Come on husband, hug me back or I'll squeeze tighter."

Paul laughed and got his arms around her.

"Welcome, Commander," he said.

"That's better. Thank you, Major."

She let him go and patted his cheek as I took her elbow and pulled her along.

"Captain William Taggart, Compound Chief of Security. Commander Wendy Vega."

She politely held her hand out to him and they shook.

I introduced her to Joshua, Ross and Wight who I hadn't been introduced to so I left out his first name and finally Jack at the end of the line.

"Lieutenant Jack Roberts, Commander Wendy Vega."

She shook his hand then paused, holding it tighter.

"Is this the Jack Roberts you told me about?" she asked out the side of her mouth, never taking her eyes off him.

I tried very hard to make an indifferent sort of noise and was surprised when a very pleased with myself 'mm hm' came from my throat. Joshua sighed angrily behind me.

"Really," she said. Jack raised an eyebrow at me and I looked as innocent as I could.

"Well," she said to Jack. "You'll have to tell me all the things Anns done lately to embarrass herself that her husband would never tell me." She leaned closer to him.

"Hm?" she said.

"Yes, Ma'am," Jack managed. Colour grew in his cheeks and I started to giggle.

"Commanders," Sig sharply said. "This isn't shore leave."

"Yes, Sir," we said at the same time and she finally let Jack go. I counted to three before he lowered his empty hand. My arm went around her.

"Captain Taggart, have you a cabin to assign Commander Vega?"

Taggart blinked as his mind worked. I guessed he hadn't known she was coming.

"Yes, Sir," he replied. "Seven East, Sir."

"Very well," Sig said. "Commanders, with me. Let's see if you two can keep it together long enough to get our briefing out of the way."

"I'll see you later, Lieutenant Jack Roberts," Wendy said as she picked up her duffel bag.

"Dear Lord," Sig said loud enough for everyone to hear. "I'm beginning to wonder if the Canadian Forces has turned in to a shameless frat party."

"My God," Wendy replied. "How much getting it on does he think happens when it's too damn cold most of the year to get your parka off?"

I burst out laughing as Sig stopped in his tracks so I slapped my hand over my mouth. Sig turned on his heel and Wendy added her hand to mine as I continued to lose control of myself. It didn't help.

"Richards, get a grip," he bellowed.

I glanced at Paul who stared at me with disbelief. He told me I'd know Wendy and I'd gone so far I'd put both her and I in trouble and embarrassed him in front of the officers and his C.O.

"Yes, Colonel," I said and held my lips shut, breathing through my nose. Wendy and I let go of each other and fell in behind him as he led us to Seven East.

"What's up with Jack?" I whispered.

"I'm just letting everyone know where my interest is so I'm not spending the evening shooting down a bunch of flirts."

"But why him?"

She seemed amused by my question and winked as she answered with another. "Jealous, Anns?"

"No," I laughed. I looked back over my shoulder. Joshua angrily whispered in Paul's ear. Paul stared straight ahead at Wendy and I as Joshua looked at Jack. I didn't know what came over me. I just knew I had a big mess walking along thirty feet behind.

We followed Sig to Seven East, on the right and halfway down the main road to the house. Wendy put her duffel on the bed and kicked her shoes off into the closet then her hat went on the top shelf.

"Did I overdo it?" she said to herself. "I didn't feel anything I shouldn't."

Sig occupied the desk chair and gestured toward the bed so I sat. Wendy opened the bag and pulled out a change of clothes.

"I have two jobs here, Anns," Wendy said.

"Wait," I interrupted. "I'm not keeping this from Paul. You know that, Sig."

"I'll straighten it out with Paul."

I nodded. Wendy hung up her jacket and unbuttoned the blouse underneath.

"Tell me about the two of Jack's men who were looking after Virtue."

"Them?" I asked. "My sister calls them 'Jack's Bastards.' They had her in a hotel room for months. Fed her, that's about it. Jack is going with us to straighten them out."

"I thought so," Wendy said. She pulled off her blouse and reached behind to unzip the skirt. Sig paid no notice. "And Patrick Fletcher?"

"Patrick is so kind," I said. "When I see him with Marie... it's like she's his. He doesn't do anything unless it's right for her and the others."

"I'm here to observe him. I thought I'd ask about the other two just in case." The skirt slipped off and she pushed down her pantyhose. She sat next to me on the bed in her underwear and pulled on a pair of socks. "I'm sorry, Anns. I overdid it and made a problem for you with your husband."

I looked over at Sig.

"Sig said you are sensitive to us. I unshielded my projections to make it easier for us to pull off knowing each other. I think it was too much."

I shook my head. "I feel so much, Wenns... love, safety. Still."

"I want to tell her, Father," Wendy said. "I shut the projections down on the road. She's still picking it up."

Sig threw his hands up. "Why the hell not?"

"You're right, Anns," she said as she took my hands and knelt on the floor in front of me. "I'm also here for Jack."

"Okay?" I replied. Jack had already earned a first and he had a second. I didn't understand what she would be assessing him for.

"Little One," she sighed. "Many years ago I lay with the man who carried the line of your brother. The one you know as Ray. My line gave yours life."

One of her palms reached for my face and I felt myself sliding down on the floor to her.

"I'm your mother, Little One."

"I feel it, Wenns," I said. "I know."

We held each other for a moment before she took my elbows and pulled me up to sit on the bed. Then she pulled my face up toward hers and kissed me softly on the mouth.

"I'm spending the night with Jack. Sometime tomorrow my line will complete its imprint of his. I'll carry his sister. Raise her. She will be my daughter. All the love you feel from me will be hers, too. When she's older I'll take her to the man who will seek her out and care for her every time the balance shifts and the lines waiting wake again to life."

I smiled as I nodded to her. I hadn't felt the love of a mother in years and was grateful for the day or two I would have with Wendy.

"That makes this cranky old man your grandfather," Wendy whispered in my ear.

I glanced over at Sig as Wendy and I started laughing again. He didn't seem displeased with what she'd told me.

"Excuse me, children," he said as he stood. "I need to sort out the Major before you get to the house."

I waited as Wendy pulled on her jeans and a dark blue tank top. She had a dagger tattooed on her right arm from shoulder to elbow and a spattering of cartoon style planets and stars in the same area of the other. Her double shoulder holster already had one gun in it and she took the other from the belt of her dress uniform and put it with its mate. The holster also had a leather scabbard and a heavy handled knife rested diagonally across her back.

She quickly threaded her belt through the loops on her jeans and pulled on a pair of runners.

"Where to, Anns?" she asked.

"The house?"

"'kay." She took my elbow and closed the door behind us. "I'm sorry if I made a problem for you."

"Don't worry about it. Paul's brother suspects something went on between me and Jack and is probably pleased as punch he's been proven right. I've been carefully avoiding his insinuations for a while."

"Well, something did go on," Wendy said as she shoved me with her shoulder and we both took a few steps to the side.

"But not what he thinks."

"But I'll be just as good," she whispered.

"Wennis," I groaned as I started to turn red. When I looked up, Paul waited on the porch with Sig. He didn't look any happier but at least the slow simmer was gone from his eyes. His arm went around me as Wendy handed me off. Sig patted him on the back and went inside.

"What you feel from me, it will fade as I get farther away," she whispered.

I nodded. She let herself into the house and went to find Jack.

"Come here," Paul quietly said and dragged me down to the end of the porch past the kitchen window. "I'm leaving it up to you to clear things up with my brother. I'm sorry. I know you don't need that right now. I've tried and he thinks I'm just blind to it."

I nodded. "What did you tell him?"

"Just that I believe you've told me everything and you both have my trust."

"Okay."

There was no point trying to convince Joshua he imagined things. I turned sideways and leaned on Paul, facing the front door just in time to see Joshua. He pulled the door shut, cutting off the sound of Wendy's laughter then he turned and glared at me, pointing where she would be inside the house. I rested my head on Paul's shoulder and closed my eyes. I had tonight with Paul and would deal with Joshua tomorrow. As long as I kept my distance from Jack and Wendy didn't waste any time getting him into her cabin, Joshua shouldn't have anything to publicly complain about. It hadn't been so bad before I left when Joshua kept finding himself around whenever Jack was. Now he was the embarrassment he claimed Jack was and publicly questioned Jack and me in front of Paul and even worse in front of Paul's men.

RJ

Chapter 29

"There's chatter about a major push on the compound in a couple of days," Paul whispered in my ear. "After you and Jack drop them off, hide out somewhere for a few days. Don't tell me where. Don't explain it to Jack until you don't return here."

I nodded as I stepped on Paul's foot. He wanted to dance and never complained about my clumsiness. His left held my right and another round of radio commercials started but we kept swaying around the living room. The DJ promised CCR and we'd make slow dancing work with that too. I kept my face tilted up, eyes closed. I knew if I opened them I'd look at the clock on the wall and know exactly how few precious minutes we had left.

"There's still lust here, Paul," I said. "I just hurt too much."

"You're beautiful," he answered as Fogerty joined us. "I waited an extra fifteen years to find you, Sugar, and I'll always be whatever you need."

"Be careful, please?" I asked as I heard boots on the stairs to our door.

Paul's warm lips brushed my jaw and moved to kiss me. I briefly tasted his tongue then he murmured words I felt more than heard as Sig knocked. His fingers stroked my hair as I squeezed him. Paul let me go. His duffel bag rubbed against his leg as he picked it up then the door closed. When the helicopter faded, I opened my eyes and went to tackle the kitchen.

A shrill ear splitting scream shot from the bathroom as I started the half empty dishwasher. I froze, hand on my gun. Then I heard it again. I connected to Jack as I unlocked the front door for him before doubling back to the bathroom.

Help, I sent. *There's someone in here with me.*

On my way, he replied and I disconnected so I could try and sense anyone in the bathroom but read nothing. Jack thundered up the stairs as I approached the half closed door.

Paul? My voice came from the bathroom then the scream set my skin crawling. I hugged the hall wall leading to the bathroom door. When Jack barged in, he pulled his gun and blocked me from moving any further.

Paul! My voice sounded more urgent.

"Do you hear her?" I whispered. Jack shook his head. "In the bathroom."

Jack put his hand up telling me to stay put as he nudged the door with his foot and took a quick peek inside.

"It's empty."

I need Pony, please! She called.

Hands kinda full, Sugar, Paul faintly answered. He wasn't in the bathroom with her.

"Look in the mirror," I said. When he turned and leaned in I noticed scratches on the back of his neck. He took another step as I flinched from another scream Jack took no notice of. After a second, his hand reached for me from the open doorway.

I stepped in to see the woman in the mirror and a three year old dark haired version of me sitting on the counter. Camille's feet squirmed in the sink. The woman tried to get a toothbrush in her mouth but Camille wouldn't open without making the sound which could only come from a little girl.

"What the hell?" Jack asked.

I didn't recognize the bathroom. Double sinks on ivory tile. A large tub behind her and open black and white striped curtains half covering the huge window.

"Do you know where she is?" I whispered. A stuffed brown bear flew past and landed in the other sink. The woman took it and popped it into Camille's reaching hands then the mouth silently opened and the brush went in.

Thank you, she said.

"Her?" Jack asked. "You mean you? In my bathroom?"

PONY! Camille's tiny voice shrieked around the toothbrush.

"We must be visiting you?" I wondered. She always warned me when I headed for trouble but since I wasn't crazy any more maybe she was sane, too. This looked like bedtime judging by the darkness outside the window behind her.

"I see her sometimes," I explained. "Always warning me of danger. But this looks normal."

Jack put his gun away as he exhaled through pursed lips and ran a palm over his brush cut.

"This it for your weird stuff?" He asked. I nodded. Camille made a noise like she was bringing up a lung before she spat.

I'm having a word with your Uncle Joshua about little girls, the woman muttered. *Close your eyes.*

She did and the woman turned Camille's back to the mirror then touched the bear to Camille's nose.

Who is it? She chimed like a doorbell.

Mmm, reading Mommy! Camille squealed and the woman laughed.

Not Mommy, close your eyes, then she put her nose to Camille's. *Who is it?*

Reading … PONY! Camille pulled her knees up, tipping sideways on the counter with laughter. The woman's smile briefly fell as she rubbed her chest and I glanced at Jack. The surprise of seeing things in the mirror had passed.

"Camille reads, Jack," I whispered as I grabbed his elbow and pointed in excitement. "It's a game, she's guessing wrong on purpose."

The woman put her nose up to Camille's again. *Reading … clean teeth,* she said as she smiled and I saw she was missing a front tooth.

"Something bad is coming," I whispered then I ran my tongue over my teeth to make sure I had them all.

"Not on my watch."

I blinked and she was gone. Just Jack and I in the bathroom. The mirror felt cold on my fingers as I reached for where Camille had been on Jack's tiled countertop. Tomorrow I would say goodbye to her and it felt like she'd just been so close. Jack moved behind me and put his hands on my shoulders.

"Are you going to be okay tonight?" Jack asked.

"It's just one night," I shrugged but wasn't so sure. I could only guess what strength Paul drew on to live up here alone without his girls. "I slept in Camille's room when Paul left in May but she's not here. I don't even want to camp on the couch."

"I'll come up and stay with you," Jack whispered. His hands slid down my arms to rest on the counter on either side of me then I turned. He didn't move his hands.

"I thought I'd ask Wendy."

"I like to whisper, too," Joshua whispered from the doorway. I startled and Jack took his hands off the counter. "I wondered why Roberts ran up here in such a hurry. Looks like I figured it out."

"Maybe you want to join Commander Vega and me for ladies night, Joshua?" I asked. He crossed his arms and leaned on the frame then he stared at Jack.

"I don't think so. Seems the *Commanders* have the night all planned."

I rolled my eyes and shouldered Joshua out of the way before I went in my room and slammed the door. It only took a minute for the apartment door to close and I sensed Jack downstairs. The other end of the apartment sounded quiet except for the occasional buzz from the dishwasher so I changed and went to find Wendy. There was no sign of her on the main floor but my blood pressure started to return to normal as I approached Seven East so I knocked.

"Come in, Little One," she called and half a second later opened the door for me anyway. Her bed was a mess and the shirt Jack wore the night before lay in the middle of her floor. She sighed as she got her arms around me. "I said goodbye to the Colonel and the Major on the way by. I'm not so sure Paul trusts me with the children."

"He doesn't know you're family, Wenns," I said. She waggled her eyebrows and smiled.

"No matter," her stomach rumbled. "Jack and I missed breakfast."

I glanced at the shirt. One sleeve inside out. "Souvenir?"

"Nope," she put a hand on her belly. "Souvenir."

"You didn't," I started to drop onto her bed then changed my mind and sat in the chair. Jack and Wendy was a topic I had no interest in. She pulled the bedding in to place.

"Don't be such a prude. I thought you knew how it works. Did you think I was going to give him a cup and a magazine?" She picked up her pillow and shook it. I made a disgusted noise but she laughed and I couldn't help but join in. "You may not have noticed but there's no kitchen in here and that's a little too kinky for a first date, even for Jack."

I blushed so I covered my ears and closed my eyes but Wendy's laughter leaked in anyway.

"Ah, inheritances. It's not your fault your memory is shot when it comes to some things. I won't bring it up again if it makes you uncomfortable."

"Appreciate it," I sighed as I dropped my hands.

"But he's got this little spot by his tail bone and when you dig your nails in he purrs like a tomcat."

"Wendy!" I shouted and covered my ears back up. When I opened my eyes she knelt on the floor in front of me.

"Do you want to feel her?" she whispered as she took my hands and rested them on my knees. "Her line? She's going to be beautiful."

I imagined Jack under my nose and took a minute to make a mirror image. Wendy nodded. "You know what you're looking for."

"May I, Wenns?" I didn't know what to do with my hand to read a line but I knew what to do with my sense. She nodded. It gently entered her chest and I looked into her eyes as I let it rest there. After a minute I picked up Wendy's line, most likely because I ignored it and focused on her daughter's. It felt indescribably new and soft like a floating dandelion seed. "Oh my," I murmured.

"A new line, Anns," she whispered. "I have a mate, you know. And a son. But this, this is the most amazing thing. I don't know why the women on your side of the family are so different from the women in mine. If I give a man on my side a sister she grows to be like you and me. A strong line, memories. But your side. Their lines are so gentle."

Wendy stood. I realized we dressed the same: jeans and black long sleeved tees. Her stomach rumbled again. "I'll have her concealed soon. If Jack picks anything up I'll act like I don't know what he's talking about. He doesn't know I'm family so would never consider he got me pregnant."

Jack did pick his sister up but in me, not Wendy. At lunch he sat with the men we brought back in the truck and kept looking at me. I tried not to look at him and instead chatted with Wendy about Camille and my sister and the others she would meet. She said she looked forward to seeing Ray again and he'd always been kind. He'd had a very short line, as she put it, when he earned his mate. He was due for one and his father handed my sister down to him as his first. She tried to catch Jack's eye to distract him from staring at me but he was oblivious to everything else in the room. I caught Joshua glaring at him from the

Officer's table. When Wendy excused herself to the washroom, Jack made his move and came and took her seat.

"You need to see the Doc," he whispered.

"Why?" I asked.

"It's fleeting but I keep picking up another line. It's here then it's gone. Baby, I think you're pregnant."

I coughed on my food. "Pardon?"

He nodded.

"I think I'd read that if I was," I said then I put a hand on his arm. "Jack, you feel guilty about what happened and might not be reading clearly. Please don't feel bad for me. I feel bad enough without the people I care about blaming themselves."

"May I?" he asked. I looked around the crowded room.

"Here?"

"No," he sighed. "Come with me."

He took my elbow and followed me around the corner into the hall and out of sight from the kitchen. We stopped outside the half-bathroom just before the infirmary.

"Go ahead," I said knowing he'd find nothing. He glanced back the way we came before his hand went up over my chest. I waited for nearly a minute before he sighed with relief as Wendy popped out and we stepped across the hall so we weren't hit by the flying door.

"Sorry," Jack said and with a small nod at Wendy he returned to the kitchen.

"I saw how he was watching you," she said. "I just needed a minute to compose myself to conceal her better. He's convinced it's not you?"

"Yes," I answered. "Will you stay up in the apartment with me tonight, Wenns? I don't want—"

"Comparing notes?"

Wendy raised her eyes and looked at Joshua behind me. He stood close. Angry warmth radiated from his body. I glanced down the hall and saw Jack watching us from his seat at the table. Wendy followed my gaze down to Jack and waved. He dropped his eyes.

"Oh my God, don't you know when to quit?" he whispered.

I quietly counted in my head and only found myself madder, not calmer.

"Shit," Joshua said and turned to walk away.

With Paul gone, Joshua's big brother instincts turned into something mean. His territory games with Jack were one thing but calling me out in front of other people pushed too far. I gave him a few steps toward the infirmary door before I charged, grabbed his elbow and shoved him in as hard as I could. Dana froze with his fork half in his mouth at the sudden explosion of commotion.

"What the fuck is your problem, Joshua?"

I would have preferred to do this alone with Joshua but had little chance of keeping the eloquence only my temper could bring out if I waited for a better time. I stared up at him from inches away as I scanned the front of the house. My anxiety rose as Wendy moved further away. The infirmary door swung shut behind and Jack stopped outside before Joshua spoke.

"My problem is you and your puppy dog ex-boyfriend parading around in front of my brother," he growled. "He thinks you're so completely perfect he'll never notice the notch on your belt for Jack Roberts."

I kept my mouth shut and tried to get a reply together while I gave Joshua more time to vent.

"Do you think I don't see it? There's no personal space between you two. No space at all. His hands are always just about to touch you and don't tell me you don't notice. You get as close to him as you do to Paul. You should be ashamed of yourself, calling yourself his wife when you're as glued to Roberts as you are to him.

"If I could skin him for letting that man get his hands on you I would. What you have is nobody's business but yours and Paul's and he dropped the ball with my little sister and let that asshole take it."

"Is that what this is about, Josh? Jack's responsible for what some other man did with his pecker when his pants were down?"

Joshua backed up. He didn't like it when I put it like that.

"You can just bet if Jack was here and you were there with me he would be grateful I had someone I trust to bring me home. That I hadn't found myself alone on that hill with two dead men and nobody who thought of me as any more than another grunt who damn well better keep it together before she became a liability."

He crossed his arms and shook his head then he wiped his eyes. I gave him a moment as I read Jack waiting outside the infirmary door. Wendy was closer. I knew that because I calmed down. Dana had turned his head away.

"Do you need to hear me say it?"

I couldn't tell if he nodded or shook his head.

"The only man I ever chose to sleep with besides your brother is Jack Roberts," I said, struggling to keep my voice down. "It happened once in a foreign hotel when I was taking him somewhere and bringing him home. It could have been a career ending decision letting my guard down like that. It's the one rule we don't break and I broke it.

"The Commander crossed the line with the Lieutenant," my voice softened as he lowered his eyes, still refusing to look at me. "I'm not ashamed. What it left us with is complicated. And absolutely I'm comfortable around Jack. I wasn't aware it was obvious and caused you so much discomfort. I'm sorry."

I waited until he looked at me.

"I know what you're doing," I said. He opened his mouth and started to say something before sighing instead and closing it. "You see what Paul and I have. How amazing we feel around each other and our little girl. You're protective and you feel Jack is a threat. I love you for that Josh. I'm proud to have a man like you for a big brother."

I put my hands on his arms and felt him start to unfold them.

"Paul knows exactly what happened and why. Jack's proven himself to Paul. He trusts Jack with my life. I think if you give Jack a chance you'll see you're both on the same side."

"I just wanted you to know how it is," I finished as he put his arms around me.

"I wish I'd been there for you, Anna," Joshua whispered.

"I know you do, Josh," I answered.

There was nothing else to say.

Chapter 30

A bottle of wine past dinner and Wendy and I settled on the open sofa bed. She abstained and decided to give in to lack of sleep from the night before. Wind cooled us through the big windows at the side and front of the room. The twilight voices of the compound came to our ears. My sleepover invitation pleased her and she moved out of her cabin after dinner, hauling her things up to the apartment. The Canadian Navy uniform went in my closet. She laughed and said to consider it a gift since she wasn't planning on packing it around from hotel to hotel. Between being half drunk and her calming influence the emptiness of the apartment wasn't completely crushing. Our packed bags waited by the door and I set up Paul's alarm clock on the end table to wake us good and early.

"You're lonely," Wendy said. "Come here, Little One."

She held out her arm. I turned off the lamp then rested my head on her shoulder and my arm around her middle.

"You know it's just a place here, right? Do you think the men Paul's been have any attachment to these walls? The men he will be?"

"No," I whispered.

"I want to help you remember something," she said. "Can I do that for you?"

I tilted my head to her and kissed her cheek.

"Is it strange I think of you as my mother?" I asked instead of saying yes. She wasn't any older than me.

"No more than my thinking of you as my daughter."

"Yes, Wenns," I answered her question.

She pulled the light sheet up over us and brushed my eyes closed with her fingers.

"Paul remembers the first time you met. When he learned he'd earned a mate. There are gaps in his memory since then but he'll always remember the first time he felt his connection to you. With your permission, I'll help you get that back."

I nodded.

"Sleep, Anns," she whispered. "I'm going to project to you and you will dream."

My eyes fluttered open for a moment before they stilled and I felt her shoulder move as she breathed. She turned to face me and shivered. Through my closed lids I knew the sun was up. My heart beat a little harder knowing we'd missed the alarm and I felt more than ticked at Jack for failing to be our backup. When she shivered again I opened my eyes to the dawn sun through the trees and the sound of running water.

"It's a big day, Little One," she whispered as her fingers dug in my ribs and I squirmed and tickled her in return. I didn't understand the language but I felt the meaning of the words. I looked at the grubby old brunette who held me. So very different from the gorgeous black woman who tucked me in. Bits of grass from the soft mat we'd bedded in tangled her nearly straight brown hair.

"Yes, Mother," I answered.

"Found a nice man for you," she laughed.

"Yes, Mother."

I rubbed my back on the ground, itching it against the rough fabric of my homespun dress.

"Are you nervous about the man or the cold water?"

"Both, Mother."

Her hand stroked my cheek then she took me to a calm corner of the river. We undressed and she cleaned me from head to toe before pulling a new dress over my head. The dress had been a sacrifice and we'd both worked hard making goods to trade for the cloth and tailoring. Then she combed my hair through with her fingers, gently braiding it and binding the end with a strip of leather.

After a simple breakfast, she embraced me and we walked from our small camp to the road. The smooth stones lining the river pushed through the coarse grass where the feet and carts of many travelers had worn dirt away. This road led us for days.

"A ways down the road you'll find three men loading a cart with river stones," she said. "Ask for the stonemason's apprentice. Tell him you are Johannes' sister and ask for an introduction to Dammo."

I repeated what she said.

"You're ready, Agnes," she said as she held her hand over my chest. "Our paths will cross again."

I nodded and bravely turned my back to her. She'd only ever left my side after leaving me in the care of my grandfather while she travelled to trade for herbs she couldn't find around his home. She'd always said there was a man for me and it was after one of these trips she returned to announce she'd found him.

I took only twenty steps and stopped; lost already without the comforting smell of her sweat and her constant humming. If I walked into the forest, I'd find a plant to calm me but I spread my bare feet on a flat wide stone instead. She taught me the purpose of every plant and how to divine the magic of any new one by its shape and smell. She taught me to heal and to cure. To prevent and encourage children and through teaching me which preparations held great danger, she taught me how to hasten the passing of those in pain which would slowly claim them. All I knew and was came from the loving woman I'd promised to walk away from this very morning.

Her hem stroked the grass at her feet as she approached and rested her hand on my back as I started to cry.

"If you choose to return to me I will be here until tomorrow morning," she promised. "Our paths will cross again and my love will always be with you."

I saw nobody for most of the morning and felt hopeful my mother could be wrong when I rounded a corner and spotted the men. My hands gripped my dress with instinctive fear, having been taught since I was small a band of men was nothing but danger to a lone young woman. One paused in his work and turned. All three were shirtless, broad of back and muscular. Each carried a stone that must have been as heavy as me yet none seemed tired by their burden. My tongue felt suddenly thick and dry as I remembered Mother's instructions.

"Hello, Little One," the man called. "Come closer or we'll scare the birds away with our shouting."

The two with him added their stones to the pile as I got my feet going. I was certain there wasn't enough air in me to speak much less shout. He neared me and the other two stayed behind. One grinned, leaning on the shoulder of the other who kept his eyes down. He pointed at me then himself and muttered in the quiet one's ear. Grime and sweat covered the three of them.

"I," I started.

"Yes, child?" He patiently answered and held a hand to me in encouragement. The tips of several fingers were missing. I glanced at the two behind him.

"I am looking for the stonemason's apprentice."

"You have found him," he nodded. I briefly bowed my head and bent my knees. Not nearly as far as I should have but I didn't trust the shaky joints to keep me from collapsing to the ground. "I am Hermannus, the stonemason's apprentice."

Air, I thought, air.

"My name is Agnes," I whispered. "I am Johannes' sister and have come to ask for introduction to Dammo." I held just enough air for that.

"My Son," Hermannus announced and the quiet one's eyes snapped up. The other shoved him as he cursed in anger and spat. Hermannus took three powerful strides to him and knocked him down, bloodying his lip.

"This is why you wait," he growled.

I backed up several frightened steps until I caught the quiet one's stare. He looked down again and I stopped.

"Yes, Father," he said and it puzzled me because they appeared the same age.

"Dammo, this is Agnes, Johannes' sister and she has asked for you."

Again I dipped and bowed but Dammo whitened as if there were suddenly six of me: male, heavily armed and headed right for him. The third man whispered in Dammo's ear, causing him to redden as he modestly crossed his arms over his hairless chest.

"Ivan," Hermannus warned but Ivan held his hands up in submission and stomped away into the trees. Brush crashed under his heavy feet and I thought how embarrassed my mother would be for him, disturbing the forest with his passage.

I took a curious step toward Dammo. My own shyness was a fault I rarely had to overcome and I felt positively brave when faced with his. I wanted to take his hands and comfort him, to let him know I knew exactly how he felt. A small push of pressure in my chest made me put my hand there as I cleared my throat to ease it.

I saw no sign of Ivan or Hermannus as I followed Dammo toward the sound of the river. He walked off without a word following our introduction and with a tilt of his head, Hermannus sent me to follow. As the flowing water came in to view, Dammo stopped and pressed his lips together in frustration.

"Have I slowed you down?" I asked.

"No," he sighed and shook his head. "You can't cross wearing that."

The river looked relatively broad and slow and wouldn't be much deeper than my knees so I reached down between my legs for the back of my skirt and pulled it up high over the front. I tucked the hem into the heavy leather thong around my waist, baring my legs. Dammo swallowed and turned his back before striding off across the water. I followed, my shorter legs working against the cold current and I had to be careful not to slip while Dammo was so sure footed I thought him part salamander. His long dark hair bound out of the way behind his head distracted me as it swayed in time with his bare shoulders.

On the other side, he waited for me to cross then remembered his manners, offering his hand as I stepped up to the shore. Thinking myself safe, I stopped paying attention and slipped. Dammo grabbed me, turning to take our weight on the rocks and slicing his elbow on a recently broken stone the water had not yet tendered. He inhaled between his teeth as I turned to see what he'd done.

"Let me see," I said. He shook his head, fingers tightly gripping the gash.

I looked up the bank and scrambled into the trees. Only a few steps in I found what I needed and pinched off a small handful of leaves and stems before turning back to the river. Dammo stood behind me still holding his arm. I shoved the bitter leaves in my mouth and forced his fingers from his elbow. The cut looked deep and the possibility of sickness from the leavings of whatever animal last shat on the rocks wasn't small. I drew my little knife and sliced a strip from the hem of my skirt as I led him back to the running water where I washed it out and pushed in the mouthful of weed before binding it with the cloth.

"Keep it on as long as you can," I said. "You know the plant. If it comes off, wash it and bind the chewed leaves to it."

Dammo nodded and I spent the rest of the afternoon following him along the bank in search of large oval stones. He pried them out with a heavy stick and I followed him back to the pile. After four such trips I made to follow him into the woods but he held his hand up.

"Thank you for seeing to my arm. Goodbye, Agnes."

He walked away and my heart broke.

I hurried to my Mother, sad and fearful. By the time I found her, my tears dried and I regretted letting Dammo walk away.

"Don't be sad, child. Don't be sad," she whispered. "I hunted a rabbit and found some good roots."

The little skinned creature looked surprised but they always did when splayed out like an X on a pair of sticks. I'd not eaten since breakfast and a full stomach with my mother would warm me as much as the fire. We tossed the sticks and bones into the water to be carried away and not tempt any night visitors and bedded down as the sun fell. Dammo's deep eyes and strong back haunted me as I slept and eventually his voice did as well.

"Agnes…"

Gritty fingers, faintly scented with river mud brushed my cheek. I reached for them as my other hand rubbed my chest to soothe building pressure. His hand felt cold and real as I worked my fingers between his and turned my head to rub my lips and nose over his palm.

"Agnes, come with me," Dammo's voice whispered in my ear. His hair fell on me as I opened my eyes and his hand gently covered my mouth, stifling my gasp. "Please."

My mother had rolled away and lay curled in a tight ball against the cool night. Just a few minutes, I thought. I could go for a few minutes. I wasn't afraid of him. Ivan, yes, but not Dammo. I nodded and our hands came off my mouth as he pulled me to my feet and silently led me to the road. We crossed and re-entered the trees, his steps as soft as mine. As we reached a small clearing, the full moon broke from the clouds and to reveal his face. Not the timid young man I followed at the river but someone as brave as I felt, emboldened by the soft darkness hiding our shyness not only from each other but from the rest of the forest. His hair hung loose past his shoulders, now covered in a simple tunic.

"I'm sorry, Agnes," he whispered. "As I walked away I imagined I could feel your disappointment. At first I thought it was with me then I realized I hurt you so I returned to the stone pile but you were gone."

I put my hand on his chest and felt his heart pound with nervousness his voice wouldn't betray.

"I watched you and your mother until you were asleep and then I came to you," he whispered as he took a step closer and put his hands on my shoulders. I nearly fell into his moonlit eyes with his next words as they filled me with happiness.

"You're the most beautiful thing I've ever seen, Agnes. I never expected a woman like you would ever come to me. I promise the only pain I will ever cause you will be the sting of our first coupling," he whispered. "I will be your friend and your lover. Your protector and guard. If you will have me I will cherish you as my own heart and never leave your side."

I let his words sit in the following silence then pressed my chest into his as my arms reached around his neck and he gasped as if he felt the deep attachment taking hold in my chest. The pressure passed leaving me with nothing in my heart but Dammo.

"I will have you, Dammo," I whispered. "I couldn't bear to watch you walk away again." Then he pulled my feet from the ground as he carried me to the edge of the clearing and lay me down on a soft bed of sweet grass and fragrant wildflowers.

Chapter 31

Paul's clock promised another fifteen minutes sleep but I had to lift my head higher than Wendy's legs to see it. She sat in the dark, smoothing my hair from my face. I felt so close to Paul following my dream. Agnes' new bond to Dammo felt exactly like mine to Paul. Through all the years it hadn't changed at all.

"That morning I watched Agnes walk away. I stood on the road for a long time just as saddened by her leaving as she seemed. Her dirty old dress lay on the ground by the river so I washed it and found a sunny spot to hang it to dry. As the afternoon wore on I felt her line still connected to mine and I worried things weren't working out with Dammo.

"A man must have earned his mate. Found it within himself to move past the self-centered mindset feeling immortal gives him. Selfish arrogant behaviours thinking of nobody but himself. It happens to the women on my side of the family, too. In his first life he's wired to listen to the grownups; they're all he knows. His second is the first of what can be hundreds of years of 'holy shit it worked.' Short, violent, pointless lives. There is no reason to offer a man in that stage of his life a mate. Imagine my daughter bound to me for centuries refused over and over again or worse bound to a man who is as much a danger to her as he is to himself.

"It isn't often they don't bind together quickly but sometimes it can take days or weeks. After I put the rabbit over the fire and the roots in the embers I went to the road to wait for her. She'd been crying so I knew she was ready for him but he wasn't ready for her. At least she thought he wasn't. I sensed him following.

"I can only arrange the introduction and send my daughter on her way. They must find each other honestly to have a strong bond. I fed her and tucked her in with me. Dammo watched us and I lay awake listening to her sleep. He woke her and led her away. It wasn't long until he made his promise to her and she accepted it. Her child's line had been bound to mine but in that moment it set and she became mated to him.

"Before dawn I put my woollen shawl and her doeskin boots with her dress. I tied them together with a leather strap then I hid in the forest and watched. Dammo brought Agnes to the quiet fire. She called to me and listened in vain. She cried. He picked up the small bundle and offered it to her. Agnes held it to her chest. Dammo whispered to her and dried her eyes. Then he put his arm around her and led her away."

"Thank you, Mother," I said.

"No need to thank me, Little One. The memory was yours. I simply shared what I remembered. You filled in the gaps."

"Oh, still woozy," I said as I sat to turn the alarm off.

"Get a shower," she laughed. "I'll fix us something then I'll get in there after you."

Jack's car crunched the gravel in front of the house as she sent me down the hall so I grabbed clean clothes from the bedroom and warmed up the shower. I dug out the Advil and washed them down with a mouthful from the sink. The summer well water tasted funny but my cache of bottled was long gone so I didn't have any choice. Paul had assured me it was safe though he made a face when he drank it. I was glad Jack would drive. When I closed my eyes to rinse I had to hold on to the wall. Too few hours passed since Wendy and I turned in.

Darkness surrounded as I pulled the bathroom door shut behind me, quieting the fan. I paused in momentary panic then picked up the sound of gunfire through the living room window.

"Wenns?" I whispered.

Nothing.

I inched down the hall then left to Paul's desk, remembering Wendy left our guns there when we went to bed but I found nothing as I knocked things to the floor. A stack of paperwork Paul put on hold to look after me scattered then the crash of his lamp and a speaker from the computer.

"Wenns!?" I tried even louder then the stink of Damian's men blew in the window.

"Wendy!" I yelled imagining the hard wind outside carried the sound of Stanton's breathing to my ears. I clutched at the stomach of my shirt with both hands as I backed into the corner. During the night, wind pushed the front curtain open about a third of the way and everything was black outside. The gunfire continued.

"Wen—" I tried again, choking out a sob. I squatted down out of sight in my corner and pulled the collar of my tee over my mouth.

"Commander?"

I didn't answer. Another burst of gunfire made me yelp. There'd been so much of it when we rescued Dana and hearing it pounded fear deep inside me.

"Anna? It's William Taggart."

"William?"

"Yes, I'm coming to you. Stay put."

"Okay," I said, feeling very small and more than a little embarrassed even though I was still scared half silly. He banged his knee on the coffee table and kept going.

"Am I close?"

"Yeah, William," I stood and reached out a hand. His brushed mine and I pulled it back in panic before trying again and taking it.

"We have a small problem at the gate," he paused when the sound of more shots came to us. "I need to get back to the radio but I couldn't leave you hollering away your location."

Taggart pulled on my hand and I followed.

"My guns—" I said.

"Downstairs, Commander Vega brought them to me. She said you'd had a couple and shouldn't be out taking pot-shots at the moon." He was unnecessarily blunt but I held my tongue, glad I wasn't alone in the dark. As we went downstairs I read Jack and locked on. There was a fresh burst of rounds.

Shit, Baby, the words appearing in my head felt angry and calling me 'Baby' felt more than slightly condescending. I didn't like being reminded I was nowhere close to being a grownup. *How about you try a little harder to NOT give my position?*

I hadn't thought about Jack sneezing in a dark firefight.

Sorry, I sent. *I'm with Taggart. Where's Wendy?*

Your brother-in-law has her and you better keep your ass in the house. Ross is pinned at the gate and we're trying to distract them.

Can any of them read far enough to know I'm here?

The front door stood part open at the bottom of the stairs.

"You got your shoes on?" Taggart asked.

"No," I answered and opened the closet to pull out a pair. He lit a flashlight for a half second so I had an idea where my runners were then he disappeared back into the common room. I heard him talking to someone between stutters of muted static from the radio. Dim light shone out from under the infirmary door and I hoped we wouldn't need Doc Flood tonight.

Fuck, Jack sent after another half minute. *This isn't a regular run on the place. They're not coming any closer or backing off. They're not really shooting at anything and won't get close enough for us to hit. Something's up.*

I thought about running south to help but without my guns I'd just be a distraction to our own men who'd have to look after me. After a quick peek into the dark common room I crept to the front door then out.

Got an idea, I sent to Jack as I made my way down the darkened front porch then over the rail and into the trees.

Get back in the damned house.

I ignored him and paralleled the road west to the warehouses.

What the hell do you think you're doing? Jack demanded.

I'm ending this bullshit stalemate before you all run out of bullets and have to start throwing rocks.

Damn it. Don't make me come after … wait … got a couple splitting off and heading west.

Really? I sent, trying to convey surprise but I wasn't really. *Tell them to turn around and go back. I was headed west first.*

Go back, Jack sent.

"Anna."

I stopped dead as cold metal pressed the back of my neck. *Jack?*

"It's William," Taggart said. "You still want to be my friend? Right now you're the best thing to ever happened to me."

Taggart has me, I sent as I raised my hands.

Good, you're safe now.

Fuck, Jack, I struggled with our connection as I tried to keep it together. *He's got me in the trees with a gun to my head.*

Shit, shit, shit, Jack sent as I concentrated on relaying everything to him like I had before.

"Keep your feet moving, money bag," Taggart said. "Dead pays enough for a long holiday on a warm beach but I prefer alive for a permanent vacation. Bet you prefer alive, too."

I kept shuffling in the dark. Hurrying over the uneven ground would put me on my face and I could still see a spot from the brief burst from Taggart's flashlight.

Be good. Do what he says. I'm coming.

"I think I'll accept your friendship, brief as it will be. You put your shoes on and quiet as a mouse you left the house and hid in the trees. Saved me the trouble of getting you out and nobody knows we're strolling un-chaperoned."

I'm gonna fucking mess this bastard up, Jack sent.

Uh huh, I replied. Taggart grabbed my hair and pulled me to a stop as two men I couldn't read stepped out in front of us. *Company, two of them.*

Ghosts? Fucking ghosts? Jack sent.

"Secure her," Taggart ordered and I felt tape go over my mouth from one as the other put a cold metal cuff around one of my wrists.

Jack? I had an idea what he meant and as he confirmed it I shook in side feeling truly blind in the dark.

Like Joshua. Can't read 'em. Not family.

"Heeler, this is Whippet," Taggart said.

"Whippet Heeler, go ahead," a voice came from his radio as the second cuff rattled shut.

"I have your morsel."

"Affirmative, Whippet. Heeler out."

Two flashes close in either side deafened me and I cried out as my knees buckled. The short chain between the cuffs caught my nose as I tried to cover my ears. Taggart pulled me up and dragged me along.

Anna! Anna! Anna! Anna! Jack sent. More than just emotion, his panic came through and spiked my already straining heart.

Here, I replied as I stumbled. *Just Taggart now.* Two green smears filled my vision and I couldn't even hear my own footsteps.

When I say so, drop, Jack ordered. I was half way to the ground anyway. I felt tears on my face and my fear frozen lungs burned as they tried to keep up with Taggart's pace through the trees.

Down, Baby.

I let my knees go as I felt Taggart's hand torn from my arm. After a few seconds of muffled struggle Jack's weight covered me.

Don't look, Jack sent. I couldn't see a damn thing yet anyway but a pair of gunshots made it to my ears as I felt Jack's hands up in my shirt then at the side of my head clipping something on my ear. A hand on my waist attached something heavier. A flashlight came on next to Jack and I looked up to see Joshua's face in it.

"Anna? You okay?"

I furiously nodded as I tugged at the tape. Jack sat me up and gently held my hands as Joshua pulled off the tape.

"Good you were on Jack's private channel. Taggart would have heard your chatter over the main one," Joshua said. I nodded again, understanding what Jack attached to me.

"They bought him, Josh," I said, probably too loud so I could hear over the ringing in my ears. "I think he shot the other two so he wouldn't have to share the bounty."

"I know, Little Sister. Jack heard everything," Joshua said. He put a hand on my cheek. I leaned forward on Joshua as Jack rubbed my back. I could be a grownup about losing one of the men who was family but I sniffled on Joshua, thinking about losing him. It would break his parents' hearts. He didn't get another shot on the other side and hadn't done anything to get caught up in my family troubles other than being Paul's brother.

"Lost your earpiece, Roberts," Joshua observed.

"Yeah, it got snagged on the brush. I'll get it." Jack answered as Ross ran up. "I'll see what I can find to get those cuffs off. Meet you at the house."

Ross and Joshua each took an elbow and helped me to the road.

"I'm sorry, Josh. I panicked with all the shooting," I said. "I went out to help and got spooked and ran the other way to hide. Then I got disoriented and told Jack where I was because I didn't know which way to go. I couldn't even tell where the shooting came from. Then Taggart was behind me. The other two showed up. They didn't even look for the radio. He killed them, Josh. There's a price on me and he wanted it to himself."

"That your statement, Little Sister?" Joshua said and put an arm around my waist as I lost my footing.

"Yeah."

"I'm going to be up all night with paperwork," Joshua sighed.

"Ah. Damn it, Josh. I have orders for you before I split." I had an idea how to get Joshua and the others who weren't family out of the compound before trouble came. Tonight's incursion had been an education for me. We reached to the road and I leaned in close to Ross and Joshua.

"Sig needs you and Lieutenant Wight to truck out with your teams by noon. Gear for an assault on some rural buildings. We think they have a big cache of weapons. Not sure if they are supplies for the men bothering us or where they're headed. Hold up in Vegas. Rest, stay sober. The Colonel will be in touch within ninety-six hours with a go-no-go."

"Got it," Joshua said. I felt bad for lying to him and relieved he bought it. "You have her Ross? I gotta deal with the other two."

Ross nodded as Joshua turned his flashlight on and stomped back into the trees.

"I know what you're doing, Anna," Ross whispered. "Paul's going to be pissed you sending half his men to Vegas."

"Ross…"

"For what it's worth I'm not going to interfere. The only man you don't outrank is the Colonel and I'd look like an idiot for trying to make you look like one." Ross put an arm around my shoulder and I leaned my head on his as we started walking back to the house. The lights were back on and Wendy waited on the porch.

"This isn't their fight," he whispered.

"Some big trouble is coming. When they come, I want you to run. I don't want anyone dying defending a bunch of wooden boxes," I said. Wendy reminded me of that. Just a place. "My daughter was born here. You heard her first cry in that house. This is my home but it's no home now when I'm here alone and Damian's men won't stop calling. Get the Doc out of here with some bullshit after Josh and Wight leave, send out as many as you can and abandon this place before they show up. Paul says they're coming in a couple of days."

"We'll need everyone to take out their nest," he agreed. "And Taggart may have given them a lot of intelligence. We'd be fools to make a stand here."

Jack ran up with an earpiece on. He took my hands and freed them.

"Wells?" Joshua called from the trees.

"Yeah, Richards," Ross answered. He disappeared toward the sound of Joshua's voice.

"Stupid thing you did," Jack said.

"Yeah? He was going to drag me out of the house anyway and nobody there to help but Doc Flood light blind from the infirmary."

Jack took my elbow and nudged me forward toward the house. "Stupid thing," he said again.

Flood ran out the front door with his medical bag and Wendy stepped out behind him. I looked behind me and saw Ross pointing into the trees then he led the Doc in. Jack and I kept going.

Wendy got her arms around me on the porch. "Anns, you okay?"

"I'm getting a shirt made, Wenns. Save you all asking."

Wendy laughed as she pinched Jack's stomach. He stepped back in surprise as he got his hands up to protect himself.

"He's so ticklish," she said as she tried again. "And pink. Look at his cheeks. Dana's on the sofa all packed. He'd be driving off without us if he knew where we're going."

"She's coming?" Jack stammered.

"You're going to hurt Wendy's feelings," I said. "Commander Vega is my replacement for the next few weeks until the Doc says I have my shit together."

"I need a word," he took my arm and pulled me to the far end of the porch. I glanced back at Wendy but her smile hadn't faltered.

"How the hell are you going to explain how we get there to her?" he demanded.

"Anything in the car; we didn't all show up naked last trip did we?"

"You ever been driving with Anns, Jack?" Wendy asked from right behind me. Her approach had taken us by surprise. "It's a fucking rush."

"I swear, Wenns, if you do the roller coaster thing again I'm dropping you off on one," I hissed. It looked like Sig told her what to expect.

"Wooooo," Wendy howled as she walked away, both arms high in the air. "Your guns are in your bag. I'll get it."

"God damn it," Jack said. "I thought the Colonel just brought her along so you'd have some female moral support."

"Which is why I set her up with you rather than hanging out with her?"

Jack reddened.

"Maybe showing *you* how I get around is what's going to land me in trouble. Maybe I'm one of the best kept secrets of the Canadian military."

"Maybe you're full of shit," Jack muttered. "I have no idea how you pulled any of this over on the Colonel."

Dana stood at the door and Jack took his bag since it looked like the weight would topple him. He unlocked the trunk and we put everything in as the Doc and Ross approached.

"You are not cleared for anything, Commander," Flood said as he eyed us loading the car.

"I need to drop off my replacement, Russell," I answered. "Then I'll be right back. I promise."

"Alright," he agreed.

"They're all dead," Ross whispered when Flood was gone. "One had a thready pulse but Doc called him when he got there. Josh has your statements?"

Jack and I nodded.

"Alright. You can sign off on them when you get back. Safe trip."

Wendy piled in the backseat with Dana. She had a bright orange iPod in one hand and powered off her phone with the other. Mine was already off in my bag and Jack took the queue to shut his down. When she finally looked up, she noticed Jack in the driver's seat.

"Jack's driving?" she demanded, half yelling over the boom boom boom in her ears. "You never let me drive."

"If you behave I'll let you drive next time," I yelled but she looked out the window and didn't hear a word so I turned and pulled out an ear bud. "Briefing… remember to close your eyes when I say so Wenns, Dana?"

"Yeah, yeah," she pouted. "Jack gets to drive."

Chapter 32

A pitch dark alley greeted us. Wendy's half cut off *ROLLERCOASTER* still rang in my ears. I stood six inches away from a dark crack in a stuccoed exterior and when I stepped back I saw it ran up both stories of a motel. Double rows of lit and unlit bathroom windows ended at a quiet street at one end and a park at the other.

"We're here?" Dana asked behind me. I turned to see Jack scanning the building. He pointed to the park end.

"Yup, they're here," he said before he glanced at Wendy and clammed up. If she heard she pretended to take no notice. We drove around to park out front as far from the building as we could get. Patrick and Mason appeared outside one of the rooms. I read Camille as we drove around and felt better than I had in days in spite of my rising anxiety. What happened with Taggart told me exactly how much I was wanted and how badly I needed to stay away from her.

"Come on, Pops," I said to Dana as I helped him out. "Let's go see our babies."

"Yeah," he said as I thumbed a tear off his cheek. We quickly approached the hotel. Patrick took Dana and me to one door and Jack got Mason by the elbow and walked off with him whispering in his ear. I hoped whatever he said wasn't pleasant.

"Virtue has an adjoining room with Ray and your sister. Marie has her own. The guard dogs in another," Patrick told me and looked coolly at Wendy. He'd learned to dislike Halford and Mason. I put an arm around her and tugged her to me when I introduced them.

"Patrick Fletcher, this is Commander Wendy Vega. She's my replacement for a couple of weeks."

They shook but Patrick showed nearly the same stunned look Jack did when he heard she was coming.

"Your sister thinks she's in labour again," Patrick continued as he glanced at Wendy before turning his attention to me. "Ray says it isn't going anywhere but she sure gets uncomfortable during the night. Just pretend she's right, please?"

He tapped on one of the doors, three and three, then Ray opened up, a little mop of brown hair on his shoulder. I dove for them and he got an arm around me as I buried my face in Camille.

"Thank God," Ray breathed. It felt like I'd been away forever. "Thank God."

"Anna?"

I looked past his shoulder to see Alina propped up sideways against the headboard of the bed with what must have been most of the pillows in their four rooms. Ray put Camille in my arms and I went to my sister.

"Dana?!" I heard Virtue in the other room and a little squeak from their baby. "Sweet Lord, Dana!"

Camille's eyes popped open at the sound of Virtue's voice and she got her hands in my hair and her mouth at my throat. Ray put a bottle in my hand as I sat on the bed with Alina and tucked baby in with her bottle. Alina rubbed her stomach and sighed.

"Patrick says the baby is coming," I said, glad she was talking to me again.

"Mm hm," she sighed again.

"You know if you were really in labour you wouldn't be talking through them, right?"

She opened one eye then the other. "Of course I know that. I'm so damn uncomfortable on these cheap beds I want it over. Ray's unnatural attraction to shitty mattresses has topped itself this time." Then she noticed Wendy standing with Patrick. Ray turned like he was seeing her for the first time. "Who is that?"

"Alina, this is Commander Wendy Vega. She's been my friend and mentor for a long time. She's, um, my stand-in for a few weeks."

Wendy came over and shook her hand.

"Wendy, Lieutenant Ray Jackson, my sister's other half."

Ray took her hand and looked at me for some insight but Wendy gasped like she'd forgotten something.

"Lieutenant!" she exclaimed. "I have something for you."

She stepped over to her bag and pulled out a palm sized box.

"Lieutenant Jackson, Colonel Iverson sends his deepest apologies he couldn't do this himself and has asked me to in his stead. He'll speak to you personally next time he sees you and promises not to get it all wrong like I'm going to." She opened the little box. It contained two pairs of small silver bars. "Congratulations, Captain Jackson."

"Captain?" Ray repeated after a moment.

"I saw Major Richards briefly the day before we left," Wendy added. "He said to pass along his congratulations to you as well and to say these weren't his. You get your own."

Ray laughed and Alina reached for his hands to see but pulled him over Camille and me to kiss him. I knew Ray well enough to know when he was uncomfortable with attention so I wasn't surprised when he changed the subject.

"Replacement?"

I looked down at Camille.

"Hey," Alina said as she turned my face to her. "What's going on?"

Camille sucked air from her empty bottle so I put it on the dented night table and put her on my shoulder. Her hair felt soft against my nose and still smelled of lavender from her bath. Wendy sat by my legs and rested a hand on my knees. I felt my breathing ease and knew she did something to help me.

"Don't tell Virtue, please? Or Marie?" I forced in a big draw of air. "There was some trouble getting Dana and I was …" another gulp of air. "Assaulted," I chose.

"No, Sweetie," Alina sighed as I watched my tears fall on my daughter. I nodded.

"She was raped," Wendy whispered. "She's off duty for a few weeks and I'll be here in her place."

"But we're safe here. You're safe here," Alina's voice shook as she shuffled closer and got an arm around me. I looked up at Ray; his hand was over his eyes, squeezing his temples.

"I killed him, Ray," I whispered as Alina started to sob. "They know. They paid off Paul's new Security Chief to try and kidnap me the night we left. You know you're all in more danger with me here."

He nodded and leaned down to hold Alina and me. Camille softly snored as Alina struggled to keep quiet.

"I think about you going through it alone, Sweetie," I whispered as I leaned on her. "The happy things you've filled your life with since. Knowing I already had those things to come back to got me home. I've kissed my husband again. I'm holding my baby. I've never been so scared but knowing what I had waiting, I never felt alone.

"I'll be back as soon as I can. I promise."

I looked past Wendy to see Dana in the door to Virtue's room, his face as wet with tears as mine. He put his hand on his heart. *Thank you*, he whispered as he bowed then blew me a quick kiss and closed the door behind him as he returned to his family.

I stayed with Camille and Alina until both slept. Alina's stomach calmed and she cuddled Camille in her arms. Ray attempted to fall back on his medical training to cope with my news and I attempted to let him but Alina shut it down barking at him to be my brother and not my damn doctor. He'd always been more my brother anyway.

Jack and Ray had to walk me out the door as dawn arrived. We stayed too long and I knew the longer I delayed the harder it would be and the more danger I put them all in. They were only a couple of hundred miles from the place we'd been found barely two weeks before and Ray needed to pack everyone up and hit the road before Alina went in to real labour.

Half way to the car, I stopped and waited for Jack to try and push me along.

"Anna?" Patrick's voice came from behind us. "Sorry, Anna. I know you have to go. Marie's up early and wants to talk to you. She said it won't take long and I don't think she'll take no for an answer."

Marie was pacing when Patrick let me into her room and crushed me over her belly before the door closed behind me.

"I was so scared," she blurted out. "They said you'd be back by morning then the next day and you didn't come back."

"I came back," I whispered, still feeling the peace Wendy projected when I gave my bad news to Alina.

"Every day you didn't and now Patrick says you're leaving us for a few weeks and I have to tell you something. You're a great friend and you've always been kind and honest and I haven't done the same and I need to be honest."

"Okay," I said. She let me go and pushed her hair back over her ears, looking away as she unhid her face. I took her hands and guided her to the bed to sit beside her.

"It's okay, Marie," I whispered unable to imagine what it could be. She breathed hard, squeezing my fingers with nervousness. "Whatever it is we're friends, right?"

She nodded then took a couple of deep breaths to settle herself.

"When I left... Keith," she hissed his name. She hadn't said it since we'd rescued her and would tune out any conversation when his name came up. "When I left over the gambling it wasn't the first time. I left him in January for the same thing. He promised it was dealt with so I went back but he lied."

"I don't understand," I said, trying to figure out why it had anything to do with me.

"He moved me out in January," she said shaking her head at my misunderstanding. "Sent me to a hotel at the other end of town. Told me not to open the door for anyone. Said he was in trouble and to keep the door locked. Then after a couple of days there was a knock. I was so scared but I peeked out the hole. It was Paul."

I knew Paul had gone to help protect her but her fidgeting worsened as I felt nervous along with her.

"I let him in. We talked for a while. He said things were bad between you and you'd left him."

"I had," I said. I'd attacked him and run off. Things were about as bad as they could get.

"I don't know what I was thinking, Anna. I was so scared and he was so supportive, calm," she raised her eyes to mine as she worked her top lip between her teeth. "I don't know what was in my head. I slept with him."

After I got the air back in my lungs I tried to speak but only sobbed as my head dropped on her shoulder. I knew exactly what happened. Paul had gone to Edmonton and asked for her, just like Keith said he wanted him to do and she'd accepted him. I held on to her and cried. I tried to remember Jack's inheritance and how Paul helped me through it. How it meant nothing to me by the time I got back to Paul. I told myself it would have meant nothing to Paul when he walked out her door and how it meant nothing now. With the exception of the word 'responsibility,' she was as nothing to Paul as Jack was to me.

"You're right, Marie," I choked out. "I'd left him. Didn't think we'd ever be together again but I didn't think ..."

I felt her nod as I straightened up. She grabbed a handful of tissues from her table and we shared them.

"He never told me," I said as I pulled myself together. "We've worked hard on us since then. Things are good. I can't fault him or you for what happened."

"Thank you," she whispered.

"We've learned so much about each other since then. It's behind us. We'll talk about it," I told her as I felt some resolve behind my words. "It'll stay in the past where it belongs."

"Thank you," she said again. "I have to tell you everything. It happened again the next night. And again two nights later. He was with me when he got a call you'd gone home ... Anna?"

My knees hit the floor hard and I got my hands out to keep from planting my face on the smelly carpet. I kept my lips sealed tight as my stomach rolled.

Unforgivable! My mind screamed. *Unforgivable!* I remembered Jack saying again was unforgivable. I remembered how Paul could have been sent out to kill himself for the unforgivable sin of trying to pick something from my line back at his Father's. I was angry with him and revolted with the consequences. Unforgivable meant no Paul. Unforgivable meant Camille with no father.

"Anna?" Marie's voice rang in my ears like I was underwater. Her hand rubbed my back and I tipped over, pressing my spine into her knee. "I'm sorry. I'm so sorry."

"Don't say anything, Marie," I begged. "Please? I can forgive. I can try and understand. Please, I love you both. I don't want anyone judging you for something you can't change."

"You fainted, I'm so sorry," she breathed. She was right about that. Punched in the gut and the head and tingly on the floor ready to run away screaming as soon as I could get on my feet fainted.

"I'm not angry at you, okay?" I tried as I grasped at something true and rational to keep from sinking any lower in front of her. "I gave too much blood for Virtue and getting Dana and bringing him here I haven't eaten or slept much. I'm upset. I'll be okay and I'm not angry at you."

I pushed myself up sitting, keeping my arms locked and my neck straight to hold my head level even though the room kept spinning. My husband was a cheater and I was a danger to my daughter and I had nothing and nobody.

"Whatever happens, Marie, telling me was the right thing. We'll figure it out," my head steadied so I pulled her up with me as I stood more for my balance than hers. She just had a month to go and didn't need to worry about me. I hugged her as I got a few deep breaths. "I love you, Marie. You're still my friend."

"Thank you," she whispered.

I held her smooth red hair to my teary cheek and kissed her through it. Then I turned my back before she could see my face and let myself out. Wendy waited outside and grabbed on to me, letting me lean heavily as I cried quietly on her shoulder. She didn't ask why.

When she let me gom she cradled my cheeks in her palms and peace flooded me.

"No, Wenns," I whispered. "This pain will last longer than you can take away."

I stared in to her brown eyes as she put a hand on my chest and kissed me; lips soft and warm on mine. "My love will always be with you, Little One. Our paths will cross again."

"Yes, Mother," I said then I turned away and walked to the car. Jack had been watching us, leaning on the trunk with his arms crossed. He opened the passenger door as I approached but I opened the rear door for myself and got in, turned towards the seat and curled up in a ball.

"Patrick gave me directions to the 94 west out of Fargo," Jack said as he got in. I ignored him. I ignored his offer of breakfast and coffee. I ignored the radio and would have been surprised with how well he sang any other day of the year but today when anything good only reminded me how dead I felt inside.

I woke once, screaming Paul's name. Jack pulled over half-sideways on the side of the highway and went over the seat to pull me up sitting. I pushed him away and turned to the window, wrapping my hands around my ears.

"Did something happen to Paul?" he anxiously asked. "Your connection to him… did you feel it flicker out for a moment?"

"No."

"Lunch? You haven't eaten much more than a bite since we got Dana. You're hungover and dehydrated in this heat. You're getting some water and food before you get sick in my car. And because I can't stand to see you like this."

Jack used the doors to get behind the wheel and pulled out.

"First diner we come to I'm feeding you."

My silence consented.

"I don't mind driving all the way back," Jack said. An hour later I'd gotten down a few bites of a burger and a couple of fries between sips of bottled water. I started to setup our jump without bothering to tell him but I was sure he knew by the worsening handling of his car. When I told him to go, he did.

Chapter 33

Early evening saw Jack and me appear in an alley in Reno. He held my elbow and steered me half-way to his car by the time I figured out we arrived.

"This isn't your place," Jack observed as he sat me in the car.

"No."

"So?"

"Reno," I sighed. "The frequencies we recovered. There's been chatter about a big push on the compound. We're still three days from check in."

"Other than the incursion when we left?"

"Have to assume so, Jack."

"Fair enough."

The alley passed behind the hotel Paul and I stayed at when we were married, the only place in Reno I really knew. I didn't think I cared if Jack checked us in or not but after a sixty second drive around the corner to the lobby, I realized I wanted to go straight home.

"Wait here," Jack said and went in.

As I watched him at the counter I decided it was better if we stayed here even though I wanted to go after Paul. Even after the long drive home there was little hope of me cooling off enough to reasonably confront him or stay silent until I could.

"You okay?" he asked when he let us in our room.

I stared, daring him to pursue the question. He knew how Alina fell apart when she heard what happened. How I'd done the same after saying bye to my baby. Then Marie.

"No, I get it," he said. "You can have the bed. I'll take the sofa."

I shrugged. I needed to burn off my rage at Paul before I returned home and wasn't going to do it in the room.

Jack sighed and put his arms around me, squeezing my crossed ones between us.

"We'll drive up in a couple of days, okay? You can have the bathroom first then we'll go out and you can blow off some steam."

That sounded good except I didn't want Jack with me when I did it. In the bathroom, I started the shower and undressed and got in.

Anna?

I paused, not sure if I heard her or not.

Anna?

When I looked in the mirror she stared at me around the curtain. I stepped out but she was faster and leaned toward me with her hands on the counter by the time I reached to it.

So what are you going to do about it?

I wrinkled my nose. She knew damn well what I was going to do.

You're going to kick Paul's ass?

I laughed.

Didn't think so. You're thinking you'll get a little payback.

Would it hurt? I whispered.

Maybe. Maybe you could think about why he did it and when you've pulled yourself together you can deal with it better.

Maybe you could let me sort this out.

Maybe lashing out at Paul isn't going to fix what Stanton did to you.

Maybe it will help.

Doing the same thing he did will hurt you both and make it that much harder. It won't undo what he did. Think about it. His wife was crazy, possibly forever. Why wouldn't he take a second? He didn't know you'd take Damian's line. You'd never know he'd done it and wouldn't be hurt by it ever. And you did threaten her.

So?

He knows exactly how big a mistake he made by going back to her.
And?
Don't make the same mistake.
I looked through the door toward Jack in the room.
Using Jack like that is a shitty move, Anna. You're right, he wouldn't tell you no but he's too loyal to you to spend like that. You know Paul would go after him even though he did the exact same thing.
What do I do? I asked.
You know what to do. You've done it before. Won't hurt anyone but yourself. When you've calmed down, go tell Paul you forgive him.
If I forgive him, I said but she was gone.

I washed up and carefully combed and blow dried over the bump on my head before I put my old clothes back on. She was right. I'd been wiped out inside before and knew exactly how to deal with it. When I stepped out I didn't look at Jack. He went in and as soon as the door closed, I pulled off my shirt and put on a tight black tank top I'd packed to wear under other things. Then I waited until I heard Jack's belt hit the floor.

"Jack?" I called from the room.

"Yeah?"

"I'm going down for off-sales. I'm not up for going out. Want anything?"

"Six-pack."

I took a twenty and his keys to slow him down then I locked the door behind me. Down the stairs and toward the restaurant. If Jack tracked me I had to look like I was going where I said. I hurried a block past the restaurant then took a right to a rough bar Denis and Ray had favoured. Men, pool. The women who went in there may not have gone in on someone's arm but they certainly left holding one. I hoped I was far enough away Jack would have to look for me.

When I entered, several sets of eyes turned my way. I stood and let them get a good look as the door pulled shut behind me. Some went back to their drinks. Some didn't. The ones who didn't watched to see if I waited for my man to follow me in. None did, so I went to the bar and took a seat. I hadn't gone looking for trouble in a long time.

"Hey," I called down the bar after a couple of minutes, shaking my money at the barkeeper. He had his eye on me and the door expecting someone to show up and take the seat next to mine.

"Miss... is?" he said, noticing my ring as he spoke.

"Gin and tonic, double," I said. He nodded and set me up. Gave me back fourteen from my twenty. Prices were steep if you weren't drinking beer. At least I thought they were; I hadn't ordered one in a bar before. I hoped someone would volunteer to buy for me before I ran out and running out would take about ten minutes. I wasn't here for conversation. I was here to drink until someone offended me and then I'd show him just how upset I was.

I pulled the dried lime off the side and squeezed the juice in as best I could. There wasn't much but I could make out a few bits of pulp on top of the ice. My nose went in the glass and pulled in the smell. It reminded me of the time the buyer of one of the cars Kenny and I stole offended me. He wouldn't take it because of the smell of the gin I'd spilled inside. I couldn't see more than brief flashes of my surroundings and Kenny managed to convince the man the car was so badly parked the owner must be passed out drunk on his bathroom floor after spilling the drink in the car himself. Kenny held my arms down as he did and pulled me back about six feet as I tried to get my fingers behind the buyer's eyes. We only received about ten percent of the usual for that one and I had to wait outside after that.

Next I wet my lips on the edge of the short glass. Then I licked them. I hadn't touched the hard stuff since I was fifteen. Except once. Stuck to beer and wine. I knew what would happen. Anna would drink until she blacked out and would hear about how bad she'd been later: fights, police cars and my father the next day. Exactly what I wanted now. Minus the police and my father. It tasted just as I remembered; a very liberal double well worth the six dollars. Half went right down.

I kept the glass at my lips and counted to ten. By nine the numb shiver I expected made its way to my feet and I took another big swallow. Ten minutes later and half way through my third, I buzzed all over. I swirled the remains in my glass and clumsily slopped as my chair shifted. My line had a nibble.

His voice wasn't particularly deep but he sounded more sober than I felt.

"I think the man you're waiting for just arrived," he said. Right to the point.

"Mm," I said without turning around as I took another mouthful of gin and put my glass down. My wedding ring was in plain sight so either he hadn't seen it or didn't care. I got my feet under me and stood, at the same time sliding over to fit between him and the bar. When I turned around he took a half step closer, dropping his eyes for much longer than necessary before looking at my face. He was my age and tanned. Even though he dressed for the seedy bar his expensive haircut and full carat earring suggested arrogance and money more than toughness.

"I have to do community service," he said. "Perhaps I could make sure you're not bothered? This is a rough place."

I felt grateful his eyes dropped because it took a moment to pull myself together after his bad line.

"You have no idea how much I needed to hear that," I whispered and his eyes snapped up. Not with surprise. Intense interest filled them and something else suggested he didn't give a shit about ever seeing me again.

"Really," he inched closer. I held the bar rail behind me in both hands, keeping myself on display.

"My master hasn't fed me much lately," I said as I lowered my chin and looked up at him. He watched my mouth move. "I chewed through my leash and ran away. Now I'm lost so I came in here. I guess I'm on the lam."

"What'll it cost me?" he asked, his words thick with something other than liquor.

"Drinks," I whispered as I let my eyes walk down him, not caring what I saw. He backed me into the bar, claiming me already, and wouldn't take it well when I said no. He was all creep and I didn't feel bad about going a round or two with him. He was perfect.

I picked my foot up and ran the inside of my knee up the outside of his. He leaned right in and got an arm around me.

"I want to go home drunk and feeling very bad about what I've done," I whispered. "Do you think you can handle that?"

"Clem?" he called without taking his eyes off mine. He pointed to my drink and held up two fingers. "The little lamb is moving to my table."

Chapter 34

I woke feeling nothing but sheets on my skin, my head split and enough light passed the edges of the curtains to chew my nerves. Jack sang in the shower. I closed my eyes and held still, hoping the pain would move on if I played dead. It didn't so I listened to Jack and the running water for another minute before I sat, pulling my knees up and the blankets over my shoulders. My hands went up, cupped around my eyes.

When Jack came out he glanced at me and finished dressing. His jeans were already on.

"Are you finished whatever it was you were doing last night?" he asked.

"Yes, did we?"

Damn that hurt. The last hangover I had was two years before with my sister and felt nothing like this.

"Did we what?" he asked as he sat too hard on the bed.

"Why am I naked?"

Jack defensively crossed his arms. "So what if we did?"

"Oh, shit," I said as I pulled the blankets up even higher over my nose.

"We didn't," he said. "Not for lack of trying on your part. You threw up gin all over us on the way back here. I rinsed out your clothes but they're going to need a wash. I thought you'd just make me go dancing or some shit. I didn't think I'd haul you out of a fight."

I noticed the half digested gin smell under the blankets. He'd taken my clothes but it was still all over my skin. It didn't help my stomach. Neither did the image of me dancing.

"I stink, Jack."

"Yup."

"How did I do?" I asked. I sort of remembered a fight and Jack showing up. More came to me as I thought about it; an alley and a dumpster, the surprised look on the face of the man from the bar when his nose started bleeding. Jack holding me back, yelling to stay away from his sister then getting all over him in the bathroom as he pulled my pukey clothes off me.

"You scored a couple on your dance partner. I didn't let you score with me. I figured you wouldn't feel the same way about me in the morning."

"Crap, I'm sorry."

"You need to do that again let me know where you're going." He sounded mad and it hurt my head. "I thought you'd gone for a fucking walk and when you didn't come back I had to go find you on foot and thank you for not losing my keys. Found you in the alley. He had you half undressed just before you broke his nose."

"I'm sorry," I said again. "Thanks for bailing me out."

Jack moved closer and hugged me.

"You stink, Anna," he said after a few seconds.

"I'll get a shower then I'll be out until tomorrow. Turn around."

Jack got up and turned his back to me as I staggered to the shower. He asked if I was okay when he heard the rest of the gin come up and when I got out I found he'd tossed my clothes in the door. I put on underwear and the top I abandoned the night before then crawled in bed.

"Here." Jack shoved a glass of water at me. A couple of pills in the other hand. I took them and sipped at the water. "What happened with Marie?"

I put my hand beside my head to shield it from the bathroom light and looked at him.

"You were upset before you talked to her and ready to put your fist through something after."

That was true but I wasn't going to tell Jack. Even if I could forgive Paul, the men in the family might not feel the same way. I dropped my eyes and wiped my cheeks dry after half a minute.

"You don't trust me," Jack flatly said.

"I trust you."

He watched me for a few seconds. "Okay."

"I haven't done that in years. It never hurt like this before."

"No?" he laughed. "How old are you?"

"Twenty-five."

Jack laughed again. "Give it a decade, kid. The hangovers only get better."

"Never doing that again," I said, catching myself from shaking my head. "I'm sorry, Jack. I knew what I was doing. I went looking for trouble."

Jack picked up my right hand and looked at the backs of my fingers. "Hurt?"

"No."

"Come help me cheat at cards."

I pushed myself under the blanket and he took my glass. The bed only smelled a bit now that I was clean.

"Tomorrow. I owe you one. I'm not very good at being good, Jack."

"Really?"

"Funny man," I mumbled. "Can you turn up the air conditioning? I'll be less trouble tonight."

He got up and adjusted the air before turning off the bathroom light and making sure the curtains were closed tight. Then he came and sat on the bed beside me.

"That's the worst set of bruises I've ever seen," he said. He would have seen them when he got my clothes off me. They were deep and taking a long time to fade. Some were still as sore as they were the day I got them.

"That's nothing," I yawned. "You should have seen the other guy."

Jack put his hand on my shoulder for a second then he went to the bathroom. I heard water running and when he came back he put a cold cloth on the back of my neck. My stomach seemed to settle and it turned the nausea and headache in to two separate smaller problems.

"I did," he said and he lay down on the blankets facing me, watching until I fell asleep.

Chapter 35

The white cowboy hat pulled low over Jack's eyes came from a hatbox in the trunk of his car. A huge silver and gold buckle above his forehead sported an eagle. Not the whole eagle; just one wicked talon lifting off after providing him with the scar running down the side of his face. It sparkled in the millions of casino lights suspended overhead. He'd hauled me shopping and bought himself a red pearl buttoned western shirt and a new pair of jeans. The silver buckled white belt holding them up said ARMY and had been in with the hat. From where he sat at the black jack table, I couldn't see it or what he called his 'shit kickers' which were the most shabby and dilapidated cowboy boots I'd ever seen. Given the satisfied rumble that came from Jack's throat when he pulled them on, I guessed they were more comfortable than they looked.

He'd won and lost for nearly five hours; winning when I could see the dealer's cards and losing when I wandered off to the slots. Based on his quick tutorial of the chips and how much each colour was worth I guessed he was up more than ten grand on the night.

Are you sure this is legal, Jack? I sent.

Telepathy? Jack grinned at his losing on purpose cards. *It's not illegal.*

I still felt stiff and bruised and wanted to get off my feet. I was also starving. Jack glanced at me as he nudged his hat down a bit more. *Let me get another couple of hands in and we'll get dinner.*

'kay, I yawned. I'd conceded to a plain white shirt and jeans that didn't smell of half used gin. I lost the coin toss over the boots and even brand new they felt damn nice on my feet. The hat was a non-starter. After changing at the hotel we took a cab out for a late lunch then another to the casino.

Jack unintentionally lost the next hand.

"Got an eye on my man Jack," a voice behind me whispered. I pulled my shoulders up, wanting to crawl away from anyone behind me especially someone close enough his whisper wasn't drowned out by the noises around me.

Who the hell is this, Jack? I sent as I took a half step away then told Jack which cards he was up against next.

Shit, Father Bard.

Who? I took a couple more steps and turned to face a friendly enough looking bald man about my father's age though sixty pounds heavier.

"Missus Roberts?" he asked and his eyes never left mine. He made me uneasy like he could see right into me.

He convinced me to stop wasting time in places like this, Jack sent then I heard him call for a card. *Worked for the Army, redirected men with bad habits.*

I didn't answer Father Bard and took another step back as Jack exclaimed "Ha!" He gathered up his chips and abandoned the table. None too soon. Bard's stare opened a black hole in my soul and weakened my legs. His smile fell a bit and he took a step closer so I backed up a little, bumping into someone behind me.

"Padre!" Jack exclaimed as he took Bard's hand and shook it just before they got their left arms around each other, Jack careful not to spill his tray of chips.

"Jack Roberts," Bard said. "I hope we're losing in moderation."

Jack, help me, I sent. My hand found a chair back.

"Always," Jack replied as he turned then shoved his chips into Bard's hands and got an arm around me.

"Why is he looking at me like that?" I whispered.

"Like what?" Jack's arm around me tightened and he lifted my chin to look in my eyes. I strained to look past him to keep an eye on Bard.

He's looking in me, Jack, I held on to his arms for fear of slipping from his grip. *What is he looking for?*

"Is your wife okay, Jack?"

"She's not my wife."

He thinks he caught us screwing around 'cause you're lookin' uncomfortable, Jack sent. *That's all. I'll explain. It's okay.*

I nodded and took a deep breath.

"Your sister?" Bard tried.

"No," Jack said as we turned to face Bard. I kept my eyes down and held on to Jack. "Let's get a table somewhere quiet, Padre. We'll chat."

The closest thing to quiet Jack could find was a round booth near a hallway leading to the restrooms and it was only quiet because we had neighbours on one side. The noise and lights from the casino reached everywhere. Jack and Bard sat across from each other and I slid in next to Jack. I still hadn't looked up, appearing much like the beaten puppy I held inside. Jack's hat went over his chips on the seat between them.

"Didn't think I'd see you in a place like this, Jack," Bard said. "You been staying out of trouble?"

I shivered as I twisted my fingers together under the table and I didn't mind when Jack's arm slipped around me. His hand gently rubbed my shoulder as I moved a little closer to him. His nearness calmed me down like when I was near Paul.

"More than most," Jack replied. "I pulled her out of a bar fight two nights ago and in return she was going to pull me out of here when I got two hundred bucks in the hole. Had a feeling she's lucky."

Bard chuckled at Jack's hat. "I'll say. So are you going to introduce us?"

"Father Bard," Jack pulled me up a little straighter as he spoke. "This is Commander Anna Richards, Canadian Forces, on loan to my unit."

"Ma'am," Bard said as he offered his hand over the table. My hand trembled as I held it out to him and shook, barely keeping eye contact.

"Hello, Father," I whispered. He offered me an honest smile and gave my hand a little squeeze.

"On which vessel are you currently serving?"

"I don't. I do odd jobs," I tried to explain, hoping he would think I couldn't talk about what I really did.

"Ah," he nodded. "A paper rank. That explains your age."

"Yes, Father," I whispered, going back to examining my hands.

"Anna was resupplying my team a week ago," Jack said.

No, Jack, I sent.

"Surveillance but a couple of my boys were picked up and we were overdue. We were able to put together an extraction right away instead of having to come back. Anna set up with Finn, remember Finn?" Jack asked. Bard nodded. "I heard she was good but man, I swear she can shoot the laces off your boots with her fuckin' eyes shut, you know?"

I put my hands over my ears but his voice still came through.

"We had more than we expected coming in after us. Finn and her made quick work of 'em but they got caught from behind. Finn got it," Jack rubbed his throat.

"Fuckin' shit, Jack," Bard said as he ran his hand up over his face.

"Yeah, asshole got Anna alone for a while if you know what I mean."

"Ah, damn. I'm sorry."

"Nothing for it now," I said quietly as I shoved my hands between my knees and squeezed them tight.

"I left him in fucking pieces," I added looking right into Bard's eyes. "Fucking pieces. Jack's taking me home tomorrow. I want to go home. I want Paul."

"Paul?" Bard asked. "Paul Richards?"

"Yeah. I met her through her husband."

I pulled Jack's arm off and slipped away to the ladies room where I locked the door behind me and sobbed silently even though the sound was more than covered by the laughter and flushing of the women in and out of the stalls. The thought of Paul at the compound fighting to protect our home was too much. Angry with him as I was I loved him desperately and needed him safe. The necklace he gave me on my birthday and my engagement ring were locked in the safe bolted to the armoury floor in the bottom of the house. I rubbed my hand on my chest and remembered the way its smooth weight felt on my skin then I put my lips on my wedding ring. When I finally left, I stopped short of the end of the hall, not sure if I was quite ready to join them. Neither could see me.

"So what are you doing with her?" Bard asked. Jack didn't answer. "Don't shit me, Jack. You two move like you're connected. You've been intimate."

"Shit happens in the field, Padre. You know that," Jack said.

"With a married woman?"

"Yes," I answered as I stepped around the corner and took my seat beside Jack, upset he was questioned about something that was none of Bard's business. They had drinks and there a glass of wine for me so I picked it up and took a sip. The waitress also brought out the food Jack ordered. I hadn't paid attention at the time and noticed everything was covered in hot peppers. "It's not a secret and I'd rather not spend the evening discussing my personal life with someone I just met. No offence intended."

Bard raised his hands in polite submission. "I apologize, Commander. Sometimes the counsellor in me takes a bit to turn off."

My stomach rumbled, still grumbling as I put my hands on the source of the sound.

"Wow, smells good," I said as I dug in, my appetite still out of control from the night's black sleep. "I had my doubts hanging out at the casino would be a good time, Jack, but dressing up like a cowboy is better than I thought. I'm glad I lost the coin toss; these boots are damn comfortable."

Jack and Bard laughed, seeming less awkward now the food pulled me together.

"Wish I had them the other night. Would have done more damage to that little pissant than with my runners. I needed to lash out, you know. It's been a bad week so I ran off on Jack to this rough bar. Let this slime ball pick me up; promised him he could roll me later if he got me drunk. There was no way I'd let him touch me no matter how drunk I got and he seemed the type to push it when I said no. Jack said I'd busted his face pretty good by the time he found me. I don't really remember much between picking him up and the hangover. Paul doesn't have to hear about that does he?"

"He's gonna hear, Anna," Jack answered.

I sighed. The emotional release of talking seemed to propel me along but only so far.

"I guess I can eat like this. Camille will be weaned by the time I see her again," I said, tossing back the last of my wine to hide my souring mood. Jack gently shouldered me to get my attention; if he put his arm around me now my white shirt would be covered in barbeque sauce. He waved the waitress over and pointed at our empty glasses. She nodded and left to get us another round.

"You and Richards have a baby?" Bard asked, giving Jack a suspicious glance. I nodded.

"That's the most you've said all week, Anna," Jack said. "I started to think you couldn't make a sentence more than three words long."

I turned to give Jack's remark an appropriately smart reply and noticed he'd tucked his napkin down the front of his shirt like a bib. Good thing too. I laughed as I wiped his chin. "It's going to take more than a paper napkin to get this stuff off. I think it stained your stubble."

"Stop it, Ma," Jack rolled his eyes and whined. "Damn it. I'm a thirty-seven year old man."

"Baby," I muttered as I added another layer to Jack's bib.

Jack ordered a pitcher of beer for them and I ordered a coffee. Their chat turned to the good old days and men they knew.

It's kinda funny, Jack eventually sent to me. His bib was gone and they were well in to their second pitcher after innumerable whiskey shots and toasts. *He's all up tight about who I've been with but his wife left him when she caught him with a pair of strippers.*

I laughed, forgetting we were still connected. Bard eyed me.

"Sorry, I was just remembering that idiot's pick up line the other night. Said he had to do community service and offered to make sure I wasn't bothered. I was thinking of my sister. She'll laugh her ass off."

Bard laughed then put his fist on his chest and belched, making his eyes bulge. "Excuse me, folks."

"I'll take you home tomorrow," Jack said when we were alone. "Then we'll finish this ass blowing assignment and get our lives back, okay?"

"Sounds real good, Jack," I rested my head on his shoulder. "Maybe you want to see Wendy again."

"Wendy?" he sounded surprised. "I'm sorry about that. I guess you heard."

"Why would you apologize? No skin off my nose. You know that."

"Suppose," Jack said as he topped up his glass. "It's hard to explain."

"Let me guess. Courtesy says you're supposed to be celibate the rest of your life, ready to step in if I become widowed?"

"Something like that," he said. I noticed his slur was getting bad. He sulked a moment. "I have you to look after now, Baby. Spending the night having unprotected sex with a stranger was reckless of me. That's what I apologized for."

"Wendy wouldn't have let it happen like that if she thought she was risking anyone and I don't think you would have either."

"Guess not," Jack pushed his hat on and closed his eyes, ending the conversation about Wendy but only for a moment. "You know, I doubt you're a real Commander though the Colonel acts like you are. He wouldn't send a replacement if he didn't believe it. And you and Wendy seem so close. I can't decide what's cover and what's the shit."

"Some day I'll tell you all about Sig and Wendy and me. But that's not going to be today," I answered. It was all bullshit anyway.

Until a year before I'd been a hermit and a nomad and a photographer. Hiding by running from everything. None of what Jack considered cover story and bullshit was anywhere close to the truth.

"Did she say anything about me?"

I pursed my lips. Much as I didn't want to talk about my sex life with Bard I was even more uncomfortable talking about Jack's. It reminded me too much of the night in the hotel which was nearly forgotten and in all honesty made me a touch jealous. I didn't want him again and irrationally didn't want him with anyone else.

"I'm guessing that's what you were talking about when Joshua overheard. That's what set him off."

Bard still wasn't back yet.

"She said you're impossibly creative," I conceded.

"Yeah?" Jack asked and as I watched I swore his ego grew half a size.

"And your pillow talk is obscene."

"You knew that," he shrugged and I turned red.

"She said you have this little spot beside your tail bone and when she grabbed you there you purred like a tomcat."

"Like the one behind your ear," Jack suddenly leaned in for it with his mouth, his hat riding up as he bumped it in to the side of my head and he grabbed my ribs, heading north. I got my hands up and pushed him back just in time. He was upright a mere second before Bard came around the corner.

You're drunk, Jack, I sent as I slid over and stepped out of the booth.

"I'm up," he announced and staggered off down the hall.

And I do not purr like a tomcat, I sent.

I glared after him as he burst out laughing. Bard picked up the pitcher for a refill then changed his mind and put it down.

"I don't get you and Jack," he said. The spicy food and beer not only turned his face red but the whole of his head. I wondered if that happened to all men and their hair just hid it.

She said you called yourself the Jack Hammer, I made up.

Privacy please.

Maybe she's seen you fight? I tried, feeling owly at him for making a pass and taking out Bard's renewed curiosity on him.

Can you please just fuck off for a few minutes?

"What's not to get, Father?" I asked.

"You're more comfortable together than most honestly happy couples I know yet I'm tempted to believe you when you say nothing is going on."

"I like you, Father Bard. I'm sorry for my reaction earlier. After what happened last week having the attention of a stranger so close behind me set me off for a bit. You're a nice smart man and you'll figure it out."

I winked at him and he scowled.

Worked in construction? I tried.

You're im-fucking-possible sometimes, Anna, he answered.

Can I wear your hat?

No.

Jack's boots made their way up the hall.

Are we fighting? I asked. *Bard just said we're like a really happy couple and it would be way out of character for us if we are.*

You'd know if we were fighting.

I shoved myself over to the middle to make room for Jack but he stayed on his feet. Barely.

"I think we're gonna call it a rodeo, Padre," Jack said. He pointed at his chips beside me and I passed them over.

"Yeah," Bard agreed. "Glad I have tomorrow off. Working for the State here in the city now. Business is good. I'm in the book, Jack. Look me up next time you're in town."

Chapter 36

Dawn hurt Jack far more than me. The motel restaurant didn't offer take out so I waited for him to be upright before we went downstairs for me to eat while he soothed his hangover with black coffee and toast. After cashing out his chips and splitting the wad of cash between our pockets, we'd taxied to the room. Jack fell asleep on my shoulder and I dragged him up the stairs to the second floor after rolling him out of the cab. I put his hat on the table and hung his shirt on one of the permanently attached hangers outside the bathroom. His first boot came off okay but the second suddenly let go, landing me on my ass as Jack fell on the floor laughing. Given my drunken behaviour two nights before and his at dinner it was a damn good thing we hadn't gone out drinking together that first night in Reno.

"What are you going to do with your winnings?"

He winced. Too loud. I pulled out my phone and put it on the table beside my coffee.

"I know we're supposed to drive back today but I thought we'd have heard something," I tried, much more quietly. "You gonna make it?"

"Yeah," Jack leaned back and closed his eyes.

"Sorry for being grumpy," I said.

"Shit, Anna," he said. "I can't believe I tried to put the moves on you. Paul's gonna pop me again and that's if I'm lucky."

If he would tell Paul everything there was nothing I could do about it. Paul would have to understand because I'd talk to him about Marie long before Jack got a chance to brief him on our behaviour.

"Yeah? Think you're in trouble? I promised a stranger sex for drinks, beat him up and thanked you for your help by getting my vomit covered body all over you."

"That's my fault and I deserve one for that too," Jack said. His eyes were still closed even at the darkest table in the room and the way his tone became firm I realized he was giving me an old fashioned parent to child lecture. "Paul warned me you're not obedient. I didn't realize what he meant until you took off. You've always been rebellious but I couldn't imagine how bad you are until I had to look after you myself."

I glared. "Screw you, Jack. I don't need a babysitter and I didn't realize I'm such a burden. I can look after myself just fine and I thought I was taking care of you since I was keeping us away for a couple of days. And while you're off screwing yourself why don't you go find something pointy and covered in splinters and pound it up your ass."

"Wow," he said after a moment. "You finished?"

"Yes," I said as I deflated. "I told you I was grumpy."

"Three day hangover or are you hormonal or something?"

"Fucker, you're going to make a six hour car ride a real treat you know?"

"Bitch," Jack answered but he didn't need to say it. His bloodshot eyes spelled it out. We stared at each other as the waitress refilled our coffee.

"Douche bag," I quietly replied after she left.

"I'm going to put you on the God damn bus to Redding and follow in the car," Jack said as his straight face started to fail.

"Yeah? Go have your period so your mood improves," I said as I started laughing. "Shit, you're a good sport, Jack. Sorry I'm grumpy."

He closed his eyes again. "Your language gets worse the more time we spend together. You know that, don't you?"

I told him the same thing I'd told Paul when he pointed it out. "I'll try and be more aware of it."

"Thanks," Jack said. "It's ... I picture you, um, not like that."

"My connection to Paul makes us more like each other. Is the same thing happening to you and me?"

He smiled. "Sorry about that. I guess I caught hormonal from you."

"If we pick up anything from each other that makes us annoying to be around we'll go see your pal Father Bard for counselling, okay?"

"Sounds good," Jack patted his seat and held his arm out so I came around and joined him. "I know you've had a bad week, Baby. I'll take you home today and it's all down hill from there, okay?"

I wasn't so sure Jack's continuing to call me Baby wasn't a put down to remind me he was the grownup and I was the child. He said it like a term of endearment but still. My phone chirped so I reached across the table for it, Jack's hand slid down around my waist.

"It's Paul," I sighed with relief. "Message says 'today?'"

I typed in 'affirmative' and put it down but it sounded again a minute later.

'ETA?'

"He wants to know when," I said.

"We don't usually ask that kind of thing but I guess he's worried about you," Jack said, putting his empty cup down and leaning back in his seat. "Tell him six hours."

I typed it in and put the phone down.

"And I don't need your help to be obnoxious," Jack muttered.

"Obviously, Jack ass," I pulled a twenty from my pocket and slapped it on the table then headed for the door.

Some days I wish the bitch would slip and fall in the shower, Jack sent. I hadn't realized we were still connected from the night before and came to a sudden stop, fists balled at my sides. At least I was nice when I was hung over.

You want to know how to make yourself more appealing to women?

I'm dying to find out. My day couldn't get any worse.

Go fall on your sword, asshole, I sent.

Been there done that.

"Err," I growled as I got moving again. *I'm gonna go drop your shaver in the shitter.*

Cripes Girl, don't make me run after you.

Then try being less of a beast, please? I'll try too. Maybe it's time for separate hideouts.

I waited outside the door for Jack with my arms crossed.

"Okay," he said when he came out and followed me to our room to finish packing. I drove the first shift and Jack navigated us free of the city before falling asleep. Within ten minutes of hitting the highway the beer and jalapeños came back to haunt us and I had to pull over and open the widows. The heat was stifling already anyway.

Apparently there were several ways to set up the seat and mirrors behind the wheel of Jack's car. One was illusive and unobtainable due more than in part to my messing with them when I drove. I stuck my head out the passenger window to avoid his bitching but he smacked the bench seat between us demanding my attention because two hours under the weight of my girly butt had destroyed his 'comfort grooves.' He claimed that's what made his head hurt; no longer the whiskey from the night before. After another twenty minutes of bickering I pretended to sleep only to be jolted upright when Jack roughly slid the seat back.

"I don't think I'm good for your blood pressure, Jack," I said.

"There's a lot of me you're not good for," he muttered.

I ignored him.

We stopped in Sacramento for a silent lunch. Jack got some of his colour back after chicken and coffee. I became more edgy and irritable, unsure what I'd tell Paul and wondering if I even should. I guessed simple was sufficient. If I stuck to the facts maybe we could avoid a blow-up. I was ashamed of my plan to get back at him and even drunk after getting it out of my system I'd still tried.

Jack filled up again in Redding and half apologized for his irritability. I didn't believe him. He didn't want to get back in the car with me any more than I wanted to get back in with him. A few days with him proved how much of a jerk he could be. He wouldn't be putting his arms around me much if at all when we got back which would please Joshua. And me for that matter. I'd only spent two weeks at most with him anyway. Paul had said most of who we were was upbringing so if Paul and I were so good together this time around Jack and I proved to be the counter example.

Jack lightened his foot as we neared the place we'd jumped the beaten up truck.

"Wha—" I started as the smell hit me and I pushed hard into the passenger door as our bags tumbled around in the trunk. The car struggled to grip its summer tires on the gravel and as we took off back the way we'd come, I turned around enough to see a couple of men on lawn chairs at the gate.

"No, Jack," I moaned. They'd taken the compound.

"Get us out of here!"

"Paul," I said as we took a corner dangerously fast and skidded toward the trees at the side.

"I can't outrun what they're driving. Do it. Now!"

I pulled off my seatbelt and knelt beside him looking out the rear window.

"Turn around, Jack," I begged.

"Did you hear me?" He bellowed, turning me around one handed and shoving me back in my seat. "There's at least ten. If we go in we won't be driving out so get us the fuck out of here!"

My mouth hung open, tears of disbelief lining my face.

"My place," Jack said, more calmly. "There's not a lot of time."

"But Paul," I blubbered.

"Whether he's in there or not he wants you to run for your life."

I glanced behind us at the still empty road but it was so windy they could be just a couple of hundred yards back and still out of sight.

"I hate you, Jack," I whispered as I forced myself to focus, picturing Paul and I making love in the trees the night we killed Archer.

Chapter 37

I found my bearings first. Jack stared off toward the far end of his backyard. I checked his hands and pockets for his keys. Nothing; they would be in the car. Then I got a heel behind his foot and a hip on him and knocked him over before I bolted to the front yard to look for the car. As I reached the front yard, Jack tackled me from behind and turned us so I crashed on him when we hit. He rolled us over and pinned me on the ground.

"No," he said. He held my wrists above my head, only tightening his grip when I struggled. "And if you break in and steal it I'll have you arrested and you can sit safely in jail."

"I hate you, Jack," I struggled.

"That makes two of us. Are you so dead set on learning every grownup lesson the hard way?"

"Paul," I gasped trying to get a thigh up hard where I could hurt him and failing.

"Paul," it came out in two patronizing whiney syllables. "I don't give a shit about Paul."

"Bastard!" I screeched as I swung my head up at his chin but he turned away. I dropped my head hard on the thick grass beneath us. Then again.

"You're only hurting yourself," Jack said. "What I care about are those four children we left behind a few days ago. I care about handing over two thirds of our leadership to my brothers for no reason at all and I care about my second even though she's doing everything she can to get herself killed. That's all.

"Paul is coddling you like a dumb mate. What were you thinking when you took my father's line, hm?"

"Get. Off," I grunted as I squirmed. Cold wet tears filled my ears and I shook my head to try and get them out.

"You thought you'd have Paul again on the other side," he said a little more softly. That was the truth. I stopped fighting turning my head away. "You thought after living out your long happy lives you'd be young and in love again. That's another lesson you have to learn but I'll save it. Nobody sees to your upbringing. It's unfair to you and makes you a danger to everyone else. If you were behind the wheel twenty minutes ago you'd have driven right in. If your heart is truly set on killing yourself fine but you're not taking Jack with you. There are children to protect and we need every man we have."

"I'm not a man," I sniffled. "I'm a woman and a mother, not a fucking man."

"Whatever," Jack said. He pushed himself to sit beside me. "Has he tried to prepare you at all?"

I glared at him as I remembered Paul's instructions to me the day I met Jack. Think like a leader. Put Camille first and the children were worth the sacrifice of every grownup in the family. Throwing myself away to get Paul wasn't a sacrifice that would help them. I opened my mouth and blinked at him, refusing to admit he was right.

"I thought so," Jack said. "You are the most disobedient child I've ever known."

"Damn you," I sighed as I rolled over, turning my back to him.

"Disconnect from me, Anna," he said. "We've been connected since yesterday. You're a mess inside and my head is still in pieces. We're feeding off each other and it needs to stop."

I pulled my sense out of Jack and listened as he got up and went around through the gate to the road out front. The car door slammed and then the trunk.

When I went inside after my private sulk I heard Jack in the kitchen. Water ran and the house filled with the smell of fresh coffee.

"Bring me your dirty clothes," he called. "We'll pack light. After dinner we'll give my motorcycle a once over and get the hell out of Dodge."

I followed Jack's voice to the kitchen. His bag sat open on the floor next to mine.

"Laundry is over there," he tilted his head to the left without looking at me.

I pulled out everything I needed washed and pushed the half open door out of the way. Jack had thrown all his things in the washer. I pulled out his new jeans so they wouldn't stain everything blue and tossed my lights in before starting it up. Jack stood in the door holding my bag when I turned to leave. He reached up above the dryer and pulled down a red and white checked shirt.

"Come with me."

I followed him out through the kitchen then down a hallway with a door on each side. He led me through a big bedroom and into the attached bathroom. The same bathroom we saw the woman and Camille in. I stared into the glass and tried to catch a glimpse of us.

"Toss me anything you're wearing you want washed. Got you a shirt to borrow if you want," he put the shirt down between the sinks and squatted down to rustle around in the cupboard underneath. He came up with a couple of fat red candles.

"They used to smell like something but I've had them for years," he ripped the plastic off and plunked them down on the side of the big tub. "It's got jets and stuff. At least the candles still look nice."

He sniffed the air then went to the window and pulled it open. "Forest always smells good. Women like that, right?" He asked, finally looking at me. Warm sweet air blew in and pushed out the closed up stale smell.

I nodded.

"Anyway," he continued. "There's nobody around for miles so I thought if you can ignore me you could have some time to yourself. Dinner won't be ready for a couple of hours."

"Thanks."

Chapter 38

"This is really good, Jack." Thick homemade soup with dumplings. All the ingredients came from the cupboards.

Jack blew on his steaming spoon and raised his eyes to me. "Thanks," he said.

"I'm surprised you weren't put in the chow rotation."

"I was. You weren't there."

I put the phone down for the twentieth time since we started eating.

"Sig not answering?" he asked.

"No."

I still had no luck reaching him. Paul was alive but I needed to know if he was in the compound or not.

"Are you sure we're safe here?" I asked.

"We'll be gone in a couple of hours. I'll get you somewhere safe to sleep it off."

We ate a while longer in silence before I tried the phone again. Still no answer. Maybe Sig thought I'd been compromised in the compound and wouldn't pick up. If I tried him enough he might be able to tell I wasn't anywhere near it and would answer.

"You know if he's in there I'm still not letting you go after him."

"Alone or at all?" I pushed my empty bowl away, then my chair and pulled my knees up to give my bruise a break. My wrists crossed and grabbed my ankles.

"At all. You know Paul wouldn't want it."

"I don't give a shit."

Jack took our dishes and put them in the sink. The light coming into the kitchen changed colour as the afternoon ended making the room feel warmer than it actually was. He pulled out a dish rack and set it up to drain back into the dish water.

"I got this," Jack said and nodded to the back door. "Garage key is hanging by the light switch if you want to pull my motorcycle out."

"Sure," I said but I didn't get up. Instead I curled around my legs, enjoying the stretch I felt as I pushed one shoulder forward, then the other.

The washing machine beeped in the other room so I got up to move everything into the dryer. When I came out, Jack stared through the walls of the house, running water almost to the lip of the sink. I pulled a sleeve up and quickly leaned past him and turned it off.

"What?" I whispered as I felt around for the plug to let a bit of water out.

"Shitfuck."

I sent my sense out in the direction I thought he looked and didn't hit anything. Whoever it was they weren't within my range so I scanned behind the house.

"Two out back," I whispered as their smell reached me. They weren't moving, just holding position.

"They got my attention first. One can read further than I can. He knows we're here alone."

"Shitfuck," I said. "Where's my weapons?"

"It won't matter," Jack said. "It's Soros."

I looked out the back window and couldn't see anyone. With the lights off inside and the sun up they would have to come much closer to see in. I took the phone off the table and hit the redial then I stuck it behind some canisters on the counter.

"Do we shoot ourselves now or will he do that for us?" I asked. "Run?"

"We can't help anyone if we're dead. Co-operate. Learn what we can," Jack said. "Don't use your charm trick unless you have to."

I picked up Soros and another man on the road and pulled my borrowed shirt up over my nose. He stunk. The shirt smelled like it had been washed a long time ago and had been in storage ever since so I tried to focus on it instead. Something caught my eye outside and I turned to see the two men step out from the trees and into the small field that had replaced Jack's back lawn during the past couple of months. Jack put his arms around me and pulled me tight to him to shield as much of me as he could as his head turned back and forth trying to keep track of them all and hopefully not finding any more. I latched on to the line of one of them and ran it forward, skipping quickly, as far as I could.

"I don't see them leaving. We'll be in the kitchen for a while, they'll split us up, but they don't leave. It can change though."

There was a knock at the door.

"Keep your distance from me, just in case," Jack said as he went to answer it.

I dropped the blinds to cover the window over the sink and checked the back door was locked as I heard the front one open.

"RJ," Jack said. He didn't greet the other man.

"Jack," the voice sounded friendly. "Big brother. I didn't think I'd miss you at all but I think I do. I've been so bored since I don't have to keep you in line all the time."

Jack made an indifferent sound as there was a knock at the back door.

"I hear you've acquired something quite rare and beautiful. I decided to stop by and offer my congratulations."

Silence.

"Well, let's not stand around. Lead the way."

Jack came into the kitchen followed by the two men. My eyes watered as their smell stung and I pulled the shirt up tighter, wishing I wore perfume or even scented deodorant to help cover it up. One of them walked past me like I wasn't there and opened the back door, letting the other two in. They were dressed like Paul's men: button up shirts, jeans and handguns. Not at all what I expected even though I'd seen the bunch on the mountain. I reached across my ribs, pulling the shirt tight around me to stop any of the smelly air from getting up into it. The other stood by Jack across the table. He watched me for a few seconds then inhaled before he spoke, putting a face to the voice of RJ Soros. I'd expected him to look like a boogeyman instead he looked a lot like my father.

"Lucky, lucky, lucky," he almost sang.

Jack appeared to know what he meant. The look on his face said he knew exactly why Soros was here. I kept my eyes on Jack as he watched me and thought about the sudsy water filled sink behind me. It hid the scary looking kitchen knife Jack used to make our early dinner. I remembered he'd put it on the right, handle closest. Paid attention because I didn't want either one of us grabbing the business end. That and the phone the Colonel hopefully listened in on were all we had.

Soros tipped his head, seeming puzzled by my behaviour, standing there with my shirt over my face. Then he turned to Jack. "You know the drill, Jack. I want to know all about her."

One of the two who had come in the back door moved around behind me and held my elbows at my sides as Jack took his shirt off. His expression shadowed to blank and distracted at the same time. Eyes never left mine. The shirt dropped to the floor as his hands dropped to his sides. I could see the long scar running down his chest and knew what was coming. My arms tensed and the man behind me pulled on my elbows reminding me he was there.

Soros held out his hand to one of the men with Jack and was given a hunting knife. Smooth on one side, serrated on the other. Tip rounded with the point to one side. He took Jack's hand and put the knife in it.

"Where, where, where," he muttered. "Mmm, here."

He moved Jack's arm so the knife was at the top of his left shoulder.

"This looks good," he traced his fingers down Jack's arm. "This way I think. If you lie or try to get to her then the knife moves. I'll start it for you."

He pinched the blade between his thumb and finger and slid it back and forth. Pain flashed on Jack's face as a narrow trail of blood ran down his arm.

"No deeper than that, you still have to work for a living," he laughed. "When you get to the bottom I want another one an inch away."

Being held from behind by Damian's stink scared me. I felt pinned down and smothered, hearing Stanton's ragged breathing in my ear, fighting the desperate urge to get out from under it. I pulled my arms forward to distract the man behind me then I picked up my foot and slammed it hard into the inside of his knee.

"Bitch..." he growled and I ground my teeth to keep silent as he pushed my elbows up behind me until my shoulders creaked.

"Want another?" I whispered, picking my foot up as he pushed higher.

Soros didn't turn, he watched Jack as the knife moved then stopped as he got control of himself. I stopped my foot in mid-air then put it down.

"Harv," Soros said, "Don't hurt her. If you can't keep her still and quiet you'll have to wait in the car."

"Yeah, Harv," I said when he let me have my elbows back.

"Keep your toes out of the water, Sweet Thing," I made a face at Soros' back. "You might not like the temperature."

I felt Harv's nose in my ear and smacked it with the side of my head. I felt the sound in my teeth. Neither of us said anything and he backed off.

"Mmm," Soros said. He had pressed himself into Jack and put his lips to his ear. "What was it like getting to know the soft side of a hard case like that my fortunate friend? Does she show that much spark between the sheets?"

Jack didn't say anything.

"That wasn't a rhetorical question. I expect an answer."

"Yes."

I could barely make out Jack's wooden whisper. The knife stayed still.

"I thought our brother, the kind and gentle Mister Walker, was having fun with me when he tried to explain how he lost you a week or two ago."

I suspected Walker was neither kind nor gentle.

"He said your truck stopped on the road... no, froze was the word he used and he drove right through it. When he looked back you disappeared. Walker's a little nuts mind you.

"Then a few hours ago I'm having my second beer at Richards' front gate when you arrived. By the time I got up to invite you in you were gone. And no more than fifteen minutes later I get a message your front door opened. Nobody else would be coming here and I know you don't drive that fast."

Soros turned and tossed Paul's phone on the table.

"It's not like you to be so punctual. Perhaps it's your new Missus?"

I bit my lips together to keep quiet. He'd either taken it from Paul or from his desk in our apartment. Both images upset me.

"Our good friend Father Bard called me very early this morning. Apparently he's most upset you've been cozy with Commander Anna Richards while you're drinking too much and gambling. I told him we'd have a word. He said you were taking her to her husband today so I knew just where to find you. If she lies, Jack, the knife moves. Sweet Thing? How did you get here?"

I looked at Jack.

"Tell him," he said.

I felt my eyes narrow.

"I moved our lines. Our bodies followed."

Soros watched the knife. It stayed still.

"You can go anywhere?" he asked.

"No."

"And why not?"

"There must be a road for the vehicle." That wasn't a lie. I'd travelled without a vehicle but he hadn't asked about that.

"Any other times, Jack?" Soros asked.

"Involuntarily," he said after a moment. "She disappeared from my side and reappeared beside Richards when Archer was going to shoot him. She knocked him clear and shot Archer."

Again the knife stayed still.

"And what about when she's in trouble?"

"She got away from Father while his knife was in her."

"Knife in where?"

"Stomach," Jack said. "Above her navel."

Soros turned his back on the knife Jack held and looked at me. Then at Harv.

"What happened to your nose, Mister Harvey?"

I glanced at Harv as he shrugged. Blood had run down past his chin.

"Nosebleed," Harv said, obviously not wanting to get into trouble for not keeping me still.

"Go clean yourself up. I'll keep an eye on her," Soros said. "And get us drinks."

Harvey nodded and walked out.

"Funny thing about inheritances, Sweet Thing. Jack and I, we have the same mother. What's given to one is given to the other."

I glanced at Jack. I saw the pain in his eyes and I took a deep breath as nausea started to build in me.

"Jack and I, we have the same mother. What's given to one is given to the other," Soros laughed at his rhyme.

"No," I whispered. I started comparing Damian and Soros as he walked around the table in just a few strides. He took me by the elbow and turned me so he stood between me and the knife in the sink. My back to Jack so he could keep an eye on the knife he held. Then he lifted my shirt taking care to not touch my skin.

"There?" he asked as I got my answer about Soros' mother.

"Yes," Jack said.

I turned and sneezed. Should have done it in his face. Soros bent his knees, lowering himself, putting his mouth near the mark Damian had left on me then at the same time they touched his hand went on my belly. I felt tickling from his nose. Not tingling like I had with Jack. I laughed with relief.

"Give it a moment, Sweet Thing," Soros whispered. My laughter turned to nearly hysterical giggles as his lips and nose kept brushing my skin.

"You won't feel it, dipshit," I pulled in some badly needed air. "You don't have the same mother."

Soros straightened, his face showing the first emotion other than politeness since he came in.

"What?" He demanded.

"Either that or you don't have the same father," I said, getting myself under control. "But you smell so damn bad you must be his."

"Pardon?" he seethed.

"I said you're a dipshit, dipshit," I spat, filling up with anger at him. Anger for Stanton. Anger for his humiliating Jack by using him as a lie detector. I wanted him to make a move on me so I could get the soapy knife to his throat.

Suddenly, I blinked tears. My head turned away. My cheek stung as Soros' hand returned to his side. From the corner of my eye I saw the knife move.

"It's okay, Jack," I said. "I got this."

After a second the knife stopped. It had moved a couple of inches.

"Say it again," Soros told me as he watched the knife.

"You... don't... have... the same... mother..." I repeated.

"How do you know that?"

"I can figure those things out, you stupid dog fuck."

Soros' face twitched. Just his eye at first, then the cheek under it. His hand went to the knife on his belt. I shoved my tongue out past my teeth and ran it around the corner of my mouth, tasting blood from the backhand as I waited to see how much madder I could make him.

"What exactly are you having trouble with, Sweet Thing?" I whispered. "That you don't have the same mother or that you're a stupid dog fuck?"

He was fast, blindingly so, but I was faster. After I disappeared I reappeared beside him, my hand in the sink around the handle of the knife. Very grateful it was where I remembered. Then I disappeared again and found myself crouched on the counter behind him, his chin in my left hand and the knife at his throat. His knife still moved forward and he stopped it as lukewarm water dripped off my elbow and on to his shirt.

He started to turn so I moved the knife as gently as I could, feeling the tension between his skin and the blade only briefly before his skin submitted, letting the knife move.

"Is that any way to treat your mother?" I said in his ear.

"What?" His lungs emptied roughly and filled again.

"You can't inherit your own mother," I said as I looked at Jack. He hadn't moved and the shock on his face was a toned down version of the expressions on Soros' men who stood with him.

"I have your off switch," I said. "Release Jack or I'll flip it."

"Come here and say that, dumb bitch. I have Jack." It wasn't Soros. One of the men behind Jack spoke. I tightened my grip on Soros and on the handle and didn't move.

"RJ doesn't have me, Baby," Jack whispered.

My nose wrinkled since the smell from Soros multiplied with the bit of blood I released from his neck. Nobody said anything for a minute as I waited. There was no way I was going to put the knife down. I read Jack and found the stink in his line didn't belong to Soros. It belonged to the man who spoke. I wasn't going to fall for that again if I ever got another shot at this.

"Put the knife on your neck, Jack," the man behind him said. Jack did. "I'm going to count. If her knife isn't on the floor when I get to five you're going to use the one in your hand to show her your tonsils."

I didn't wait for him to start. The knife hit the floor as my feet popped out on either side of Soros and I sat behind him on the counter.

"Put it back on your arm, Jack," Soros said. He seemed to have himself under control again. "That it for the games, Sweet Thing?"

I put my hand over my mouth to yawn as I nodded.

"Wrong," he said, grabbed my arm through the damp shirt and pulled me from the counter, past the sink and canisters to the stove. Soros put my left hand over the burner about six inches and set it to medium.

"Jack, if her hand moves then the knife starts. It moves until she puts her hand back."

I could see my phone between the two middle sized canisters. Just a bit of the display where the timer was but if the line was open the light would have turned off long ago. I couldn't feel any heat yet from the element and didn't think I would feel much anyway but it still had high and my hand could get lower. Soros stepped away from me to the table. I heard them fill their glasses and smelled whiskey on his breath when he returned to stand close behind me.

"If you don't answer promptly, the burner warms up or I will lower your hand. Yes?"

No, I thought but I answered "yes."

"I hoped to inherit you," Soros breathed in my ear. "Even more so after hearing what you can do. Our son would be a great asset to Father's line."

He put his mouth on my neck and inhaled.

"You're in heat, Sweet Thing. My timing couldn't have been better. But now my plan is ruined and you've pissed me off."

My back stiffened and I leaned my head toward him to push his face away from me. Soros turned the burner from five to six.

"Let's get through this quickly. I have other business when I'm done with you."

I nodded. Quickly sounded good. I wanted a nap and a good breakfast in the morning before the black sleep came.

"You escaped Father like you dodged me?"

"Yes."

He turned and stood beside me leaning on the stove, glass to his lips as he watched the knife in Jack's hand.

"Then you killed him?"

"No."

"It's moving, Sweet Thing."

"I killed him the next time we met."

"Mm, it stopped," Soros said, pausing to take a drink.

"When and where?" He caught me with my lungs empty and as I filled them to speak he grabbed my hand and lowered it an inch. Bastard.

"February, the plane crash wreckage by my house."

"Were you merciful?"

"No."

He turned the burner to seven. "That's because you should have been. He's a devoted family man."

I didn't comment. My hand felt hot, uncomfortably so, and I imagined the element turning a little orange, like an angry blush.

"Why weren't you?"

"Revenge for my sister and for what he did to the dead woman and her baby."

"Mm," he said between sips. "What did he do to the bitch Alina?"

"He beat her, chewed her shoulder up with his teeth."

"She would have asked for it. Your cruelty was unjustified. And the others?"

"He made their bodies move," I said, remembering the eerie wailing coming to me through the flames and acrid smoke. "They screamed. She only had an arm left after the crash. He took her baby away and I had to get it back."

Eight. I wanted my hand back. I remembered the labour I was in then. The pain I rode up and down for hours. My eyes closed as I breathed, trying to disconnect myself from my hand like I had from the contractions.

"I caught up to him with the baby. I shot him twice in the leg with his gun and ran away..."

"Keep going," Soros said pushing my hand down a little further. "When you're finished you can have your hand back."

"I picked up the baby, took him to his mother. He bragged about my sister... told me what he'd do to my baby. I shot him in the shoulder where he bit Alina then in the knee of his good leg and he went down."

I knew the element held its temperature and didn't warm further but the damage the heat had done already made the hot air coming up hurt even more.

"I approached him... shot the fingers off the hand still holding his knife. The only good limb he had was the same one the mother had. I... I..."

Nine. A deep breath as I heard the dial move.

"Dropped on his good arm and put my knife in his heart. His life started to bubble out of him. The last breath he took came from my lungs and then he was still."

After a long second I heard the dial click and Soros lifted my hand.

"Release him."

Then Jack's arm was around me as he pulled me to the sink. I heard the plug come out and the tap came on as welcome coldness covered my palm. The hand holding mine was cut and bloody down to the wrist.

"I wish even half my men had her constitution," Soros said.

Sounds of a bottle on the lip of a glass. Then again. My stomach tried to heave so I breathed hard through my nose to keep dinner down. He wasn't going to see me lose it now. I turned and pushed my face into Jack. Then my sleeve came up and I felt the sting of a needle.

"I'm not inhumane," Soros said. "Leave her at the sink, Jack, if you want your arm closed."

"I'm sorry, Jack."

"I'll be right behind you," Jack answered.

I lowered my head on to the counter, putting it as close to the canisters as I could then I cleared my throat and sighed.

"Can you hear me?" A small quiet voice next to my head said so I cleared my throat again.

"He wasn't there."

The call disconnected.

I struggled to stay awake as the water ran then someone turned it off and wrapped up my hand. A hand under my elbow and another under my arm took me to the table and put me on a chair next to Jack. He didn't look at me. Soros hummed, putting stitches in the deeper parts of the cut to his arm and Jack's other hand held a half-full glass.

Then Jack pulled me up from the next chair over. I must have fallen on it when I fell asleep. Jack had a hand on either side of my face and looked into my eyes. I looked back into his, feeling nothing but his palms on my cheeks.

"Jesus, RJ. How much did you give her?" Jack's voice only went in one of my ears at a time. Someone picked me up around the middle and hauled me away. I watched Jack's face get smaller until it disappeared. My head hit something hard and I landed on something soft. The pain was gone so I dozed a little longer.

Paul

Chapter 39

The little clock beside the bed said one in the morning when I picked up Jack's gun from the mattress in front of me and climbed out of bed. My face felt sticky with half dried tears. I might have slept a bit, leaned against the wall, but I don't think I stopped crying. The carpet felt soft under my sock feet as I tipped my head back and took a few deep breaths to try and clear my nose.

I wasn't sure I should even bother trying the door. It made an extra click after Jack and Soros walked out and I guessed I'd been locked in. When Soros' man tossed me in here I hadn't paid much attention to what the knob looked like from the outside. If it wouldn't open I'd have to link to Jack and ask him to come to me. We avoided telling Soros about the way we communicate during his little get to know us session and I hoped he couldn't tell if I did it now. I could still smell him in the house, weaker but still pungent. Soros and the three who had shown up with him were still either downstairs or outside. Jack was in another room on the top floor.

I double checked the safety on Jack's gun. Holding it under my chin with my finger on the trigger and the safety off was stupid but it got them away from me. Well, it would have been stupid if I was bluffing but at the time I meant it. They hadn't even taken it from Jack and I'd grabbed it from his waistband.

I understood Jack had no choice but to take Soros up on his offer. I didn't have any choice either. Jack was dead either way. If Jack and I gave Soros what he wanted then Camille and I would live. Jack would be dead once we got to his Father's and I'd have at least nine months longer. And that was if we succeeded in giving dead Damian Howard the grandson Soros couldn't. Don't hesitate to act on a tough decision, Paul told me. Damn him, I couldn't afford to.

After I crossed the room to the door I still had to feel for the knob. Night was dark like this at home in the compound, unless the moon was out, and there was no moon tonight. I took a deep breath and turned the knob as silently as I could then I pulled. Cool air came in as the door swung past. Even surrounded by tall trees, enough light entered through the evening to warm my room. Weak light came up stairs and I heard a radio or maybe TV with it. I would have to pass through the light by the top stair to get to Jack's room.

I wiped my eyes on my forearm and walked as softly as I could to Jack's door. It didn't open after a minute. Maybe he slept. Maybe he thought I'd let Soros take us into the woods at dawn like he'd promised if we didn't get down to business. It was like the charm. The pain of tearing my marriage to pieces along with the pleasure Jack would have to take in sleeping with me. The alternative was the pain of whatever other charm games Soros invented. And the death of my daughter when Soros called the men tracking her and told them to move in; or failed to call to tell them not to.

My knuckles only paused a moment before I tapped a few times on Jack's door. There was no noise from inside so I knocked again.

"Jack?" I whispered, hoping my voice wouldn't carry downstairs.

Then I heard the soft rustle of bedding and a single complaint from his mattress followed by a creak of the floor. His door opened a few inches and I heard his voice but I couldn't see him.

"Hi, Anna," he said.

I waited a moment but he didn't say any more.

"I want to return your gun. I'm sorry I took it."

The small crack in the door didn't widen. I didn't blame him. It was only a few hours since I'd told him I'd rather shoot myself in the head than ever let him touch me again; standing there shoulder to shoulder with his asshole brother. I said it to lash out at Soros but there had been real hurt on Jack's face. Soros laughed and patted Jack on the back before pulling him from the room.

"May I come in?" I tried, not quite ready to apologize. "Please?"

He sighed and the door opened the rest of the way. Jack's hand appeared in the dim light and took my elbow, gently pulling me in. His other found his gun and took it. The door shut as I passed it and he put the gun on a dresser.

"You can tell when I lie, can't you?" I asked.

"Yeah," he answered. "I didn't think I could read you like that. Some of us I just can't. You're an incredibly truthful person and when you lie it's very subtle."

He stood to my side, his hand still on my elbow.

"Can you tell if your brother is lying?"

"Yes and he isn't," Jack answered.

"He can change his mind later though..."

"If he's going to do that he hasn't decided to. I'd feel it. Right now, he intends to keep his word."

I sighed through my half unplugged nose and nodded in the dark.

"I've been listening to you cry for hours," Jack said. The forgiveness in his voice made me feel even worse.

"Don't be sad." I felt his other hand on my chest, just under my throat. "I know you feel a broken heart. This won't be your fault. It's a small price to pay to protect your baby. And you. The grownup in Paul will understand but I know you're worried your husband won't. I can't promise he will."

I nodded again, trying to breathe and keep the tears away. The hand on my chest moved to my shoulder and slid down to hold my other elbow. I sniffled as quietly as I could and raised my hands, resting them on his bare chest.

"Sshhh, Baby," he whispered as my breathing grew shaky again. "Sshhh. Accepting me wasn't that bad, was it?"

It hadn't been.

"Hm?" he asked.

"No," I whispered.

"Did you ask for me again to make me feel good?" His hand came up and tried to lift my chin to his. I let him but turned away so his lips brushed my cheek. "It's okay to tell me if it was mediocre. My ego can take it."

"It wasn't."

"Mm," he breathed as his other hand slipped around my back. "Then maybe I left you unsatisfied, that's why you wanted me again."

"Ah," I sighed as I remembered that night. The things I'd forgotten. "You didn't leave me unsatisfied. That's why I wanted you again."

He pulled at my shirt as he tried my chin again.

"When did you fall in love with me?" I whispered to his lips.

"That night. I know you don't feel the same way. I don't expect it to be the same this time. I just have to give you something, right?"

I let him put his lips on mine but I didn't return his kiss.

"Little help please, Baby?" he asked.

I thought about it and felt more tears on my cheeks.

"Jack," I whispered. "The last man I slept with hit me in the head with his gun and threw me face down on Finn to... to..."

"Please don't say it."

"You have no idea how much I don't want to be touched."

He gave up on my mouth and slipped his hand up my shirt as he kissed my neck. It seemed to work for him as I shrunk away inside and hoped as long as I kept the water works under control, it would be over quickly.

"Don't rank what he did to you with anything you've ever done with Paul or when you accepted me or even with now. I've wanted you since that night but not like this. Not when you have to fight so much just to let me near you. Think about your baby. Think about revenge. I love you more than enough for this."

I let him pull me into the bed and I pulled up the blanket to hide us even in the blackness of the room. Then I closed my eyes, forgot about Jack and thought about Camille.

Chapter 40

Sun must have been coming in Jack's bedroom window for a while when my eyes opened. I woke as alone as when I'd finally fallen asleep. Jack's Spartan room only seemed lived in by the amount of clothes on the floor. He'd tried to comfort me but I pushed him away, rolling as far to the side of the bed as I could. 'Please,' he whispered, needing comfort as much as he needed to give it and when I didn't answer he walked out. It had been as miserable for him as it was for me. Struggling to make love to a woman who wouldn't stop crying.

By the time I felt angry enough to deal with Jack and the smell downstairs it was past nine-thirty. I pulled on my jeans and tank top from the day before and left Jack's shirt on his floor. Hadn't been able to do up my bra with one hand so I left it off. The pain under the bandage completely woke so I kept it still. I returned to my room and found the bed had been slept in. I hadn't gone under the floral blanket when I was in there but now it lumped over the foot of the bed so it must have been Jack. My bag sat on the counter in the ensuite so I brushed my teeth.

On the way downstairs, I felt somewhere between fearless and disinterested in my own safety. As long as they didn't hurt Jack again I'd do what ever I wanted. I pulled back the bandage enough to see my wedding band carried the heat around my finger. Blisters on my palm and wrist. I could tell they were all in the kitchen but the breakfast smells were no match for their stink. I'd sit with them but wasn't so sure much would go down.

I paused in the doorway to see four of them around the table. Nearly empty plates. Coffee mugs. Harvey refilled the coffee maker, his back to me.

"Come in, Sweet Thing," Soros said, patting the chair next to him. The one facing Jack. The red line I left on Soros' neck had scabbed over.

His men indifferently looked at me and Jack didn't look up from the mug in front of him. White with dark blue letters in various styles spelling out 'stud.' I had no doubt it was Soros' idea. I remembered seeing it in the back of Jack's cupboard as I set the table for dinner.

"Mister Steele," Soros said pointing to the man who held Jack the night before. "Get the little mama some breakfast. Mister Steele went all the way to town this morning for groceries and hurried right back to cook."

The man got up and after a minute a plate of salt and cholesterol sat in front of me as Soros slipped his hand over my thigh and squeezed.

"Thank you, Mister Steele," I politely said. Fuck you, I thought, putting Soros' hand on his own leg.

"You're adorable when you use your manners," Soros said.

I nodded and forced down a small mouth full. Then I hooked my sense to Soros' line and rewound until I came into the room. He watched my breasts until I sat down.

Figured.

He didn't react to my connection to him so I rewound more. He put my guns in the drawer at the bottom of Jack's booze cabinet. As I rewound further I saw him in the bathroom, hands on the wall and swinging his hips so his urine traced a circle around the bowl. Teal underwear.

"Morning, Jack," I said.

He looked as I rubbed under my nose. When he connected, I sneezed into my elbow then excused myself in the direction of the downstairs bathroom, keeping my elbow there like I sneezed on it.

I'm sorry for provoking him, I said.

He'd have done worse to me and less to you if you hadn't. Would you be upset if I told you that was the worst sex I've ever had?

I knew he was hurt and angry I'd treated him like he wasn't there even though he'd told me to. It was the only thing I could think of doing to have a chance with Paul.

Would you be if I agreed with you? I asked.

No.

I took a left to the living room and grabbed my guns before heading to the bathroom to run the water for a few seconds as I strapped them on.

There's a limit to how good I'm going to be for this asshole, Jack. If it means you'll get hurt again I'll smarten up otherwise I don't give a shit about his feelings.

Language, Baby, Jack warned.

Sorry.

Soros noticed right away I returned to the table armed as did his men. I took my seat and tried to get another bite down.

I didn't realize you'd woken up with such a death wish, Jack sent. *Maybe it was worse than I thought.*

"Sweet Thing, where did you get those?" Soros asked.

I pointed toward the living room until my mouth was empty.

"Drawer under the whiskey cabinet," I said, forcing myself to look puzzled he didn't know where they were. He was the one who put them there.

Soros glared around the table. "Who told you where they were?"

"You did," I shrugged.

Jack struggled with his coffee. Soros' put his hand on my back and slid it up into my hair before he grabbed a painful wad of it and turned me to face him.

"Hi," I cheerfully said. He tightened his grip. "Okay, you didn't. I pulled it from your head."

"Damn it, Anna," Jack muttered.

Soros thought a moment before he let me go.

"Everyone at this table can read," he said. "I don't keep dumb grunts around me who can't like my compassionate brother Jack does. No two are the same. Mister Steele is very good with control. Mister

Roberts can detect lies. I don't think an intelligent paragraph could describe what Mister Travis can do. Mister Harvey? What do you do again besides make good coffee?"

"Read farther than anyone?"

"That's it! And Father finds me most valuable because of my gift with the ladies," his arm went around me as he smelled me again. "Mmm, delicious timing. The scent of a woman's line tells a lot about her reproductive state. He's very busy and doesn't have days to spend in bed."

I nodded as I took another bite.

"That's always been at the top of my list," I said. "Finding a man who knows when his bitch is in heat."

"Exactly," Soros seemed pleased with my apparent enthusiasm. His hand felt its way further around me and he pinched my back. Then he grabbed my chin with his other hand and pulled me to face him.

"What else can you see about me," he whispered. His voice was soft but his fingers pressed through my cheek right to the bone.

"Are you sure you can get by without me for a day or so, Mister Soros?" I asked as politely as I could.

What the hell are you thinking?

He's not going to let me live long enough to give your son his first feeding, Jack. Or see my daughter again unless I can make myself invaluable.

"You're not going anywhere," Soros said.

I raised my eyebrows, showing surprise at his honest misunderstanding. Enjoying playing him.

"Things drain me," I said without specifying which things. "I'll have a wee coma for a while as I recharge."

He nodded. "Mister Travis is occasionally plagued with the same thing."

He wouldn't tell me that if I had any chance at all, I sent to Jack.

I'm sorry, Baby.

Let him think the sleep is from reading him... disconnect.

I felt Jack leave me as he got up for more coffee.

"I hear random things: past, future. Hit and miss with most people. When I force it most are just plain miss."

"Stop stalling," he said squeezing harder.

"Face me, please."

He pushed his chair back and turned it as I swung my legs around. He hadn't let go of me. I unbuttoned his black silk shirt and put my palms on his chest. Hopefully he would think I needed contact and permission.

"May I?" I asked even though I already had his line.

He nodded. I watched his eyes for the first few seconds I ran him back then they lost focus as I looked out through his.

"Going backwards," I murmured. "You watched how my breasts moved under my shirt when I first came in for breakfast... putting my guns in the drawer."

"We know that," he interrupted.

"Sshhh," I said. "Nobody's looking; you helped yourself to a mouthful of whatever is in the big bottle on the right. Then back, you're in the bathroom, hands on the wall drawing circles in the bowl with your pee."

I felt his grip loosen just a bit.

"Is that really a colour for men's underwear?" I asked and felt his hand tighten again.

"Future now, Sweet Thing," he whispered. I smelled the coffee he'd been drinking and the lingering odour of the garlic in the potatoes and the whiskey. He let me rock my head back and forth as I worked.

I skipped ahead further than I intended. He stood in a doorway watching me at the counter struggling with a dull knife to cut an orange while I laughed and looked out the window. I turned to face the room then my eyes closed. I threw something.

"Sweet Thing?" he sounded distant and if I hadn't gotten to know him better maybe even a tiny bit of concern.

"You're holding a rifle on me," I whispered, seeing myself in the long grass of Jack's backyard. Talking to something large and brown behind me. It was hard to be selective about what I told him. Touching him made the connection so intense it overwhelmed. I spoke to the brown shape and it disappeared at light speed then the rifle fired, missing me. I saw myself struggle to stand as the black sleep sunk in and I fell.

"You watch it discharge... the smoke. I make it half way up, holding my chest but I go down."

"Enough, Anna," Jack's voice. Hands gently shook my shoulders.

Further forward Soros stands over my bed. He puts my guns on the table beside me. He takes one out and holds it on me before putting it back.

"You," I felt come from my mouth. He sits on the bed beside me, puts a towel under my hand and carefully unwraps it. Cleans it then some white cream before he wraps it back up and puts the old dressing in the garbage.

"I…" the shaking became urgent. Soros carefully picks me up and sits down at the head of the bed, leaning back on the headboard. Arm around me stroking my face. 'I'm sorry, Mother,' I hear and watch his tears fall on my cheek. Pain in my shoulder intrudes.

"Maybe," I whisper. Maybe not this time. Maybe on the other side Soros will be ready for the coming peace. The reconciliation and healing the family needs.

"Anna?"

My eyes focused on Jack's. I lay in the living room on the same end of his couch where Paul held me a couple of months earlier. Jack's thumb dug into my shoulder to try and rouse me.

"Hi, Jack," I said.

He sighed and let go of my shoulder. "I don't know, RJ. I've never seen her react like that."

"Never," I echoed. I'd never had contact with someone I was reading. And if Soros believed I needed it all the better. "Like what?"

"You only breathed in to talk. Your lips were turning blue. You wouldn't stop shaking."

"Leave, Jack," Soros ordered. He put his hand on Jack's shoulder and pulled him away from me. Jack didn't hesitate but he kept eye contact as he stood. When we were alone, Soros crossed his arms. His shirt was still unbuttoned and open. "What are you going to pull to make me shoot you? Hm?"

"I'm not planning anything," I said. "Maybe it's not at me. I don't pick up everything. It could read different again even now."

He studied me.

"Can you pretend you trust me for a few seconds?" I asked as I took the guns off and tossed them to the other end of the couch. I didn't remember seeing them on me when I watched myself through Soros' eyes.

He nodded. I stood and put my hands on his waist. He stiffened. I stepped closer and pushed my arms around him until I pressed up against his body. He involuntarily reached around me.

"I felt you'll need this later. I'm not sure why," I sighed as I rested my head on his shoulder. Then I let him go and walked back into the kitchen.

My barely touched food waited where I left it on the table so I put it in the microwave. Jack sat back at the table with Soros' men and the coffee maker was working again. When I turned, Soros stood in the doorway.

"What can Mister Travis do?" I asked. I felt that was a fair exchange.

"Turn your back to him," Soros told me so I turned to the counter and started cutting up an orange with an old knife. "Where is he?"

I read behind me and picked up everyone but Travis.

"His chair is empty," I said as I looked out the window. Not just empty, he was plain gone. Something big moved in the trees. I laughed. A bear.

"Are you certain? Turn and look."

The microwave beeped so I pulled out my plate and added the oranges and a couple of raw eggs. I heard bears liked eggs. Then I turned.

"His chair is empty," I said because it was. Jack looked at the seat next to him. "Can he block my vision and my sense?" I asked.

"We can all see him, just can't read him," Jack said.

"No shit?" I asked. "Sorry, language. I can't. He's invisible."

I closed my eyes, probing his seat then around it. Nothing came. I pulled my sense back and after a couple of seconds felt his presence tease me like the Colonel's did. There when I ignored it and disappearing when I sought it.

"You're like the faint stars, Mister Travis, gone when I look but I can see you move in the corner of my eye when I turn away. I'll find you."

I kept my eyes closed and reached behind me for an egg, cool in my hand. Smooth yet rough enough I could make out the faint vibration on my skin as I turned it.

"Mmm," I said as I concentrated on the colour of the egg. Brown ones. Could be light. Could be dark. Travis seemed to tug at me from the door opposite the one Soros stood in. I needed to be sure or I would make a mess. The hard edge of the counter pressed into me as I leaned. I put the egg to my lips and inhaled the cool air from its surface. Travis' presence became insistent; unhappy with being ignored.

"Gotcha," I said as I threw the egg at the door and listened. There was no crash, instead the soft slap of it landing in his palm.

"I'd like to trace your parentage sometime, Mister Travis," I laughed as I turned back to my plate. "A most intriguing line."

The bear approached a few feet into the yard, maybe forty or fifty feet from the house. It stood absolutely still, watching the window. I glanced back and Travis took his seat.

I paused my hand on its way to pick up my plate and covered my mouth to yawn. Travis and Soros talked.

"You saw it," Travis said. "I didn't move until after her eyes were closed. She picked me up."

"But she couldn't see you."

I took a couple of bites with my fork and considered the bear. I giggled and sent my sense out to it. Or her, I realized. She pushed herself up and appeared to snort at me. I couldn't hear her from inside. Soros would see me out there talking to her. She would run away when he went to shoot her.

"Mister Steele? Breakfast is excellent," I said.

Steele didn't answer.

"Mister Soros?"

"Yes, Sweet Thing?" he answered.

"If you're at Jack's table tomorrow morning I will kill you," I said. "I need some fresh air. May I go eat outside?"

The table filled with laughter.

"She's so much like having breakfast with Father," Soros replied. "Keep an eye on her Mister Harvey,"

"Uh huh," Harv said. But he didn't get up. He didn't have to. If he could read further than any of the others he would have no trouble catching up with me long before I passed from his range.

I carried my plate to the door with my good hand and put it down to get the door unlocked and open. Then I gingerly balanced it on my left hand as I closed the door behind me. Jack had a faded cedar table and chairs out on the stone patio. Dried out planters. His small trees looked okay and the grass had done great for a while until it dried out. I imagined the field around the pond at home would smell the same.

The bear hadn't moved, other than tilting her head.

"Hello," I said, keeping my sense in her for no reason I could explain. At the bottom of the short run of stairs I paused and pulled my sense back. She shook her head, then pushed herself up off the ground and exhaled hard as her paws slammed down. Angry. I took a couple of steps back and put my sense in her and she sat.

"Good girl," I said and approached.

My plate still balanced on my left hand so I picked up a sausage and tossed it. It landed in the grass a few feet in front of her. After a couple of seconds, her nose stretched toward the sausage and she took a couple of slow steps before her head disappeared into the grass. Her tongue slid back into her mouth as her head came up.

Next a quarter orange. I'd only cut it in fours because the knife was lousy. The orange disappeared. I kept walking, tossing her a couple more tidbits as I went, until I was less than ten feet away.

"Still hungry?" I asked. She seemed skinny to me but then I new nothing about bears.

Another sausage and she ate it up. I took a couple more steps and sat in the grass, watching; careful not to move my sense from her. I held out a piece of orange and waited. She seemed to consider how much she wanted it and took a couple of steps and stopped. As I tossed the orange, her attention shifted to the house and I heard the door open.

"Jesus, Anna. Back up, slow!" Authoritative. Quiet. Jack.

I reached my hand up and waved him away, my attention on the bear.

"RJ," Jack hissed then there was more commotion behind me.

"Fuck," Soros said.

I turned my back on the bear and rose to my knees between her and the crowd gathering on the stone patio. An egg remained so I picked it up and held it in my palm behind me.

"Eat fast," I whispered over my shoulder as Soros stepped out with a rifle. I felt her huge nose in my hand for a split second as the egg disappeared. Her teeth made quick work of the shell and her satisfied tongue worked to keep it from running from her mouth. Then I picked up the last two pieces of orange and held them out.

As those went down, I felt pressure in my chest and absently wiped bear spit on the front of my shirt. I watched Jack as Soros raised the gun.

"Run," I said as I pulled my sense back. She startled at the sight of the men on the patio and bolted. There one second then nothing more than a torrent of sound as she crashed through the brush and into the trees. The pressure passed and relief washed over Jack's face. A new line was starting in me. If we'd failed we'd be dead.

I saw the smoke from Soros' rifle as his shot struck a tree behind me. Then pain in my chest. From the inside and out at the same time. Was this what it felt like to lose Paul? To have my connection to him ripped from me? I started to stand then paused remembering my plate but I only got my hand part way to it before the pain spiked. My finger nails dug into my skin through my shirt as my legs pushed under me and my strength failed. The black sleep had me before I hit the grass.

Chapter 41

Three days of chest pain passed as it felt like my line tried to cut its way out. I hid it around Jack and the others during the day but in the morning I woke up with my arms tied down and fresh gouges on my chest. Blood under my nails. I couldn't read Soros and his men any more, only a blessing since I no longer noticed their smell. I hadn't decided if the pain was fair exchange.

"Jack?" I yelled, no answer.

"Mister anyone?"

Nothing.

I slid down in the bed until I got my teeth on the gauze they'd restrained my hands with and freed one then the other. Then I dressed and left my room. I heard Jack's shower running and couldn't find anyone downstairs. Even without the smell, pain ensured I had no appetite. The window over the sink let in bright sun and a view of the overgrown yellow grass waving in the good breeze.

I decided not to wait for permission to go out and unlocked the door. Nobody came after me. They could all read where I was anyway. Matted grass marked where I fed the bear so I curled up there in the sun and waited for the ache to forgive my movement.

"Anna?" Jack called.

I grudgingly pushed myself up so I could see over the grass. He stood in the door wearing nothing but a towel. The long cut down his arm stood out deep red even from across the yard.

"I'm here," I replied and lay back down.

"Will you come in, please?"

"No."

Jack sighed but I didn't hear the door close. The wind in the trees soothed and I felt nothing more than the change in temperature when it picked up.

"Why are you ignoring me?"

My eyes popped open to see Jack standing over me. He had a couple of pillows and a heavy blanket in one arm and some notebooks in the other.

"I didn't hear you say anything," I said.

"I didn't... and you don't sneeze either."

I put a hand over my eyes to shield them from the sun but I didn't say any more. I'd failed every time I'd tried to connect to Jack during the past three days. It was like he wasn't even there.

"I want to show you something," Jack said. "Can I join you?"

I patted the grass beside me so he spread out the blanket and put the pillows at one end. He took the one farthest from me and I rolled over on to the other. Jack hadn't had much to say to me in the past few days. Only Soros touched me, pinching and pulling my hair. I tried to hit him the day before and he pushed me into the wall, telling me to keep my hands to myself unless I wanted the other hand wrapped up and him wiping my ass. I chose the pinching.

Jack put a stack of old books down. Nearly ancient, like something my great-grandmother would have kept for reasons known only to her. I expected if I looked inside there would be columns of figures and names. There was a new book at the bottom. A pen and a pencil on top. I pulled back the bandage on my hand.

"I'm going to get tan lines if this doesn't hurry up and heal," I said.

Jack didn't answer. Instead he stared, still hurt and angry after our fight on the way back from Reno and my lack of enthusiasm with him a few nights earlier. I didn't know what he'd wanted or had worked himself up to expect in spite of saying he understood how hard it was for me. Actually, I knew exactly what he wanted. Anna hungry for him and pushing him to keep up with her. No wonder he was more than disappointed.

"I can't read a thing since the pain started," I said.

"Yeah, that's what I thought."

"Are the others here?"

Jack shook his head. "RJ doesn't like your wardrobe. He's gone shopping for you."

I could only imagine what Mister Touchy would want to see me in.

"I suppose the rest went for moral support," I thought out loud.

Jack's eyes bored into me so I turned on my stomach and buried my face in the pillow to try and hide. He sat up and leaned toward me.

"What's on your back?"

My shirt had come up a bit so I pulled it down over my jeans and firmly held the hem.

"Nothing."

"Let me look," he insisted.

"Whatever," I said as I let it go. Jack pulled it up a few inches to get a better look at the red welts Soros left. The bad ones turned in to fresh lip shaped bruises easily distinguishable from the browner bruises from Stanton.

"What is that from?"

"Your brother has been getting amorous when nobody is looking." I ran my fingers through my hair and came away with a handful of strays. I hadn't bothered to brush it when I got up. "He fixes my hair, too."

"Bastard," Jack sighed. "I'm so sorry."

"I tried to put my fist in his face yesterday for it and he threw me into the wall and offered to burn my other hand so he could look after my toileting needs. He's very thoughtful."

Jack pulled my shirt up a little more.

"It's the waiting for it to happen again that's the worst," I said. "Well, nearly the worst. The worst is when he walks by and does nothing. When he does it's over really quick and only hurts for a couple of minutes but at least it doesn't happen again for a while."

"He still thinks of you as his even though he couldn't inherit you. He's so drawn to you. But he's angry with you for what he sees as refusing his inheritance."

I thought of Soros so carefully cleaning the burn. Letting me hold him briefly and holding me in my bed. He'd been the one tying my arms down to spare my skin and trying to medicate the pain away when I slept. The one who threatened me and pulled my hair. Pinched me, twisting sometimes until I thought my skin would tear or slapping the back of my head. I was still so shattered inside since Stanton and Marie and every bit of torment from Soros made sure I went back into the hole of self loathing I kept climbing out of.

Jack leaned close, his breath softer than the wind in the trees above us. His finger passed over one of the marks. I started to argue about touching me but as I filled my lungs to do it the pain's grip weakened, low in my back. The rest hurt just as much. I exhaled as he grew bolder and let the rest of his fingertips graze my skin. I wanted his hand off but short of the sedated sleep this was the first relief I'd had.

As painlessness spread further, I sighed. Jack swallowed and put his whole hand against my skin. I turned my head enough to see he faced me so he could judge my reaction. His hand pushed up and his fingers made their way up under my shirt as he followed with his eyes. Then his other hand joined the first, sliding across my back, barely touching me as he inhaled.

"Jack," I whispered, wanting to tell him he stopped the pain but instead I trembled and lost my voice as I reconnected with the things the pain had taken. My absent connection to Paul was the most precious. Much fainter than it had once been but after three days without it was enough to fill me. If I moved or spoke I was scared it could disappear.

"Mmm," he mumbled as his hands moved up my sides, guiding the growing numbness and removing more sharp agony. He misread my reaction to my returning senses as desire for him to go further. Again I was torn between hands off and relief. Between leading Jack to frustration and feeling my husband again. Selfishness won out, much to my disappointment. Tell him, I thought, tell him he's just taking the pain or tell him to stop and take the pain yourself. But instead I rolled over and put his hands on me, one just below my bra and one in the very centre of my ribs, almost inside it.

"Here, Jack," I breathed as the pain disappeared and I shook as Paul completely reconnected to me. Part of me wondered if he'd felt the disconnection or if our connection had always been there and I hadn't sensed it.

"Yes, Baby," Jack breathed, half on top of me. He had one of his hands around under my shoulders; the other found its way up into my bra as he tried my lips. At first, I kissed him. An unexpected reflex. I didn't want the pain to return but it would when I said—

"Stop."

I pulled his hand out of my shirt and I turned away to get my mouth out from under his. His fingers still tried to touch me as his face turned with mine.

"Stop," I said again.

"Son of a bitch, Anna," Jack grumbled in my ear then rolled away. Pain immediately seeped in. Gradually. Steadily. Taking over.

"Aahhh," I sighed as I pulled my knees up and scraped at the scabs from the night before.

"I'm sorry, Jack," I wheezed as the deep sharp pains returned. My back arched and I kicked at the blanket in a futile attempt escape. It felt like two men fought with knives inside me, never landing blows on the other. Only on me.

"Jack?"

"What exactly is going through your miserable cruel head?" he demanded as he turned. "Do you think I would tell you no?"

"It stopped hurting," I whispered through my teeth. My breathing eased as the pain peaked. "I could read again, when you touched me. I'm sorry I let it go so far. That was selfish and cruel, you're right."

He didn't say anything.

"I'm sorry," I said. "I'll get through this. I won't lead you on like that again."

"You're shaking," he finally said as he pulled my fingernails from my ribs.

"It's worse now," I admitted.

"Roll over."

I turned on to my stomach and without hesitating he put his hand up my shirt and between my shoulder blades. The pain shrunk again, more quickly this time, as I put my head down and he watched my face relax.

"Thank you," I said.

I knew what to expect when my sense returned to me. My breathing stayed steady and the shaking was limited to a few small twitches. I welcomed Paul, hoping if he felt the disconnection he felt the reconnection, too. Jack didn't move and when I briefly opened my eyes he watched.

There was a new line in me, that I knew, but conceiving Camille never felt like this. Or fertilization as Soros said. It was too soon for Jack's son to be stuck permanently inside me. I pushed my sense down from under my nose and let it settle in my chest. At first all I felt was me. Then another line between mine and Jack's hand. Soft, yielding. I relaxed more. I let my sense settle around it and found I understood a little bit about why this one felt so different.

"He's immature, Jack, but he's picking things up already," I said.

"Who?" he asked.

"Your son."

"My son," he laughed through his nose. "I want to kiss you, Anna. Just a little one on the cheek. May I?"

I nodded and he did, stroking my skin with his nose before pulling away.

"He's reading already?"

"Yes, I think so," I whispered. "But not understanding, just reacting to things. He's been badly frightened."

I opened my eyes to look at Jack. I saw concern and anger. Anger at whatever his son's line felt threatened by.

"You comfort him. His line is so still. I can't soothe him like that. My line is bound to Camille."

Jack moved closer. As he did, his hand slipped off my skin for only a second but it was enough to tell me exactly what frightened him. I read it as the pain closed in, blinding me. The soft line split in two. Identical in the way they felt to me and in their terror at the presence of the other. Their sudden flight pushing them farther from my line than they should be hurt me. They demanded Jack much faster than when I told him to stop.

Jack startled at my reaction and put his hand right back. "What?" he asked.

I caught my breath as they calmed down and the pain disappeared again. The two small lines regained their equilibrium. Taking their place again between my line and where Jack's hand rested on my back. They settled down in the same place and appeared as one again. My lungs emptied before I spoke.

"I know what scares him, Jack."

"Yes?"

"His brother," I whispered. "They scare each other. They don't understand. It hurts me when they flee so far from my line."

"Brothers?" he said before kissing my cheek a second time.

"Yes," I yawned. I hadn't slept much in the past few days.

"I know you wouldn't have done it if there was any other way to keep your daughter safe."

I nodded, deeply sad. I didn't have a lot of hope I'd return to my family alive.

"Thank you for my sons," Jack said. "My first and I never had any. Between Father interfering and her second we never had a lot of luck. We were only together a few months this time before Father found out. Her upbringing was a problem. She loved me but I wasn't what her parents wanted for her and she wasn't going to disappoint them. She slept with me a few times but she never enjoyed me. I think I fell in love with you that night because you enjoyed me as much as I enjoyed you. You fell in love with me but it wore off."

He shrugged.

"That's expected. You're with your first. I expected it to fade from me but it didn't. I'm not jealous of Paul. I love to see you so happy with him. Loving you is what I need to put the lives of you and Camille ahead of mine."

I nodded.

"What did you want to show me?" I asked, remembering the books he brought out.

He gave me a little smile and put the stack of books in front of me as I pushed myself up on my elbows to look.

"I haven't shown mine to anyone. The others who share with me let me keep theirs and I keep them up. Father's property is a big old house on the east coast. The house is more like a castle. He made sure the title would go to him when he returned and I kept these things there until I had to face separation from him was inevitable and moved them out here. I bought this house when I found my first, hoping we could raise a son here."

"I'm sorry, Jack," I whispered. The house he bought her turned into a hideout. "I'll stop pissing off your brother. You can raise your sons here."

He sighed. "Paul would be within his rights to send me to the other side as punishment for sharing my bed with you. Or he could break it off with you and leave. Or let me live while he stayed with you or let me live and leave you. If he wishes they'll be his sons to bring up. My line but he would see to their upbringing. It's the wronged man's decision."

The thought of Paul as the wronged man accentuated the repercussions of having Jack's children even if it was to spare Camille. Jack didn't know about Paul and Marie. About me being the wronged woman. More wronged than Paul.

I looked at the cover; plain old leather worn by years of handling. What I first took to be several books were actually one. The binding had failed and the sections had shifted.

"Can I open it?"

"Yes." Jack propped his head on his bent arm and kept his other hand on me, fingers tracing circles on my skin.

The book's old smell came up while I carefully lifted the cover and lowered it to the side. The first page contained a long list of names, more than twenty. The first half dozen had partial or complete dates. The second to last name on the list was Willem Larsen, the name he gave at the hotel. 1943 - 1969. The last name on the list was Jason (Jack) Bradley Roberts. No end date. Not yet.

"Is this all your lives?" I asked with appreciation of the truly enormous amount there could be for him to remember.

"I'm not sure. It's all the names I can remember and I'm not sure about the order in places. Some could be names of others in the family but I'm not certain. I remember less about the older ones and more about the newer ones, of course. In the late sixteen hundreds me and a couple of the others froze to death. The winter was devastating that year. As I slipped away I saw something that really stuck with me. On the other side I tried to make some sense of it but there was no way I could. I died that time in my early twenties, I think. I'd been in a fight and had taken a few to the stomach. Internal bleeding. It wasn't quick and I welcomed rest when it came. I saw images very similar to when I died before. They added to my previous experience though they confused me even more.

"When I returned I made an effort to learn to read and write. I started drawing. I was pretty terrible but I've improved. That's when I started this book."

"Paul says it's muscle memory. You remember how to do things but the body still has to relearn."

"Yes," Jack said. He straightened the arm under his head and let his neck rest for a moment before getting up on his elbow and pushing his hand around to my side. "Okay there?"

"Mm hm," I replied. I was so curious to find out what the pages contained and a little uncomfortable intruding into something Paul would never speak of. He wouldn't even tell me what his name was when he was with Catherine. I didn't remember her family name and only knew her first because whoever Damian was then said it.

The next few pages had one name each. Recollections of occupations, names of men in his family. His father. His first. Names of towns. Memories which stood out to him in the seventeen hundreds when he started writing things down.

"I left some space because I thought more would come to me but it didn't," he explained. "My memories of many of the things I wrote are gone."

Then the entry for sixteen-ninety. It started with the same sorts of details as the others only much more specific. Not just a list of statistics. The memories here seemed more alive, like the person who wrote them many years later remembered the feelings associated with the recollections. Then it said End of Life and a brief paragraph.

"All I remembered was a woman on the ground, screaming next to a dead man," Jack said. "I didn't know her or him. It troubled me, her hurting. Not over his death but with pain. I thought he died in a fire because her arms were burned."

The next entry was for seventeen-thirty, when Jack said he died of internal bleeding.

"I saw a strange building, something I'd never seen the like of. It was on fire. I knew it was the same woman from her long orange hair. There were symbols on the building I hadn't seen before. She struggled, trying to run, holding something. When I came back on the other side I knew something was going on. I knew the experiences were related and the woman was the same."

The next entry started in the same handwriting as the first two. A name, a date. There were several pages of the details of his life then again the heading End of Life. After that the handwriting changed.

"I couldn't write about his experience of course until my next return," Jack said. "She was in a fire, part undressed. I saw her face and the metal houses around her. The shape of the man who followed her."

Jack turned the page.

"Jack... I," I struggled to speak as I turned to him.

He'd filled both pages with the place Damian died: the torn pieces of fuselage, the fire. The half naked woman with the long hair seen from behind, standing over the dead man on the ground. The nightmare in which I walked through the wreckage, noting the location of everyone who died. Memorizing them so when the time came to walk through the real crash I would know which of the bodies shouldn't be there; which one was Damian's.

"I know it was you," he whispered. "And this is where you killed him. It made sense when you told RJ about the plane crash. I thought maybe there was more hidden meaning in what I saw but it was exactly what it was. The burns on your arms were the tattoos, your hair orange in the light of the flames. The metal houses were parts of the plane. When we met a few months ago and saw your face in the daylight, felt the inheritance in our skin. I thought you only looked like her, but you're the same."

I took a deep breath and looked at the page. The woman in the drawing was insane. There to cut the line from Jack's insane father thereby curing them both. Him with the real death of never remembering his past lives, freeing him from the insane personality dominating him and her earning freedom from the evil man she lived as before who made sure she didn't fail.

"This is the exact place, Jack. Where he died," I whispered. "He said "I'll see you again bitch." He didn't know he wouldn't. His chest started to heave to get air in. "Let me help," I said and I filled my lungs. I pinched his nose closed and blew my air into him and when his line broke free I inhaled it. I bound Pilot's gift of reading to me using your father's line. Kept it."

Jack sat up, crossed his legs next to me and kept his hand on my back. He kept turning pages. There were several more drawings. None showing my face even though he had seen it. Each showed a different part of the wreckage. I knew each and every one. I could still picture precisely where they were. Knew the fastest way to get from one to another; the faces of the dead who surrounded them.

My shoulders tired so I sat next to him. He put his legs on either side of me so I picked up the book and leaned back on him. His hand moved around in front of me on my lower ribs just off to the side.

"I dreamed about the crash ever since I was a kid. Always the same. Like you dreamed of it, I guess. I know every single place you've drawn. Walked past them all what feels like hundreds of times."

"Why don't you look at the other one now, Baby," Jack said. "You've seen the part in mine I wanted you to see. I needed to know what my experiences meant."

I nodded and covered my mouth to yawn.

"Then we'll go in. I'll put my hand on your back and you can sleep as long as you need."

"Thank you, Jack."

The other book was new. I picked it up and slowly pulled the cover back. There were only three names listed.

Catherine Adams 1777
Andre Laporte 1944
Anna Irena Richards (Creed)

"This one is for you," Jack said. "I never knew Catherine's surname so I used my father's since they were married. I came the next day with food and firewood and found what my father left behind. Catherine, a man and a tiny baby. I was certain my father was insane. I took the bodies to the woods and built a cairn. I found Father and put him down that very day, thinking I'd cured him. I took his knife. It's been lost since."

"It wasn't lost, Jack. It was loaned to me to cure your father. I've returned it. Its place isn't with me."

I felt Jack's head slowly shake behind me so I turned the page. There was just Catherine's name and the date at the top and several blank ones. I would be sure to add Agnes to my book as well.

"Think about what you want to say about her," Jack explained. "I can write it for you or if you want to keep it private you can fill it in yourself."

I nodded. "Paul and his group don't talk about who they were. So many of their relations have been lost over time. They think talking about it means you're crazy. I've been crazy, Jack, and talking isn't crazy. I think they only share enough to make a connection to the ones they knew before. I found four sons I've had so far. Three of them didn't know I'm their mother. The fourth I read after his death so I don't know what he knew."

"Did you hear what you said?" Jack asked.

I shook my head as I ran my fingers across Catherine's name and down the blank page. The shadows of the trees above touched the edge of the book as the wind picked up.

"You said his group. Not 'our' group. Why would you see yourself so separate?"

I thought. "Have you ever seen anything like me?"

"No, Baby," Jack said, putting his cheek beside my head.

"I'm Paul's wife. His lover. The mother of his daughter. His friend. His mate and partner. He's such a part of me I could never describe where I end and he begins. His men put up with me. As do yours and your brother's. It'll be a long time before any of those groups stop seeing me as different. I can fit in, but I don't fit. Even with the other women."

Jack's hand moved with me as I sighed. He turned a couple of pages to Andre's.

"I remember Andre. I was with Father on that island. I was able to get a hold of his service picture. Father knew who Andre really was."

The soldier in the photograph looked very different from the man I remembered. Chin tilted up and to the side. Wearing a dress uniform with a tie and a hat. The face I recognized but otherwise the only thing familiar was the sepia tone of the print. It was the same as the faded dirt and blood I saw on Andre's uniform.

"When you were Willem?"

Jack answered by opening his book and turning it to Willem's page.

"Andre remembered him," I said when I saw Willem's picture. "He watched as your father took far too long to beat Andre up. Willem flinched with each blow. Andre didn't think much of the strength of his stomach."

Jack laughed. "Father didn't either. In my mind he beat a woman. That's all Andre's line was. Gentle, thin. A stark contrast to Andre himself. He was truly terrifying. Willem had seen him fight hand to hand several times. The wounds he left the enemy with were hard and devastating yet carefully planned. The men he hurt never survived although they lingered in great pain. Sometimes we had to follow him and do the humane thing he wouldn't."

"I only ever saw Andre as a dead man when he haunted me, Jack. The big hole in his neck. Crooked glasses, one eye not pointing in the right direction. Blood on his uniform dried and faded. In life he never felt pain. I think that's why he was so good at what he did. He was incapable of empathy.

"I can't describe what it was like being Andre's woman. He only wanted to cure your father so he could have peace. The woman he loved wrote him. She was pregnant by his brother and all Andre wanted was death. I was just a difficult tool he had to keep in line. He couldn't do it without my flesh."

Jack slipped his other arm around my shoulders and I tipped my head back so my cheek was on his neck.

"When Alina started college she had a friend. Boyfriend hit her once. I beat him senseless. She never talked to me again and he was a prince after that. I'd promised to kill him if he was ever anything less.

"I'm ashamed I wound up with a man like that. How could I tune up a ghost? Whispering to me with a voice only I could hear. I could cut the line from any man and did from four including your father. Andre said he would use my hand to kill Paul if I wasn't good. He bruised me. Slept with me. I would cure your father as long as I had Paul at the end. Andre used that to push me along. Threatened the thing I loved most."

Jack piled the pillows up and pulled me over with him. I lay on my back with my book perched on my stomach.

"Paul talks about balancing the present and the memories but how can you balance them if you shut them off?" I asked.

"You know I approached him like I approached you. He pretended he didn't hear me." Jack put his nose in my ear so I pushed it away with my head. He laughed.

I laughed with him. "He would. That's okay. Sharing a mate with your father was no doubt difficult. I know I have things I'd like to forget. He has his reasons and I won't debate them. You've found balance, Jack. This isn't insane... it's something really beautiful. Like a baby album. I wouldn't remember how much Camille weighed when she was a week old or the colour of her hair without the little piece in her book. I share it, too. Ray and Alina have it and will keep it up for me."

"Turn the page, Baby," Jack said.

This one had my name at the top. A recent picture of me in the centre and pictures of Paul and Jack on either side. Camille next to Paul.

"I remember that day," I said as I looked at mine. I sat on the porch feeding Camille in the shade. Paul had been with us, his arm around me until the phone rang with the orders which would send him away that night. It was the day after Paul hit Jack.

"I waited a long time for you to lift your head. You wouldn't take your eyes off her."

The pictures of Jack and Paul were their service pictures. Old ones at that. They were both younger than I was. I laughed. "Look at you two kids."

Then I touched the picture of Camille.

"I stole it from Paul's desk. I think the printer at the photo shop broke he had so many copies."

"I'm glad you did. This and the one in my wallet are all I have of her. I thought I'd be going home."

I closed the book and held it to my chest. Jack rolled me to face him and held me as tears ran silently down my face.

"Thank you, Jack," I whispered. "You're the only person who would understand how much this means to me."

After a few minutes we awkwardly stood. Jack only had one arm he could use. We gathered everything and carried it in. The pillows and blanket were tossed on my bed since it was too small for the both of us and the books went in a fire proof safe bolted to the floor of his closet. The sun came in, warming the room, so we opened the window and curled up on the bedspread; Jack's arm wedged around and underneath me so it wouldn't come off.

"How long will we be stuck together like this?" I asked, hoping he would know.

"I've never seen twins, Baby," he answered. "A single reader would have no reason to react like they do. You know I want you. I won't complain."

I nodded, feeling his chin behind my head.

"I love you, Anna," he whispered.

I didn't answer. Instead I reached up and put my hand on his cheek and softly moved it up over his ear to feel the short hair on the back of his head before moving my arm back in front of me. I was asleep before my hand touched the blanket.

Chapter 42

When I woke, Jack still had a hand on me but he sat half-off the bed checking his gun with his other. The movement of him climbing over to his bedside table shook me from sleep. I pushed myself up as the smell of Soros downstairs made its way in the open bedroom door.

"I can't make out the voice with RJ," Jack whispered. "He's not family."

I pushed my sense downstairs as I moved closer to Jack so he didn't have such a reach. I picked up something familiar, like Mister Travis only I was much better at reading him. The Colonel. He coordinated our intelligence and having him here could mean he'd involved himself with Soros and Walker as well. Maybe playing both sides. Or maybe he'd changed sides.

"I can. It's the Colonel."

Jack froze, looking at me.

"God damn two timing old fart SOB," Jack went on as his voice quieted.

"He better have a good explanation. Maybe he thinks he's negotiating for our release?"

"Maybe," Jack answered but he didn't sound like he believed it.

Jack tucked the barrel of his gun into the front of his pants and I stood, first beside him with his hand in the back of my shirt then I stepped in front of him.

"No," he whispered.

"Yes," I insisted and refused to move though not to protect Jack. I worried he'd react too quickly to the Colonel.

He angrily sighed as he reached around my ribs. I felt his other hand between us on the handle of his gun. We heard them on the stairs and had a clear view of the landing at the top from where we stood.

"Hear him out," I told Jack.

"Damn, you're pushy."

"Pulling rank."

Jack snorted.

"I protect my pregnant mate," he whispered but he didn't move. "Not the other way around."

Soros crested the stairs first, his head already turned in our direction. As Sig reached the top, Soros' eyes narrowed as he saw Jack's hand up my shirt then they dropped to my exposed stomach. His mouth opened as soon as Sig turned to us then he pulled his lips back and worked the tip of his tongue between his teeth.

"Stay put, RJ," Sig said as he approached.

Jack's arm tightened around me and his hand moved on his gun.

"Colonel," I said.

"I'm not here as the Colonel," he said. "RJ and I have a similar understanding to the one you and I have, Anna."

I nodded. Something I didn't expect was going on here. Something family.

"RJ called me in to help understand the pain you're experiencing. It doesn't look like she's in any pain now, RJ."

"No it doesn't," Soros said.

"What the hell is going on, Anna," Jack whispered in my ear but I ignored him.

"Jack and I figured it out, Sig," I said.

Sig nodded. "Anna, please make sure Jack is aware of his manners."

I reached behind and pulled Jack's hand off his gun then slid it out from under his waistband and put it on top of his dresser. He didn't try and stop me. Instead, he stepped away like he suspected I was a traitor, too.

"Jack," I said. "I expect you will listen and not speak. You won't ask Mister Soros or me about Sig's presence here now or later. Neither one of us will talk about him and we won't with each other. Sig is..."

I paused and Sig nodded to go ahead.

"Family," I continued. "You won't hear any more about him than that."

I turned to Jack as he took a heavy breath to say something so I put a hand on his mouth.

"Not a word. If he's here to check on me then something is seriously wrong."

His lips tensed under my fingers.

"Please, Baby," I whispered. "Trust me."

His eyes widened when I used his pet name for me and I felt him relax as I moved my hand to his cheek. He nodded.

"Okay," I said to Jack then turned back to Sig. "There are two, Sig, reading each other already but they don't understand what they're reading. They're scared of each other. Jack calms them. Their lines were trying to get as far away from each other as possible and that's what hurt me."

Sig digested it for a moment.

"That makes sense," he finally said. "There have been twins before but not like these."

"They demand Jack immediately when he takes his hand from me and are calmed more quickly each time he puts it back than the time before."

Sig approached and Jack tensed. Then he held his hand over my chest. Soros moved to the doorway.

"May I, Anna?" he asked.

"Yes."

I reached for Jack's hand and held it. He was getting anxious again. Sig's hand didn't move as he stared through Jack.

"There's damage to your line. They've torn it. Your line is unexpectedly sturdy and should heal in time. I want to feel what happens when Jack takes his hand off you."

I felt Jack shake his head. "I don't want to hurt you."

"Just a few seconds, Jack," I said.

"Go ahead," Sig said.

Jack took half a step back and pulled his hand away. My breath stuck in my throat as pain seized me and my hands flew to my chest. My nails pulled at their beds as I tried to make a hole to let the pressure out and my knees buckled as I got faint. A sharp whistling noise stopped as my lungs emptied and I couldn't pull any more in.

"Grab her," Sig said then I found myself sitting on the bed with Jack's arms around me and his hand on my back. Even Soros looked alarmed.

"I don't want you separated from her for any more than a few minutes at a time, Jack," Sig said. "No more than a couple of times a day. She'll heal and I believe they'll stop reacting like this but I can't tell you how long it will take. Could be until they're born. I believe they'll get stronger before they stop pulling at you.

"Back to bed," Sig said. "I can only imagine how much having my line torn would hurt."

I lay on my side and Jack sat next to me.

"Your husband was with me, Anna, when you called last," Sig picked up my burned hand. "He's very interested in finishing you off, RJ. He also figured out what you would motivate Jack to do when your inheritance failed and he's gunning for Jack. After he finished insisting he pay for the damage to my office, I told him your call came from an area in south Florida and right now he's AWOL. He'll calm down."

I nodded.

"When he turns up, I'll make him aware of the details of your arrangement with RJ," Sig said as he stepped away. "And of my instructions to you and Jack. RJ, I recommend you move Jack and Anna as soon as you can arrange it. This house will be on his list of places to look for her and I doubt he'll stop to listen to any of us if he catches up."

I didn't hear Soros say anything so he must have nodded or given some other acknowledgement.

"Downstairs now, RJ. I'll be with you in a minute."

Sig's old knees popped as he knelt down beside the bed. When I opened my eyes, he was close.

"Gerald Walker will know how you two communicate. I picked it up back at the compound. I don't know if any of the others can. Be cautious," Sig said. "I'll check in on you in a couple of weeks, Anna, where ever you are. Okay?"

"Okay," Jack and I said at the same time.

"Sig," I asked. "Please take us from here."

But he shook his head. Lines of worry stood out around his eyes though he patiently smiled. "Removing you would put your daughter in danger and your presence at Jack's family home will offer protection to the women and children there.

"I'm just a man, my child," Sig added. "I have the same responsibilities as you. To treasure our children first. Perhaps RJ's motives aren't so different. He has insurance now for the young lives in his home.

"Jack, she's gone above and beyond for us before and is doing it again. She'll disobey you and Paul in the interests of the family. Best you mind her."

Jack nodded and pushed my hair back from my face as my eyes closed. I was more tired than I thought possible after three days of little rest. Jack got in bed behind me after Sig left and I rested with my head on his arm.

"Can't ask?"

"Can't answer," I replied. "I bet Soros will have his men lining up for me."

"Not really, they wouldn't think of asking without Father's permission," Jack said.

I relaxed but I didn't sleep. Paul worried me. He heard what Soros did and was after us. If he didn't understand how bad it would be for me without Jack I'd be in a lot of trouble if he finished Jack off.

It was a long time before Soros and Sig stopped their quiet talk downstairs. Sig drove off alone and Soros' men were allowed back inside. They spread through the house, gathering things up and the front door opened and closed as they made trips out to their truck.

Soros joined us when the noises downstairs settled. Jack thought I slept and kept brushing his nose over my hair. Soros' weight gently shifted the bed as he sat and it was a while before he said anything. I didn't stir.

"You've bought yourself some time," Soros finally said.

I felt Jack's chin move as he nodded.

"Fallen in love with her?"

Jack nodded again.

"It won't be long before she starts to return it in fact I wouldn't be surprised if she's started to already. Don't suppose you have the stomach to break it off."

"No," Jack whispered. "She knows she's never going home."

"Perhaps if she keeps making herself useful," Soros said. "When she wakes we'll eat. Then we're going to Father's."

Soros got up. His footsteps in the carpet sounded off balance when he returned. I heard him put something down and then chair legs being pushed through the pile. He picked up my hand and started removing the dressing.

"Can't believe she's not complaining about this," he said around an object in his mouth.

As cool air touched my palm, it started to hurt so I thought about the pain my line had been in and considered myself lucky it was all I had to deal with. I ignored it as he took off the dead skin and wrapped it back up.

"She took it to protect you. Like I said, she's rare and beautiful."

"Yes," Jack said.

"God, you've gotten soft. You'd cut it off to have her want you again."

Jack didn't say anything but he breathed a little faster.

"Get some sleep, Jack," Soros said as he walked out. "You're driving midnight to six. We're pushing straight through."

Jack's nose went into my hair and he worked his way over until he found the remains of the bump Stanton gave me. He kissed it. I waited until Soros was back downstairs before I spoke.

"We're in a lot of trouble, aren't we?"

"For now, no," Jack said. "Walker will get to know us like RJ did and even RJ won't get in his way. I thought you were sleeping."

"Thinking."

"About what?" Jack asked.

I shifted my legs and leaned against him.

"I met Paul a year ago today. I was thinking about how much my life changed since then. Before we found each other I'd only ever been kissed twice, by the same boy when I was sixteen. Never had anyone. Then Paul. I had him in bed after little more than an hour. Never thought I'd be pregnant a month later and married by November. A killer a couple of weeks after that."

"Why did you accept him so quickly?"

"The only reason I can think of is faith, Jack."

He didn't say anything.

"My mother died when I was fourteen. She withered away, heartbroken to leave us. I lost faith in everything and spent the next year and a half drunk stealing cars. Wound up arrested. Drunk driving a stolen Lexus. Record. When I finished high school at sixteen I got on my bike and ran for eight years until I found Paul. Within a few minutes I knew I could stop running. I didn't know why. I only understood I had faith it was right.

"I know I'll be dead at twenty six. I won't see Paul or Camille again."

I wiped tears from my face.

"Peace is coming to the family. Reconciliation. Not in Anna's life but I know there are still things I can do to help it along. Something bigger than me wants it and I'm not going to argue."

"I have faith, Jack. I'm not afraid."

Jack backed away and rolled me to face him.

"Would you be disappointed in me if I didn't share your faith?" he asked.

"This from the man who spent three hundred years trying to understand a woman in a fire," I smiled. "You're teaching your faith to others including her. When you found her you knew it was time to lead your men away, into her world to be part of something she has faith in. You've wanted to comfort that woman since long before Jack met Anna. Now she's yours are you disappointed by what she is?"

"No," Jack said. "Every minute with my first I felt guilt for deceiving her. She'll never know who and what I am. I can be who I truly am when I'm with you. Could you love me if you didn't have Paul?"

I watched his face for a minute as I thought. Jack didn't have faith because nobody had faith in him. He wasn't ready yet to see himself the way I did. I put my hand on his cheek and kissed him.

"I already do, Jack. I already do."

"Say it, Baby," he whispered.

"I love you, Jack."

After a minute he said. "You're not lying."

"I love you, Jack," I said. "Is it because I'm having your sons?"

"Partly. Being pregnant with my children makes the feelings you already have much stronger. And I know you love Paul. I'd be disappointed if you didn't."

Jack leaned toward me and I let him taste my neck. I giggled as his nose found the little spot behind my ear.

"I know you won't sleep with me, Baby," he whispered. "You won't sleep with anyone now. I won't ask. I know how badly you feel about the last time. My end will be the same. It doesn't matter if I never touch you again or if we love each other a thousand times. I won't say no if you ask but you have to say it."

I nodded and tucked my head under his chin when he lifted his head.

"Rest, Baby," I said. Jack reached back for the blanket and folded it over us.

Chapter 43

The sun had moved and I woke to sounds in the kitchen and Jack's soft breathing at my side. I'd rolled over and he leaned away, his hand almost off me. I put my hand on his and pulled him closer to be sure it didn't. He mumbled and went back to sleep. I had to use the washroom and decided to see if I could make it on my own. I knew how bad it would be and decided I could manage the minute or two it would take so I wouldn't have to wake him. If I could get away with it then I could try a shower.

I pushed myself up as gently as I could and sat, keeping Jack's hand on me. He was still out cold. I guessed he'd been up with Soros looking after me. I scanned for the others and found Soros in one of the upstairs bedrooms. Steele was in the kitchen and the other two were out back. I took a few deep breaths and let Jack's hand go.

Pain snapped in right away and I pulled in another lung full and started around the bed. Jack's bathroom was on the other side. After three steps, I made it to the foot still forcing air in and out but the pain in my chest was already unbearable. I read nothing and realized I could no longer hear the air passing in and out of my throat. The other corner of the bed looked so far away. I pushed another step and almost made it before I heard a thump. Maybe something downstairs, I thought, as I kept going for the door, feeling nothing under my feet.

I looked down to see Jack's legs at ninety degrees to mine. Shit, he fell out of bed. Now I'll get caught, I thought.

"Damn it, Anna," he said.

I shook my head, upsetting the little lines in my chest even more. It wasn't my fault he fell.

Then my lungs moved easily again and Jack was on the floor with me, hand on my ribs.

"I have to pee," I said.

"Not on my carpet."

"Not on your carpet." I got my bearings sorted out. "I thought I could make it without you having to get up."

"How did that go?"

I shook my head. The last thing I wanted was Jack and I having to go to the bathroom together all the time. At first I didn't want to share the shower but I felt more uncomfortable about the bathroom.

"Come on," he said.

I glared at the toilet.

"I'll turn my back. Think of it as the public restroom. You hear everything in there."

"I'd rather burst," I said as Jack put his hand down the back of my shirt and turned around.

"No getting around it," he said. "I promise I won't eat anything nasty."

It hadn't occurred to me I'd have to come in here with him.

I sat. I went. Jack didn't peek or move. Then he went, not bothering to zip his pants up. I wasn't sure how he would do it with one hand anyway.

"You want a shower? We won't get one for a few days."

"Alright," I said. I realized I hadn't had one since the day we arrived and faced two solid days of travel. Jack started it running and we quickly went to my room to get my bag. Soros waited at the top of the stairs.

"Potty time?" he asked.

Neither Jack or I said anything so he laughed and went downstairs.

The shower was awkward. Jack with one hand on me and me with my bandaged hand in the air trying to coordinate soap and shampoo without touching each other. I thought Jack brushed up against me on purpose and I kept my eyes up. He didn't. By the end we'd taken so long the hot ran out. I'd rinsed but Jack hadn't and he laughed as he turned under the cold trying to keep it off me. I figured he needed the cold shower anyway.

We wrapped up in towels and returned to the bedroom. The door had been closed and a couple of items waited on the bed. A pale yellow long sleeved button up ladies shirt and new jeans. Sandals and a fitted grey jacket with a zipper. It wasn't what I expected.

"I thought he'd get me something really sleazy," I whispered.

"You're married, Anna, pregnant. A mom. Sleazy wouldn't be appropriate," Jack lightly said before becoming serious. "We don't mark our bodies with ink. I know that's not the case for Paul and his men. If Father found a man with a tattoo he compelled him to remove it himself. He would deny a man his mate if she turned up like that. RJ would like you to keep them covered in respect of our values.

"I like them on you," he whispered. "But you need them covered at Father's. It will be tough enough there. They think of you as breeding stock. You'll be fed, clothed and exercised. You'll have a place to sleep. Don't count on much else. If we get word Paul has recovered the children we'll run for it. He can have justice on me when you don't hurt any more."

"He'll have to judge us both. I crossed the same line you did to protect them. If he doesn't have the strength he'll have to be a grownup about it."

"Generous girl..." he lifted my chin and this time I didn't turn away. I tasted the bit of toothpaste on his lips and lifted my arms up around his shoulders. "Please say you want me now."

"I know I'll never see him again but I'm still his wife, Jack. Until he's dead or doesn't want me I'm still his wife. I could say it. It could even be the truth but my faithfulness is his."

"I know, Baby," Jack sighed. "I just wish it was mine.

Chapter 44

Thunder in the distance announced our arrival downstairs. Jack pulled my regular seat beside Soros around to the end of the table so he could keep one hand on me while he ate with the other.

"Sweet Thing?" Soros said as he pushed his plate back. "Stand up and let me look at you."

I paused with my mouth full then quickly swallowed as I stood.

"Turn," he said, gesturing with his hand.

"Thank you, Mister Soros," I offered but his tone suggested my thank you might be a bit late. Jack's hand trailed around my stomach. "They fit perfectly, very comfortable."

"You are most welcome, Sweet Thing." He sounded pleased with the complement and when I finished turning I was relieved to see he didn't look angry. "Your old clothes will remain here, I'm afraid."

"Yes, Mister Soros," I answered. Then I smoothed down the front of the jacket and glanced at Harvey. A sudden turn of his head got my attention. Soros noticed as he pointed at my chair so I sat.

Harvey said one word.

"Richards."

The others turned in the same direction. I felt my cheeks whiten as I sent my sense out but picked up nothing. Paul was still too far away for me to read. Soros stood as Jack pulled me to my feet.

"Mister Steele, Mister Roberts, take her to the front door. Mister Travis and Mister Harvey, get the lights please."

Steele had my elbow and dragged me along as the lights started to go out.

"Jack?" I anxiously said as I reached for him. More lights went out and each time the sudden increase in darkness made me jump inside.

"Keep your bitch quiet," Steele said.

By the time we reached the front door of the dark house I read Paul down the road. His truck lights out front lit us through glass panels on the hinge side of the door. Jack's hand touched my face.

"We're going to save your daughter," he whispered.

"We can't save him, Jack," my voice shook as I leaned on him.

Then the smell of Soros crept out of Jack's skin and I knew I was on my own. Whatever games he had planned I was just a play piece. The other was my Paul. I saw his shadow in the headlights but I couldn't see him from where we stood at the window beside the front door.

"Are you up for a bit of fun, Mister Steele?"

The chill in Steele's laugh said he was. I felt someone take my hand and put it on Jack's elbow. As it pushed my fingers up his forearm I ran them over the knuckles of his fist then drew back as I touched the cold metal of his gun.

"You will stay on your feet and convince Richards to leave if you want to keep him alive. If you want to keep your sons from tearing your line to shreds you will lie to him. If you tell him the truth Jack will pull the trigger."

"Jack," I whispered as I felt Soros' pawns slip into place. A quick glance showed Paul in the headlights. I had a chance to keep him alive for Camille. Jack and I would worry about getting away from Soros later when she was safe. He connected to me as I dropped my head to his shoulder.

Baby, I know you won't feel me, he sent. *But I'll stay here in you. It'll be enough to get you through.*

"*JACK ROBERTS!*" Paul yelled, a weak flash of lightning followed his shout. I counted as my father taught me when the earth shaking noise used to scare me. Thunder rolled over us softly after a half dozen seconds, muffled by the trees.

We can do this, Jack sent. *I'll get you through it. We all walk away alive.*

The front door opened as we all stepped back from the light. Fresh sweet summer air washed over us, briefly cleansing me of the stink from Soros and his men before it closed in again. I could barely make out Paul in the middle of the road. His black silhouette looked even darker than his long shadow stretching away to our right. Even his face was nearly invisible.

"Roberts," he called again.

"Answer him," Soros whispered as he shoved my shoulder from behind.

"I'm here, Paul," I called. He scanned the house, his head turned as he did, not centering on the door until he finished. Paul's weight shifted as he turned his shoulder to us, making himself in to a narrow target. Metal flashed at his hip.

"Stay on your feet, Sweet Thing," Soros whispered then he pulled Jack's hand from my skin. I gasped, feeling like a knife slid into my chest. Paul's hand went to his as he staggered back a step. He felt the disconnection just as I did. Steele grabbed my elbow as I locked my knees and let out a sob before I filled my lungs. Air moved in and I struggled not to moan as I let it out.

"Paul," I called to reassure him. I could only imagine he thought me dead.

Steele pulled me toward the door. I picked my feet up and put them down, only moving forward because he was. Paul put his hand on his sidearm as we stepped out and Steele pulled me in front of him.

"Stay put, Richards," Steele said and I felt his other hand tap my shoulder. I looked to my right and briefly saw a gun before he put his hand behind me. Paul raised his hands and stood still as Steele half dragged half carried me down the steps to the walk.

"Go back to the truck, Paul," I said. The vibration of my own voice aggravated the boys' lines even further. "Leave. There's nothing for you here."

"Not likely," Paul replied. From the bottom of the stairs I could tell why he'd been so hard to see. He wore fatigues, face painted to match. The headlights showed me the glint of his eyes against his black and green cheek. He took a small step and widened his stance as a semi-automatic hidden behind him swung in to view.

Steele escorted me half way down the walk then pushed me forward. Each step I took closer to Paul hurt more as my distance from Jack grew. Paul's head turned, watching Steele disappear over to my right toward a large tree in the center of Jack's yard. Paul approached when his footsteps stopped.

"Sugar," he whispered, his arms out but I backed up. "I didn't feel you for three days. No pain, just gone. Then today I did. I closed my eyes and knew exactly which way to go to find you. Now I don't feel you again."

I nodded. Every second the man he'd come to kill had his hands on me he could feel our connection. Horrible, horrible irony. Wind picked up above our heads and the trees groaned with discomfort as they pushed against each other.

"Come," he held a hand out as he glanced at the bandages on my left.

"Do you think I'm going to leave willingly?" I asked, trying not to sag under the pain. He paused, hand on his sidearm as he looked at the door. His lips came up in a half smile. I had to break his heart although I doubted even then he'd leave without me.

"I went back to Jack. The need from the inheritance never left us. It ate away at me for two long months until I went to get Dana. Just once more, I thought. To get him out of my system but it made his pull on me so much stronger." I wiped my eyes with the shame of my words. Even though they were untrue the pain of Marie's confession still stung and I felt sick with guilt from trying to do the same to him. "I wasn't prepared for the cold on that mountain. I spent the night in his shelter with him. Just for survival at first but it didn't take long to realize there was something going on we couldn't fight."

"I don't believe you," Paul whispered but the hurt on his face said part of him did.

"I won't lie to you," I lied. "You know that."

"I palmed the pills from Doc Flood," I whispered as I put my hand on my stomach. "I couldn't take a chance and I'm glad I did. He's Jack's. I know it."

Steele laughed behind his tree as Paul pounced, covering the few paces between us before I noticed he'd moved. There one second and his arms around me the next. He picked me up and ran around the side of the house and into the shadows of the forest, closer to the lights of his truck.

"Stop," I shouted. The tearing inside me strengthened as I moved too far from Jack. "Stop."

Paul did. My hands came up between us. One to push him away and the other found its way between the buttons on my shirt to dig in.

"What do you think you're doing?" he hissed then he took my elbows and pulled me close. His voice wavered with fatigue, anger and hurt. I rested my head on his shoulder as I pushed down on the ground with my feet. "You wouldn't have done that and you've never lied to me."

As I pushed away, he took my burned hand and held it on his chest.

"Why don't I feel you anymore?"

"Leave, Paul," I tried, weakening as the prolonged separation from Jack became too much. "Jack? It's been too long."

I kept backing up, each breath followed by a retch as my stomach heaved in an attempt to clear the twisting knot in my chest. Then Jack's arms were around me, his hand up in my shirt and I turned and held on. The pain was gone but the effort of remaining conscious left me barely so.

"Get your hands off her," Paul growled as Jack kept backing up with me into the open space of the yard. He held me in front of him and when I turned I saw why. Paul's gun was drawn and pointed just over my head. At Jack's. It wasn't cowardice. If Jack died it was only a matter of time before his sons tore themselves free, taking my line with them. I would never survive the miscarriage. It would be the real death for me. If I died now I'd return on the other side.

"No," I said, reaching up to hold Jack's head in my hands. "You won't hurt him."

He won't go, Jack, I sent. *He doesn't believe me. Even if he did he'd forgive.*

"You don't have to move, Sugar," Paul whispered over another rumble of thunder. "I can take his head off from here. You won't get a scratch."

Please, Jack. Make him hate me.

"No," I begged as I pulled Jack's head closer, cradling it beside my neck. Lightening flashed, turning the sky white and the trees black as rain began to fall. It battered the trees with the wind.

"You wouldn't have known, my family didn't," Jack said over the growing howl above. "And you wrongly believed my son would kill her. Didn't matter to me any; I was going to walk away with another responsibility regardless.

"There hasn't been an inheritance in such a long time. Nobody knew the effect the little bit of rubber would have on me. Her insisting we use it. She didn't fully accept me. It was enough for a strong connection but it didn't end cleanly. I walked out of that hotel room just as in love with her as you are."

Jack gestured toward his porch, the hedge rustled next to it.

"After *she* and I killed Archer together you cloistered her with the children then you only let her get Dana because it meant she'd be back under lockdown with Ray. After Stanton you retired her. She's not a child, Paul. She's a woman just as responsible and powerful as we are but you're so off balance between Paul's life and family you've neglected almost everything, especially her.

"I held her that night on the mountain to keep her warm but I didn't sleep. She was in my arms, trusting me to protect her as soft and peaceful as I'd dreamed she'd be. Then she murmured your name and started moving against me. I told her no, it's Jack. But she turned, wide awake and said she knew who I was. She said she loved me."

Paul took a step toward us, his gun shaking in his hands.

"Step away from her you son of a bitch," he demanded.

"Why, Paul?" I sobbed. "For Christmas with your parents? Joshua's sideways remarks about his so-called nephew? For Christ sakes, you're the only man in the family who keeps in touch with the man and woman who raised him. It's you who's messed up. Not me."

Paul's breath quickened as he took his left hand off his gun and put it on his head. I heard shoes on the porch to my left as the light came on. Paul glanced that way but I didn't. It would be Soros coming to tell me I'd run out of time to save my husband.

"Just come with me," Paul pleaded, his voice breaking. "Jack crossed the line, Sugar. We'll work this out."

"No, Paul," I yelled with my last attempt to make him walk away. "I went to him. He said it was unforgivable. He said he could pay with his life. If you're taking revenge on anyone you'll take it on me."

Paul stepped back as Soros came down the stairs. The gun wavered.

"If you can't do that," I bit out. "Then you're a coward."

"No, Sugar," he moaned.

"Don't make me choose," I warned as menacingly as I could. "I carry Jack's twins. Do you think my connection to you stands a chance against that? Are you prepared to lock me up to keep me?"

You're a fool, Paul, I thought. You're so caught up in chivalry you can't see when your only choice is to save yourself.

"No," he said again as his voice strengthened. "Something is fucked up."

I felt Soros reach his arm around me with Jack's then take his hand and I cried out as he pulled it from me. Jack quickly got his other up in my shirt but not before Paul grabbed at his chest as he figured out why he felt the disconnection.

"What the hell have you done to my wife?" He breathed as the anxiety of my absence settled down. Paul stomped his foot as he moved several feet closer, cupping his gun hand with his left.

"Finger off the trigger, Mister Richards," Soros softly said from my side. Again his smell came from Jack. Paul groaned and I watched the strain on his face for several seconds before he pulled it out of the guard and laid it straight on the side of his handgun. "Mister Roberts, draw your weapon on Mister Richards."

"Please, no. Mister Soros," I breathed as he pulled me away from Jack. He tangled his hand up in the side of my bra tight enough that his knuckles kept contact. Wind whipped up under my shirt.

"Sweet Thing, you're going to choose whose life will be spared tonight."

Soros grabbed my arms to hold me up as I leaned on him for support.

"No," I whispered. "Please, tie Paul up and take us from here. Please, Mister Soros."

He lifted my chin and put his lips to my wet cheek. "Choose, Sweet Thing. Whose life will you save tonight?"

I closed my eyes against the stinging drops as his ear touched my lips. Thunder rocked through me, rattling in my chest. It was my dream, the one I had on the helicopter. A premonition then, an answer Jack called it. I finally understood the question. I couldn't save them both or myself. Jack thought knowing the question would save us all. He was wrong.

"Camille," I whispered. I couldn't choose Jack or Paul even though I knew choosing Paul would cost me my line. I would take Camille over the three of us. "I don't care who walks away. Just keep your promise to protect my daughter."

"I see," Soros muttered, heavily sighing in my ear.

Soros approached Jack from behind, pushing himself in close and slipping his left arm around his waist.

"Don't speak, Jack," he whispered as he brushed his nose on the back of Jack's neck. "She didn't ask to save you."

Jack's eyes widened as he turned to me, shaking his head. Paul laughed. I caught a whiff of Steele from Paul's direction so I was sure who had him.

"As much as my dear brother Jack is sentimental and unambitious, Mister Richards, he is very, very useful. He can read when a person is lying," Soros explained. "Jack, you are going to aim directly at your Missus' knee. If you hear any lies you will shatter it with a bullet."

I stood still as Jack struggled to keep his arm from moving. Hate filled his eyes as he took aim and when he looked at me I could only look away.

"You bastard," Paul breathed, barely audible over the wind above.

Soros shrugged, invisible to Paul from his position behind Jack. "Sweet Thing? Did you ask me to spare Jack?"

"No, Mister Soros," I answered not knowing who Soros would spare. If any of us. Jack's children enhancing his Father's family was Soros' second choice and maybe not so desirable in hindsight. Jack would believe I chose Paul. A choice that would not only cost him me but his sons as well.

"Sorry, Jack. I intend to let Mister Richards pull the trigger," Soros said as he looked down, watching Jack's silent gun before he took it and tucked it in the back of Jack's pants. "You're very helpful, Jack, and your contribution has been admirable but I'm not sure even you can keep your willful Missus in line."

Steele stood off to the side between Jack and Paul with his arms slung around Travis and Harvey's shoulders. Porch light lit their faces. Harvey's boredom contrasted Travis' rapt attention on Soros. Steele whispered first in one of their ears then the other causing them to laugh.

Jack glared at me as Soros approached Paul, stopping behind him with his head on Paul's right shoulder. Lightening flashed and Soros waited for the thunder to quiet before he spoke.

"Any of you gentlemen care to ask for the Missus while there's still time?" There was more laughter from his men. "No?"

Soros hand came up under Paul's as Soros attempted to look down the sight on Paul's gun. "Where are you thinking, Mister Richards? Maybe see if you can empty it before he hits the ground?"

"I would if my wife wasn't watching," Paul said.

"I can't see through your head," Soros whined as he tipped his back and forth to see where Paul aimed. "But you've always been a better marksman than me. A clean head shot then?"

Soros pushed Paul's hand up to accommodate.

"Yes," Paul said as he nudged it up a little further.

"Good, good," Soros said. "But not there."

He took Paul's wrist and pulled back and up, bending his elbow until the bore touched his temple.

"Dear God, no," I blurted out and tried to step to Paul but Jack pulled me to him.

"Didn't I say Mister Richards would pull the trigger?" Soros asked in surprise. Steele held Harvey and Travis even tighter as he laughed. I stared at Paul, my eyes as wide as his. If he was scared he didn't betray it as I did; sobbing and shaking.

"Mister Soros, please," I begged as I tried to get away from Jack again. Jack couldn't speak but I guessed what he thought. I hadn't begged for him.

Lightning flashed once then again, burning the image of Paul with his own gun to his head into my memory.

"We need to get on the road, gentlemen. Let's wrap this up," Soros said. "I'm counting down from ten. Then you pull the trigger, Richards. Ten."

He'd wasted no time in starting the count. I dug my nails into Jack and pulled his hands free of me, shrieking in sudden pain as Soros said nine. By five I'd shuffled the half a dozen steps to Paul and tried to pull the gun from his head but he held firm. My body was already shutting down without Jack's touch.

"I'm sorry, Paul," I cried as blood rushed to my ears and coldness sunk through me. I hung on his arm as all feeling left my legs.

"Four."

"Look away, Sugar," he whispered.

"I'm sorry," I tried again.

"Three."

"Look away."

I couldn't feel my hands covering my ears as I turned to the dimming porch light. My scream muffled Soros' 'two' and I felt my bladder let go at one.

The sound of the gunshot knocked me off my feet then I saw nothing but black.

Chapter 45

Soft fabric brushed against my shins and I felt warm sun down to my nearly bare feet. Pressure between my toes told me I wore flip-flops and I laughed, tipping my cheeks to the sun. Our connection felt so strong, filling again after the days of pain and distance. I realized a skirt tickled my legs and thought we must be wherever the in between place was before we went to the other side. I didn't recall ever owning a sundress.

His hand moved on my shoulder as I pressed deeper under his arm and gently kissed his neck. Our lines so close felt like joy inside me. I remembered the guns and the thunder at Jack's house like it was a lifetime ago. Sunshine and a park bench and the sounds of life around us suited me just fine. I could wait years for the other side; I felt nothing but peace curled up here.

"It's beautiful," I whispered and felt him shift, turning toward me as his hand slid up my right arm squeezing as it went. He smelled a little different but the buttons running down the center of his chest felt the same. I grabbed a handful and swung my knees to the left, up over his thigh and lost a shoe. Beyond the little warm groove where his jaw met his throat, my nose touched his ear and set off a little rumble I imagined I could taste. We had no need for physical touch in this in between place but we both felt it.

"I didn't think there would be anything before the other side, Paul, just over then being a kid again."

He sighed and took my elbow, pushing me away enough to get my lips off him.

"Don't open your eyes yet," he whispered. My left hand tensed and pain spiked up my arm. Too late I relaxed and the throbbing wouldn't go away.

Paul sounded wrong.

"You're right," he whispered. "For most of us that's it. An experience as the brain shuts down then childhood."

"Is this my experience?" I asked. "Are you my guide for my first time through."

He palmed my cheek and brushed his thumb over my lips.

"It's Jack, Baby. Open your eyes."

"No, Jack." I crumbled. His red eyes puffed with exhaustion. A great sob came from me then I wailed, barely hearing it as I clung to him, weakening as I chilled in the breeze.

"Please, Baby. Stay with me," he begged. "Please, don't shut down. Don't make me put you through this again."

It was like a punch to the stomach, reintegrating with the memory of the countdown and the gunshot. I'd done that to Paul: failed to send him away, told him Jack had me pregnant before I ridiculed him. And still his last thoughts were to spare me as much as possible by telling me to look away. I buried my face in Jack's shoulder and cried out at the pain in my cheek. My hand came up and I looked at Jack in panic. Wondering where the mysterious pain came from distracted me from sinking into complete despondent grief.

"Your feet tangled as you turned toward the house," Jack whispered. "You fainted before you could even try to get your hands out."

I nodded, remembering the fall but not the landing. My hand went to my chest as I felt pain from the boys' lines in spite of Jack's touch.

"The connection you feel is to me. I'm your mate now and you're mine. It spared you the pain of him leaving you. I don't think your damaged line could have taken it otherwise. I hope I don't disappoint you, Baby. I'm so sorry. We did our best."

I started to cry again as he cradled me.

"He didn't suffer," Jack added, his chin on my forehead tipped my head back and he stared into my eyes. "You need to stay calm. I've told you five times what happened and you fall apart and withdraw then you pull yourself out of it after a couple of hours thinking I'm him. Then I have to break your heart again. When you're so upset it aggravates them and they tear at you. Stay calm, please?"

"Is she staying with us now?" Soros asked. The killer. Talking about Anna who failed to save her own husband from him.

"Yes," Jack answered.

"Alright, bathroom then in the truck. I need to redress her hand."

"I'm right here," I spat as I contemplated running out on to the road. Half hoping to get hit by a car and half hoping if I ran fast enough to Jack's then it wouldn't be too late to save Paul. As I looked past Jack I saw we sat at a dirty bus stop.

Soros ignored me and Jack pulled me up, helping me to the gas station bathroom then to the truck. I sat by the window and Jack in the middle, the same positions we sat at the bus stop and Soros took my hand and rested it on Jack's leg. I hissed as the air touched my burned palm.

"Skin is growing back," Soros muttered to himself as he worked. "No new dead skin to clean up. Keep her calm, Jack."

Jack's head turned toward me and away from his brother as he made a point of looking as if he ignored him. Soros the compassionate asshole.

"Sweet Thing?"

I turned my face more toward Jack to ignore Soros as well. I didn't care about Jack's twins or Damian's grandsons or Soros' brothers or nephews or whatever the hell they were. Not right now at least. My heart filled with a traitor's connection to a man I'd only found feelings for the day before.

"Sweet Thing," he continued. "If I have to spend the next forty-some hours in this damn truck listening to you boo-hoo-hoo even more than I already have neither of you will live to see the rest of the family. You won't meet your obligation to me so I won't hold up my end. Every time you wind it up Jack gets stitches until you push me too far, you understand?"

I nodded.

"Do you think you can manage that or are you going to need some help?"

"Help, Mister Soros," I whispered as I covered my mouth with my hand. "Help."

"Good decision," Soros said as he wrapped my hand then I felt cold alcohol on my arm and the sting of a needle. "You haven't slept either, Jack. Lights out."

I woke to the sound of a cell phone beeping as Soros dialled in the front seat. I let my eyes flicker half open then closed them and pretended sleep. I remembered Soros drove when we pulled out from the gas station but now Harvey was behind the wheel. Steele sat on the other side of Jack and Travis up front.

"My dear brother Gerald," Soros said. "It's RJ."

"We are fantastic." He emphasized each word. "You?"

"Good, good. We expect to arrive at Father's late tomorrow night, possibly early the next day if the roads become unfavourable."

"Mm," he said. "Unfortunately Jack's inheritance wasn't mine to share. It appears the Richards woman was my bitch."

Soros listened for a moment.

"No, the happy couple is alive and quite well. Jack most generously agreed to stand in for me. And she did too when she learned we know where their hidden children are!"

"Yes, truly," Soros laughed. "I always suspected Jack was a terrible lover. All those selfish years of paid entertainment. She cried the whole time."

He laughed some more. I was surprised he hadn't woken Jack. My mouth felt dry and I tried to swallow.

"And the best part is he has her in the family way already, Gerald, yes, twins. Jack's Missus doesn't do things half way. They read each other already, frightened of each other they are. Jack must keep in contact with her or they'll rip her line apart to escape each other and get to him."

"Mm, I agree."

Soros listened again. I heard the voice but I couldn't make out the words.

"She's most amazing, Gerald. She gets around just like you said. She's beautiful. You've never seen such a thing."

Gerald spoke again.

"No, Father is dead, Gerald. By her hand. Any man who asks for her risks his displeasure on the other side. I feel the score has been settled but I wouldn't speak for you. He will be most pleased with how mating her to Jack turned out."

"Jack is in love with her. He'll do anything to keep her now that Richards is no longer a concern."

I heard Soros turn in his seat and felt his hand on the side of my face.

"I don't blame him. She's absolutely precious. Spirited. Fearless. She can do more than just travel. It would be a shame to dispose of her."

"Absolutely, I won't ruin the surprise. I know how it disappoints you."

Soros' fingers made their way down the front of my dress before he sat down.

"Love to you, Gerald. Toodles," he said.

"Mister Walker is most excited by our good fortune, Mister Travis. I have missed being home. I can't fucking stand California. I should have made Jack slice an extra line on his arm for making us drive all the way out here."

"Returning home is good news, Mister Soros," Travis said. "Mister Roberts' odd little house always smells funny."

Soros burst out laughing, causing Jack to stir. I put my hand on his cheek and rested my lips on his forehead until he went back to sleep. Jack was all I had. He understood my loss. Betrayed Paul as I had to keep my daughter safe. I knew how much Jack wanted me as his mate in every way possible and there were some things he would have to wait for. He could have my love and companionship but I wouldn't cross the line in bed with him again for a long time. If ever.

I thought about Camille growing up without Paul and me. Like she had told me she would when I travelled to see her before I killed Damian only we had just a few months with her instead. Jack held me tighter as I cried as silently as I could. I sniffled once and Soros threw the box of tissues at my head. I wasn't spirited at all. Reliving the rape in my head while I let Jack give me what I needed to give him his sons followed by three days of pain while Soros hit and pinched me every chance he got had taken my spirit from me.

The evening of our second full day in the truck I sat up a little straighter and buried my face in Jack's neck, memorizing his smell and the sound of his heart. Then I took a deep breath and pushed my pain away, forgetting everything but the gentle thump, thump in his chest and the way it moved when he breathed. I didn't feel alive inside and I clung to him to remember what it felt like.

It was nearly five in the morning when we arrived at the family home. The change from pavement to dirt road under the tires woke me and I sat up beside Jack to try and get the kink out of my back. The others woke as well. My spine wouldn't straighten so I put my arms around Jack as he kissed my cheek. After what felt like nearly twenty minutes of bumping along, Jack stopped and four armed men appeared in the headlights. Soros rolled down his window letting their unmistakable stink in.

The one nearest his window approached and spoke.

"Mister Soros, welcome home."

"Thank you," Soros exclaimed. "Drive, Jack."

Jack's arm tightened around me as the truck started rolling again. Soros grabbed my knee.

"Aren't you excited, Sweet Thing?"

"Of course, Mister Soros," I replied.

"Good girl," he said as he patted my thigh.

It only took another few minutes to reach the house. It was massive. Three floors and I made out unfamiliar old trees surrounding it in the dawn light. Jack took us around to the left and then to a gravel parking lot with ten or so other vehicles in it. As soon as we stopped he opened the door and pulled me out, dragging me a dozen feet away. Soros didn't seem alarmed. There was no place for us to go.

"Don't be scared, Baby," he whispered. "You're pregnant so he won't hurt you. Co-operate, okay? He's going to hurt me. More the longer it takes. Do your best and don't feel bad for me. It's going to be hard. It won't be over until he feels I've hurt enough no matter how good you are.

"I love you no matter what happens."

"I love you, Jack," I whispered as Soros and Harvey grabbed us. Travis stayed behind to unload the truck.

"Take their things to Jack's room," Soros ordered. "And my first aid bag."

"Certainly, Mister Soros," Travis replied.

Soros led Jack and I through the back door to start our brief lives together.

Thank you for reading Deadly Deceptions. Writing it has been an amazing experience and sharing it with others has made that experience even better. Other readers would love to hear your thoughts on this book (or any others you have enjoyed!) Please take a moment to visit the online store from which you downloaded it and share your thoughts. Your support helps small publishers and independent writers continue to provide great and original stories!

Thank you.

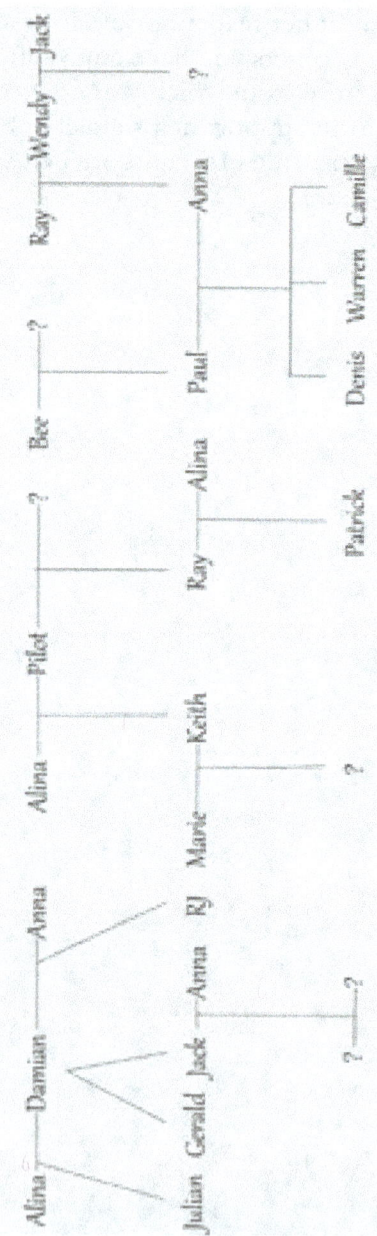

Anna's Family Tree, Book 2

www.ingramcontent.com/pod-product-compliance
Lightning Source LLC
Chambersburg PA
CBHW070850250626
47159CB00003B/1018